ACT
TWO

Other books by Denise Grover Swank:

For more check denisegroverswank.com

ACT
TWO

A Magnolia Steele Mystery
Book Two

Denise Grover Swank

Copyright 2016 by Denise Grover Swank

Developmental Editor: Angela Polidoro
Copy editor: Shannon Page
Proofreaders: Carolina Valdez Miller
Cover design by James T. Egan, www.bookflydesign.com
All rights reserved.

chapter one

"What the hell are you doin', Magnolia?"

My hand froze in midair, holding the pastry bag suspended over the tray of hors d'oeuvres. I brushed a stray hair out of my eyes with my forearm. "I'm doing what you told me to do. I'm filling the shrimp puffs."

My mother put her hands on her hips and gave me her best *How did I give birth to someone so stupid?* look. I'd grown accustomed to it during my teenage years, but she'd dusted it off and used it more times than I could count over the last three days. "With *buttercream frosting?*"

I lifted up the bag and squirted some of the creamy filling onto my finger, then cringed after I tasted it. Definitely not cream cheese. "I must have grabbed the wrong bag."

"Just how many people at the art gallery show are gonna want to eat Cajun shrimp puffs filled with buttercream frosting?"

The answer was so obvious I saw no reason to respond.

She moved closer to the stainless steel table, taking in the trays lined with savory pastries. "And just how many have you done?"

Yesterday she'd berated me for dawdling, so in the moments before she'd shown up, I'd been giving myself a mental pat on the back for picking up the pace. I cringed. "Almost all of them."

Momma sucked in a breath and held it for three whole seconds, her face turning red, then flung her hand toward the front door. "Get!"

"What?"

"Get out of here! Go! *For three days* I've let you work in the kitchen. *For three days* you've screwed up everything you've touched! Now get out of here so I can make them all over again."

"Lila!" my mother's best friend barked, slapping down the spoon she'd been using to stir a pot on the stove, and turned around. "Maggie's tryin' her best." I'd never heard her use such a harsh tone with my mother, but then again, I could always count on Tilly to have my back.

"She's a failure in the kitchen, Tilly. *She's hopeless.*"

Tilly crossed her arms and gave my mother a disapproving glare. "Then we'll find somewhere else to put her."

Act Two

"Where else are we gonna put 'er?" my mother asked. Her Alabamian accent was always stronger when she was exasperated—which, around me, was a lot. "Maybe we should dump all the folders she just organized in the file cabinets and let her file 'em again."

Anger burned in my chest as I jerked off my plastic gloves and threw them onto the stainless steel table. "You know I've never been good in the kitchen. I'm trying the best I can!"

"It's not good enough!" Momma shouted.

I tugged my apron strings loose, then ripped the apron over my head and flung it onto the table. "I never asked you for this job!"

"I'm leaving my half of this business to you!" my mother shouted. "You need to learn how to help Tilly run it!"

Before she died. She didn't say the words, but we were both thinking them. In that moment, though, my temper eclipsed my grief over my mother's death sentence. "Then maybe you should get my perfect brother to run it, because I quit!"

"Magnolia!" Tilly shouted in dismay.

But I was already making my exit stage left, stomping across the kitchen and through the swinging door to the reception area. I didn't stop until I was on the sidewalk in front of Southern Belles Catering. Only then did I realize it was raining.

Great.

Of course, it was April in Middle Tennessee; it would have been more remarkable if it hadn't been raining.

I ran toward the pizza restaurant at the end of the street, Mellow Mushroom, where I was supposed to meet my sister-in-law, Belinda, for lunch at noon. I was fifteen minutes early, but I was also newly unemployed. I might as well get a beer.

Moments later, I was sitting at the bar in the garishly decorated restaurant, staring at a mural of cartoonized famous musicians while I sipped a pint of Guinness. As I took the first sip, I lamented that my life had gone so drastically off course in one month.

Three short weeks ago, I had been poised to make my debut as the lead in *Fireflies at Dawn*, the hottest new musical to hit Broadway in a decade. But then I discovered that the director—whom I'd been living with—was screwing my understudy . . . and to say I didn't take it well would be an understatement. The understudy and I got into a brawl onstage on opening night, much of which was captured on video and posted on the internet. People especially loved the part where Woman on a Train #3—aka my boyfriend's new lover— ripped off the front of my dress and exposed my 34B breasts to the world.

After I lost my job (fired), lost my home (that asshole Griff kicked me out), and found myself destitute (said asshole had convinced me to sink most of my money into the musical), I had no choice but to max out my credit card on a plane ticket to Nashville, Tennessee, take another Guinness," I said, making my voice sound sweet and light. "Put it on my sweetie Colt's tab."

The bartender shot me a glare before stalking off to get the drinks.

"What was that for?" Colt asked, leaning away from me. "I was about to ask for her number."

I laughed and sat back up. "Just how many numbers do you have?"

He shot me a smug look. "I've got yours, so don't laugh too much."

"And we both know that's because you needed it for work." But that wasn't all. Despite the hard time I was giving him, I considered Colt a friend. I knew I could call him if I needed help. Now that I'd decided to stay in Franklin for the indeterminate future, I'd need all the help I could get.

He snaked an arm around my back and graced me with his sexy eyes. "We can change the reason I need it."

Things inside me began to stir, and it wasn't the beer sloshing around in my empty stomach. I may have decided not to become involved with Colt, but I wasn't dead. I was usually good at not letting guys affect me, but I'd let two men get under my skin since I'd come back to my hometown. Colt was not a safe bet. A good time, sure. But these weeks in Franklin hadn't gone easy on me. I'd become a murder suspect on my first night in town, and no sooner had I cleared my good name than I'd found out about my mother's terminal illness. Then there was the other thing . . . the one I still didn't like to think about. The memories I'd zapped from my mind so I could show up on my mother's front doorstep in Franklin. My welcome home had been bumpy, to say the least, and not just because it was my first visit in a decade.

"Hey, Maggie Mae," a man said over my shoulder.

I turned around to find Colt Austin, fellow Southern Belles employee and womanizer—though not necessarily in that order—bestowing his sexy bad-boy grin on me. His short blond hair was styled, and he'd recently shaved the scruffy beard he'd been sporting. I thought he looked better clean-shaven, but I knew better than to tell him so. His ego was already a force to behold.

"Did Tilly send you to find me?"

"No," he said, sitting on the empty stool beside me and snatching the glass from my hand. "I was thirsty." He took a sip and grinned again, his blue eyes dancing.

"Get your own," I grumbled, snatching the glass back and taking a healthy gulp.

"Had a run-in with Lila, huh?" he said, waving his finger at the bartender. She came running with a bright smile plastered on her face. Colt had that effect on women—unfortunately, he knew it. "Hey, darlin'," he said, laying on the accent as thick as molasses. "What stouts do you have?"

The bartender batted her eyes and listed off his choices. Then they discussed which was her favorite and how long she had worked there, and by the time he'd finally settled on what to order, I'd nearly finished my drink.

Before she could walk off, I wrapped my hand around Colt's arm and laid my head on his shoulder. "I'll before running away from Franklin ten years ago had finally come back to me, but I had no clue what to do about it.

I was, simply put, in no shape for a fling. My heart was too raw. I couldn't risk falling for Colt Austin, master charmer and—I was quite certain—lover extraordinaire.

I lifted an eyebrow. "And become lay number two thousand three hundred and sixty-seven?" I released a derisive laugh. "No, thanks. I have *some* self-esteem left."

He covered his chest with his hand. "You wound me, Maggie."

"I'm sure Mindy will help you through it."

"Who?"

Shaking my head, I pointed to the bartender. "The woman you're trying to lay. Perhaps you should have taken at least one glance at the name on her name tag instead of zeroing in on her cleavage."

He shuddered, but his eyes twinkled with mischief. "So crass, Magnolia Steele. And here I thought you were a lady."

I lifted my shoulder into a shrug. "Shows what you know."

Mindy came back with our beers and gave me an assessing glance.

"I don't want Colt," I said. "He's a free man."

She gave me a dubious glare.

"No, really. You're more than welcome to him. I've already used him up, and now I'm moving on to . . ." I spun on my seat, my finger extended as I scanned the quickly filling restaurant. My mouth fell open, and I found myself pointing at an older man with a pot belly and thinning hair. I recognized him from when I was a kid, but I hadn't seen him in fourteen years.

"Him?" Mindy asked in shock. "You're giving up this hottie for *him*? Why?"

"Because Colt has chlamydia," I said absently as I hopped off the stool. "He's a carrier."

Colt quickly—and loudly—protested my statement, but I was too busy trying to determine if I'd correctly identified the man sitting alone at a table for two.

I stopped next to his table and hesitated. What if I were right? What would I do?

I was still working on my approach when he looked up and gasped. "Magnolia?"

I wasn't surprised he knew who I was; the question was *how* he knew. The last time I'd seen him was when I was fourteen, and although I'd aged—barely!—I still looked a lot like I had as a teen. But the more likely reason he recognized me was that I'd made every gossip site and tabloid in the U.S., and Nashville had paid particular attention to the fact that I'd come back to Franklin to lick my wounds.

I could only imagine the attention I would have faced if my name had been released in connection with Max Goodwin's murder. Thank God it hadn't come to that.

"Mr. Frey?" I asked.

He rose from his chair and shook my hand. "Magnolia, I haven't seen you in years."

Precisely fourteen years and two months, in fact. The date he was referring to had been etched in my mind ever since.

It was the day my father had disappeared.

I'd had a dentist appointment that morning, and Daddy had taken me to his office for a little while. Something strange had happened right before he brought me back to school on his lunch break. Before we could board the elevator down to the lobby, a frantic Walter Frey, who had looked remarkably the same then as now, only with slightly more gray hair, had come barreling out of it. I remembered what happened next like it was yesterday.

Mr. Frey grabbed Daddy's arm and said, "Brian, I have to talk to you *now*."

Daddy glanced at me and stiffened. "I'm taking my daughter back to school, Walter. This will have to wait. I talked to Geraldo."

"It can't wait. *He knows*."

Daddy's face paled, and he stared at Mr. Frey for a couple of seconds before he said, "Are you sure?"

"Yes."

Daddy nodded, taking a deep breath, then letting it out. "We can't talk now," he whispered. "Even if Magnolia weren't here. Meet me tonight at eight. You know the spot."

Walter nodded, bouncing like a bobble head.

Daddy pushed Walter back onto the elevator, but instead of following him in, he reached out an arm and held me back.

"We'll take another one."

"Why was that man so upset? Who was he talking about?" I asked.

Daddy looked into my eyes, and I didn't like what I saw in his gaze. Fear. "You forget what you heard, Magnolia. That was business."

"Why would he be so upset over business?"

"I'm a financial planner," he said. Another elevator dinged, and he led me into it. "People trust me with a lot of money. Sometimes it makes them anxious."

"Do you ever lose their money?" I asked.

"Sometimes, but I try really hard to make sure they lose as little as possible." He pressed the button for the lobby. "That's why Mr. Frey was upset . . ." I could see the wheels turning in his head as he talked. "He heard that a stock was doing poorly."

"But he said *he knows*," I said. "That didn't sound like a stock doing poorly."

"It's just business talk, Magnolia. You need to let it go."

And I had, mostly because I worshipped my father and making him angry at me was the last thing I wanted. But I knew it wasn't typical stockbroker stuff. Especially because he stopped by my room before he left that night to make sure I knew where his handgun was hidden. It was the last time I'd ever seen him.

The police had questioned Walter Frey based on my statement, but from what little I'd gathered, Mr. Frey had told the police the eight o'clock meeting had never happened, had never been discussed, in fact. The reason he'd come looking for Daddy that day was to discuss his Roth IRA account. The police had quickly dismissed Mr. Frey as a suspect or as a source of information.

His lies had infuriated me, but as Momma had so tactfully said, if given the choice, who would *I* believe? A flighty fourteen-year-old girl prone to drama or a respected real estate attorney?

Life had gone on after Daddy's disappearance, and I was told to accept that there would be no answers. Anytime I brought it up, my mother told me I was too young to worry myself over such things.

Well, I was all grown up now and Walter Frey had fallen into my path.

It was time to get my answers.

chapter
two

I motioned to the seat in front of him. "Would you mind if I take a seat?"

He looked flustered. "I'm . . . uh . . . I'm meeting someone."

Was he nervous to be talking to Brian Steele's daughter, or to Magnolia Steele, naked internet sensation? The way he kept eyeing my chest told me he knew me as both.

I sat down anyway. "I want to ask you a few questions."

He looked over his shoulder and then sighed and sat back down, placing his shaking hands on the table. "What about?"

"My father."

His face paled, and he glanced over his shoulder again. "There isn't anything to discuss."

"Actually, there is—and you know it. You were supposed to meet my father the night he disappeared."

"That was a long time ago, Magnolia."

"And yet I still want answers."

He finally met my eyes. "I told everything I know to the police."

No use mincing words. "What you told the police was a lie," I said, staring right back at him. "I want to know if my father showed up at your meeting that night."

"There was no meeting."

I leaned forward and lowered my voice. "Don't lie to me, Mr. Frey. I was there that day. I remember you talking to my father. I know you were supposed to meet him at eight at the *usual place*."

He looked torn, but I'd made it good and obvious I wasn't leaving until I got what I wanted.

He cursed under his breath and then said, "I can't talk about it here. Not right now."

"You're going to tell me what really happened. I'm not leaving until you do."

"I told you I can't talk now. I'll talk to you later." He sounded frantic as he looked over his shoulder again.

"You have to meet me tonight." I looked out the window. "At the Embassy bar."

"Fine. Eight o'clock. *Now go.*" Apparently that was his go-to time for meetings, but before I could say as much, he gave my hand a slight shove.

I had half a mind to be offended, but then I noticed a well-dressed middle-aged woman had walked through the door. She was the apparent source of his anxiety. I didn't blame him—she reminded me of my elementary school librarian, Ms. Burke, who used to patrol the aisles like a storm trooper. Rumor had it an exceptionally rowdy boy had been thrown into "the hole" for misbehaving in the library. Though never substantiated, his story had put the fear of God into us, and the suspicious gleam in Ms. Burke's eyes had offered little reassurance. This woman had that same glare.

I stood. "If you're not there, I'll come to your office tomorrow." I gave him a tiny smile. "I know you're a real estate attorney. You shouldn't be too hard to find."

The woman approached and stopped in front of me, looking me up and down with a pinched expression. "Are you here to see Walter?"

"I'm just saying hello. Walter and my father were old friends."

She cocked her head slightly. "And who is your father, dear?"

"Brian Steele."

Recognition flickered in her eyes. If she was Mr. Frey's wife, I'm sure she would have remembered my father's name. The police took Mr. Frey downtown to question him. Something told me that wasn't a common occurrence for this man.

"I see," she murmured, shifting the strap of her handbag on her arm. "If you'll excuse us, Walter and I have a few things to discuss."

"Of course." I almost reminded Walter of our meeting, but I couldn't see Mrs. Frey setting her husband loose to meet me. "It was good to see you again, Mr. Frey."

He nodded slightly, then looked down at his clasped hands.

When I returned to the bar, Colt was waiting for me. Shaking his head and laughing, he said, "It's a bad day when you strike out with an old guy, Maggie Mae."

"Eww . . . that's disgusting. He was a client of my father's." I picked up my beer and took a sip as I glanced back at Walter Frey's table. My vantage point gave me a good look at the side of their table. The woman was leaning forward and—judging from the look on his face—giving him an earful.

"Didn't your father run off when you were in middle school?"

I jerked my gaze back to Colt and asked defensively, "How do you know that?"

He held up a hand. "Whoa. Calm down. Tilly told me. What's with all the antagonism?"

"Because unlike everyone else, I *know* my father didn't run off with Shannon Morrissey."

He paused. "Then who *did* he run off with?"

I looked into Colt's eyes. "He didn't run off with *anyone*. My father was murdered, and I'm pretty damn sure Mr. Antsy Pants knows what happened."

Colt gave me a hard look. "You think that weaselly-looking guy killed your father? I hate to typecast, but he really doesn't look like a cold-blooded murderer."

"He didn't do it." I shook my head. "Or I don't think he did. Look, all I know is that he was supposed to meet my father the night he disappeared. My father left for the meeting, but he never came home."

"Magnolia . . ."

The pity in his voice did nothing to ease my mood.

"What are you doing here, Colt? Tilly *did* send you, didn't she?"

"I heard all the shouting between you and your mother, so I decided to come check on you." He bumped his shoulder into mine. "It can't be easy going from living in New York City to living in Franklin. And then there's dealing with your mother 24/7. I know I couldn't do it."

"I just feel so guilty," I said, looking into my glass of beer. "I want to move out so badly, but I know I need to stay."

He took a sip of his beer, then asked, "Why do you need to stay at your mother's? Is it money?"

Well, crap. I'd almost spilled the beans on Momma's cancer diagnosis, and she definitely didn't want anyone but me and Tilly knowing (even if she didn't realize my brother knew). While I felt guilty about leaving her alone, I didn't know how much more I could take of being her houseguest and employee. Soon I might be tempted to finish her off before her cancer did.

"I have to move out." I turned to look at him. "And I need another job."

"Whoa. Don't get crazy now. You're working at the catering business."

"I suck at the catering business." I sighed as I rested my forehead on my hand. "The only two things I'm good at are waiting tables and working in the theatre. But the last time I worked as wait staff at Momma's party, I became a person of interest in Max Goodwin's murder. Besides, I'm the star of a very unfortunate viral video. I'm too much of a distraction for Momma and Tilly to let me out in the public eye."

"There are plenty of other things you can do to help with the business. Look at me."

I narrowed my eyes. "I see you there all the time, but I don't see you doing a whole lot of anything. How do I get *your* job?"

He shot me a look of mock disgust. "I work. I bartend at events, and I help with loading and driving the van, as well as a host of other errands for the *belles*."

"So what do you propose *I* do? I'm hopeless in the kitchen, and my history prevents me from waitressing."

"Maybe you could work in the office."

"I already got them caught up. Their whole system is digital now, everything from filing to appointments."

"Well, you're just too efficient, Maggie Mae. You need to slow your roll." He waved his flattened hand in front of him as if he were icing a giant cake.

I lifted my eyebrows. "Slow my roll? What decade is this?"

He winked. "Sure. That's right. You go ahead and deflect."

"Deflect?" I shook my head. "You don't seem like the kind of guy to say deflect."

"And you're still doing it," he drawled. "Anything to take the focus off the *real* issue—your delusion that your father was murdered."

I heard a gasp, and I turned to find my sister-in-law Belinda standing behind me, wide-eyed. "I had no idea your daddy was murdered. Roy told me that he ran off with a client's wife and took a bunch of money with him."

I wasn't surprised to hear Roy was touting the company line. After all, he worked for my father's ex-partner and appeared to be doing very well for himself.

"He wasn't murdered," Colt told Belinda, lowering his voice. "But for some reason, Magnolia thinks Elmer Fudd over there killed him." He picked up his glass and stuck out his index finger to point to Mr. Frey.

"What are you doin'?" I asked, pushing his hand and making his beer slosh. "You can't just *point* at him. That's rude."

"So you're sayin'," Colt said playfully, licking the spilled beer off his hand, "accusin' him of murder quietly is *polite*."

"I didn't accuse him of anything," I said defensively. "I only want to ask him some questions."

Colt chuckled. "If you aren't accusing him of anything, then why were you glaring at him so hard?"

I scowled. "I wasn't."

Belinda continued to watch our exchange with a look of shock.

Colt let out a pained sigh and then leaned closer to my ear. Whispering so my sister-in-law couldn't hear, he said, "Maggie. I know what you're goin' through, but I'm asking you to think this over. If you start down this path, you're bound to be disappointed."

I leaned back and gave him a hard look. Was he speaking from personal experience? Colt was hiding something, but I didn't know what. It didn't seem right to ask since I had so many secrets of my own.

"I'm sure you're wrong, Magnolia," Belinda said. "I can't see Walter Frey hurting a fly."

I started to ask if she knew him, but she quickly changed the subject. "Colt, Magnolia and I are having lunch," Belinda said. "Would you like to join us?"

He drained the last of my beer and set the glass down with a thud. "Nah. I've been eating too much Taco Bell lately, so I'm having a liquid lunch today." He patted his belly. "I'm getting a little pouch, and I need to work it off." He winked at me. "Call me later if you want to start a workout plan together." Then he sashayed out the door.

"That man is something else," I said, eyeing my now-empty glass with a frown.

Belinda watched me as she said with measured words, "Yeah, he is."

I rolled my eyes. "I'm not interested in Colt Austin. I know my mother thinks I'm stupid, but I'm not *that* stupid."

"He's a good-lookin' man."

"A man who has slept his way through Middle Tennessee. No, thanks. That's one lesson I've learned. Not interested."

"Good," she said. As we followed the hostess to our table, Belinda added, "Because I like Colt well enough, but I'm sure he's a heartbreaker."

"You're preaching to the choir, sister," I mumbled.

We took our seats and ordered a pizza, but I kept casting glances toward Walter Frey while we waited for our food.

Belinda leaned forward, worry filling her pale blue eyes. "Do you really think your father was murdered?"

I took a sip of my water. As tempted as I was to order another beer to replace the one Colt finished off, I knew it wouldn't solve my many issues. "Do I believe Daddy stole all that money and ran off with Shannon Morrissey? No."

She linked her French-tip-manicured fingers together and rested them on the table. "Roy's told me that you and your father were very close."

"Roy was talking about me?" Considering how much my brother hated me, he mustn't have said anything good. In fact, after all of the nasty interactions I'd had with him since coming home, I couldn't believe Belinda was here with me now.

She ran her finger down the side of her water glass, swiping at the condensation. She seemed to measure her words before she said, "He said you didn't handle his leaving well."

That was an understatement.

"He said that you saw your father's abandonment as a betrayal." Her eyes lifted to me. "A betrayal you couldn't accept."

The way she said it invited a confidence, and I wanted to confide in her. Belinda was pretty much my only friend in Franklin now—not counting Colt—but how much would she tell Roy? How much did I want him to know?

Maybe it was best if I kept my meeting with Walter Frey to myself.

"You're right," I said, glancing down. "I couldn't imagine my father leaving me behind. Murder was the only way I could excuse it."

Her hand covered my own, and I looked up into her sympathetic face.

"Oh, Magnolia. Of course you did. So why were you asking Walter Frey questions?"

"He knew my dad."

She lifted her eyebrows. "So? I'm sure lots of people knew your dad."

"He was supposed to . . ." I let my voice trail off, reminding myself that the less she knew, the better. I forced a smile. "You know, this is silly. You're right. I should let it go."

The waitress brought our pizza, which gave me a chance to change the subject after she walked away. "I need to find a job."

Her eyes widened in surprise. "I thought you were working for Lila."

"It's not working out."

Belinda picked up a slice of pizza. "I know Lila can be a difficult woman . . ."

"True, but I'm terrible. The only thing I'm good at is filing—which is all done—and waitressing—which I don't dare do. I ruin everything I touch in the kitchen. I would prefer my last days with my mother to be as pleasant as possible, so I think it's best if I find somewhere else to work."

Belinda set down her pizza. "Your mother's last days?"

Well, crap. My brother had let me know he was aware of my mother's terminal cancer diagnosis. I'd just presumed he'd told his wife.

I had two ways to go about this—try to smooth it over with some lame excuse, or tell her the truth. Selfishly, I wanted to be able to confide in her.

"Momma is dying, Belinda."

Tears filled her eyes. "Are you sure?"

I nodded. "I'm sorry. I was sure Roy told you."

She dug around in her purse, retrieving a tissue. "No. I had no idea." She looked at me as she dabbed the corners of her eyes. "Is that why you came back home?"

"No," I said with a derisive chuckle. "I came home because of my walk of shame. I only found out Momma's diagnosis the day Amy . . . died."

The police had concluded that Amy, personal assistant to country singer mega-star Luke Powell, was guilty of murdering both Max Goodwin and Neil Fulton, an entertainment attorney. But her supposed motive was paper-thin—they claimed Amy had held a grudge against Goodwin because he'd wronged her when she'd first come to Nashville as a country singer. And Neil was guilty by association; he'd represented his sleazeball friend. The official story was that Amy had killed herself over the guilt.

But the more I thought about it, the less I bought it. Up-and-coming country singer Paul Locke had signed all his rights and money away to Max Goodwin, and a month before the murders, he had lost his legal battle to get them back. And of course Neil Fulton had represented Goodwin in that case too. Locke seemed to have the stronger motive.

I told myself that Amy's death wasn't my concern, but I couldn't help feeling guilty that her death had exonerated me as a suspect. Still, I wasn't about to tell Belinda any of that. Amy had been Belinda's friend, and I hated to stir up more emotional trauma.

Totally clueless about my inner struggle, Belinda asked, "How much longer does she have? *What* does she have?"

"She refuses to give me many details. She said she has cancer in her blood and she's known for a couple of years. They've told her she has three to six months left." I paused. "Tilly's the only other person she told, because of the business."

"But you said Roy knows."

"He told me he knew when I went to see him in his office. The day I was going to go back to New York." The day my brother had attempted to bribe me with fifty thousand dollars if I left town and never came back. Which Belinda had admitted she knew about.

"How did *he* find out?"

"I don't know," I said. "But Momma didn't tell him. She only wanted me to know because if I got on that plane, I probably never would have seen her again."

"So you stayed."

"I couldn't leave. Especially after she gave me some very blunt advice about self-respect."

Belinda smiled and wiped a tear off her cheek. "That sounds like Lila, all right."

I studied her for a moment. "I'm not sure you should tell Roy you heard this from me. He obviously didn't want you to know."

But would she pay a price if he found out she was keeping a secret?

She nodded. "I'll give it some thought." Then she absently rubbed her forearm, confirming my concern. Her pink cardigan went to her wrists, and I couldn't help wondering if it covered new bruises on my sister-in-law's arms. I was sure my brother was an abuser, but I had no idea how to help Belinda leave him. She seemed determined to stay.

"Okay."

We ate in silence for a few moments before Belinda said, "Are you sure you want to get another job?"

"Yes. I love my mother, but at the moment, I want to strangle her—and I'm sure she feels the same way. We always butted heads when I was a kid. It seems we haven't outgrown it."

"Do you have anything in particular you want to do?"

I shook my head. "I'm not qualified for much. Waiting tables and working in a theatre, and given my notoriety, waiting tables seems to be out."

Her lips pursed as she concentrated. "I'd hire you, but I just hired a part-time assistant."

"I'm not sure I'd be a good assistant." Besides, I was probably too jaded to work for a wedding planner. "And maybe it's best if I don't work for family."

"Hmm . . . you could be right." She let out a sigh. "What about retail work?"

"I've never done it, but I'm willing to try."

"I know the owner of a retail shop downtown— they sell gift-type items but some vintage pieces too. It's very unique and charming. Alvin's business is growing, and I know he needs help."

"Full-time help?"

"No, just part time, but it's a start. Maybe you could still work part time at the catering business. You know, do the office work and help load the van."

She had a point. I would still be part of the catering business, but I wouldn't be underfoot looking for something to do. "Would the owner be willing to work around my catering schedule?"

She smiled. "It can't hurt to ask him. How about we walk down there after lunch? I'll introduce you."

It felt a lot like my mother walking me to kindergarten, but I really needed a job. I wasn't about to blow off a good lead out of pride. "I still need a place to stay."

"You're moving out too?"

"It seems for the best, but it will have to be something close to downtown. I don't have a car."

She cringed. "That will be difficult. Everything downtown is pricey."

"Then I'll have to keep living with Momma for now. One step at a time."

After we finished lunch, we walked down to Rebellious Rose Boutique and Belinda introduced me to Alvin Blevins, the owner of the store. He was a well-dressed and trim middle-aged man with shockingly dark black hair and piercing brown eyes that told me he didn't miss much. It was obvious he loved Belinda—everyone did—and he offered me the job based on her recommendation alone. Did I dare risk working for someone who seemed so keenly observant?

"Can you start tomorrow?" he asked, glancing at a customer who had just walked in the door.

"Yes. Of course," I said, surprised by how enthusiastic I sounded. One month ago, I was the lead in a Broadway musical. Today, I was excited over working in a gift shop.

"The pay isn't much, and I can only give you about twenty hours a week, but I'll try to work with your catering schedule."

"Thank you," I said, shaking his hand. "You won't regret it."

Alvin nodded. "Be here at ten and convince me that I won't."

Belinda and I went out onto the sidewalk. "When are you going to tell Lila?"

Act Two

"I don't know yet." I wasn't sure how she would react to the news about my second job, and I didn't want to piss her off.

I needed her car tonight. I had a date with Walter Frey.

chapter three

When Momma came home, nothing was said about the way I'd stormed out that morning, but I did tell her about my new job. She merely nodded and told me she thought it was a good idea since it was obvious I couldn't cook to save my life. The business end was probably what I needed to know anyway, and it would be good for me to spend some time in the public eye in a harmless setting.

I hadn't considered that part of it.

Then she went up to bed. She'd worn herself out in the catering kitchen, presumably remaking all those shrimp puffs.

The thought gave me a pang of guilt, but it did make borrowing the car easier; she'd never even know I'd left.

My stomach was knotted into a tight ball as I drove to the Embassy bar. I'd hoped to have more time to prepare my questions for Mr. Frey, but I decided I'd had fourteen years to prepare. I knew what I wanted to ask him. I just had to make sure I wasn't so antagonistic he'd up and leave.

The day-long rain had let up, but the streets were still wet. The parking lot was full for a weekday night, but I found a space and crossed the parking lot toward the entrance.

I'd never been in the Embassy bar, but I'd always admired the outside décor when I was a kid. The outside reminded me of one of those old 1950s nightclubs. In my head, I'd envisioned moody, romantic scenes filled with men in black suits and women in low-cut, slinky dresses. What I found wasn't anywhere close. The lights were dim and the place reeked of smoke. Several middle-aged men leaned on the bar, nursing their drinks, and a few middle-aged couples were scattered around the room. An older guy stood on a makeshift stage about a foot off the ground, strumming his guitar and singing a Johnny Cash song. But it was obvious I'd gotten there before Walter Frey.

At least I hoped he was coming.

I walked up to the bar, and the bartender—a thirty-something guy with a name tag that said Chuck—came over and shot me a grin. "The gentleman at the end of the bar would like to buy you a drink."

Shrugging off my jacket, I glanced down at the group of men. An older man lifted his beer bottle and graced me with a semi-toothless grin.

"Yeah," I said. "Tell Snaggletooth no thanks."

He laughed. "Snaggletooth. For that, I'll give you one on the house. What'll it be?"

"A Guinness."

He wandered off to get my drink, and I turned around on my seat to scan the room and make sure I hadn't missed Mr. Frey. Given how empty the place was, it didn't take long to verify he wasn't here.

Chuck returned, his grin even bigger. "Now Snaggletooth's friend wants to buy you a drink." He pointed to a bald guy next to the toothless guy.

The bald guy flashed me a big grin.

I picked up the beer and took a sip. Lord knew I might need more than one to get me through this night. "What is he? About seventy?"

"Eighty-two. He's excited because, besides me, you're the youngest person to walk in here in about six months."

I laughed. "Lucky you."

He leaned forward on his elbow, and a devilish grin lit up his face. "So what do I tell him?"

Shaking my head, I let out a sigh. "Tell him no. I'm not sure I'll be here long enough to drink another. I'm waiting for a guy, and he hasn't shown yet."

Chuck gave me an appraising look. "He must be in the hospital with a coma. That's the only reason I can come up with for a guy standing you up."

I resisted the urge to roll my eyes. "It's not a date. It's more of a . . . business meeting."

"What's he look like? There's a guy who came in ten minutes ago and immediately went back to the restroom.

If it's a business meeting, it might be your guy. Otherwise, no way."

"Middle-aged guy, I think in his fifties. About my height with thinning light brown, graying hair. He has a sagging chin and a bit of a belly. He was wearing a white shirt and brown pants when I saw him earlier today."

"Sounds like quite a catch."

"I told you, it's business. Not that it's any of *your* business." I added a bit of a sting to the last sentence, but Chuck only laughed.

"If it's none of my business, then maybe I shouldn't tell you that you've just described the guy who went back there."

"Are you just shitting me?" I asked, skeptical.

He held up his fingers in the shape of a V. "Scout's honor."

"That's the Vulcan sign for—never mind." I set my purse on the counter and hopped off my stool, pointing to the hall. "That way, you say?"

He laughed. "You going to take your meeting in the bathroom?"

Ten minutes in the bathroom was a pretty long time for a guy. Maybe he'd gotten cold feet and needed a little encouragement. I took one more gulp of the beer. "If that's what it takes."

"I'll keep an eye on your bag," he said with a wink. He was grinning from ear to ear as I headed down the hall.

There were three doors on the same wall. The first two were marked as the ladies' and the men's restrooms, so the third one probably led to a storage room. The door at the end of the hall was marked exit. I debated what to do, but I had to know if Mr. Frey was even there.

I knocked on the door of the men's room and called out, "Mr. Frey?" After he didn't answer for several seconds, I knocked harder and said louder, "Mr. Frey? Are you in there?"

The door opened and an older man walked out. Looking me up and down, he said, "I'm not Mr. Frey, but I'd be happy to fill in for him."

Ew. Gross. I forced a smile. "I'm looking for the *actual* Mr. Frey. Did you see anyone in there?"

"Sorry, sugar."

Now what? I cast a glance at the door at the end of the hall. The words painted on it—*emergency exit*—seemed to mock me. I suspected Walter Frey had taken Door #4 and escaped. He'd ditched me.

But why? Why show up just to leave?

Oh shit. Something had scared him.

I pushed the back door open and looked around the nearly empty parking lot. The only two vehicles back there were a pickup truck and a dark sedan parked several spaces apart. But then something to my left captured my attention. Walter Frey lay flat on his back, his eyes closed and his jacket partially open to reveal his white shirt.

"Mr. Frey?"

He didn't answer.

The hair on my arms stood on end as I walked around the door and called out his name again. The sky was spitting a light drizzle, and I shivered as I moved closer, dread making my stomach clench.

"Mr. Frey, are you okay?"

I knew something was wrong with him, but while the last man I'd found flat on his back, Max Goodwin, had been stabbed in the chest, Walter Frey looked like he'd fallen asleep on the grass.

But as I crept closer, slowly inching my way around his side, the small hole in his left temple and the blood pooling on the rain-soaked ground told me I was wrong.

Walter Frey was dead.

The back door opened, and Chuck peeked his head around the corner. "Hey, Pete said he saw you go out the back door . . ."

I glanced over at him, and his eyes widened when he saw the figure splayed beneath me.

"Oh shit. Looks like you found him," he said, his voice shaking. He looked liable to drop my bag, which he'd brought from the front. It was obvious finding dead guys behind his bar wasn't a common occurrence for him. "Is he alive?"

"I don't know. I didn't check." I dropped to my knees, sinking into the soggy grass, then placed a trembling finger on his neck as I searched for a pulse.

"So? Is he alive?" he repeated.

I shook my head, my stomach roiling as I stared at the blood still trickling from his head. I felt dangerously close to throwing up, but Detective Holden's voice echoed in my head. He'd been pissed because Amy and

I had almost vomited at the scene of Max Goodwin's murder.

Detective Holden had been eager to pin the last murder victim I'd found on me. What if he did the same this time?

"Oh, my God," Chuck said in a shaky voice. "What if the killer's still out here?"

His panic was infectious, but logic told me that whoever had done this was long gone. Otherwise, I was fairly certain I'd already be dead.

I took several deep breaths, pushing back my panic and trying to figure out what to do. "I need my phone," I said, settling my butt back on my heels. I felt too lightheaded to stand. This couldn't be happening. Not again.

My memories of the murder I'd witnessed ten years ago, on the night of my college graduation, had only surfaced a few weeks ago—dredged up by my return to Franklin and the sight of Max Goodwin's bloody body. Up until then, the only thing I'd remembered about that night was a sense of dread so strong it had set me running all the way to New York.

"What?"

I held out my hand for the phone. Chuck's reaction confirmed that he, at least, did not have a habit of stumbling upon dead bodies. "My phone. It's in my purse. Pull it out."

"Who are you going to call?" he asked, sounding nervous.

"The police."

He grabbed my phone and handed it to me, still holding on to my purse. As I started to unlock the screen, I noticed that I had a text message from a blocked number.

If you're digging into the past, be careful what you reveal.

I gasped and looked down at the bloodied man in front of me. Had *he* sent the message?

"Are you gonna call?" Chuck asked, sounding freaked out.

Of course, this wasn't the first cryptic message I'd received since my return to Franklin. At first I'd assumed they were a practical joke, but then my memories of that night had returned. Now I knew they were something more—warnings from the long-ago murderer who'd chased me out of town. And he hadn't just left texts . . .

I gave myself a mental shake. I'd figure out who had sent the text later. I needed to deal with this first.

"Yeah." I pulled up my contacts and started scrolling, thankful I didn't have to scroll very far. When he answered, I nearly cried with relief. "Brady?"

"*Maggie?*"

"I need your help."

"Where are you?" His voice became stern and professional—very cop-like. "What's happened?"

I glanced up at Chuck. Would my alibi be enough? I wasn't quite sure I could trust Brady. A few weeks ago, I'd gone to the Franklin police station to report what I'd remembered about the night of my high school graduation. They had assigned Brady to talk to me. I'd realized it was a huge mistake before I started talking. They'd think I was crazy, plain and simple, and I had no concrete information to give them. There was no body, no open case, and any evidence had gone cold a decade ago. Besides, the murderer had threatened my family, and the texts I'd received since returning to town were proof he was watching me.

Brady had insisted on taking a walk with me—as my friend, not as a police detective—and I'd foolishly let my guard down. The problem was that he hadn't realized my connection to the Goodwin case. Once he did, he told his partner all of the things I'd shared with them—things that made me look guilty of Max Goodwin's murder. It had caused me a good bit of trouble, and while Brady hadn't had much choice in the matter, I couldn't help but see it as a betrayal.

What if he betrayed me again?

"Maggie?"

It was the worry in his voice that worked my tongue loose. "I'm okay, but there's a man behind the Embassy bar. I think he's dead."

"Is there anyone else around? Are you in immediate danger?"

Was I? I glanced up at Chuck. "No. It's just me and the bartender. He walked out right after I found him."

"Keep everyone away and don't touch anything. I'm less than ten minutes away."

"Okay. Thanks." My voice shook on the last word.

"You okay?" he asked quietly.

"No," I said past the lump in my throat. Now that I'd passed over the mantel of responsibility to a professional, I was close to breaking into tears.

"I hate to ask you this," he said softly, "but I need you to watch over the body and make sure no one disturbs the crime scene."

"Yeah, of course," I said, feeling close to vomiting again as I stared at the hole in Walter Frey's head. "I'll stay."

"If it's too gruesome, you can turn your back." I was surprised to hear guilt in his voice.

"No," I said. "I can do it." I felt like I owed at least that much to the dead man in front of me.

Walter Frey was dead, and I was a hundred percent sure it was my fault.

chapter four

I stuffed my phone into my pocket and looked over at the poor bartender who was still standing in the doorway. "The police are on the way," I said. "He said to try to keep people away from the crime scene."

"That didn't sound like a 911 call."

"It wasn't. I know a Franklin police detective. He's on his way." I suddenly wondered why I had called Brady instead of 911. Did I expect him to protect me? Because he hadn't really followed through with protecting me in the past.

Chuck looked dubious. "Maybe I should call 911 anyway."

I wasn't sure if that was a good idea or not, but I preferred to let Brady make that decision. "He'll be here in a few minutes. Do you want to stay out here with me?"

He shook his head and cast a glance inside. "I need to get back in there. I guess I better tell my manager. He's gonna want to know."

"I know you have to tell your boss, but can you keep it from everyone else until Brady shows up?" I'd worked enough hospitality jobs to know that customers loved gossip and drama. The last thing we needed was for everyone in the bar to rush out here like poor Walter Frey's fate was reality show fodder.

"Yeah, yeah. I won't tell anyone," he grumbled as he went back inside, leaving me alone with the dead body and the drizzle. I'd found two dead men within a very short period of time. I had no idea how high the odds were of something like that happening, but I suspected most people had a better chance of winning the Powerball lottery.

Lucky me.

But this was different. My involvement in the Max Goodwin investigation had been an accident; Mr. Frey had been murdered outside the bar where we'd agreed to meet to discuss the night of my father's disappearance. If the police had tried to blame Goodwin's death on me, what would they do now?

I leaned over his body, trying to see if there was anything lying around to potentially incriminate me, but common sense told me to get up and back away. Brady would be here any minute, and while he was arguably the least threatening person in the Franklin Police Department, that didn't mean he would grant me any favors. He might—rightfully—think it was suspicious that Walter Frey had been murdered at the site of our secret meeting.

It only took a few seconds to figure out that the only thing around the body was a bloody puddle and trampled grass.

Trampled grass. The grass behind Mr. Frey's head was flattened, and I was fairly certain I could make out a set of footprints leading to the parking lot. That had to be in my favor.

I sat back on my heel, about to call it good, when something caught my eye. Mr. Frey still held his cell phone in his fisted hand, but sticking up behind it was a folded piece of white paper, like a piece of typing paper folded multiple times. Scribbled across the exposed part were three lines of writing, partially blurred from the ink running on the damp paper: Gerry Lopez, —rritt, and — ogers. I guessed the last two lines to be names, but they were too obscured for me to be sure.

The sound of car tires splashing through water caught my attention before the headlights spotlighted me. The car came to a stop in the middle of the parking lot, pointed toward me. The rhythmic sound of windshield wipers set my nerves on edge. When the car door opened and Brady got out, I tried to tell myself everything was going to be okay. While he'd turned me in to his partner in connection with the Goodwin case, I truly believed he hadn't done it to hurt me. If he'd held back information, it would have made things worse for both of us in the long run.

Which meant he might arrest me now if he deemed it necessary.

He started across the pavement toward me, the car's headlights still focused on the body and me. He glanced down at the trampled grass and then back up at me.

"Maggie, you okay?"

I nodded, suddenly dangerously close to tears. "Yeah."

"I'm coming around behind you. Just stay put, okay?"

I nodded and put my hands in my now-wet lap, then started to shiver.

"Where's your coat?" he asked as he walked around the curbed patch of grass.

"Inside. I hadn't planned on coming outside."

"Did you hear something?" He'd made it over to the sidewalk leading to the back door.

"No," I said, then took a breath. Brady seemed like the kind of guy who respected the truth, and I hadn't done anything wrong. I'd be better off trusting him. "I was supposed to meet him here, and the bartender said he'd headed to the restroom about ten minutes earlier. So I went to check on him. I found him out here."

"You know who he is?" he asked as he walked through the grass toward me.

"Walter Frey. He's a real estate attorney here in Franklin."

He reached out for me, and I grasped his hand, letting him help me to my feet. "Did you touch or disturb anything?"

"No. I just knelt next to him to check for a pulse. Chuck the bartender came out less than a minute after me. He thought I was leaving and brought me my purse. As soon as I realized Mr. Frey was dead, I called you."

"You didn't have to stay right next to him. You could have stood by the door." He shrugged off his jacket and set it on my shoulders.

I pointed to the grass. "I saw the footprints. I was afraid to get up and disturb anything."

"Good call." He gave me a gentle push toward the sidewalk, then bent over and felt for a pulse.

"Are more police coming?"

"Yeah. I called them as I pulled up. They'll be here in a few minutes." He looked down at the body, then over at the patch of grass. "Are you buying real estate?" he asked as he straightened.

It took me a moment to get the gist of his question. "Uh . . . no. He was my father's client. I saw him at Mellow Mushroom at lunch this afternoon and asked him to meet me here."

He swung his head around to study me, his questions obvious yet unasked.

I might as well tell him everything I could. "My father disappeared when I was fourteen. He had a meeting with Walter Frey the night of his disappearance. Daddy left for the meeting but never came home."

His eyebrows lifted. "Was he ever found?"

"No. But I was never satisfied with Mr. Frey's answers to the police, so when I saw him today, I asked him to meet me and tell me his version of events."

Brady started to ask me another question, but the wail of approaching sirens cut him off. "Why don't you wait inside? I'll be in to ask you more questions in a bit."

I nodded, a lump filling my throat. "I didn't do it, Brady. I didn't kill him."

His eyes widened in surprise. "I never said you did."

"I know how it looks . . ." I waved toward poor Mr. Frey. "How many people stumble onto two murder scenes in less than a month?"

The sirens grew closer.

"Despite how things went with the first case, I promise you'll be treated fairly this time. Besides, Amy Danvers confessed to the murders at the Powell estate before killing herself."

Red lights from the approaching police cars bounced off the pavement on the side parking lot.

Brady moved closer to me and put a hand on my upper arm, searching my eyes. "Magnolia, if you didn't do anything, you have nothing to worry about, no matter how it looks."

I told myself this was how it happened on all those documentaries. The detective lulls you into a false sense of security so you'll let your guard down and spill your secrets. While I had nothing to hide—other than what had happened the night of my high school graduation— I was still nervous. "So it looks bad?"

He glanced over his shoulder at the two police cars that had pulled up behind his sedan. "Just go inside and wait for me, okay? Don't talk to anyone else. Tell them you're waiting for me."

Nausea churned in my stomach as I watched several uniformed policemen heading toward us.

"*Maggie.*"

I glanced back up at him, his dark brown eyes intense as they held mine. "Trust me."

Tears filled my eyes and my voice hardened. "I did that before, Brady. Look how that turned out."

He paused. "That night when we went out for coffee, you asked me if I was fair when I looked at evidence, and I assured you that I am. I'm not Detective Holden. Believe me. I want to find the real perpetrator." He paused and the side of his mouth tipped up into a small smile. "You must trust me a little if you called me instead of 911."

"How do you know I'm not taking advantage of *you*?" Oh, God. Why had I blurted that out? But as bad as it sounded, I needed to know if this semi-trust went both ways.

His smile reached his eyes. "Because I always follow my instincts." He put an arm around my back and ushered me to the back door, which Chuck had left propped open. "Now go order some coffee or tea to warm up and wait for me to take your statement."

Call me a fool, but I believed him, which made me equally frightened and furious with myself. He opened the door and waited for me to walk inside, but I slipped off his jacket and handed it to him. "I think you need this more than I do."

As soon as he took the jacket from me, he turned to face two of the policemen who now stood behind him.

"We need to set up a perimeter past the strip of grass," he said, his voice now professional and in charge. "Block off the rear parking lot for now."

His voice faded as I let the door close behind me. I went into the bathroom and pressed my back to the wall for a couple of minutes while I tried to get control of myself. Now that Brady had taken over, I felt lightheaded and nauseated.

What had I done?

When I felt a little more composed, I checked my appearance in the mirror. My hair was covered in tiny rain droplets, but my mascara was only slightly smudged. My cheeks and nose were red from the cold, and now that I didn't have Brady's jacket around me, I couldn't stop shivering.

Deciding I didn't look *so* bad, considering, I swiped away the smudges under my eyes and headed back to the bar.

Chuck made a beeline for me as I approached my previous seat. "The police have already been inside asking everyone to stay put."

I nodded and grabbed my jacket from the stool and slipped it on before sitting down. "I don't suppose you make expresso drinks here?"

He quirked a half-smile. "You're lucky to get decent coffee here."

"Then I'll try my luck. Cream and sugar, please."

He gave me a nod before he walked over to an ancient-looking coffee pot.

"*Magnolia?*"

Stunned at the familiar voice, I spun around in my seat. "*Colt?*"

"What the hell are you doin' here, Maggie?" he asked with worry in his eyes.

"I guess you've heard the news."

"That there's a dead man lying on a patch of grass behind the building? Yeah, Chuck was quick to tell me." He hefted the weight of the guitar case in his hand.

"I told him not to tell anyone."

His eyes widened with realization. "Oh, my God. *You're* the one who found him."

I leaned forward and grabbed his arm. "Shh! Don't shout it!"

Colt moved closer. "What the hell, Maggie?"

"I didn't kill him!" I whisper-shouted.

"I didn't say you did."

I glanced around the room to see if anyone was paying attention to us, but everyone seemed lost in their own worlds. "What are you doing here?"

He lifted the guitar case. "I thought this made it pretty obvious. I have the next set."

"You play here?"

"Hey, beggars can't be choosers. I need the rehearsal time, and you never know who's gonna be listening. The question is what are *you* doin' here?"

I cringed. "I was supposed to meet the dead man out back."

"Maggie." There was worry and a hint of disappointment in his voice, although I had no idea why he would be disappointed with me. "Oh, God. You were meeting Elmer Fudd, weren't you?"

Chuck banged on the bar. "Dude, we're payin' you to play, not to hit on the customers. Get up there and dedicate a song to her or somethin'. Everyone's waitin' on you."

Colt shot him a glare, but I shook my head.

"We'll talk later." I gave him a tiny push. "Go do what you need to do. You literally have a captive audience."

He put a hand on my arm. "Are you sure? I'll blow them off if you want me to sit with you." He ignored Chuck's scowl.

I glanced toward the hall. "No, I'd like to hear you play."

"I'm here for you, Maggie. I mean it."

I felt my guard loosen as I looked up into his crystal blue eyes. Colt had declared himself to be my friend, but I'd always kind of assumed he was playing the long game to get into my pants, even after his rough encounter with my brother. Studying his face now, though, I finally believed he meant it. "Thanks."

He nodded and walked over to the stage, which had indeed been vacated. The previous musician was nursing a beer in one of the booths, barely looking at the face of the woman sitting across from him as she leaned over the table to show him her sagging cleavage.

The life of a musician.

"Here's your coffee," Chuck said as he set the cup in front of me. "It looks remarkably similar to car oil, and there's no guarantee it doesn't taste the same."

I grinned, even though I was sick with worry about how my questioning would go. "I guess I'll take my chances."

The coffee wasn't as bad as Chuck had warned it would be. Colt pulled his guitar out of his case, then sat on the low stool and adjusted his microphone.

"This looks like a crowd who can appreciate the classics." He broke out into a slightly updated version of Waylon Jennings's "Good Hearted Woman." While he was singing, he cast a glance at me and winked, and cheesy though it was, it filled me with reassurance.

Several uniformed police officers walked in and started talking to the patrons one-on-one, but Colt kept on singing. And he didn't once shift his gaze off me.

I'd heard him sing the night of Max Goodwin's murder, but this was the first time I'd heard him sing alone. He broke into a Vince Gill song next while the police continued to make their rounds. To my surprise, they steered clear of me, but Brady had promised to question me himself.

When Colt finished his song, he shifted his guitar. "I'd like to switch gears and ask my friend Maggie Mae to help me with this next one." He smiled at me. "What do you say, Maggie?"

I cringed. I was waiting to be questioned in connection with a murder. This was most likely a very bad idea.

"I think she needs a little encouragement," Colt said, facing the room with a grin. "Why don't you all help her out?"

A lukewarm applause broke out, not that I was surprised. Colt wasn't kidding about using this place as a rehearsal. But I hadn't performed in weeks, and there was no denying I was itching for an excuse to sing somewhere other than in my shower. Besides, what better way to escape my fear and worry for a few minutes? I slid off my stool.

A look of triumph stole across Colt's face. "And here she comes," he said with his Southern drawl, reaching out his free hand and helping me up onto the foot-tall stage.

"Got anything in mind?" I asked away from the microphone. "My knowledge of country songs is limited to the top twenty hits."

He winked again. "I think you'll know this one. Lady Antebellum's 'Need You Now.'"

"Trying to tell me something?" I teased.

"Nothin' you don't already know," he growled. Then he started strumming the intro on his guitar.

Tapping my hand on my leg to keep the beat, I leaned into the single microphone on the stand and started the female singer's first verse. He leaned his face close to mine—wearing a huge grin—and joined me for the chorus.

"It's a quarter after one, I'm all alone, and I need you now."

Colt shot me an *I told you so* grin as we sang, and I couldn't deny he was right—our voices blended well together. We were better than I'd expected, and it felt amazing to lose myself in the music.

After he sang the male singer's second verse, I pulled out the mic and held it between us as we moved into the chorus again.

Somewhere in the middle of the song, a movement to my right caught my eye. Brady was standing in the dark hallway with his shoulder leaning against the wall. His gaze caught mine, and something inside me coiled tight as I held his gaze and continued to sing about needing a vague *you.*

I was a performer. Singing with other men—and women—was nothing new, and neither was singing to an audience, but something in Brady's expression had me spellbound.

So much so that Colt noticed. He gave me a strange look, then tracked my gaze to Brady before turning back to me with a quizzical expression.

That was enough to snap me out of my daze, my face flushing with embarrassment. Why was I so attracted to Brady Bennett? I'd originally been fooled into thinking he was a genuinely nice guy, but I'd quickly realized he was just another good-looking charmer with an agenda. His particular agenda just happened to be finding out who'd killed Walter Frey. Which would probably put us at odds. Again.

So why was I still drawn to him?

Probably because he seemed like the exact opposite of every guy I'd been involved with in New York City.

Ignoring Brady, I turned my attention to Colt, professing how much I needed him and putting a little acting into the performance. Colt put himself into it, selling his role as hard as I was selling mine.

We finished the song, and to my surprise, a respectable applause broke out. I smiled and gave a wave of thanks.

"That was Maggie Mae, everyone," Colt said as I stepped off the stage. "I suspect we'll be hearing a lot more of her."

I looked over my shoulder, trying to figure out what he had meant by that, but he'd already launched into "The Gambler" by Kenny Rogers. Talk about musical whiplash.

When I turned around, Brady was walking toward me.

A jolt of electricity shot through me as I watched him. He was definitely a *very* attractive man. He was tall, with thick, wavy brown hair, expressive deep brown eyes, and a broad chest that I knew from experience was firm and muscular. I'd been pressed against it outside the coffee shop.

When we'd kissed.

Looking back, I was still shocked I'd kissed him. I wasn't prone to public displays of affection, let alone with a man I'd just met. Every relationship I'd had in New York had been superficial . . . initiated because I was lonely or wanted sex. I'd lived with Griff, but I'd never been in love with him or any man. Though my mind had protected me from the memories of graduation night, some part of me had internalized the murderer's threat: don't tell anyone, or else. I'd kept an emotional distance from people without realizing why.

Now that I remembered everything, I *knew* I couldn't let people get close. If I did, the murderer would know, and they'd be in danger.

Which meant I needed to be on guard more than ever. And that definitely did not entail dating a police officer.

Yet there was no denying that there was something about Brady that drew me in like a moth to a flame, no matter how I tried to reason it away.

The kiss had been an indulgence, but it had seemed safe at the time. I'd never expected to see Brady again. I had planned to head back to New York to reprise my role as Scarlett in *Fireflies at Dawn*. My scandal had sold plenty of tickets, but the understudy/slut who had replaced me had sucked. The producers had tried everything they could think of to try to get me back, and truth be told, if Momma hadn't told me about her terminal illness, I would have taken the job back in a heartbeat—especially since they had fired Griff and assured me I wouldn't face any kind of sexual harassment and intimidation on set. My agent was beside himself when I at first kept turning down the producers' offers, only to have him tell me what a "smart girl" I was when they then sent in higher counteroffers in response.

But I had stayed, and now Brady was standing right across from me.

It didn't matter that there were sparks between us though. I needed to keep this professional.

Steeling my back, I said, "Where would you like—"

"How about we go—" he said at the same time. He smiled. "Ladies first."

"I was going to ask you where you wanted to do this."

He cast a glance at Colt, who was still singing about his poker hand, then returned his gaze to me. "How about we go somewhere quieter?"

The coil inside me tightened and my imagination ran wild as I considered where someplace quieter might be and what we might do there. I quickly tamped it down. *Get control of yourself, Magnolia.*

Brady sensed my hesitation and gave me a half-smile. "I'm starving. I was headed to a late dinner when you called. How about we head over to the Red Barn Café?"

I was torn. The side I'd let loose with him wanted to feel something again. But I knew better. I had to tell him no, but I couldn't bear to do it.

To buy myself more time, I walked over to the bar to get my purse and then headed for the front door, turning back to give Colt a wave goodbye. His eyes penetrated mine, but I quickly turned and walked outside. I stopped on the sidewalk, under an overhang, as I tried to encourage myself to do the *sensible* thing.

Brady followed me and stopped a respectable distance away . . . far enough away to let me know he was still there but I was totally in charge of what happened next.

He shoved his hands into his jeans pockets. "We don't have to go to the café. We can sit in your car or mine if you prefer."

"Don't you need to stay?" I asked, gesturing toward the police cars in the parking lot.

"I wasn't officially on duty when you called. I've handed the case over to another detective. I only stuck around long enough to make sure the transfer went smoothly."

I gasped. "I'm sorry." But that meant he wasn't in charge. So maybe I *would* become a suspect.

He gave a slight shake of his head. "I'm not. You have no idea how relieved I was that you felt safe calling me. Especially after our last conversation." As if sensing my hesitation, he added, "But this is a professional interview, Maggie. I don't want you to feel intimidated in any way, and I definitely don't want a repeat of what happened in the Goodwin murder case. So you tell me what will put you at ease."

I looked down, unsure of what to say. Our last conversation had taken place on the sidewalk outside a restaurant downtown. He'd tried to convince me that what we'd shared had been too special to just throw away. He wanted to give a relationship between us a try. I'd told him that I didn't trust him enough to start over, but apart from the look we exchanged while I was onstage, so far he'd come across as completely professional, if not overly compassionate. "If you passed off the case, why are you taking my statement?"

"I told Owen I'd handle it for him. You're not a person of interest, Maggie. This is merely a witness statement. They already have a statement from the bartender that you were gone for only a minute or two before he came looking for you. The grass was trampled like there had been a confrontation, with large footprints leading away to the parking lot. And finally, there's the fact that the victim was shot and you didn't have a gun."

"How do you know I didn't?"

He gave me look that said *please*. "You weren't wearing a coat, so the only place you could have hidden a gun was in the back waistband of your jeans, covered by your shirt."

"How do you know I didn't do that?"

"Because when I put my arm around your back, I didn't feel a weapon."

I gasped. "You were patting me down for murder weapons with your arm?"

"No." His voice deepened. "I was trying to get you inside out of the rain—and maybe give you a little comfort at the same time."

I wasn't sure how to respond.

"Maggie, I told you I trust my instincts, and they told me you didn't kill that man. I will admit that I'm worried he was murdered at the very location he was supposed to meet you, which is why I requested to take your statement. I want to make sure *you're* not in any danger."

"Oh." I had to wonder if he was right. I already knew I was in danger from the murderer from ten years ago, but what if I'd put myself in a different spotlight of danger? It definitely wouldn't hurt to tell a police detective about my father's disappearance. Or the text I'd gotten after finding Mr. Frey's body.

But he mistook my hesitation. "I know I hurt you, but this is—"

"Brady," I said, wondering if I would ultimately regret this but going for it anyway. I was scared, and at the moment, Brady represented safety. I was going to indulge the illusion, even if it was only for an hour. "Let's finish this discussion at the restaurant."

chapter five

He smiled, and the way his eyes lit up sent another jolt of electricity through me. Falling for Brady was a very, very bad idea, I reminded myself. He would find out about my own disappearance when I was a teenager—how I'd disappeared from my graduation party and showed up hours later covered in mud and grass—and then he'd ask questions I couldn't answer. What would I do then? I had to find a way to protect my heart.

Find a role. When I found myself in a situation that made me anxious, I'd always found a role to play, a character to impersonate. But at the moment, none came to mind.

"How about I follow you there?" he said. "Do you know where it is?"

"Yeah."

He walked me to my car and opened the door. I reminded myself of why I should keep my distance from him. But Brady had missed his dinner, and if I went, it meant I'd have a captive audience. Maybe I could convince him to reopen the investigation of Daddy's disappearance. Part of me felt bad using Brady like that, but the rest of me knew I was deluding myself to believe that was my only reason.

I almost chickened out a dozen times during the short drive to the restaurant. In the end, the only reason I didn't turn around was the pesky fact that I was about to give Brady my official police statement. I was stuck.

While I parked a good minute before him, I was amazed by how quickly he parked, got out of his car, and intercepted me.

"It's like you think I'm about to pull a runner," I half teased.

"As skittish as you're acting, I considered the possibility." He lifted his eyebrows. "Before I reasoned that you were nervous because you were a person of interest in a murder, but now I'm thinking it's me."

Play a part. I found one, settling into the young woman with secrets to hide and seeking help from a man she couldn't trust. The fact that my role was the exact situation I was in meant nothing. I'd played this game too many times to count. I only had to believe I was playing someone other than me.

I laughed, showing more confidence than I felt. "You don't need to look so cocky. For the record, I could still be a person of interest. Someone else is in charge of the investigation."

"But I already told you you're not."

I lifted my eyebrows in challenge. "And yet I'm still concerned."

A frown was his only comment. He walked past me to open the door, then waited for me to walk in first. The restaurant was nearly empty well after nine on a Tuesday night, and given the late hour, I was surprised when the hostess showed us to a table. It overlooked the Harpeth River, although the view was lost on us with the dark and the rain. We sat down and gave our drink orders—water for both of us—then sat in silence for a moment.

I ran through everything I'd said to him since I'd called, trying to remember if I'd incriminated myself in any way. Then something hit me full force. I put my hand on the table, striking a pose as I lifted my chin. "You didn't seem very surprised when I told you I was at the Embassy bar. The last time we talked, I told you I was leaving for New York."

He leaned back in his chair, looking uncomfortable. "I already knew you hadn't gone."

"How?"

His demeanor changed, as though he'd decided to own up to it. "You work downtown. I work and eat downtown." He shrugged. "People talk."

"About me?"

"You can't be all that surprised. You're a celebrity."

"No. I'm not. Not really."

"You don't see it?"

I shook my head. "No. I'm just the latest internet sensation, and I will soon be forgotten." At least I sure as hell hoped so.

He started to say something, then stopped and switched gears. "Tell me about your father."

"You don't want to jump right into my statement about finding poor Mr. Frey?"

"We'll get there. I'm not going anywhere. Are you?"

He held my gaze in a challenge, and I felt my defenses weaken. *Stay strong, Magnolia. But maybe he can help with Daddy* . . . "Don't you need it right away to catch whoever did this?"

"I've already passed what you told me on to Owen. Your statement is a formality. Besides," he added, "I suspect the information you're about to give me will be far more helpful." His gaze held mine. His eyes were warm and kind, and the fortified wall around my heart crumbled a little. "Now tell me about your father, Maggie."

"He was a financial planner and partner with JS Investments. He worked in downtown Nashville. Walter Frey was one of his clients."

Brady sat up and pulled a small notebook and pen out of his pocket. "How long had he worked there?"

"You're serious," I said in amazement. "You're really interested in this." After all the times people had told me to let it go, that Daddy had just run away, it felt amazing to have someone believe me.

He looked up in surprise. "The coincidence is too great. I want to know everything you remember. Now how long had he worked there?"

"Since before I was born. Around the time he married Momma."

"And how long ago was that?"

I did some mental math. "Thirty-one or thirty-two years."

"Did your father act suspiciously before his disappearance?"

I nodded. "Yeah. I was fourteen when it happened, but he started acting paranoid about six months before. He took me to the firing range and told me I needed to learn to protect myself."

Brady's gaze flicked to mine. "Protect yourself from what?"

"He never said. I asked him why he didn't teach my brother Roy too, but he said Roy and I were like night and day, and that it was up to me to protect my family."

"Protect your family? Did he say what you were protecting it from?"

I shook my head. "No."

"And who was in your family at the time?"

"Roy—who's two years younger—and my mother."

"Did your mother remarry?"

"No. Daddy was officially declared dead about seven years ago, but Momma was never interested in other men."

"So no hurry to collect on the insurance?"

I shook my head. "No." I'd been so furious when I'd found out that Momma had declared him dead, but she'd countered my argument with her favorite trump card: I'd run off to New York City and never looked back. That meant I had no say in the matter. Besides, Daddy was never coming back and I was deluded to think otherwise. The anger in her voice hadn't shocked me. It was the absolute grief in her words that had shaken me.

"Was there very much money?"

I narrowed my eyes, a seed of anger sprouting in my chest. "If you're suggesting my momma did something unsavory to my father, you're barkin' up the wrong tree. She *loved* him."

He looked up with a slight grin. "I love how you sound more Southern when you get riled up."

Crap. That was a nasty habit I'd picked up from my mother. "Nevertheless." I made sure to enunciate the syllables. "I know there wasn't much money involved. For all I know, she put it toward her catering business." The timing of the opening of their Main Street location fit.

"She didn't tell you what she did with it, and you didn't ask?"

"I was in New York."

He gave me an odd look. "You didn't talk much on the phone?"

"My mother and I didn't see eye to eye."

"She didn't approve of your career choice?"

"Um . . ." This was starting to delve into dangerous territory. "Let's just say Momma and I had our moments."

"What made you decide to come back home to stay?"

I gave him a guarded look. "Is that part of the investigation?"

He gave me an unreadable look. "Perhaps . . ."

"My reasons don't seem pertinent to this discussion."

He studied me for a few seconds before he said, "When did you go to New York?"

"I'm not really sure what that has to do with this investigation either." The curiosity on his face told me that was the wrong answer. I'd only made him more intrigued. Somehow I had to regain control.

The waitress came back with our waters and asked, "You two ready to order?"

Brady gave me an apologetic look. "I didn't give you time to look at the menu."

"That's okay. I'm not ordering anything."

He grinned and the dimple on his right cheek appeared. "You have to order *something*. If you don't, can you imagine how bad I'll look if I eat in front of you? My mother would be mortified."

"Do you always order food for the witnesses you interview?"

"On occasion."

That surprised me. Was it for women he was interested in, like me, or just because he was a nice guy?

I suspected it was the latter and felt guilty for being so suspicious of him when he was clearly trying to put me at ease.

I grabbed the menu and quickly scanned it, then looked up at our waitress. "What's your soup of the day?"

"Creamy baked potato."

"I'll take that."

"And I'll take a club sandwich," Brady said. He handed our waitress the menus, then waited until she was out of earshot. "You said your father was behaving strangely."

"Yeah," I said, relieved he was letting go of my more current history. "Sometimes he'd think someone was watching him. He started going to evening meetings. He'd never done that before, but he told my mother that the market was tight—we were in a recession—and that he had to soothe his clients' concerns. Which meant night meetings. More meetings than my mother had liked."

"What did your mother say about his behavior?"

I was quiet for a moment. "She and my father were at odds." I gave him a smile. "My mother is a very strong woman, but my father was a strong man, so you can imagine they butted heads frequently. I was used to it, but this was different. As Daddy became paranoid, Momma grew reserved—something totally unlike her."

"Tell me about the night he disappeared. How did you know your father went to meet Walter Frey?"

"My father took me to the dentist that morning. Then I spent some time at his office before he took me back to school during his lunch hour. I saw Mr. Frey then."

"You were living in Nashville?"

"No, we never moved from the house I grew up in, here in Franklin. My parents bought the house before I was born. My mother still lives there."

"Most people who live in Franklin go to the dentist here rather than drive into Nashville. Did he take you there because it was closer to his work?"

"I don't know," I said, searching my memories. "We usually went to the dentist here—Dr. Murphy on Cool Springs Boulevard." I shook my head. "For some reason, I saw a new one that morning."

He shifted in his seat as he scribbled in his notebook, then looked back up at me. "Was it a special appointment? An orthodontist? Oral surgeon?"

"No." My eyes widened as a memory hit me. "It was my first time there. A new dentist. Momma didn't know."

He stilled and cocked his head. "What do you mean your mother didn't know?"

"She was helping out at my brother's school that day. They left early together." I paused. "I think he had a field trip, and they had to be at school an hour or two early. They'd only been gone a few minutes when Daddy told me that I wasn't catching the bus. That I had a dentist appointment." How had I forgotten that? "I told him that Momma had taken me to the dentist a few months before, but he told me not to worry about it. That it was just a consultation."

"Did anything unusual happen at the dentist appointment?"

"Daddy walked into the exam room with me, which I thought was odd. I was too old to have my father go with me. Then the dentist walked in and gave me headphones to watch TV. He looked in my mouth for less than a minute; then Daddy told me he and the dentist needed to talk about something. I was worried something was wrong, but he assured me that everything was okay. They were discussing something else. Then they stood by the window and talked."

"But you didn't hear what they said? Because of the headphones?"

Tears stung my eyes. I felt like a fool. "No."

He wrote something in his notebook, then looked up and waited for a few seconds. "You okay?" he asked. "You need a moment?"

"Why didn't I realize that meant something?"

"You don't know that it actually did. They really could have been talking about your teeth."

I narrowed my eyes. "Do you really believe that?"

He paused. "No."

"But if I'd told the police. Or my mother . . ." What if I'd ruined any hope of finding my father?

"Maggie." He waited until I looked into his warm brown eyes. "You were fourteen. You weren't Nancy Drew. You weren't expected to put *anything* together. He was your father. You trusted him. It sounds like he purposely tried to hide whatever he was doing from you. As well as from your mother."

"But the appointment was a front. He used me as an excuse to meet someone."

"Maybe."

I took a sip of my water while I viewed every memory I had of my father through a different lens.

"Do you remember the dentist's name?" he asked.

I searched my hazy recollection. "No. I never went back."

"That's okay," he reassured me. "We still might be able to figure out who he saw. For now, let's keep going. After they talked, what happened next?"

"Daddy told me that the dentist said everything looked good and we could go. Then we hung out at his office for an hour or so before he took me to school."

"During his lunch hour, right? And no one in the office thought it was strange you were there?"

"No. Momma often brought Roy and me to see him."

"But for you to stay with him for an hour or more?"

"We'd go spend part of the day with him during summer breaks. Usually only me . . . Mom would send me there when Roy's and my bickering got on her nerves. I loved to come to his office. Usually I'd sit in one of his client chairs and read, but sometimes his assistant would give me simple jobs to do, like making copies or filing. Roy only tolerated it whenever he went. He preferred hanging out in the woods behind our house with his friend."

He nodded and continued to write in his notebook. "You said you saw Walter Frey when you were leaving?"

I told him about the bizarre incident outside the elevator, how Daddy had said he'd already talked to someone named Geraldo, how Mr. Frey had rebutted with, "He knows," and how they'd arranged to meet that night at eight at "the usual spot." It still hurt to talk about how Daddy had lied to me afterward, saying Mr. Frey had only been upset over a bum stock.

Brady gave me a soft smile. "You were close to your father. I can tell."

"Much more so than my mother," I admitted. "Momma and I butted heads regularly. Daddy said it was because we were too much alike. After a disagreement, he would often take me out of the house." I pushed out a breath. "On that day, Daddy took me back to school and told me there was no need to mention the trip to the dentist to Momma since everything was fine. We didn't want to worry her. Momma and Roy came home after school, and then Momma made us dinner before she went out with Tilly for their girls' night out."

"Tilly?"

"Momma's best friend. They own the catering business together."

"So your mother went with Tilly, leaving you with your brother and father?"

"Yeah. After she left, I went to my room to do some school work. Around seven thirty, Daddy came into my room and sat next to me on my bed. He asked me if I remembered where his gun was."

Brady stopped writing and looked up. "Did you?"

"Yeah, it was in the padlocked box in the basement. But I didn't get it." Not then, anyway. But I *had* retrieved it the night of Max Goodwin's murder. "Daddy kissed me on the forehead, told me he loved me, and left." A lump filled my throat. "I never saw him again."

He held my gaze. "I'm sorry."

I wiped a tear from my eye. "It happened fourteen years ago."

"And yet you're still hurting."

There was no denying that.

The waitress showed up with our food, and Brady took a bite of his sandwich as I dipped my spoon into my soup.

"Daddy never came home, and Momma sat up worrying," I said, scraping the bottom of the spoon against the lip of the bowl. "She wanted to know where he'd gone, and I wasn't sure what to tell her. I didn't think Daddy wanted her to know. But I was worried sick. So around midnight, I told her. She was *furious* with me for keeping it from her." My voice broke as the memory filled my head. Her words had cut me deeply that night. I set the spoon down. "She called the police, and I told them what I knew—that Daddy had arranged to meet Walter Frey at eight o'clock, but that I didn't know where. They questioned him, but he denied there had been a meeting. In fact, he claimed he had no idea what I was talking about or where my father had gone. His wife provided his alibi."

"Did they find any leads that you know about?"

"One million dollars was missing from one of his client's bank accounts. And Mr. Morrissey's wife was missing too. My mother had told the police about all of my father's evening appointments, and they decided my father had been having an affair with Shannon Morrissey. The two of them stole the money from her husband— her name wasn't on the account—and ran off together."

"But you obviously don't believe that."

Anger and grief blended together, mushrooming in my chest. "My father would never steal anyone's money. He would never run off with some other woman. Daddy would never have just left me." As I stopped my tirade, I realized how juvenile and naïve I sounded. But I knew Daddy had loved me. He'd been the rock I'd clung to throughout my childhood and early teen years. He knew how much I needed him. He was the only person who had truly understood me. I just didn't believe he'd abandon me like that.

"Maggie." Brady reached across the table and covered my hand with his. "I'll try to figure out what happened to your father, but what if you don't like what we find?"

It didn't escape my notice that his words echoed Colt's. But when it came down to it, I could either believe in my father or not. I could either let fourteen years of memories fortify my belief in him, or let a forgotten memory about a dentist appointment plant a seed of distrust.

I believed in my father.

"I want to know."

chapter six

"So you said you saw Walter Frey at Mellow Mushroom this afternoon?"

"Yeah," I said, looking down so he couldn't see the tears filling my eyes. *Keep it together, Magnolia.* I'd shown more emotion in the three weeks I'd been back in Franklin than in the ten years I'd spent in New York, but maybe that was simply what happened when you stopped running.

When I finally met his eyes, the compassion in them amazed me. "Are you always this kind with the people you question?"

His answer was immediate. "I am with the people who've been hurt. Or people who are scared."

"But not with criminals."

He watched me for a second, indecision wavering in his eyes. "I believe everyone is innocent until proven guilty."

"Are you being nice to me now because you feel sorry for me?"

"I'm being nice to you because you found a dead body and your father disappeared fourteen years ago and you're still grieving his loss. I won't deny that you intrigue me, Magnolia Steele, but I'm willing to let things ride for now. Something tells me you need a police investigator more than you do a boyfriend. Right now, anyway."

A tingle skated down my spine, but I tried to remain detached. "So you are still interested?"

His gaze held mine. "I won't lie. I respect you too much for that, and I want to be up front so there's no mistaking my intent. I hope you change your mind at some point and give this a chance. But in the meantime, I'm willing to wait."

"Why? Because I'm Magnolia Steele, former Broadway star, internet embarrassment?"

I half expected him to become angry, but he smiled, his dimple showing again. "No. You're forgetting that I was intrigued by you before I ever knew who you were. I'm interested in Maggie, the woman who ran across the street to accuse her potential stalker." He lifted his eyebrow. "Not that I recommend you do that again, but you have no idea how hot that was."

It had happened minutes after we'd first met in a sandwich shop near Southern Belles. I'd realized he was walking in the same direction as me, but on the opposite side of Main Street. When I'd caught him watching at me, I'd crossed the street—in front of moving cars—to

call him out on it, going so far as to poke him in his chest
to prove my point. He'd only been amused. The next
time I'd seen him was at the police station.

"Well," I said in my defense, "you *were* going in the
same direction and watching me."

"Promise me something."

I stiffened. I didn't do promises. "What?"

"If you really think someone is watching or
following you, either call me or 911, okay? Don't
confront them."

But someone *was* watching me. My heart started
beating double-time in my chest. Did I trust Brady
enough to tell him about the night I'd blocked from my
memory, like I'd originally intended that night at the
station?

The old fears came roiling back. What if the killer
hurt Momma? Or Roy? I was no fan of my brother, but
I couldn't let him get killed because of me.

But maybe there was one thing I could tell him. The
text I'd gotten tonight was more likely connected with
Mr. Frey's murder than with my other texter. "I got a text
tonight. Before I found Mr. Frey's body."

His smile was instantly gone. "What did it say?"

"Something about some things being better left in
the past."

Anger filled his eyes. "And you didn't think to tell
me that sooner?"

I couldn't tell him the truth, that I'd held back
because I didn't know who'd sent it—Frey's murderer or
the one who'd been stalking me—or what "things" it

meant. So I went with the most asinine excuse ever. "I forgot."

The look of disbelief he gave me was almost comical. "You *forgot* you were threatened?"

"I wasn't exactly *threatened*," I said dismissively.

"You've got to be fucking kidding me, Magnolia."

His anger caught me off guard. "I told you now."

"You should have told me when I found you next to a dead body an hour ago. You're in danger."

As if in agreement, I felt my phone buzz in my jeans pocket.

Oh, God, what if it was *him*?

I'd let myself get lulled into a false sense of security, but if the killer from my past knew I was socializing with a police detective—*again*—there was no knowing what he'd do. Why had I agreed to this?

I needed to see what that text said. "I have to go," I said, setting down the spoon.

"What?" He looked stunned. "*Now?*"

Good God. Pure panic surged through me, which probably only made me look more suspicious. I needed to get as far away from Brady Bennett as possible. "I hadn't planned to be gone so long, and I promised my mother I would have the car back by ten."

When he looked at me this time, his eyes were guarded. It didn't take a genius to discern this was his cop face. "It's only nine thirty."

I grabbed my purse and stood. "I'm tired. I had a fight with my mother and quit my job; then I found a dead man who might have been the last person to see my father alive. It's been a shitty day, Brady. I want to go home."

He stayed in his seat, looking up me. His expression softened just a little. "I know, and I'm sorry, but I need to ask you a few more questions, and I need to see that text."

Well, shit. Of course he did. But I couldn't show him my phone, not right now. I didn't know what the new text said, and I hadn't deleted the other threatening texts. I'd left them on my phone as a reminder to be careful.

"Can I go to the restroom first?" I asked, summoning tears. It wasn't hard to do. I was close to losing it.

Brady stood but kept a few feet between us. "I'm sorry, Maggie."

They were such simple words, but he obviously meant them. To my embarrassment, the dam to my emotions burst, and I started to cry.

He gently pulled me to his chest, wrapping his arms around me, and damned if I didn't let him. I fit against him perfectly, which made me cry all the more. I'd finally found a man who knocked down my walls, but I couldn't risk being with him. He was too dangerous.

His hand pressed against my back, his fingers moving gently up and down in a comforting gesture. I sank into him more, starting to relax, and my crying subsided. It had been a long time since I'd let anyone hold and comfort me.

As hard as it was to give up the comfort of his touch, I made myself take a step back. "I'm sorry."

He kept his arms wrapped around me, leaving inches between us as he searched my face. "You're right, Maggie. You've had a shitty day, but it scared the hell out of me that you were so lackadaisical about that text."

I chuckled, wiping tears from my cheek. "Lackadaisical? You get that word from your fancy Belmont education?"

He looked pleased. "You remembered where I went to college."

I remembered everything from the night we'd strolled down Main Street together.

But Brady Bennett was dangerous. Why did I keep forgetting that?

I took a step back, out of his hold. "Can I go to the restroom and clean myself up?"

"Of course. You're not a suspect. You don't need to ask permission."

"Thank you."

I headed straight for the bathroom, digging my cell phone out of my jeans pocket before the bathroom door even closed.

The text was waiting for me on the screen:

Someone is being a very bad girl. Are you willing to pay the price?

It was accompanied by a hazy photo of Belinda standing next to her car.

Oh, God. Oh, God. Oh, God.

Did communication with a hidden number work both ways? Would he get my text if I answered? I had to try. It took three attempts to type it out with my shaking fingers:

I haven't said anything about that night. To anyone.

I held my breath as I pressed send. To my relief, I didn't get an error message.

I waited several seconds before a text came back.

Then everyone is safe. For now.

Whatever it took, I had to protect Belinda.

I took screenshots of the texts about Belinda and deleted them. Once that was done, I scrolled back and pulled up the old texts, one by one, and did the same thing.

Welcome home, Magnolia. I've been waiting.

The first message had arrived on my first night back in Franklin. After Max Goodwin's murder. The number was blocked, and while it had terrified me, I'd tried to dismiss the seriousness of it.

Secrets don't make friends.

The second was more ominous, but Belinda had just dropped me off after a Bunco night with some vicious old high school friends, including my ex-best friend Maddie. My memories hadn't yet returned at that point, and I'd considered the possibility that Maddie's husband might have sent the text. He was the last person I'd seen that night before everything went blank. But while Blake Green may have chased me deep into the woods that night, I'd lost him before stumbling into the abandoned house in the woods.

The third message wasn't a text, but a card that had been left on my front porch with a magnolia blossom. There was nothing to delete—the photo I'd taken of the flower and the card was already stored elsewhere on my phone, but I remembered exactly what the card said.

I'm still watching, Magnolia.

That "gift" had arrived the morning after I'd ventured out into the woods and found the house from my nightmares. I'd entered the old house, and all my memories had come tumbling back. That was when I'd gone to the police station to tell them everything—only to change my mind.

If I'd harbored any doubt as to who had sent the texts and the flower, another text had arrived about a week after I'd decided to stay in Franklin.

If you talk, there will be a price I'm sure you're not willing to pay.

That very afternoon, I'd found a dead cat on my front porch. A cat that looked almost exactly like my childhood pet. Momma and I were both horrified, but when I told her that I would bury it at the edge of our backyard and the woods, she said, "Don't be silly, Magnolia. That's what animal control is for."

Of course, I couldn't let animal control see that whoever had killed the poor thing had slit it open from stem to stern, and carved a backward C with a line through it on its back. The same mark the killer had dug into my right upper thigh. Especially when I read the next text, sent later that night.

A cat is such a simple thing. I much prefer people. Be careful.

After I finished taking the screen shots and deleting all the original texts except the one I'd received after finding Mr. Frey, I stuffed my phone into my pocket and wet a paper towel to clean myself up. When I looked into the mirror, I was startled by the look in my terror-filled eyes. I had to get myself together, or I was going to look even more suspicious. I wiped my face, trying desperately to come up with a plan.

I needed to play a role. I was a frightened young woman who'd found a dead body. I would tell Brady nothing about my past.

But there was one problem. I now knew for certain that the text Brady wanted to see wasn't from the man who killed Mr. Frey. The killer from my past had sent it.

I couldn't let him see it. What if he managed to scrape the number somehow? If the killer found out, he'd hurt Belinda first and ask questions later. Scrambling for a plan, I dug out my phone again. Maybe I could get someone to send me an identical text. Later I could pretend to "figure out" who the sender was. But who would help without asking too many questions? I dialed the first person who came to mind.

"Colt," I said as soon as he answered. "I need your help."

"Maggie? You okay? Who was that guy you left with?" His voice deepened. "Do you need me to come get you?"

"No. I'm not in that kind of trouble. I need you to send me a text, but it has to be specific, and I need you to try to hide your number."

"What the hell are you talking about?"

I shook my head, trying to think rationally. Maybe it would be better for him to send it from his own number. I could pretend I'd only processed the message, not the sender. "No, scratch that. Send it from you. The message is: *Some things are better left in the past.*"

"Why the hell do you want me to do that?"

"I'll explain it all later."

"Does it have to do with Elmer Fudd behind the bar?"

"Yeah. The guy I'm with is a police detective. I told him I got a text at around the time I called him. I . . . I can't show it to him. I want you to send it, but he might ask to talk to you."

He was silent for a moment. Just as I'd suspected, he didn't ask more questions—Colt was good like that. He just said, "That's not gonna work, Maggie. He's gonna see the time stamp."

"Oh shit." My voice broke as I started to panic again, and I began to breathe in heavy pants.

"I'll help you figure it out, okay? Do you trust me?"

I wasn't sure how much I trusted him, but there was no denying that I needed his help. "Yeah."

"Get rid of the text and tell him you accidentally deleted it in all the confusion. Then I'll send a text in a few minutes telling you that it was insensitive of me to have badmouthed your Broadway musical. Then I'll ask if I can still spend the night with you."

I sucked in a breath. "What?"

"He'll buy it. Trust me. Especially after he watched us sing."

"How do you know he watched us sing?"

"Come on, Maggie. I know finding a dead body can addle anyone's brain, but this is your second go-round. You should be desensitized by now. Use your head."

"Colt!"

"Maggie," his voice softened. "When you were up onstage, that guy was staring at you like you were a blue plate special after he hadn't eaten in three days. Are you interested in him?"

Yes. Much more than I had any right to be. "I don't know. Maybe."

"He's a cop, Mags. He's gonna dig into your past."

My heart skipped a beat. "What are you talking about?" My voice sounded strangled.

"Come on. It's me you're talking to here. I don't know what cockamamie story you've been selling everyone else, but I'm not buying. You ran off ten years ago without warning and without a backward glance. Nobody does that unless they're hiding something. Or running. And now you want me to mimic a text about leaving things in the past."

"I didn't say . . ." Oh, God.

"Maggie," Colt said, his voice gentle and soothing in my ear. "You should know by now that I'm not gonna ask you any questions. I respect your need for privacy, just like I need you to respect mine. But he's a cop, Mags. He's gonna ask questions, and he's not gonna accept the same bullshit answers everyone else does."

Colt wasn't telling me anything I didn't know. But if I let him send that text, I'd lose any hope with Brady.

That was a good thing, wasn't it?

My heart warred with my head, but my head had ruled for so long that the wrestling match was short-lived. "Okay."

"Good girl. How much time do you need? A few minutes? Are you at the police station?"

"No," I said, wiping my new tears away. "Red Barn Café."

"He took you out on a date?" he asked in disbelief.

"It's not like that."

"Oh, it's *so* like that," he said. "You just watch his reaction when he sees my text."

Colt was right, and I wasn't sure I could bear it.

"Call me when you leave the restaurant," he said.

"Colt . . . Thanks. I owe you."

He laughed. "I'll just add it to your tab. Be sure to delete any record of this call."

"Good thinking."

"That's why you called me, babe." Then he hung up. I took a screen shot of this evening's message, deleted it like the others, and then deleted the record of my call with Colt.

When I finished, I left the restroom. I wasn't sure I could go through with this. But I had to.

Belinda's life might depend on it.

When I walked back into the dining room, my stomach tied in knots, Brady was watching for me. He stood as I neared the table.

"You look exhausted," he said.

That was a kind way to say *you look like shit*. I knew I did. I'd just walked away from a mirror, after all. "It's been a long day."

"Then let's get this wrapped up and figure out where to go from there." He gestured to my chair and waited until I took a seat before he sat down. "I really need to see that text, Maggie."

"Yeah, of course." I pulled out my phone and unlocked the screen. Then I checked my messages and pretended to be confused. "I don't understand. It was there earlier."

"You can't find the message?"

"No."

He took the phone from me and examined the screen. "What happened to it?"

"I don't know, but now that I think about it, I'm not sure *who* it was from."

"I thought you said it was blocked."

I shrugged, still feigning confusion. *Think fast, Magnolia.* "I saw it when I called you, but obviously I was a bit frazzled. Maybe I accidentally deleted it while I was waiting for you. When I grabbed my phone to text my friend Jody."

He looked up at me. "It looks like the last time you texted Jody was yesterday afternoon."

"I started to text her, then remembered she was on the stage." At least that part was true. He gave me a weird look. "She's in a touring production of *Wicked*. She's not done until well after ten, closer to eleven."

The phone vibrated in his hand, and he stared at the screen, his face expressionless. Finally, his gaze lifted to mine. "Could your text have been from *Colt?*"

I paused for a moment, then gasped, trying to look embarrassed. "Oh, God. How could I have been so stupid? We had an argument . . ."

He tilted his head slightly to the side and said, "Colt just sent a text apologizing for encouraging you to leave your theatre life in the past. He hopes he can still Netflix and chill with you *again* tonight. He can be there in fifteen minutes."

I maintained my role and tried to look even more embarrassed. It wasn't a stretch. "Oh."

He remained silent as he stared at the phone screen.

"I'm sorry to have worried you for nothing."

"Who's Colt?"

I didn't miss a beat. "The guy I was singing with tonight. He works for my mother and Tilly."

"You're seeing him?"

Play your role, Magnolia. Colt was right. Brady asks too many questions.

I gave a slight shrug and played coy. "I wouldn't call it seeing him."

Brady remained quiet, studying me.

I waited several moments before I said, "We're friends."

"With benefits." It wasn't a question.

"Is there anything else you need from me? I thought we were keeping this professional, and if we're now delving into my personal life, I really need to go."

His eyes turned cold. "I'd hate for you to miss your Netflix and chill plans."

"My personal life is no concern of yours, Brady Bennett."

"As you've made glaringly obvious."

That stung more than I cared to admit, but Colt had been right about this too. The ploy had worked out perfectly. I swallowed my tears. "The text was from Colt, so I guess I'm not in danger."

"Not necessarily. The man you were planning to meet was killed before you could talk to him."

"Because Mr. Frey had information he didn't want me to have. Which means I'm safe."

He watched me closely, as if trying to figure me out.

"Do you want to take the rest of my statement?" I asked.

"Yeah." He buried his head in his notebook. "Tell me again about going to the bar and finding Mr. Frey."

I spent the next several minutes recapping what I'd already told him, including seeing Mr. Frey at the restaurant at lunch.

My nerves felt frayed and raw, so when he remained silent for nearly a minute, looking over his notebook, I stuttered out, "Is there anything else?"

"Yeah," he said, looking up. "What's your father's name?"

"Brian. Brian Royland Steele."

"Can you give me his birthdate and physical description?"

I hesitated. "You're still going to look into my father's disappearance?"

His mouth sagged a little. "You think I wouldn't do my job because you're sleeping with somebody else?"

"Well . . ." I'd hoped he would, but I had prepared myself for the possibility he might drop it. My father was likely beyond anyone's protection, and as much as I wanted to know what had happened to him, it was more important to protect Momma and Belinda.

"I'm digging deeper into your father's disappearance because it's pertinent to this case. Not because of any personal connection to you."

My face burned. "Of course."

"Now about your father's personal information."

I gave him Daddy's information. He'd been forty-two when he'd disappeared, but most people had thought he looked younger. He'd been tall, around six feet, and trim—he was a runner. I'd inherited his dark hair but not his brown eyes.

"Any distinguishing marks on his body?" Brady asked. "Tattoos? Piercings? Birthmarks?"

I shook my head. "No."

He nodded and closed his notebook. "Then I think we're done. You're free to go."

I started to apologize, but I couldn't. Besides, what was I apologizing for? I'd told him three weeks ago that whatever spark we felt was never going to amount to anything. "Sorry to interrupt your dinner."

I stood, and he stood too. "Magnolia. Don't apologize. I'm glad you called me." He paused, looking out the window before turning back to me. "I'm still worried about you, but I suspect you're right. It sounds like someone killed Walter Frey to keep you from finding out what happened that night. Which means he won't consider you a threat. But don't be setting up any more meetings with anyone else. Let me take care of it, and I'll let you know when I find something."

"Thank you, Brady. This means a lot to me."

"You want answers about your father. It's my job."

And just like that, I'd become another victim.

The reclassification hurt more than I cared to admit.

But then I realized something else. I had never told him about the note I'd seen.

chapter seven

When I got to my car, my phone vibrated with a call.

"Why didn't you call me?" Colt asked.

"I just got done."

"Good, I want you to meet me at a house downtown on Fourth Street."

I groaned as I started the car. "Not tonight, Colt. I'm not playing any games. I've had a shitty day, and I just want to go home."

"I think I'm about to make your shitty day better."

The ego of this man. "Yeah, I've heard *that* before."

"Did my plan work?" he asked.

"Yeah. It worked." My tone was sullen, but it was the best I could do.

"Sorry, Mags. I know it sucks, but I just proved you could trust me, didn't I? Trust me on this one too. You'll love my surprise."

All I wanted to do was crawl into bed, but I had to admit he had saved me. I couldn't imagine why he would want me to meet him at a house downtown this late. "Okay, I'll come, but I'm only giving you five minutes."

"Five minutes should be more than enough."

"You only need five minutes, huh?" I teased. "Good to know for future reference."

"Very funny. Glad to see you still have your witty sense of humor." He gave me the address, then hung up.

When I approached the intersection, I found him standing next to his truck, which was parked curbside in front of a restored Victorian-style house. I parked behind him and got out, taking in the property.

"If you tell me I have to participate in TPing this house as payback for your help, you're out of luck."

He laughed as he walked toward me. "You seriously think I asked you here to toilet paper this house? It's a little close to the police station, don't you think?"

I crossed my arms over my chest. "I can't imagine what else we'd be up to. You obviously don't live here."

"No, but you do."

I dropped my arms as he placed his hand on the small of my back and pushed me toward the driveway. "What are you talking about?"

"Just keep walking," he said as we continued up the drive.

"We're going to get in trouble for trespassing," I whispered. The last thing I needed was for Brady to show up.

"*Relax*. We're not gonna get in trouble. We're checking out your new home."

"I can't afford this house, Colt."

"No shit." He laughed. "You can't afford the crumbs in a Taco Bell wrapper. But you're not gonna be living in the house."

"Then what in tarnation are you talking about?"

He pointed to a detached garage. "There's an apartment up there." Then he walked around me and climbed up a flight of stairs built into the side of the garage.

I stopped at the bottom of the stairs. "Wait. *What?*"

He laughed as he unlocked the door at the top with the keys in his hand. "Come on. Come check it out."

I glanced back at the house, certain the owner had already called the police. "Are you sure we're supposed to be here?" I asked as I climbed the stairs.

He shook his head. "Come on, Mags. Would I get you into trouble?"

I stood next to him, about to say *hell yes*, but he put his finger to my lips and grinned. "Don't answer that." Then he moved to the side and flipped a switch on the wall. "Welcome home."

A lamp turned on, filling the small space with warm light. Bookcases lined one wall on either side of a TV. The opposite wall was red brick, and an overstuffed sage-green sofa sat against it. The coffee table with the lamp was arranged between the sofa and a floral overstuffed chair. Behind that was a small kitchen with an island with two barstools.

"It comes furnished," Colt said as I walked inside, the heels of my shoes clicking on the hardwood floor.

"I don't understand . . ."

"What's not to understand?" he asked as I walked into the kitchen. "You need an apartment. This one's available."

I turned back to face him, shaking my head. "I can't afford this."

"You don't even know how much it costs."

I gestured toward the small but very cozy living room. "I know I can't afford *this*."

"Check out the bedroom and bathroom."

"I don't see the point."

Colt groaned. "Jesus, Mags. Just check it out." When I hesitated, he said, "This is Franklin. It's not New York City."

"Real estate is still expensive here." This I knew. In my desperation to get away from my mother, I'd already looked.

"Will you just check out the bedroom already?"

I still didn't see the point, but I had to admit I was curious. The bedroom was small, but there was a queen-sized bed with a pink and cream floral comforter and lots of pillows. The walls were a soft cream color. Next to the simple wood headboard was a nightstand topped with a white ceramic lamp, and there was a tall dresser against the opposite wall. The window overlooked the house and the street.

"The closet is small," Colt said. "That might be a problem."

"Not as much as you might think," I said as I headed toward the door and into the bathroom. I'd only brought two suitcases stuffed with clothes with me to Franklin. I was sure Griff had either sold the rest or given my things away to a thrift store.

The bathroom was small too, but all the essentials were there—a pedestal sink, a toilet, and a shower. The floor and shower were both covered in tiny white tiles. It was obvious it had recently been remodeled to give the room—the whole apartment—a vintage feel to match the house.

Colt stood in the doorway, leaning his shoulder into the window jamb. "What do you think?"

I shook my head. "How did you find out about this place?"

"A friend."

"How much?"

His grin spread. "Six hundred a month."

I narrowed my eyes. There was no way the price could be that low. "You're always complaining about your roommate. Why don't *you* live here?"

"Because Ava—the homeowner—doesn't want a guy living here. She wants a girl."

"Six hundred seems pretty cheap."

"Well . . . there *is* a catch."

I knew it. "What is it?"

"You have to clean her house once a week. Just the floors on the first floor, her kitchen and bathroom and her bedroom."

"What makes you think I know the first thing about cleaning houses?"

He laughed. "You were raised by Lila Steele. It's a given."

He had a point.

"What do you say?"

"It still seems too good to be true. How long's the lease?"

"Six months."

"I might have to leave sooner than six months."

"Because Lila's dyin'?"

"You *know*?" I asked in disbelief.

"Maggie. Believe it or not, I'm a pretty smart guy. I can put two and two together." I wondered if he was talking about more than just my mother's situation, but I didn't dare ask.

"So what do you think?" he asked, dangling two keys on a small chain. "You ready to break free from your mother?"

I felt guilty. I only had a few months left with her; did I really want to miss any of that? But we got on each other's nerves like nobody's business when we were sharing each other's space, and I was sure this was the solution. She'd said so herself. Still . . .

"What do *you* get out of it?" I asked.

He laughed and backed up so I could leave the bathroom. "Consider it a good deed."

"You don't seem like the good deed kind of guy, but you've done more than your fair share of them lately. What's your endgame?"

He plopped down on the sofa and rested his arm on the armrest. "You really are paranoid, aren't you?"

I stood in front of him with my arms crossed. "Let's just say I know your type."

Grinning, he shook his head. "Don't be so sure about that." He patted the space next to him. "Come on. Try it out."

This place was so tempting. Truly an answer to my prayers, had I been keen on saying them. It was an amazing opportunity, but I couldn't help but wonder if there was a catch to it—something more onerous than one afternoon of cleaning per week.

Colt stood. "Okay. I can see how maybe I sprung this on you too quickly. I'd planned to tell you tomorrow, but after your crap day, it seemed like you needed some good news. How about I give you a minute to hang out and think it over? I'll be right back."

Then, before I could answer, he was out the door and I was alone.

I'd never had my own place. New York was expensive, so I'd always had at least one roommate. I couldn't imagine living completely alone, but with the killer watching me, maybe it was a good idea to distance myself from everyone.

I wandered into the kitchen and opened cabinets, surprised to see dishes, glassware, and pots and pans. There was even a stackable washer and dryer in what I'd mistaken for a closet. By the time Colt came back in, carrying a brown bag, I was sitting at the island.

"It's pretty great, isn't it?" he asked, closing the door behind him.

"Yeah," I said grudgingly. "It's pretty great. How much is the deposit?"

Ignoring me, he walked to the cabinet and grabbed two juice glasses. He walked over to the sofa and set the bag and the glasses on the coffee table.

"Don't we need to get out of here?" I asked as he flopped back down on the couch.

"Nope. Ava gave me the keys to give to you. It's yours."

"Don't I need to sign a lease? Or give references?"

His mouth twisted into a half-grin. "You can figure out all the details of the lease later. Your name was enough to get you the place."

I hopped off the stool and stomped over to him, getting irate. "She wants to rent to *Magnolia Steele*? I'm her claim to fame?"

"Calm down, Yosemite Sam," he said, raising his hands, palms out. "She rented it to you because you're Lila Steele's daughter."

"Oh." I supposed her name carried the weight of responsibility. Too bad I was nothing like her.

He patted the seat next to him. "Come on. You need this."

I sat next to him, eyeing the package. "What's in the bag?" I asked.

"Something to help celebrate your new apartment." He pulled down the paper to reveal a bottle of Jameson whiskey.

I snorted. "Most people celebrate housewarmings with wine or champagne."

"Well, we're not like most people, are we?" He poured a generous amount into both glasses, then picked them up and handed one to me.

I took it and he clicked his glass to mine, all humor gone as he said, "To new beginnings. And to leaving our secrets behind, buried deep in the past where they belong."

I looked deep into his blue eyes. Though a part of me was itching to know what secrets Colt Austin was hiding, it felt good to have a friend who understood my situation, if not what had caused it. "Amen."

We both took sips of our whiskey, and I leaned back into the overstuffed sofa, amazed by how comfortable it was.

"Do you want to talk about the text you were hiding from Detective Hot Stuff?"

I snorted whiskey, then coughed for a good minute before choking out, "Detective Hot Stuff?"

He shrugged. "He's a good-looking guy. I'll give him that."

I grinned. "Jealous?"

"Jealous?" He burst into laughter. "I don't do relationships, which means I never have a reason for jealousy. Just making an observation."

Studying him, I decided he was telling the truth. "No, I don't want to talk about the text. I thought it might pertain to poor Mr. Frey, but I was wrong."

"It was from your past. The secret you don't want to get out."

Maybe it was the whiskey, or maybe it was just the stress of the day, but I was starting to get pissed. "You must have short-term memory loss, because if I remember correctly—and I do—we just toasted to leaving our secrets in the past."

"True enough, but it's always good to know how many people know about your secrets. How many, Mags?"

I took a long gulp of whiskey, then leaned back into the cushions, closing my eyes as I cradled the glass to my chest. "One. And I plan to keep it that way." Time to change the subject. I sat up a little bit. "How long was your set at the Embassy? And how'd you have time to rent this apartment?"

"My set was an hour. I found out about the apartment earlier tonight. Like I said, I'd planned on telling you tomorrow."

"And the whiskey?"

He sat back, kicking his feet up on the coffee table. "I've had it in my truck. I was supposed to meet a couple of buddies later, but after you called tonight, I canceled."

"Why would you cancel your plans?"

"Because you need a friend tonight. And I wanted to give you something good in a day full of shit. So chill with the third degree."

I turned my head to study him. He was closer than I would have liked, but I didn't think he was trying to hit on me. The look on his face told me that he really was here as a friend. "I'm not sleeping with you," I said, just in case.

"News flash, Magnolia Steele, internet porn star—I don't want to sleep with you."

"I'm not a porn star."

"Fair enough," he conceded with a grin. "But I still don't want to sleep with you."

I wasn't sure whether to be relieved or insulted that notorious man-whore, Colt Austin, didn't want to have a go at me.

"Tell me about the detective," Colt said, looking down at his glass and then back up at me. "That was some pretty intense chemistry for two people who'd just met over a dead body."

I cringed. "That's disgusting."

"Which makes it all the more unlikely."

I took another sip of liquid courage. "That's because we met three weeks ago."

"He was the detective trying to pin those murders on you?" he asked in disbelief.

I found myself telling him more than I'd intended, from how Brady and I had met to how he'd betrayed me by sharing stuff we'd talked about in private with his partner.

"*Jesus.* I hope you kicked him in the balls."

Scowling, I took another drink.

His mouth dropped. "You *didn't?*" When I didn't answer, he shook his head in disgust. "I never pegged you for one of *those* women."

I sat up and set my glass down on the coffee table with a thud. "*What* women?"

"Women who let men treat them like shit and go back for more."

I turned to face him, my anger rising. "I didn't. The day I was planning to go back to New York, I ran into him downtown, and he apologized. Said he was only trying to protect me but he'd like to start over." It wasn't exactly verbatim, but it was close enough. "I pretty much told him to go to hell."

He gave a slight nod of approval. "So just bad freakin' luck that he was assigned to the guy behind the bar tonight?"

"Yeah." I was already piling up the lies and secrets with him; what was one more?

"You like him."

"He used me."

"Yet you like him anyway. You already told me so on the phone. You went to that restaurant with him."

"Well, he doesn't like *me* anymore." I gave him a begrudging grin. "Your Netflix and chill comment stopped him in his tracks."

Colt's face beamed with pride. "You're welcome." His smile fell. "On a scale of one to ten, how badly do you want your secret to stay in the past?"

I looked into my nearly empty glass. "I think you know the answer to that. A ten."

"Then you can't date him. You know that, right? He'll start diggin'—he can't help himself; he's a detective—and then he'll unbury your secrets."

"Yeah." I sighed and sat back, sinking into the cushions. "I know."

We were silent for half a minute before he refilled both of our glasses and then said, "I cared about someone once."

I glanced at him in surprise. He'd told me he'd never been in love and hinted that he'd never even come close.

He handed my glass to me, then sat back next to me and stared up at the ceiling. "It was a few years ago. I was bartending in Nashville. She was a waitress." He turned his head to face me, and a woeful smile tipped up the corners of his mouth. "She made me break my five-date rule."

"Your five-date rule? If they don't put out by date number five, you break up with them?"

"No," he said in disgust. "I get laid *long* before date number five. What, are you crazy?"

"Wow," I murmured. "Such a gentleman."

"The difference between me and *Detective Brady Bennett* is that I never pretended to be a gentleman."

That stung more than I would have liked, but I had to admit he had a point. "Go ahead, enlighten me about your rule."

"I make sure there never *is* a fifth date." He returned his attention to the ceiling.

It occurred to me there was more to Colt's motivation to be a man-slut than I'd suspected. He was hiding in plain sight. He kept the people he dated at a distance to avoid revealing himself to them.

Wasn't that exactly what I had done in the past? Sure, Colt had undoubtedly slept with a lot more women than I'd slept with men, but maybe we weren't so different. "So you dated her more than five times?"

He gave me a bitter smile. "Oh, yeah . . ."

"What happened?"

"She found out my secret."

"And she left you?" I asked in disbelief. "What a bitch."

His eyes were full of emotion—anger, regret, and something I couldn't identify—when they snapped to mine. "She's not a bitch. She's a good woman."

"If she loved you, she wouldn't have thrown you away just like that."

"Detective Brady sold you up shit creek without a paddle, Mags, so don't go throwing stones."

"First of all, he's not in love with me. And I don't excuse him for what he did. Well, I understand why he did it, even if I don't like it."

He took a big gulp of his whiskey, then let out a loud sigh. "We're like two peas in a pod, you and I."

"So what's your big secret?" I asked, starting to feel a buzz. "What scared her away?"

His eyes darkened. "Some things really are better left in the past, Maggie. You want to share your secret first?"

"No." Most definitely not.

chapter eight

My first two observations as I blinked my eyes open were that my mouth felt like cotton and I had a crick in my neck. The pale sunlight shining through a window in the kitchen indicated it was early morning.

I sat upright on the sofa, my head pounding and nausea clutching my stomach.

Colt was next to me, his feet up on the coffee table. What had I done?

I looked down at my body, relieved to see all my clothes were still on, with the exception of my shoes. Colt was still dressed too.

He stirred, his feet knocking over the half-empty whiskey bottle. "Shit," he muttered, sliding upright.

The clink of the glass on the wood shot an arrow of pain straight through my head. I pressed my palm into the side of my head. "You suck, Colt Austin."

"Me? What the hell did *I* do?"

"You made me drink all that whiskey."

"I did no such thing." He ran a hand over his face, then cupped his hand over his mouth and shuddered. "Jesus. My breath smells like Taco Bell farts."

"What the hell is your obsession with Taco Bell?" I asked, getting pissed, which only made my head hurt worse.

"Who doesn't like Taco Bell when they're drinkin'?"

"Me! I don't like it when I'm drinking! I don't like it at all!" I said, getting to my feet. "And this most certainly *is* your fault. You kept refilling my glass."

"Well, you didn't have to keep drinkin' it."

I ran my hands through my hair, pressing them against the sides of my head. "I'm supposed to start my new job today. How's it going to look when I show up with a hangover?"

"So chase some aspirin with plenty of water and coffee, take a shower, and you'll be good as new. If I avoided social interaction every time I had a hangover, I'd be a hermit."

Why was I not surprised? "Good to know," I said, digging my phone out of my pocket. "Oh crap. It's six fifteen. My mother is probably already up."

"So?"

"So! I have her car. She's going to want to know where I went." Did I need to cop to my meeting with Walter Frey? Was there any way to keep it from her? Doubtful.

"I doubt the first thing Lila does when she wakes up in the morning is peer out her bedroom window to make sure her car is still in the driveway. And you're a grown-ass woman," he said, groaning as he stood. "Don't tell me you have a curfew."

"She's going to want to know where I was. She'll never approve of this." I gestured between us. "And she sure wouldn't understand."

He grinned. "Obviously, because I'm too good for you."

I stumbled into the kitchen and pulled a glass out of the cabinet.

"I forgot you don't have a car." He sounded more serious this time.

I pressed the ice dispenser on the refrigerator door and cringed as ice clinked into the glass. "Actually, I *do* have one. It's currently inoperable."

He waited for me to continue.

Filling the glass with water, I shot him a quick glance. "Apparently my mother still has the car I used to drive in high school. She stored it in the garage."

That perked him up. "You're kidding."

I still wasn't sure what to make of that. Had she held on to it expecting that I'd eventually come home? That I'd ask for it one day? Whatever the reason, she'd stored the vehicle in the garage, but now it was surrounded by a bunch of Roy's junk and boxes of files. "It won't start. As far as I know, it hasn't been driven for ten years."

"Why haven't you fixed it?"

I took a long drink of the water, which felt good on my parched mouth. "I don't exactly have the money to fix it."

"It's probably just a battery. Surely you can afford that."

"I suppose I can after I get paid on Friday."

He shook his head. "How can someone who's been all over the internet be so destitute?"

"Just lucky, I guess."

He pushed out a loud sigh and ran a hand through his hair. "What's your schedule like today?"

I gave him a suspicious look. "I'm working at Rebellious Rose Boutique this morning, but I'm not sure for how long. Then I'm helping Momma and Tilly prepare for the cocktail party tonight."

"Yeah, me too. I'm tending bar." He scrubbed his face, and his eyes looked a little more alert when he dropped his hand. "I have the code to your momma's garage. I'll ask Lila if I can go take a look at the car before I'm due to show up at the catering office."

My mouth dropped open. "You have a code to the house?"

He shrugged and took the water glass from my hand. "Yeah. But just the garage. If Lila wants me to go inside, she leaves the door to the kitchen unlocked."

"She doesn't give that out to just anyone, Colt."

He looked me in the eyes. "Then maybe you should take a cue from your momma and trust me a little more." He took a long drink, draining the glass, then handing it back to me. "I'll text you later."

"Wait," I said as he walked toward the door. "Where are you going?"

Laughing, he opened the door, his back still to me. "Just because we slept together doesn't mean you get to know every detail about my life. Don't be so clingy, Maggie."

"We did *not* sleep together!" I shouted, sending a stabbing pain through my head.

"Miss Ava's a morning person, so you should probably stop by to find out when she wants you to clean. But it's more likely she'll stop you on the way out."

The door closed behind him before I could ask him for more details. Just like a man.

But it was kind of nice to be alone in the apartment for the first time. It was small—you could fit the entire space into a bigger living room—but it was clean and cozy, and it had enough character to make it interesting. More importantly, it felt like home. Nowhere had ever felt that way since I'd left from Franklin. Sure, I'd spent the past few weeks in my childhood bedroom, but it wasn't the same as an adult. I felt like a guest.

I put the glass in the sink and grabbed my car keys and the keys to the apartment off the island. Moving in wouldn't be hard. I only had two suitcases. But how would Momma take the news? And what would I do if I couldn't get my car running? This place was only a few blocks from downtown, so I could walk to my jobs. The grocery store was another story. I remembered Franklin having a trolley system, but I had no idea where it stopped or when.

I locked the door behind me and headed down the stairs. I had just made it to the bottom when a woman called out to me from the house. "So you're Magnolia."

The sun had started to rise, which sure didn't help my pounding head. I squinted to find her. "Yes, ma'am."

The woman laughed and stepped out the back door of the house. I'd expected someone older, but she had the unmistakable air of Southern gentility. "And you have good manners. But then, Lila Steele is your mother, is she not?"

I moved closer warily, feeling like I'd been caught doing something untoward. I wished Colt had stuck around to introduce us. "Yes, ma'am, she is."

"I'm Ava Milton. Colton tells me you're working for your mother, but you need reduced rent because she's not paying you much."

"Um . . ." It wasn't Momma's fault, actually—she'd given me $5,000 a few weeks ago, back when she'd thought I might leave town for good, but it had mostly gone toward paying my credit card bills. "I also work at Rebellious Rose Boutique, but a break on the rent would be helpful. Thank you."

"Have you ever cleaned houses before, Magnolia?" she asked, her tone now brisk and superior.

I was suddenly questioning this decision. I hated cleaning, but I wanted that apartment. And not just because my mother was getting on my last nerve. "Yes, ma'am. My mother is quite the taskmaster when it comes to cleaning her house."

She nodded, her mouth pressed into a thin line. "Good. Too many young people don't know the first thing about cleaning." She opened the door wider. "Come on in. We can discuss your schedule and the lease agreement."

I resisted the urge to check my phone. If I wanted this to work out, I couldn't just leave, no matter how late it was getting.

As I got closer, I realized Ava Milton was a fair bit older than she looked from twenty feet away. I would guess her to be in her late sixties, but her face was so smooth it was hard to tell.

I followed her inside the house, and she showed me where she stored her cleaning supplies. "I have a Bible study every Thursday morning," she said, standing in the closet doorway. "Can you clean on Wednesdays?"

"I'm sure I can work it out."

She arched her tiny, over-tweezed eyebrows. "Either you can or you cannot; which is it, Magnolia?"

I couldn't help startling at her tone. "Yes, ma'am. I can do it."

She gave me a sharp nod. "Very good. Then let me show you the house."

The house was bigger than I'd expected and also more dated. Ava had vintage furniture and antiques, most of which looked dainty and fragile. Given her request for a female tenant, I suspected there was no Mr. Milton and that she rarely entertained men.

"How do you clean hardwood floors, Magnolia?" she asked in a superior tone that told me she had a preferred answer, even if she'd likely never cleaned a floor in her life.

"Vinegar water, of course," I said, trying not to sound smug. Of course, it could be argued that the knowledge of how to mop hardwood without leaving streaks was nothing to feel smug about.

If the cast from *Fireflies at Dawn* could see me now . . .

I gave myself a mental shake. Ava had moved on.

"I prefer a ratio of one gallon water to two tablespoons of vinegar," she said. "I know some people try to skimp on the vinegar because of the smell, but if you add a bit of—"

"Lemon juice," I said. "But in the winter, Momma always added pine oil."

"I'm sure she did," she said in a snotty tone. "But in my house, you will use lemon juice."

"Yes, ma'am."

She gave me a grudging nod of approval. "This might work out after all."

She led me to the kitchen and showed me a form on her kitchen table. "The contract says you'll clean on Wednesdays and pay the rent on the first of the month." Then she gave me a long list of rules, starting with no parking on the street. Her pinched look might as well have screamed, "first warning," since my momma's car sat in front of her house, bold as brass. The rest of the rules were about what I'd expected. No loud parties. No loud anything. No parties at all. She was looking for a quiet tenant who kept to herself.

"Colton told me this morning that you were accepting the apartment," she said with a disapproving glare. "So I know he spent the night." She folded her hands and took a deep breath before continuing. "I realize times have changed from when I was a young woman, so I know it's unrealistic to expect you not to entertain male suitors, but I would prefer for you not to bring home a variety of different men." She lifted her chin. "I wouldn't want my neighbors to think I'm running a brothel."

I tried not to gasp; instead, I nodded my understanding. "You have nothing to worry about, Miss Ava. Colton is merely a friend. I'm not seeing anyone."

"There will be no more than one man as an overnight guest per month, and you must have a one-week minimum between men."

Was she really dictating my love life? Was that even legal?

But I wanted the apartment enough to see my new landlord as an eccentric challenge rather than as a controlling nuisance. "It won't be a problem."

She waved her hand as she walked toward her coffee pot. "That's what they all say. Just sign by the X's. And I'll need your first and last months' rent by the end of the day."

That was a problem. I had enough for one month, but not two. "Can it be later this evening?" I asked. "I'm working at both of my jobs today, and I'm not sure how much time I'll have between them to run a check to you."

She turned around to look at me. "How many hours does that keep you busy?"

I wasn't sure if I saw a look of approval or disgust, but I wasn't about to be bullied. "I'm not sure yet," I said. "I just started working at Rebellious Rose, and I'm working out a new schedule with my mother."

The crafty smile that lit up her face told me that I was in trouble even though I didn't know how or why. "I will need your help with my Bible study. Can you manage to get time off from your other jobs?"

I resisted the urge to gasp. "Um, I'm not sure what help I'll be. I haven't been to church in years." As soon as the words were out of my mouth, I regretted them. I suspected Miss Ava Milton didn't appreciate heathens living on her property.

But to my surprise, she breezed right on by my lost soul. "*I* will lead the Bible study. I merely need you to help manage the refreshments."

In any other part of the country, a Bible study would mean donuts and stale coffee, but this was Franklin, Tennessee, where even Bunco nights were a competition in hospitality. I might have just met her, but I already knew Ava Milton wasn't the kind of woman who'd let anyone else outdo her. "I'm more than willing to help," I said. "I have to warn you, though: my mother may be a caterer, but I'm impossible in the kitchen."

Her delicate eyebrows arched again, and the fact that she could actually move them like that proved she was a genetic winner, not a Botox consumer. "You're Lila Steele's daughter and you don't cook?"

"Trust me, you don't want me anywhere near your stove."

She only allowed herself a brief frown. "Well, no worries. Your presence will be enough."

"Why?" I asked. "Is there a Bible study quota?"

She laughed at that, catching me by surprise. "Colton said you were witty."

"How do you know Colton?" I blurted out.

She hesitated. "Colton has proved himself to be a very loyal resource."

Ava Milton didn't look like the kind of woman who associated with men like Colt on a regular basis. I had to wonder what he'd helped her with.

She waved her hand. "No, I don't have a quota. I'll need you to maintain the refreshment table, make coffee—" She looked alarmed. "You *do* know how to make coffee, don't you?"

"Yes, that's the one thing I'm good at. Out of necessity."

She nodded. "Very good."

"How much will you be paying me per hour, and what hours will you need me?"

"You're a cheeky girl, aren't you?" she asked with a chuckle. "I think we'll get along just fine." She took a few steps closer. "I'll need you here by nine o'clock. Bible study is from nine thirty to eleven thirty, but plan on staying to help me clean up afterward. No need to wear a server's uniform. Just simple garden party attire. Can you manage that?"

I wasn't sure what garden party attire was, but I knew how to Google. "Yeah, uh . . . I mean, yes, ma'am."

"Very good. I'll need you to start tomorrow. I already have someone scheduled to clean today, so you can start that next week."

I didn't know my schedule at Rebellious Rose Boutique yet, but I bit my tongue before I said so. It was evident that Ava Milton did not take no for an answer. If I was about to potentially lose the job I needed to pay the rent I owed her, I needed to make sure it was worth my while. "And how much are you paying?"

"Fifty dollars. Now sign."

I was glad I'd asked. That would end up being five dollars more than the fifteen dollars per hour I had intended to demand. "Maybe I should wait to sign until I have the first and last months' rent check."

Her eyes narrowed. "Does your word mean anything, Magnolia Steele?" The challenge in her voice was obvious.

"Well, of course it does. But I'm not sure I'll be able to get you the check today, so it doesn't feel right to sign until I have it."

Her mouth pinched again as she considered it. "Then bring it as soon as you can. Now sign."

I flipped through the pages, surprised to see the Bible study arrangement was included in the document. She'd already expected me to accept her offer. That gave me second thoughts, but then I thought about living alone in an apartment that didn't reek of cat urine and BO. I picked up the pen and signed my name.

"Very good," she said with her genteel smile. "I think this is going to work out just fine."

I only hoped I hadn't signed away my soul.

chapter nine

Y ou're living *where?*" Momma demanded, the vein on her neck pulsing.

To my surprise, Momma hadn't even realized I'd been gone all night. Feeling like a teenager again, I'd snuck upstairs to take a shower. I'd also packed my clothes for the move, although I'd been too chicken to stuff my suitcases in the car and tell Momma right away. I was still warming up to the idea myself.

We had driven downtown together because she and Tilly had agreed to meet there at nine. Which meant I had an hour to break the news about my apartment before heading off to my new job.

Unfortunately, it wasn't going so well.

I was sitting in a chair between their desks, so I turned to Tilly for help. But Tilly quickly looked down at her computer keyboard.

Well, crap. That was an ominous sign.

"I'm really confused," I said, leaning forward. "Is it the fact that I'm moving out? Or that I'm moving into an apartment over a garage?"

"Neither," Momma said. "It's that snake you're gonna be living with."

I gasped. "What? I am *not* moving in with Colt!"

"Colt?" Momma asked. "Why would you be livin' with Colt?" Her eyes narrowed. "Are you sleepin' with Colt Austin?"

"No!"

"Now, Lila," Tilly said. "Colt is a very nice young man. He's very helpful. We would never manage without him."

Momma's face reddened. "That's the problem. He's *too* helpful. He helps any woman under the age of fifty-two out of her clothes."

"Lila," Tilly said, giving me a reassuring smile. "I'm sure he's just waiting for the right woman." Then she made a sweeping gesture toward me. "Maybe Maggie's the girl to tame him."

"*I am not sleeping with Colt!*" Now that I had their attention, I added, "Please give me more credit. I do have *some* sense in my head."

That settled Momma down. "Then why did you mention Colt?"

"Because he helped get me the apartment."

"An apartment owned by a snake." Momma's anger was back.

"Miss Ava?" I asked.

"*Miss Ava*," Momma said in a mocking tone. "And it's no wonder Colt got that apartment for you." She and Tilly exchanged a meaningful look.

"What does that mean?" I demanded. "What do you two know?"

My mother shook her head. "I'm not repeating gossip."

That was no surprise. I hadn't expected an answer from her. Tilly, on the other hand, loved gossip more than she had a right to. She was also usually correct. I turned to face her. "Spill it, Tilly."

Her eyes alight with excitement, she cast a glance toward the door, then back at me. "Rumor has it that Colt used to visit Ava Milton after dark."

"You mean at night? So?"

"So?" Tilly said in exasperation. "He was showing up for a booty call."

I sat back in my seat. "What? Colt and Miss Ava hooking up? No way." The guy had to have *some* standards, and I suspected Miss Ava was a lot older than fifty-two.

Tilly gave a mock, nonchalant shrug. "Maybe they did. Maybe they didn't. But rumor has it he still stops by to see her."

Was that Colt's big secret? That he was hooking up with a sixty-something? Would that have been enough to scare his girlfriend away? Miss Ava had called him a loyal resource. As prim and proper as she was, it was hard to believe he'd been using his "resources" to help her find a big O.

"Whether they're hooking up is beside the point," Momma said. "You're not living with that snake."

"Technically, I'm not living with her," I said. "I'm renting the apartment over her garage."

"Can you imagine what people are going to say, Magnolia?" Momma asked in disbelief. "You paying rent to that woman instead of living with me."

"They'll say I'm an independent woman, making my way in the world. Beside, two days ago you were on board with me getting my own place. You said I was getting on your nerves."

Tilly gave my mother a comforting look. "She's right, Lila. Magnolia's going to live in an apartment separate from the house. It's not like they'll be fraternizing with one another." She glanced over at me and nodded. "Isn't that right, dear?"

Oh crap. "Uh . . . Actually . . ."

Momma's eyes narrowed. "What?"

Fear snaked down my back. What had I done? "I agreed to clean her house every Wednesday for reduced rent."

"You're Ava Milton's cleaning lady?" Her voice was amazingly calm—like the eye of a hurricane.

Obviously there was some history between my mother and Ava Milton, not surprising since both were headstrong women. It also explained why Ava had looked so giddy when I'd agreed to help with her Bible study.

I was going to kill Colt.

Might as well get everything out in the open. "There's more." I paused, summoning the courage to continue. I had an inkling that this wasn't going to go over well. "I'm helping with her Thursday morning Bible study."

"When you say helping," Tilly said quietly, searching my face, "what exactly do you mean?"

"Um . . . I promised to help with her refreshment table. And making coffee." Momma paled and a sick feeling washed over me.

"Magnolia, dear," Tilly said, grabbing my hand and holding it between her own. "I don't want to alarm you—"

"If that's true, then don't start out the sentence with *I don't want to alarm you.*"

"We're sworn enemies," Momma said in a tight voice. "She's had it out for me since we started the Belles. She was an amateur caterer, and we took a lot of her business. She was furious."

"Oh shit . . ."

"Oh shit is right," Momma said. "She vowed to make me pay. She said she'd get her revenge even if it took twenty years, and now she's gotten it."

"Your daughter working as her hired help." No wonder she'd been so eager to get me to sign the contract. She was worried I'd tell Momma and she'd talk me out of it. Killing was too good for Colt; I was going to rip him into pieces. "Momma, I had no idea. Surely it can't be that bad."

"Why didn't you tell me before you signed that contract?"

I shrugged and started to pace. "I don't know. Colt set the whole thing up. He took me there last night after we sang together at his set at the Embassy."

"You were at the Embassy last night?" she asked. "I didn't know you even left the house."

"Didn't you wonder when I arranged things with Miss Ava?"

"I figured you saw the apartment yesterday afternoon and just found the courage to tell me." Worry filled her eyes. "I've seen the news, Magnolia. I know there was a murder there last night."

I grimaced. "It's not as bad as it looks." Lie.

"But you're involved somehow?"

"A tiny bit."

"Oh, my God," she said, sitting back in her chair. "What were you doing there?"

No point lying about that part. She'd find out sooner or later. "I was meeting him."

"The dead man?"

So the police hadn't released his name yet. Well, she was about to get even more upset. "Momma, maybe I should get you some water. It's not good for you to get so upset. It messes with your immune system."

She took a breath and pushed it out. "Who were you meeting, Magnolia?"

"Walter Frey."

I expected her to blow up, but instead she became very small and pale. "Why were you meeting Walter Frey?"

Her reaction scared the crap out of me, and I found myself telling her almost everything—how I'd bullied Mr. Frey into setting a meeting with me, only to find him dead in the back of the bar I'd chosen as our rendezvous point. Of course, I kept out the part about the text message and the note.

Tilly covered her mouth with her fingertips. "Oh, my word."

"Are you a suspect?" Momma asked in a quiet voice.

"No," I said. "The bartender is my alibi, and I didn't have a gun. Plus, there were footprints that looked like they were from someone who ran off to the parking lot. I'm not a suspect."

Momma's eyes sank closed. "Thank the Lord."

"Maggie," Tilly murmured, patting my leg. "How do you manage to find yourself in so much trouble?"

Momma sat up and turned to me. "You have to let this go, Magnolia. Your father's gone. He's not coming back. Asking questions is pointless."

She knows something. I could count on one hand the number of times I'd seen her scared. She had to know more about Daddy's disappearance than she'd told the police.

But then again, what *had* she told the police? They'd dismissed his disappearance so quickly . . .

I wasn't sure how to handle this. Part of me was furious with her. How could she have withheld information that might have helped someone find him? On the other hand, she'd loved Daddy with her entire being. If she was keeping something quiet, she had her reasons.

"Promise me you'll let this go," Momma said, some of her color returning.

The more vague a promise is, the easier it is to get out of it. Momma's fatal error was not specifying what she meant by *this*. While she obviously wanted me to stop digging into my father's disappearance, *this* could also refer to our current argument over his disappearance. "Yes, Momma. I'll let this go."

She pushed out a breath of relief.

"Good girl," Tilly said, and I suddenly felt like I was her dog Pete.

"But we still need to deal with the Ava Milton mess," Momma said. "I want to know what happened last night first. All the details."

I sure as hell wasn't telling her everything, but the more I told her, the better. There was less of a chance I'd slip up this way. When I got to the part about Brady, I decided to continue with my partial-honesty-is-the-best-policy decision. "When I found the body, I called a detective I'd met during the Max Goodwin investigation."

Momma's face became guarded. "Which one?"

"His name is Detective Brady Bennett. He didn't believe I murdered Max Goodwin, so he gave me his cell phone number in case I needed help. So I called him."

"And he doesn't believe you killed Walter Frey either?" Tilly asked.

"Exactly. He assured me I'm not a suspect."

Tilly put her hand on her chest and pushed out a long breath. "Thank God. I'm not sure I could handle you being involved in another murder case."

The look on my mother's face suggested she couldn't handle it either.

"But Colt showed up to play a set at the bar, and he told me about the apartment. He'd planned to tell me about the place today, but he brought me there last night to cheer me up."

"After hours?" Momma asked.

"He had a key."

She gave me a skeptical look.

"He said Miss Ava had approved me right away because . . ." Oh crap.

"Because?"

"Because you're my mother." I shook my head. "Does Colt know? Is this his idea of a sick joke?"

"No," Momma said, sounding reserved. "He may have tuned into some tension, but I doubt he knows the whole story. This happened long before he started working here, and Tilly and I never discuss it."

That eased my mind. Whether or not he realized it, I had put a lot of trust in Colt—something I never did—and I wasn't sure how I'd handle his betrayal.

"I suppose there's no getting out of it," Tilly murmured.

"No," Momma drawled. "But we can use this to our advantage."

I really didn't like the sound of that.

"Magnolia can tell us what she's up to," Momma continued.

"Momma, do you really think she's going to make me privy to anything that will interest you?"

"You'll just have to earn her trust."

"Like a double agent," Tilly said. She looked deep in thought, and her head bounced up and down.

I was about to argue that I wasn't about to take on a 007 role when the buzzer for the front door went off.

"Who could that be?" Tilly asked. "I thought our first appointment was at eleven."

"It is," I said. I'd kept track of the appointments since I'd started working there. I stood. "I'll go take care of it."

"We're not finished with this conversation, Magnolia Mae," Momma called after me.

Of that I was sure, but at least I'd bought myself some time. I had no desire to spy for my mother. In fact, the entire scheme seemed more like Tilly than her.

I walked down the stairs from the second floor office and made my way through the empty kitchen. Thank goodness no one had been making spicy food in there today. Thanks to lots of water and enough ibuprofen to make my liver protest, my headache was nearly gone, but my stomach was still regretting last night's excesses.

I pushed through the swinging front door to the small reception area, fully expecting to find a passerby who wanted to talk to the Belles about catering. We had an appointments-only policy, but there was a sign on the door encouraging visitors to push the buzzer to speak to the staff and set up an appointment. The person who was standing there wasn't a potential mother of the bride or a businessman wanting to get a quote for an awards dinner.

It was Brady.

There was no way he could have found out anything about my father this soon, which meant this was likely a personal visit. I took a deep breath, pushed it out, and then unlocked the door and opened it a crack. "We're closed."

He looked slightly amused. "I can read the sign. Can I come in?"

I took a step back and let him inside, closing the door behind him. "Can I help you with something?"

He took a while to choose his words. Finally, he said, "I owe you an apology."

My eyes widened in surprise and I took a step back, feeling lightheaded from shock and fear. "Oh, God. Are you here to arrest me?"

"What? No! No, Maggie. You're fine." He grabbed my arm to steady me, then realized what he'd done and slowly dropped his hand. "I assure you that you are *not* a suspect."

Still feeling lightheaded, I sank into the sofa Momma and Tilly kept for waiting guests. Brady sat down beside me.

"Then what are you apologizing for?" I asked.

"For treating you so unfairly. You have a right to your personal life. The night we took our walk, I asked you if you had a boyfriend and you said no." His mouth twisted with a grimace. "It was presumptuous of me to assume that was still the case, especially since you made it perfectly clear that you weren't interested after I told my partner about our conversation. And even more so after I told you that I was willing to wait. You don't owe me anything."

"I was angry, Brady. And hurt," I said, looking down at my clasped hands. "But you need to know that I'm not angry with you anymore."

"But you're involved with Colt?"

I sighed. Maybe I should lie and tell him I was desperately in love with Colt, but I doubted he would buy it. And in the end, I just couldn't bring myself to do it. "It's complicated."

"You implied he was just a friend with benefits. Do you want more with him?"

"No." I kept staring at my hands, wondering what I was doing. I'd given him the perfect excuse to leave me alone, and here I was ripping it to shreds. I needed to figure out a way to salvage this without lying. Because for some reason, I hated every lie that came out of my mouth with Brady. My hair fell over my cheek, and when I reached up to push it back, Brady's deep brown eyes tracked the movement. "But I obviously don't trust you. The first thought that came to mind when you showed up was that you were here to arrest me."

"What if I could rebuild your trust in me?"

"Are you still investigating my father's disappearance?"

"Yes. But I'll be turning everything I find over to Owen."

"The detective who's in charge of Mr. Frey's murder?" I asked.

He nodded. "Owen Frasier. He's a friend of mine, and he's busy working on another active investigation too, so I convinced my boss to let me dig into your father's disappearance. He agreed the coincidence is too great."

"Thank you."

"Is your mother here?"

That caught me off guard. "Why?"

"I need to speak to her. About your father's disappearance."

"Oh." I stood. "Right. Of course. She's upstairs." I wasn't sure how Momma was going to take this. She'd made it very clear I needed to stay out of this, so she was liable to be ticked that I'd told Brady so much.

I turned to head toward the kitchen, letting Brady follow me through the swinging door.

He glanced around the sparkling clean kitchen. "You said your mother is upstairs?"

"Yeah. This way." I continued through the kitchen and up the stairs. My mother wasn't going to take kindly to his line of questioning, especially after what we'd just discussed. I considered warning him, but he'd discover soon enough on his own.

Brady followed, keeping a respectable distance between us.

"Momma," I called out as I stopped in the threshold of the office. This was not going to go well. For any of us. "Someone is here to see you."

She was sitting at her desk with a pen in her hand. "Who is it?"

I stepped to the side, and Brady moved into the doorway. "Mrs. Steele? I'm Detective Bennett with the Franklin Police Department. I'd like to ask you a few questions."

Momma's gaze darted to me before settling back on him. "What's this about?"

"Your husband's disappearance. May I come in?"

Tilly's gasp filled the quiet, but Momma kept her steely gaze on him.

"I gave my statement after he left. A long time ago. The case is closed."

He took several steps into the room. "Nevertheless, I'd like to ask a few more questions if you don't mind."

"What does it matter?" Momma asked with an edge in her voice. "I had him declared dead several years back. It's a done deal."

Brady moved even closer. "You're correct, but it's not closed. There were no bodies, and he and Mrs. Morrissey never turned up."

"So why look into it now?" she asked, but the look she shot me told me that she already knew. And she was not happy.

"Magnolia told me that she set up a meeting with Walter Frey last night to talk with him about your husband. As I'm sure you know, Mr. Frey was murdered."

She lifted her chin, and her eyes hardened with irritation. "Magnolia is as mistaken now as she was fourteen years ago. Brian was not meeting Mr. Frey that night. This is her way of excusing her father for running off with that woman." She turned her attention to me. "Your behavior was understandable fourteen years ago, but you're old enough to know better now. Especially after that director stole your money and your dignity, only to fire you and replace you with someone younger and prettier." Her jaw set. "Grow up, Magnolia. Men want the newest model. Your father was no different."

Tears swam in my eyes. I knew in my heart that my mother didn't believe that—she'd pretty much admitted as much earlier—but why would she humiliate me like that? Especially in front of *him*?

Brady cast a quick glance back to me, but I looked down, trying to avoid his gaze. He turned back to my mother and cleared his throat. "Nevertheless," he said, his voice hard, "I would like to ask you some follow-up questions."

"I don't suppose I can say no."

"It would suggest you have something to hide."

"How about it suggests I have something better to do with my time?" she demanded.

"Ma'am," Brady said, pulling out a notebook, "I'm sorry, but I still have to insist that you answer my questions. It might help lead to the apprehension of Walter Frey's killer."

"My answers aren't going to help you do shit, but if you insist on wasting both of our times, then by all means . . ." She gestured toward the chair I had sat in earlier, then looked over at me. "Don't you have a new job you need to get to?"

I looked over at the clock on the wall. It was only nine forty-five, but it definitely couldn't hurt to show up early on my first day. Besides, I was more than ready to leave. I grabbed my purse from beside Brady's chair and took off without a word.

"Maggie," Tilly called after me.

I practically ran down the stairs, but I heard Tilly clomping behind me, so I stopped and waited at the bottom. I didn't want her to hurt herself trying to catch up with me.

"She didn't mean that," Tilly said quietly.

"Which part, Tilly?"

"All of it."

I shook my head. "I'm not so sure she didn't mean what she said about me." I closed my eyes, close to breaking down. "She doesn't want me here. I keep screwing everything up."

"That is not true, Magnolia," Tilly said in a firm voice, pulling down my hands. "She's so grateful you're here."

"She sure doesn't act like it."

I heard Brady's faint voice. "Mrs. Steele, in your statement you said that your husband had been leaving frequently in the evenings."

Then Momma started to lay into him about his reading comprehension level.

Tilly took my hand and pulled me deeper into the kitchen so we couldn't hear their voices. "Magnolia, Lila is trying to protect you. Surely you can see that."

"I'm not a child, Tilly. I have a right to know what happened to Daddy. You and I both know he didn't run off with that woman. Why wouldn't Momma want the truth to come out? She hated how much people whispered behind our backs. They said such terrible things about Daddy and how he'd up and left us."

She grabbed my hands. "Sometimes we have to give up our pride to protect the people we love."

How much did Momma know? How much did *Tilly* know?

My hand fluttered to my chest. Of course she'd tell her best friend. "You know. You know what Momma's hiding."

"That your father had an affair and abandoned his family?" she immediately responded. "The whole town knows that one." But the look in her eyes—confusion and maybe a little guilt—didn't match her tone.

I was desperate to find out what she knew, if anything, but she'd never betray my mother's confidence. Besides, I already knew it was dangerous to press for information about Daddy's disappearance. Someone had seen fit to kill Mr. Frey. What if someone I loved was next?

Maybe I needed to let this sit.

I pulled Tilly into a hug and kissed her cheek. "I love you, Tilly. You're a wonderful friend to both of us. Thank you."

"You know I love you like a daughter."

I leaned back and smiled. "And you know I love you like a second mother." I laughed. "Sometimes I wish you were my first one."

She gave me an uncomfortable look. "You hush that nonsense." She gave my arms a squeeze and pulled away. "You need to listen to your momma and let this go. You hear?"

"Yes, ma'am. I hear."

"You go to work and have a great first day. Break a leg."

She followed me out the front door and locked it behind me, leaving me with plenty to think about.

chapter
ten

Thankfully, I didn't have to stand on the sidewalk and wait for Alvin to open the doors at ten. He praised me for my punctuality, and I resisted the urge to tell him that I hoped he didn't get too used to it.

Some things were best discovered on their own.

He introduced me to an older woman named Rhoda, who gave me a skeptical look, making it obvious I was going to have to win her over. Then he told me about the merchandise, which was half-new and half-vintage home décor, and jewelry he purchased from antique dealers.

"You'll just work the floor today," he said, then winked. "We'll start you on the cash register tomorrow."

"Um . . . about tomorrow . . ." I said hesitantly. "I know we haven't discussed my schedule yet, but I've been asked to help someone with an event she holds every Thursday morning. She says she needs me until noon. It's only a couple of blocks away, so I can walk over as soon as I'm free."

His eyes widened. "An event every Thursday morning and only a few blocks away? Is it Ava Milton's Thursday morning Bible study?"

"Well . . . yeah. How did you know?"

He looked ecstatic. "*Everyone* knows about Ava's Bible studies. Are the Southern Belles catering? That's surprising. Supposedly Ava always does her own cooking."

Crap. "The Belles aren't catering."

"So you're working for Ava?" he asked in surprise, then leaned closer. "Do you have any idea what goes on in those meetings?"

"Um . . . they study the Bible?"

He laughed and swatted my arm. "You poor naïve girl. You really have become a city slicker, haven't you?"

Did people still say city slicker? But I had more important things to worry about. Like what went on during those meetings. "So what do they do?"

"The city's finest women come together to determine everything to do with our town's society."

"Franklin has society?" I asked in disbelief. I could see that kind of thing happening in Belle Meade, but Franklin?

"Oh, just you wait," he said, shaking his head. "I can already tell you're goin' to be a riot. Of course you can have Thursday mornings off, but I expect a *full report*." He narrowed his eyes. "How did you get that job anyway?"

"I'm living in the apartment over her garage."
Which reminded me that I'd never gotten around to
asking my mother for the rest of my rent money. My
check on Friday would more than cover it, but I hated
asking her for an advance.

"*You're living in Ava Milton's apartment?* How did you
manage that?"

I gave him a sidelong glance. "I needed an
apartment and she had one?"

"She doesn't just rent that apartment to anyone.
She's extremely picky."

I couldn't very well tell him that the goal of
embarrassing my mother had probably been her
motivating factor. "Just lucky, I guess."

"You lead a charmed life, Magnolia Steele," Alvin
said as he walked to the front of the store and reached
for the "open" sign on the door. "Broadway star and Ava
Milton's chosen one all rolled into one beautiful package.
I knew I made the right decision when I hired you."

Rhoda glared at me, but I turned away to straighten
a stack of scarves. I already had enough negativity in my
life, and Alvin's enthusiasm wasn't any less worrisome.

Our first customer pushed open the door as soon as
the sign was flipped over.

Of course it was Brady Bennett.

I couldn't seem to escape the man.

"Detective Bennett," Alvin said. "Did your mother
like those candlesticks I suggested?"

"Yes. She loved them. You were right. As usual."
He headed straight for me, searching my face before

turning back to Alvin. "Can I borrow Magnolia for a moment? Police business."

Police business? Great. This was exactly what I needed on my first day. I hadn't even lasted fifteen minutes. While I was curious about his meeting with Momma, she held on to her secrets like they were the presidential nuclear codes, so he probably didn't have anything new to tell me. All this was going to do was make me look suspicious in front of my new boss. Still, I wasn't about to tell him I wanted to wait. Maybe he *had* gotten something out of Momma.

Alvin looked worried. "Of course."

"We're going to head out to the parking lot," Brady said. "I'll only keep her for a few minutes."

Rhoda gave me a look that suggested she expected to see me led off in handcuffs, but Alvin nodded. "Yes. Of course."

Brady motioned to the back, and I pushed out a heavy breath as I preceded him. He held the back door open for me, then nudged a brick into the threshold to keep the door cracked once we were both outside. Without saying a word, he led me into the parking lot.

"The parking lot?" I asked as I crossed my arms. We were in the shade, and the breeze had a slight chill.

He gave a slight shrug. "Alvin is known for his gossip."

The fewer people who knew about this, the better. Especially in light of poor Walter Frey's fate—but I was presuming Brady was really here for official reasons.

Maybe he wasn't. "I hope this is about my mother. You're going to get me fired on my first day."

He gave me a slight grin. "First day, huh? That explains why no one told me that you were working here."

I rolled my eyes.

"I didn't ask," he volunteered. "But if you show interest in something, people in this town are always eager to share information."

"Great," I grumped, wondering if that was how he got a lot of his information. I'd tuck that away for future interest. "I suspect everyone knows you as *Detective* Bennett. Do they all think I'm a fugitive?"

He grinned. "You can't be a fugitive if you're living out in the open, and no, they don't think you're a criminal. They think I'm interested in you. A few have offered to try to fix us up."

I found myself smiling back, despite my better judgment. "And did you take them up on their offer?"

His grin spread. "No. I don't usually need help, but I'm a whole lot less confident in regard to you, so I'm starting to rethink matters."

"Thanks for the warning."

His smile faded and he glanced toward the door and lowered his voice. "Your mother wasn't very cooperative, but I finally convinced her to give me a brief statement."

"Tell me your secret," I teased halfheartedly. "I've been searching for the power of persuasion over my mother since the day I was born."

His lips twisted into a tight grin. "At the risk of losing your admiration, it took a threat of taking her downtown."

My eyes widened. "Would you really have done that?"

His grin spread. "No, but she didn't know that."

Too bad I didn't have that trick up my sleeve.

"Your mother insists you made up the incident with Walter Frey at your father's office. She says she knew your father was having an affair with Shannon Morrissey, but that she kept it from you and your brother. The story she's telling now doesn't match with what she initially told the police, but she later recanted. Said she no longer saw the point of denying the truth."

I sucked in a breath as I wrapped my arms tighter around myself. "I see. So you're questioning my statement?"

"No. On the contrary. I'm sure your mother is hiding something."

I was too, and that worried the crap out of me. Should I recant my own statement? It was obvious Momma didn't want anyone pursuing this, and I didn't want to put her or anyone else in danger. But Walter Frey deserved justice, didn't he? And besides, I'd set this ball in motion. I suspected it was too late to call a halt now. "What do you plan to do?"

"I'll ask more questions."

"Who are you going to ask?" When it was obvious he wasn't going to answer, I lifted my eyebrows. "You're not going to tell me what you're doing, are you?"

"I'll take care of it."

"If I had a dollar for every man who's told me that," I said in a teasing tone.

But Brady didn't laugh. "Maggie, I'm trying my best to earn back your trust, and I assure you that I'm taking this seriously. In the meantime, if you feel unsafe, I want you to call me or 911. Promise? It's always best to be aware of your surroundings, but you should be extra vigilant until we catch Walter Frey's killer."

"I understand this is police procedure, Brady, but I was meeting with Mr. Frey to get answers. You're asking me to trust *you* to get them when no one else took this seriously before."

"A man is dead, Magnolia. I'm a police detective. Let me do my job."

I'd flipped a switch and Detective Bennett was answering—not Brady. But maybe that was for the best, especially if he was the impartial, fair investigator he claimed to be. "How do I know you're not doing some bullshit investigation just to appease me?"

His eyes hardened slightly. "I've already told you I think there's a link, so why would I bullshit you? To lie my way into your good graces?"

I groaned and turned away from him. Sometimes I could really be a bitch. "I'm sorry. You're right."

His eyes lit up with amusement, and maybe a dash of surprise. "After what happened with the Goodwin murder, I understand your concerns." He paused. "I'll keep you in the loop. I won't tell you what I plan to do, but I'll let you know what I find out. Okay?"

I crossed my arms and gave him a skeptical look.

His face softened. "If I were in your place, I'd want answers too. I'm trying to help you, Magnolia. Will you let me?"

When he put it that way, how could I refuse? But I'd been on my own for so long, it was hard to give control to someone else. Even in this. "Okay." I could see Alvin peeking out the window and pushed out a sigh. "Is that all? Because I'm about to get fired, and then I'll never be able to pay the rent for my new apartment."

He looked surprised. "Your mother said you lived with her."

She was obviously still in denial.

He pulled out his notebook and a pen. "I'm going to need your correct address for the current police report. I'll give it to Owen."

"What?" I teased. "You can't find out from your vast array of informants?"

He gave me a sheepish look.

"I'm teasing." I rattled off the address, then looked up at him, hugging myself tighter against the gusty wind. "Thanks for taking this seriously."

He stared into my eyes with an intensity that caught me by surprise. "Trust me when I say that I think there's something here. But . . ." He hesitated. "While this investigation is ongoing, I need you to keep your involvement in Walter Frey's murder to yourself. It's safer if you don't talk to anyone. There are details we're not releasing to the media. And if you tell the wrong person . . ."

"Like Alvin?"

"Exactly."

He followed me back inside, then stopped next to Alvin. "Thanks for letting me borrow Maggie for a few minutes. She had some very helpful information for an investigation I'm conducting."

"Of course." Alvin nodded, his eyes widening in excitement.

Brady turned back to give me one last glance. "Maggie, are we still on for dinner tonight?"

My mouth dropped open like a trap door at the gallows. "*What?*"

His grin spread. What the hell was he doing? I'd never agreed to dinner, but he'd also just told me that Alvin was a purveyor of gossip.

I put a hand on my hip. "Sorry, Detective Bennett. I have other plans for tonight."

"More important than going out to dinner with Brady?" Alvin asked in disbelief.

Brady's grin turned mischievous. "I know it can't be to wash your hair. It's gorgeous just the way it is."

I'd pinned back the front strands, but the rest hung halfway down my back in natural loose waves. Definitely nothing special. "Nice of you to notice, Detective Bennett," I said in a dry tone. "I had no idea you were so infatuated with women's hairstyles."

His grin spread. "Only yours."

Damn him.

Before I could respond, he took a step toward the door. "If you have other plans, I'll take a raincheck."

Then he walked out the door, the bell clanging behind him.

"I'm pretty sure that was police harassment," I said in a low breath.

"He can harass me any day," Rhoda said, fanning herself with a greeting card as she watched him walk away. "With handcuffs."

That was not an image I wanted to entertain.

"Damn, girl," Alvin said. "How can you tell that boy no?"

"It helps that it's a one-syllable word."

My phone vibrated with a text a minute later, and I was surprised to see it was Brady.

I figured it might help the rumor mill if there was a personal nature to my visit. Better to keep the focus off your involvement in the case.

I was tempted to scoff, but he was right about Alvin and Rhoda. Alvin didn't seem at all disturbed by my short break. Instead, I spent the next hour deflecting questions about where and how I had met Brady.

Shortly after lunch, the bell on the door dinged, announcing a new visitor: my ex-best friend Maddie. We'd been friends all through school up until graduation, but she'd taken my unexplained and sudden departure to New York City as a personal insult and hadn't talked to me for years. We'd reached a tentative truce in the produce aisle of a grocery store a few weeks ago, but I hadn't seen her since. Now she was here with an older woman I didn't recognize, pushing a baby stroller.

My heart leapt to my throat. I had no idea how Maddie would take seeing me, and I really hoped it wouldn't cause a scene.

She and the woman huddled around a display of silver picture frames while I stood in the back, rearranging a stack of scarves that were already lined up with military precision. Maddie's face lifted and her mouth parted in a small O when she saw me. She leaned in to say something to the woman and then headed straight for me, leaving the stroller with the older lady. I squared my shoulders, wondering if I should prepare for a verbal assault in case she'd agreed to the previous truce in a moment of insanity. But she gave me a hesitant smile.

"Hey, Magnolia."

"Hi," I said softly, suddenly nostalgic for the simple life I'd lived before I'd run away. I missed her. I missed my old life. I missed the simple feeling of belonging, which I hadn't felt in a long, long time.

I missed not having to look over my shoulder at every turn.

"Are you on lunch break from the Southern Belles?" she asked.

"No," I said with a hesitant smile. "I work here."

She looked surprised.

I lifted a shoulder into a half-shrug. "I work for Momma too. This is just extra money."

"Working in a boutique?" Her question wasn't unkind, but I sensed a condescending attitude.

I forced a smile. "Are you out shopping with the baby today?"

"And my mother-in-law."

"So that's Blake's mother," I said, trying to stifle my unease. Maddie's high school boyfriend (now husband) Blake hadn't been a nice person ten years ago, and after our recent encounter at Maddie's Bunco night, which I'd unwittingly attended with Belinda, he hadn't improved.

"Yeah." Maddie looked around the shop, then back at me. "I just can't believe you're working here."

"Yeah, well . . ." I could tell her I was here because Momma was dying and I couldn't bear to leave her, but that would be a betrayal of my mother's trust. Besides, if Momma told me tomorrow that her cancer had been magically cured, I'd still stay in Franklin. Brady had convinced me that he was really going to look into my father's disappearance, and I was hoping for answers this time.

Maddie looked uncomfortable, especially when she realized the older woman was staring at us. "Well," she said. "I better head home and get dinner started."

I lifted my eyebrows. "Yeah. You only have about four hours to whip up a meatloaf and mashed potatoes."

My tone certainly left something to be desired, but the look of pain in Maddie's eyes caught me off guard. Based on our childhood plans and dreams, her life was unfolding exactly as she'd hoped. I was tempted to ask what was wrong, but she mumbled goodbye before I could get any words out. As I watched her and her new family leave the store, I had to wonder if our friendship had run its course. Our lives were vastly different now, and the image of what my life would have been like if I'd never left Franklin didn't bring warm and fuzzy feelings. Domestication had never been for me.

As the rest of the afternoon progressed, I could see why Alvin had hired me—it would have been too much for two people. But thankfully things slowed down around three, when I needed to leave to help with the catering business.

"So tomorrow I'll come in as soon as I'm done with Miss Ava's Bible study," I said, feeling ridiculous since Alvin had insisted scripture wouldn't play much of a part.

Alvin winked. "I can't wait to hear all about it."

That's what I was afraid of.

My phone rang almost as soon as I stepped out the door. I smiled when I saw it was Belinda.

"How was your first day?" she asked.

"All in all, it was good. I think Alvin likes me, but Rhoda acts like I'm a serial killer who took the job just to get close enough to drop her down a well."

"Some people don't like change. She'll love you soon enough."

I wasn't so sure about that, but God love Belinda for truly believing it.

She sighed. "Hey. A client just walked in, but I also called to see if you could meet me for lunch tomorrow."

"I can't." I considered filling her in on the Ava Milton mess, but it would take more time than she had. "But maybe Friday. I'll let you know when I get my schedule from Alvin."

"Sounds good. I'll talk to you later."

It was a good thing I had Belinda's cheery voice to brighten my afternoon. My mother was still in a foul mood when I showed up, but the kitchen was bubbling with activity. They'd learned better than to put me in charge of any food prep, but I could transfer food to pans and gather all the other necessary items.

Colt was already there, but he just gave me a grin and returned to work. I glanced up at the clock on the wall, feeling anxious. I still hadn't asked for an advance on my salary.

Momma went out the back door to check on a loose shelf in one of the vans, and I took advantage of her absence to corner Tilly in the kitchen.

"I have a huge favor to ask," I said.

Worry filled her eyes. "Your mother is in a mood, Maggie."

"You don't even know what I'm going to ask."

"It's obviously something that will upset her if you're asking *me*."

She had a point. "I need to get my paycheck early."

Tilly looked me over like I'd misplaced my brain, then pushed out a sigh. Understanding filled her eyes. "You need rent money."

I nodded. "Momma gave me money when she thought I was leaving town, but I used it to pay down my credit cards."

Her mouth pursed as she glanced toward the back door. "Lila has a firm policy about not giving advances."

"But I'm her daughter."

"All the more reason she'll refuse."

Would Ava wait? I suspected not, but then I remembered that she'd tricked me into signing the contract before I saw Momma. She'd take the check late, but I wouldn't hear the end of it the entire time I lived there. In hindsight, I shouldn't have signed anything without the money in hand. But all the Ava drama aside, I loved that place. I didn't *want* to get out of the lease. "So I'm out of luck?"

A sly grin lifted the corners of Tilly's lips. "Now I didn't say that, did I?"

"What are you saying?"

She lowered her voice. "Just because Southern Belles doesn't give advances, doesn't mean I haven't given out a personal payday loan every now and then."

My eyes widened. "Oh, Tilly. I can't take your money."

"You most certainly *can*. Besides, you'll pay me back on Friday."

"Tilly"—my voice broke—"I don't know what to say."

"Imagine that," Momma said as she walked through the door behind us. "Magnolia Steele without something to say."

I spun around and gave her a glare.

"What are you and Tilly up to?"

"Nothing," I murmured.

Tilly turned her attention to the sauce she had been stirring on the stove. "I'm not sure what you're talkin' about."

"Uh-huh," Momma grunted. "You both look guilty as hell. I thought you were supposed to be some kind of hotshot actress, Magnolia, but from what I can see, you can't act your way out of a paper bag."

Her barb struck deep, and I wondered once again why I'd stayed in Franklin. Momma clearly didn't want me here.

I looked her in the eye. "Funny thing, Momma," I said, ignoring the hitch in my voice. "I had no idea I was supposed to be acting with *you*."

Pain and sorrow filled her eyes before she spun around and started barking orders.

I was dangerously close to tears, so I eagerly agreed to take a pan out to the van.

Colt was out there rearranging things, and he turned to take the pan from me. "You okay, Maggie Mae?" he asked quietly, sympathy in his eyes.

"Of course," I said with a shrug.

He grimaced. "I may have stirred up shit and made her cranky. I asked her about working on your car. Sorry."

I pushed out a breath. "Don't worry about it. She was already ticked." I looked into his eyes. "Did you know she and Ava Milton are mortal enemies?"

Something flickered in his eyes, brief enough that I would have missed it had I not been looking for a reaction. "Really? You don't say."

A non-answer if ever I'd heard one.

"I suppose Lila filled you in when you spilled the beans about your new place."

"Yeah. And I dug myself deeper by agreeing to help Miss Ava host her Thursday Bible studies."

His eyes widened. "You're helpin' with her Thursday morning meetings?"

"Why is that so surprising?"

"She doesn't let just anyone into those meetings."

"What are they doing? Picking out the pope? What's with all the secrecy?"

"I've never been to one, so I have no idea what they do, but I doubt there's much reflectin' on the Bible."

"That's what my new boss at the shop implied. Should I be worried?"

His hesitation to answer ratcheted up my blood pressure. "You should probably be cautious."

"I'm not a guest, Colt. I'm the hired help. She's paying me fifty dollars."

"It's still best to stay on your toes."

"What the hell, Colt?" I demanded. "Is she some Southern Godfather wannabe? I've got enough shit to deal with."

The look on his face . . . was he afraid?

I gasped and grabbed his arm. "Are you shitting me?"

He laughed, then shook me off, rolling his eyes. "For a city girl, you're pretty damn gullible."

"Not funny, Colt."

"Aww, come on. Don't be like that. I really don't know what goes on at her meetings, but I can assure you that you have nothing to worry about, Maggie Mae. Miss Ava's weapons of choice are rumors, and you've got plenty of those floatin' around about you already. What more could she do?"

I really didn't want to find out.

"Mags, I'm sorry. Really, I was just shittin' you. You'll be fine as long as you don't piss her off."

"Hello? Have we met? Pissing people off seems to be my specialty."

He chuckled. "She obviously sees something she likes if she invited you."

"She didn't *invite* me. I'm supposed to help her serve refreshments."

"Like I said, you'll be fine. I'm just surprised. Most people have to earn her trust."

This had something to do with my mother, no doubt about it.

"Do you plan on shootin' the breeze all afternoon?" my mother asked from behind me. "Or are you actually gonna work?"

I headed back inside to help package up the rest of the food. When we were almost done, Tilly sidled up to me and handed me a folded piece of paper on the sly. I gave her a questioning look, and she winked. "Our secret."

I leaned closer. "Is this an advance?"

"No advance," she said with tears in her eyes. "A welcome-home gift."

I turned my back to the room and then opened the paper, gasping when I saw she had given me a check for two thousand dollars.

"Tilly," I whispered. "I can't accept this. It's too much."

"No, my sweet girl. I can afford it," she said, patting my arm. "You need something to get you started, but don't put it toward your credit cards. Splurge on something for your new apartment. And don't tell your mother."

"I won't." I leaned over and gave her a quick peck on the cheek. "I love you, Tilly."

Tears filled her eyes. "I love you too, girl."

"If you like, I'll invite you over for dinner so you can see my new place."

She laughed. "If that's your way of showing your appreciation, I think I'll take it back."

I could have been offended, but I knew it had been said in love. I laughed and gave her a hug. "Maybe we'll order out."

She grinned. "There we go."

I stuffed the check into the pocket of my purse before I drove to the event with Colt. They had me help out in the back, where the risk factor had been deemed the lowest. Several hours later, we brought everything back and washed the pots and pans so we could work on another event the next evening. And I was utterly exhausted.

Colt offered to take me home to get my already packed suitcases and then on to the apartment. It was a good thing too—Momma still wasn't speaking to me. She got home just ahead of us and went straight to her room and shut the door. I gave her closed door a long look, tempted to knock on it and insist that she tell me what had really happened with Daddy, but I knew from personal experience that now was not the time. There was a cycle to her anger. I needed to wait her out, so leaving was actually the best thing I could do.

I carried my luggage downstairs with a heavy heart.

Colt, who was waiting by the door, gave me a reassuring look as he took the bags from me. "She'll get over it, Mags. I've seen her like this before. Just give her time."

"But she doesn't have time," I said as we walked to his truck.

He put the bags into the back of his truck, then pulled me into a hug. "I know. I'm sorry."

I leaned into him for a moment, realizing how good he smelled. I pulled away and grinned up at him. "How come I smell like cocktail sauce and you smell good?"

"Noticin' how I smell, huh? I knew I'd win you over." He winked, then swatted my bottom. "I don't have time to be seduced, woman. I have to drop you off and head to rehearsal."

I laughed and walked around the truck, thankful that he was teasing and things weren't awkward between us. I suspected Colt would be on board should I decide to start something, but it felt like a breath of fresh air to just be friends with an attractive guy and not worry that he was trying to get into my pants.

"Are you playing at the Embassy again?" I asked once he'd pulled out of the driveway.

"Nah. I'm filling in as guitarist for a band on Sunday night, so we're gonna run through the set."

"How often do you play in bars?" I asked.

"Plenty enough to know if this was gonna happen, it probably would have by now," he said, sounding more serious than I'd ever heard him.

"You're good, Colt," I said. But we both knew Nashville was chock-full of talented musicians. Sometimes it boiled down to luck.

"You interested in singing anywhere?" he asked, draping his hand over the wheel.

I laughed. "I'm not a singer. I'm an actress."

"Could have fooled me last night. You were a natural."

I shrugged. "I was performing. I guess it's all the same. Convincing the audience you're sincere with what you're saying or singing."

"I'm playing at the Kincaid in Nashville Friday night," he said, casting a sideways glance at me. "You should sing with me."

"What are you talking about?" I laughed. "Last night was a one-time thing."

"Performin' is in your blood, Mags. You loved bein' on the stage."

I had to admit he was right.

"There's money in it."

That perked me up. "How much?"

"Tips."

"You mean like street musicians?" I asked in disgust. I knew it was a common practice, but considered it the equivalent of begging.

"Don't be such a snob. You don't even have to sing the entire set. How about a few songs? I'll even let you pick them. We'll split whatever we pull in."

I was tempted. I definitely needed the money, even with Tilly's extravagant gift. But if we were playing for tips, we'd definitely have to put on a show to earn them.

"What else are you doing Friday night?"

"I think Belinda wants me to go to Bunco."

The last time I'd gone with her had been a disaster, and Colt knew it. We both looked at each other and grinned.

"So what do you want to sing?" he asked.

We settled on repeating "Need You Now," a few other songs, and one of my solos from *Fireflies at Dawn*. He told me he could pick up the accompaniment as long as we practiced a few times before the gig, and we agreed to meet up late Friday after I got off work.

Colt drove around Miss Ava's house and parked in a bay to the side of the garage. "I'm sure this is where Miss Ava will have you park once we get your car running."

"You know, I shouldn't let you be seen here. She counts you as a gentleman caller," I teased. "I only get one every few weeks lest I turn my apartment into a brothel, and I'm not sure I want to waste it on you."

"So you got the speech?" He laughed, then added an air of sophistication to his voice. "So you plan on entertainin' gentleman callers, Miss Steele? I didn't know you were pursuing a suitor."

I shook my head as we got out. Colt grabbed my suitcases and followed me up the stairs.

When I opened the door, he set the bags inside, then looked over his shoulder. "I know you're stuck out here without a car, so call if you need anything, okay? I'm not far away."

"I still have to pay Miss Ava, only I still have a check I need to deposit before there's enough money in my account."

He winked. "I'll stop by and talk to her. Just give her a check in the morning and deposit your money into the bank on the way to your first job tomorrow. She'll agree to it."

I had to wonder what he had on Ava Milton to wrap her around his finger like that, but part of me was scared to ask. Especially since it was working in my favor.

Then he left and shut the door behind him. I stood in the middle of the room and spun in a circle, amazed that this apartment was all *mine*.

I put my clothes away, which didn't take long since so many were dirty. I tossed those onto the floor of the closet. I realized I needed things for the apartment—like laundry detergent and a host of other toiletries and household supplies, so I found a pen and pad of paper in a drawer in the kitchen to make a list. But my stomach growled as I sat down at the kitchen island to compose my list, reminding me that while I'd been around food all evening, I hadn't eaten much of anything. I looked up the number for Marcos Pizza and placed an order for delivery, making sure to tell them I was in the apartment over the garage, figuring I had plenty to do during the thirty-minute wait.

About ten minutes later, I had finished the list and was on my laptop searching for additional songs for my set with Colt. If I was going to sing with him, I might as well do my part to earn tip money. I'd already written down several possibilities when a hard knock landed on the door. At first I was surprised the pizza had already arrived. But I realized my mistake as soon as I opened the door. It wasn't my dinner.

I was face to face with my very pissed brother.

chapter eleven

Roy," I gasped. How did he know where I lived? A surge of fear filled my head, but I pushed it aside, pissed to give him any control over me.

He pushed me aside, barged into my apartment, and shut the door behind him before he looked around. "Who are you sleeping with to get a place like this?"

I'd been caught off guard, but I quickly regained control. "What do you want, Roy?"

He walked into the kitchen, then pushed open the bedroom door to peek inside. "I bet this place is quite the fall from living with that director in New York City."

"What do you want, Roy?" I repeated with more force. My anger had kicked in, but I still felt a healthy amount of fear. A few weeks ago, he'd physically hurt me, and I was certain he beat Belinda. I had no idea what he'd do here with the two of us alone, especially since I could see he was pissed. The question was why?

"I know it's not that loser Momma insists on keeping as her employee." He opened a cabinet door, closed it, and circled the island back toward me, holding my gaze. "Colt Austin's broke."

I remained silent. He obviously had an agenda, and I'd only be playing into his hands if I begged him to explain. I refused to give him the satisfaction.

He rested his palm on the island counter next to my laptop. "Guess who came by my office today, Magnolia?"

"I haven't the slightest idea, nor do I care unless it was the FCC there to arrest you for insider trading."

"Very funny," he said with deadly calm. "You've always considered yourself to be so clever." He shoved my laptop off the island and sent it crashing to the wood floor.

I resisted the urge to try to save it. One, I would never reach it in time, and two, my brother had begun to slowly advance toward me.

The dead look in his eyes scared the hell out of me. He was twice as big as me, and while I knew self-defense, it still wouldn't be a fair fight, especially considering most of my maneuvers ended with me running for my life. As much as I liked my new apartment, there wasn't much room for me to run.

I had a can of pepper spray in my purse. If only I could get to the other side of the room . . .

I took several steps in that direction, away from him, and a spark lit up his eyes. He saw my move as a challenge. A predator with his prey.

"Guess again, Magnolia."

I lifted my chin and gave him a haughty stare. "Since my guess was wrong, why don't you save us both time and just tell me?"

His eyes darkened, and I took another step. My purse was on the bookcase, five feet away.

"The police, Magnolia. The police came by my office."

"So I wasn't too far off after all," I said in a snotty tone.

His jaw tensed. "They wanted to know about our father. The night he ran off with Shannon Morrissey. The night he ran off with my client's money."

Which made absolutely no sense. If Daddy had helped steal Mr. Morrissey's million dollars, why would Mr. Morrissey want my brother as his funds manager? The whole thing smelled more rotten than a fish out in the noon sun. But I had more immediate concerns. Like the fact that the police had been to his office.

"They questioned you?"

"Yes, and Bill James."

I wasn't surprised. It stood to reason Brady would question Daddy's partner. "So?"

"What have you done, Magnolia?"

"I know you like to blame me for everything, but *really*, Roy . . ."

"I know about Walter Frey."

I gave him a look that told him he was being ridiculous. "I didn't kill him."

A vein on his temple began to throb. "But you had something to do with it."

Of that I was sure, but I'd done a pretty good job of ignoring it for most of the day. If I was going to admit my guilt to anyone, it wasn't my brother. "That's ridiculous."

"There was no drama before you came back. No one had mentioned Dad for years. But you've been back three weeks, and all hell's broken loose."

"Aww . . ." I said, knowing it was like poking a sleeping bear, yet I couldn't stop myself. "You missed me."

He lunged forward and grabbed my arm. "You don't belong here."

I forced myself to remain still, even though his fingers dug into my arm. "I hate to break it to you, Roy, but I lived here before you were even born. I have just as much of a right to be here as you do."

His grip tightened, pinching my skin. "I'm not playing around."

"And neither am I," I said in a firm voice, looking into his angry eyes.

He pulled me closer. "I gave you every opportunity to leave. I offered to pay you. You should have taken the money, Magnolia."

"We all should have done things we didn't. You should have done a better job of mowing the lawn when we were kids, and I should have gone out with Billy Peeler—who knew he'd become *People*'s hottest man alive?—yet here we are. A little bit older and a whole lot wiser. Well. I'm wiser, you . . . not so much."

I never saw his hand coming, so it caught me by surprise when his palm connected with my cheek. He hit me hard enough to make it sting, but not hard enough to leave a bruise.

Just like I'd thought, he was obviously an experienced abuser.

I tried to pull back, but his hand tightened on my arm. "Oh, no, Magnolia. We're not done yet."

"Wrong, Roy. We're completely done." I hadn't taken off my shoes, and thankfully I'd had fashion in mind earlier that morning. I'd worn flats, but they had a bit of a pointed toe, so I kicked him as hard as I could in the shin.

He grunted and dropped his hold.

I stumbled back and lunged for my purse, but he quickly recovered and shoved my stomach against the bookcase.

My chest and stomach hit the shelves with a loud thud, and I cried out as he grabbed my left forearm and twisted it around my back.

He leaned his mouth next to my ear. "I'm not finished, Magnolia."

"You're hurting me, Roy," I forced out through gritted teeth, wrapping my free hand around one of the shelves to keep him from pushing me harder. "You get off on that? Hurting people physically weaker than you?"

"I don't want to hurt you, but you left me no choice. You *will* listen to me."

I pushed off from the bookshelf, trying to break free, but he shoved me back even harder this time, pushing my arm higher. I fought to keep my panic in check, but the pain in my arm brought tears to my eyes.

"Why must you always be so stupid?" he asked in disgust.

"Fine," I said hatefully. "Say what you have to say and get the hell out."

"In case you hadn't noticed, I'm the one making the rules." I heard the smile in his voice and felt like throwing up. How could we have grown up in the same household? How could the little boy who used to play endless games of Connect Four with me have turned into this monster?

My purse was on the shelf to my right but slightly out of reach. Even if I broke free from Roy's hold, I'd have to dig through my purse to find the pepper spray.

"Do you know how hard I've had to work to be taken seriously at my firm?" he asked. "I had to practically beg Bill to hire me, and I've had to work my ass off to get him to trust me. Three years, Magnolia, three fucking years I've kissed that man's ass."

"Go work somewhere else, you idiot. It's not the only financial planning firm in Nashville." Even as the words left my mouth, I knew *I* was the idiot. He was going to beat the shit out of me. But I was tired of backing down. I was tired of being a victim. I was taking charge. Even if the only thing I could do was mouth off.

He shoved me harder, and I released another cry of pain. "I don't want to work anywhere else. I want to work at JS Investments, and you are ruining *everything*, Magnolia. Just like you've *always* ruined everything."

He spun me around and dropped his hold on my arm, but he placed his hands on the shelves on either side of my shoulders, trapping me in front of him. The loathing in his eyes scared me.

"Why do you hate me so much?" I whispered, my voice shaking.

"You're so stupid. You don't even know."

"Then enlighten me."

"Everything you touch is blown to smithereens."

I had no idea what he was talking about, but I had no desire for him to elaborate. "Fine. I'll stay out of your life and you stay out of mine."

"If only it were that easy, but you seem incapable of it."

That sounded ominous, and I wasn't going to wait to see where he was going with this. I lifted up my knee and rammed his crotch as hard as I could.

He grunted and hunched over, no longer blocking me in. I took advantage of my freedom to dash for my purse and then backed into the kitchen and around the island as I frantically dug for my pepper spray.

"I'm going to kill you, Magnolia," he sneered, stumbling into the kitchen.

My panic increased as Roy rounded the island. Did he mean it literally? Where the hell was the spray?

"Get out of my apartment, Roy," I said, near hysterical. He was still bent over at the waist, and the look on his face told me I was going to pay for what I'd done.

Just as he was about to reach me, my fingers wrapped around the metal tube. I swung my purse at his head with my left hand, but pain shot through my shoulder from the spot where he'd pinned my arm.

He easily deflected my weak swing, but it was enough to catch him off guard as I flipped the tab on the top of the metal cylinder. I held it up and took a step back.

"Get out," I said, keeping my voice firm.

He froze when he saw the can in my hand.

"Get the hell out of my apartment," I continued. "Or I'll spray the shit out of your face."

He lifted his hands in surrender. "Calm down, Magnolia."

"Calm down?" I shrieked. "*Calm down?* You show up at my apartment and hurt me and threaten to kill me, and now you're telling me to calm down? *Get the fuck out!*"

He took several backward steps toward the door, and I followed him, keeping enough distance so that I was out of his reach.

He grabbed the doorknob, then sneered, "Stay out of my life, Magnolia, and leave what happened to our father where it belongs. In the past. If you don't, I'm not responsible for what happens." Then he flung the door open and stomped out into the night.

I ran over and shut the door and locked it before I collapsed on the sofa and burst into tears. Why did my brother hate me so? A few weeks ago, he'd implied it was because I'd gotten so much attention from our parents, but surely there was more to it. That was a matter for a different day, though, or maybe a therapist's couch—something *today* had made him angry. It had undoubtedly embarrassed him to have the police show up at his office, especially if they were asking about his father, who had supposedly embezzled his client's money, but beating the crap out of me was an excessive response. Even if he did beat his wife.

Belinda.

I found my phone and typed out a text with shaky fingers.

Roy's furious with me and I'm scared he's going to take it out on you. Be careful.

I hit send and felt close to tears again. It would be my fault if Roy hurt her. But I shook my head as the thought floated through. That was a typical enabler excuse. I would not take ownership of my brother's abuse.

I heard a knock at the door and startled. With the pepper spray in hand, I moved over to the door and looked through the peep hole—something I should have done earlier, though I would have opened the door to my brother anyway. But this visitor was standing at the top of the staircase with his back to the door, holding a pizza box with the Marcos Pizza logo.

I ran a hand over my hair, worried about what I looked like. After setting the pepper spray on the table, I ran my thumbs under my eyes to wipe away any mascara that might have smeared from my cry. Then I opened the door and asked, "How much do I owe . . ."

But my voice trailed off because I knew who it was before he turned all the way around.

"What are you doing here, Brady?"

He was grinning, but his smile fell as soon as he saw me. "What happened?"

I shook my head. "Why do you have my pizza? Why are you here?"

"*What happened?*"

"Who said anything happened?" How bad did I look? "What are you doing here?"

"I promised to tell you what I found. I considered asking you to meet me at the station tomorrow, but after what happened last time, I thought it might make you more comfortable if I came here."

"Oh."

"Can I come in?"

"Yeah."

I turned my back to him and started toward the kitchen, resisting the urge to cringe. There were still signs of my struggle with Roy—not many, but Brady was sure to pick up on them, especially since he already thought something was wrong.

To his credit, he didn't say a word as he set the pizza box on the counter.

"What did you find out?" I asked as I squatted and picked up my laptop. The lid had been opened, but thankfully the screen wasn't cracked, and the sign-in page opened when I swiped my thumb over the trackpad. I closed the lid and set the computer on the other side of the island, then picked up my purse and returned it to the bookshelf.

I eyed the pizza box but was now too nervous to eat.

"Why don't we sit down?" he asked. "Where would you be most comfortable?"

There was that word again. *Comfortable.* He was here with bad news. No one ever made sure you were comfortable for good news.

"The barstools."

I took a seat and he sat next to me.

"I talked to several people today," he said, looking into my eyes, "including your father's boss and Shannon Morrissey's husband, and they all said the same things— your father was having an affair and he conspired with Mrs. Morrissey to take one million dollars of Mr. Morrissey's money."

"And?" I asked. He didn't seem like the kind of guy to be so easily dissuaded, and yet I sensed his hesitation. As though he was holding on to bad news.

His eyebrows rose. "And I talked to your brother."

"You talked to Roy?" Roy had told me that, but I didn't trust him. "What did he say?"

He looked into my eyes. "Maggie, your brother confirmed that your father was having an affair."

"I see," I said. "And did he say how he knew for certain?"

"He said that he caught them."

I stared at him, hiding my disbelief. "Did he give any details?"

"He said something happened about a month before your father disappeared. You were at dance class one night, and Roy hung out with your father. They stopped at a coffee shop so your dad could talk to a woman. Shannon Morrissey."

"So? That doesn't mean they were having an affair."

"He said he saw them kissing."

"Did you talk to anyone else?" I asked.

"Maggie," he said, his voice low. "Even if I thought there might be something there, my boss has told me to drop it. The case was closed, and he wants to leave it that way."

"I see." And I did. All too well. Roy had lied his ass off. I hadn't taken a dance class since I was ten—something I had lamented after moving to New York. My brother had deceived Brady to throw him off the trail, and then he'd come over and threatened me to stay away too.

All after Walter Frey had been killed.

Something terrible had happened to my father, and my brother was helping to cover it up.

chapter twelve

The real question was what I wanted to do with this information. "You think my father ran off?" I asked.

He gave me a sad smile. "Yeah, Maggie, I do. I'm sorry."

I nodded. Should I tell him that my brother was lying? If Brady's boss had told him to let the investigation go, I didn't see the point. I was sure Brady would take my brother's word over mine after my emotional outbursts and my admission that I'd been close to Daddy. My statement was biased. What if I told him about my brother's visit fifteen minutes ago?

But there was my mother to consider. I'd seen genuine fear on her face. One man was dead. What if she was next? We didn't have much time left together, and I wanted her last months to be as peaceful as possible.

I'd sit on my suspicions for now. "So what happened to Mr. Frey?"

"He was robbed." He stiffened slightly and studied me closely. "His wallet and his phone were missing."

"*His phone?*"

"Yeah." He hesitated and seemed to choose his next words carefully. "I know you mentioned seeing his phone. So I need you to think back and be certain you saw it."

Shock reverberated through me, leaving me speechless. I was positive I'd seen the phone. I almost asked him why someone would have taken it, but the answer was glaringly obvious. I said instead, "Did you find anything else?"

"Like what?"

I'd already told him about the phone, which was mysteriously MIA, so why hold back? "I thought I saw a piece of paper under his hand. Did they find it?"

His cop face was back. "You didn't mention that."

"I just remembered it earlier. I hadn't had a chance to tell you yet."

He hesitated for a split second, then shook his head, looking wary. "To the best of my knowledge, nothing else was found. However, it was raining and windy. The paper could have disintegrated or blown away. Did you see anything on it?"

It was possible he was acting, but if so, he deserved a Tony Award.

That begged the question of what had happened to the paper *and* the phone. Because both had been firmly wedged in Mr. Frey's hand. Someone had taken them. I'd bet my only pair of Louboutins that the names on that paper had something to do with my father.

If Brady wasn't investigating my father's case anymore, I was going to have to do some digging of my own. Which meant I couldn't tell him. He had begun to earn my trust, but what if he was involved in this somehow? Even if he wasn't, there was a chance he could unintentionally tip off the person who'd taken them.

"Did you see anything on the paper?" he asked again in a quiet voice.

I shook my head. "I was freaked out and it was all a blur. Maybe it was trash."

"Are you sure? I need you to be honest with me, Magnolia."

I couldn't read the emotion in his eyes. Fear? Worry? Did he think I was losing my mind? "Nothing."

He looked disappointed with my answer. "Did you remember anything else? Anything at all?"

"No. Nothing else." I ran a hand through my hair, suddenly exhausted. "I'm sure it was nothing important."

Thankfully, he let it go, but the topic he moved on to wasn't an improvement. "What happened in your apartment before I showed up?" When I gave him a confused look—I'd have to get used to this role: innocent girl, no secrets—his eyes narrowed. "The laptop?"

"Oh," I said, pretending to feel like an idiot. "I accidently knocked it off when I heard you at the door."

"And your purse?"

"The same."

"So why is there pepper spray on your table by the door?"

"A woman living alone can never be too careful."

"I see."

And that was the problem. He did, all too well.

He leaned closer and lowered his voice. "You know I can help you, Magnolia, right?"

"Like you helped me before?" I asked, inserting just enough bitchiness to get him to back off.

"That was a unique circumstance. Even you have admitted that."

I leaned my head back and groaned. "I am not having this conversation again."

Brady stood and moved toward the coffee table, scanning the room.

I got to my feet and followed him. Part of me wanted to tell him about Roy's attack, but my mother was already pissed at me. How would she take it if I had Roy arrested? She seemed in denial that Roy's violent streak was a mile long, so she'd likely blame it on me. And what good would it do? He'd probably get what amounted to a slap on the wrist, and for all I knew, he might take it out on Belinda. It would serve me better to let Roy think he'd won the war and do some digging on the sly. Brady wasn't going to keep investigating, and I was more certain than ever that Daddy had met foul play. Despite the dangers, I couldn't let it go, not now. Rather than put me off, Roy had only convinced me to keep digging.

"What are you doing, Brady?"

"Admiring your new apartment. Has your brother stopped by with a housewarming gift yet?"

Oh shit. If he was dropping my father's case, why would he make that leap? Probably because he knew my brother had been physical with me before. "My mother is my only family member who knows about my new apartment." Which begged the question: How *did* Roy know where to find me?

"Do you happen to have any boyfriends in Franklin other than Colt?"

"What?" Oh shit. He really *was* trying to put things together. "No."

"And Colt? How well do you know him?"

"He works for my mother."

"Does he have a temper?"

"No. Colt would never put the effort into threatening someone."

He turned to look at me, his face serious. "I never said anything about a threat."

Double shit. "A man is dead, Brady. That seems pretty threatening to me."

"Fair enough." He turned his attention to the bookcase. Several books had fallen out in a haphazard manner, and a figurine of a woman in old-fashioned clothes and a bonnet lay on its side. He set one book back in place, then picked up the figurine and examined it.

I had to get rid of him. "Thanks for paying for the pizza. Do you want me to reimburse you before you go?"

He turned to look at me. "So you're kicking me out?" He carefully set the figurine back on the shelf, as though to mock the violence that had toppled it to its side.

I crossed my arms in front of my chest, flinching when I touched my sore ribs. "It's been a long day, and I'd like to go to bed. I'm helping with a Bible study tomorrow, and I'd like to look fresh." That was partially true. I was hired staff, but Miss Ava would want me looking my best.

Brady's brows rose. "*A Bible study?*"

I dropped my arms and balled my hands into fists. "Why do you sound so surprised? Do you think I'll burst into flames?"

"No," he said, shaking his head. "It's just surprising is all."

"Well, a job is a job. Beggars can't be choosers." I pushed on his arm and nudged him toward the door. "Thanks for dropping by."

A war raged in his eyes, but his shoulders finally slumped as he accepted his defeat. He walked to the door and stopped next to it. "Maggie, I know you don't trust easily, and I've got even more to make up for after . . ." His voice trailed off, but his eyes held mine. "But I'm genuinely worried about you."

"I'm not sure why. I'm fine."

He searched my face, lifting his hand to the cheek Roy had slapped, brushing his thumb close to where it had stung. Horror washed through me. Was the mark visible?

"I want to help you," he whispered. "Please let me help you."

"I'm fine."

He sighed as he dropped his hand. "I live ten minutes away. Call me if something scares you. Anything at all."

I almost protested, but I had to admit it felt good to have someone care about me. And since I was in literal danger, it was nice to know that someone also had a gun. "Okay."

He gave me another long look and walked out the door. I shut it behind him, locking the door knob and the deadbolt. Then I went into my new bedroom and watched him through the window as he made his way down to the driveway.

Brady's car was parked at the curb, but he was looking around the bushes and close to the house as he walked to his car. If I hadn't known better, I would have thought he was casing the place.

I glanced over at the house and noticed a curtain flutter in the back window. I had no idea how closely Miss Ava had been paying attention, but I had definitely had three gentleman callers in the space of a few hours.

I was in deep trouble.

I rushed over to the island and opened my laptop to search for the only whole name on the list. "Gerry Lopez" struck pay dirt. Gerry was actually Geraldo Lopez, a dentist in Nashville. His office was only a few blocks away from my dad's office. I couldn't remember much about what the dentist I'd visited as a kid had looked like, but my vague memories aligned with the images popping up on the screen. Plus, there was his name. Daddy had said something to Mr. Frey about Geraldo. It was definitely worth paying Dr. Lopez a visit.

I then set to work looking up "–rritt" and "–ogers" in combination with Dr. Lopez's name with no luck at all. Considering I didn't have complete names, I wasn't all that surprised. At least I had the dentist.

It was a start.

I tossed and turned for most of the night. When I wasn't waking up in a cold sweat from nightmares about my brother beating the crap out of me, I was trying not to get paranoid about Walter Frey's phone. It had definitely been in his hand, but the police claimed it had been stolen. Was someone in the Franklin Police Department dirty? I wasn't too shocked given my own experience, but I'd attributed that to Detective Holden, the man who had seemed out to get me. As far as I knew, he was nowhere near this case. What bothered me the most was the question of Brady's possible involvement. In the end, I decided he was just as much in the dark about the phone as I was. He'd insisted he was trying to prove himself to be trustworthy, so why would he tell me the phone had been stolen when he knew I'd seen it?

The next morning, my first thought was worry for Belinda, followed fast by the realization that my whole body was sore. Thankfully, she sent me a text while I was in the shower, telling me she was okay, which put me somewhat at ease. Of course, she could have been lying, but I decided to play Pollyanna and take her at her word. Maybe I could find the time to drop in on her later and see her for myself.

I tried to push it all out of my head when I knocked on Miss Ava's door at 8:55. I hoped my punctuality would help make up for my evening activities.

She opened the door and looked me over with a critical eye through the screen door. I was prepared for that. Since I still hadn't figured out what garden party attire entailed, I'd worn a pale pink dress and cream cardigan with kitten-heel, sling-back shoes—ivory, of course. Miss Ava was old enough she might still stick to the "no white before Memorial Day" rule.

She kept the door closed after assessing me from head to heel. "You don't *dress* like a hussy."

"That's because I'm not." I'd been prepared to beg, but I couldn't bring myself to do it. "I have a perfectly rational explanation for my visitors last night."

"Go on then," she said in a brisk tone. "I don't have all day."

I wasn't sure why I needed to justify them at all, but it *was* her property, and she'd made her wishes known. "You know Colt was here last night. He gave me a ride home. He said he was going to stop by and tell you that I'd bring your check this morning." I pulled the folded paper from my pocket and held it up.

She looked pleased . . . though still a little grumpy. "I'm surprised. Most young folks don't know how to write checks these days."

"The second person was . . ." Did I want anyone to know Roy had come to see me? Probably the fewer the people who knew, the better. "Was a family friend. I'm sure you noticed that he didn't stay long. He just wanted to say hello."

"And the third?"

"Detective Brady Bennett. With the Franklin police."

"Are you in some kind of trouble with the law?" she snapped back.

"No," I assured her, lifting my hands. The check was still in my right hand, but I figured it couldn't hurt to wave it at her. "I haven't done anything wrong. Colt and I sang at the Embassy the other night."

"A man was killed there."

"Yes, and I was the one who found his body. Detective Bennett took my statement and came by to check on me last night. To make sure I felt safe and give me an update." I wasn't sharing the intricacies of the situation, but why should I? Everything I was saying was true—to a point.

"Are you in danger?" she asked.

"No. Detective Bennett was just being cautious."

"I see."

"I assure you, Miss Ava, I am a very quiet and low-key tenant. I'm working two jobs—three if I count helping you. I won't have time to stir up trouble, much less have a social life."

"Well . . ." she said, her gaze narrowing on my check. "I guess I can overlook things this once. Just don't make it a habit."

"Yes, ma'am."

She pushed open the screen door and let me in, snatching the check from my hand as I passed her. After showing me around her kitchen and discussing the menu, she put me to work setting up the dining room table in an elaborate tiered display. She'd obviously prepared all of the food herself without any help.

"What time did you start cooking to get this ready?" I asked.

"Five."

"If you need me to come earlier next time, I'd be more than happy to."

She gave me a sideways glance. "What about your evening activities? Won't they interfere?"

Her tone of disapproval summoned images of wild parties and orgies. "No. As I said, I'm not much of a socializer."

She pursed her lips, looking like she was in deep thought. "We'll see how today goes, then discuss it later."

Based on the elaborate setup, it was easy to see Miss Ava was a perfectionist; but then, so was my mother. I took it as a good sign that she gave me direction and had few corrections.

Once the guests arrived, my job was simple—stay behind the table as much as possible, greeting everyone with a pleasant smile and a "salutation." I was to learn their names so I could greet them personally in the future (*if* this worked out, Miss Ava added). I was to make sure there was plenty of food and drink, and when the Bible study began, I was to remain in the kitchen until called upon to return to the table to clean up.

"Do you have all of that?" Miss Ava asked.

"Yes, ma'am. I'll take care of it." Just as I said the words, the doorbell rang.

"Oh, dear. I forgot to tell you about the special drinks."

"Special drinks?"

"Have you ever bartended, Magnolia?"

I blinked. "Yes, ma'am."

She looked pained when she said, "There will be a few guests who wish to have their drinks doctored. I trust you to keep it discreet, and not to overindulge them. Only procure the special libations for them if asked. The alcohol is in the cabinet next to the refrigerator."

Who drank at a Bible study? At nine thirty on a Thursday morning, no less. But then again, Colt and Alvin had both implied there wasn't anything sacred about Miss Ava's meetings. "Yes, ma'am," I said with a nod. "I'll take care of it."

"I guess we'll see if you do," Miss Ava said.

The guests arrived in a trickle, then a gush until there were fifteen women—sixteen, including Miss Ava. When the first guest approached the refreshments table, an elderly woman in an expensive silk blouse and linen pants, she gave me a wary once-over.

I greeted her with a bright smile. "Good morning. I'm Magnolia, and I'm helping Miss Ava today. If you need anything at all, be sure to let me know. Would you like me to get you a cup of coffee?"

She looked a little taken off guard by my chipper attitude. "What happened to Lori?"

"Who?"

"The girl who used to do this before you? Lori."

"I'm not sure. But I'll be more than happy to help you. Would you like coffee or tea? Miss Ava also has some fresh-squeezed orange juice."

She looked irritated. "She always has orange juice. I'll need a little vodka added to mine."

"Yes, of course."

I hurried to the back and poured vodka into her juice glass, then, reflecting on her curtness, poured a little extra. When I handed it to her—adding an orange slice for a garnish—she took a sip and broke into a wide smile. "Better than Lori's."

"Thank you."

I'd won one woman over. After Miss Ava's pronouncement of "we'll see how it goes," I was fairly certain this was an audition. At over fifteen dollars an hour, I was going to give it my all. Which meant I had fourteen women left to charm.

The women—most in their sixties and seventies, although a couple looked to be in their fifties—made their way to the table. While they all helped themselves to plates of food, well over half requested mimosas, screwdrivers, or Bloody Marys, all of which I had to make one by one. The odd part was that none of them ever asked for the drinks by name—instead asking for tomato juice with "a wee bit of alcohol" or an orange juice "that special way." Unfortunately, there were a few ways to make orange juice "special," so I began to ask if they wanted the kind with bubbles or without, which seemed to earn brownie points with some of the women.

I ran myself ragged getting their drinks, but all with a smile on my face and a cheerful attitude. The women stood around talking and eating, making no move to actually start their meeting. Thankfully, none of them seemed to make the connection of who I was. I learned about half of the women's names by eavesdropping on their conversations, and when some of them returned for refills—drinks, not food—I was able to call them by name.

At first I was an oddity, but within a half hour, most had accepted my presence and had begun to act like I wasn't there. I was rearranging a tray of mini quiches when I heard one woman say, "I can't believe what happened to Walter Frey. What's going on in our town?"

"It's goin' to hell in a handbasket," the woman beside her said.

"They're saying it was a robbery," a woman named Blanche said.

"I don't believe it for a moment," the first woman announced, louder than she'd probably intended, because she lowered her voice to continue. "I heard he was mixed up in some sort of mess."

"What kind of mess, Gretchen?" Blanche demanded.

"I don't know, but I suspect Ava does."

Ava stood several feet away, talking to a small group of women, so Gretchen patted her arm. "Ava, what do you know about Walter Frey?"

Miss Ava gave her a disdainful glare, then shot a sideways glance in my direction. I was still straightening the table, thank goodness, so she didn't realize I was paying attention. "We'll discuss it later. It's on the end of the agenda."

At the meeting.

Finally, around ten thirty, Miss Ava announced it was time to start. While the women made their way into the living room, she told me to clear all the savory food dishes from the table and start cleaning the kitchen.

I cast a curious glance toward the living room while grabbing a plate of mini quiches and a breakfast casserole. The women were seated in multiple rows of dining room chairs, and Miss Ava stood in front of them. I'd been to enough Sunday school classes as a kid to know this wasn't the usual way to conduct a Bible study. Most were conducted in a circle. But then our snacks had been Goldfish and Kool-Aid. Maybe this was the sophisticated version.

After bringing the plates into the kitchen, I came back for two more, dawdling longer than necessary in the hopes I'd hear them discuss Walter Frey. But Miss Ava saw me and shot me a glare. "Magnolia, you may remain in the kitchen until we call you out."

"Yes, ma'am," I said as I took the plates into the kitchen. I spent the next five minutes putting away food and washing the dishes while periodically approaching the swinging door to the dining room. But all I could hear from my vantage point was murmuring. I had to get closer without being seen. The dining room was too dangerous; there was a sliver of a wall to hide behind, but I'd be discovered in an instant if someone headed to the kitchen. I considered going outside to listen under a window, but I doubted I'd hear anything, and I could only imagine what Ava would say when her neighbors told her a woman in a pink dress had been seen prowling around her bushes.

But I had another idea.

When I was a girl, I had a friend who lived in an older house in downtown Franklin. One of my favorite things about going to her house was using the hidden staircase. It wasn't really hidden, but its door was a panel in the dining room that popped open to reveal a spiral staircase the servants had used back in the day. I'd seen a door in Miss Ava's dining room, and while it could have been anything, the way it fit into the wall led me to believe it was a secret staircase.

Think about what you're doing, Magnolia. If I got caught, I had no doubt I'd lose both my job and my apartment. I'd be forced to move back in with Momma.

But Ava knew something about Walter Frey. I was sure of it. And that meant it was worth the risk. I only hoped I hadn't missed their discussion.

Act Two

Slipping off my shoes to avoid making noise, I looped the backs over my fingers, then crept through the door to the dining room, making sure to stop the door from swinging shut when I was on the other side. I pressed my back to the wall with the panel, waiting to hear if I'd been noticed. Ava's voice continued in a low tone, too low for me to make out her words, but her tone led me to believe they were discussing something important.

I only hoped I wasn't too late.

Holding my breath, I pushed on one side of the panel. Nothing happened. Had I been wrong? But then I pushed on the other, and it sprang open, making a tiny squeak.

I froze, but there weren't any changes in the low murmuring in the other room. I needed to get the door closed before someone saw it and came to investigate.

After I shut the door behind me, I hurried up the tight circular staircase and then pushed another door open at the top. It revealed a hallway that ran through the middle of the house, ending at a semi-circular staircase in front.

I tiptoed to the end, squatting down when I got close to the staircase. I pressed my back to the wall and sat far enough away from the edge that I could make out the room and the backs of the women. Miss Ava stood in the front, but she was no longer talking. A woman in an Easter-egg-blue suit was standing and addressing the room.

"I can't believe we're discussing a Mother's Day tea when we should be discussing the murders in this town."

"Murders aren't new, Georgine," the woman who'd ordered the first screwdriver said. "They've been around since Cain and Abel."

Georgine turned to stare at her. "You can't tell me that these murders are run-of-the-mill crimes."

Ava gave Georgine a stare that would have made most people wither. "We will discuss it after we finish the arrangements for the tea."

Georgine sat down, but if her back hadn't been to me, I was sure I'd have seen her spitting nails.

They spent the next five minutes discussing some mother-daughter tea before Ava stood in front of the group and cleared her throat, giving the group a stern look.

"As you are all aware, a respected member of the Franklin community was tragically murdered two days ago."

Murmurs of sympathy spread across the room.

"We need to keep Ruby in our thoughts and prayers." She turned to face a woman in the front row. "Eddy, will you set up a covered dish plan? I think two weeks will suffice."

The woman nodded. "Yes, of course. Consider it done."

"The funeral is tomorrow, and I think we ought to show our support. Ruby Frey has asked that money be donated to the Boys and Girls Club in lieu of flowers."

Ava folded her hands and held them at waist level. "That just about finishes our new business. Does anyone have anything to add?"

Georgine shot out of her seat. "You can't be serious."

Ava's eyes narrowed. "You disapprove of donating to the Boys and Girls Club?"

"I have no problem with the donation. It's the fact that you refuse to discuss Walter Frey's murder that I object to."

"And what more is there to discuss?"

"You know that Walter was mixed up in some sort of messy business. Ruby admitted to as much before she quit last year."

"Maybe he was. Maybe he wasn't. That's for the police to decide," Ava said airily.

"Then why did you try to handle that situation yourself two years ago?" Georgine demanded. "You know something you're not telling us."

"What I may or may not know is none of your concern," Ava said in an icy tone.

"This is not a dictatorship, Ava Milton," Georgine shot back. "You owe us answers."

A collective gasp shot through the room, but there were also some murmurs of agreement.

To her credit, Ava didn't look the slightest bit ruffled.

"Ava's got things under control," another woman called out.

"I'm not so sure she does," Georgine said in a snooty tone. "When she handled that problem two years ago, it sprouted two more."

"Both manageable," Ava said in a stern tone. "You can't expect to take care of messy situations without a touch of cleanup."

"So we're expected to just take your word for it?"

"No. I expect you to judge the results."

Miss Ava turned to the side, glancing out the window, and let out a long sigh. I looked out the window over the front door and saw a man in a suit approaching the house. "And there's Reverend Brown," Miss Ava said. "Mabel, will you go to the kitchen and ask Magnolia to make him a cup of coffee?"

Crap.

I got to my feet and padded down the center of the hall, staying on the rug to muffle my footsteps, then made my way down the steps as slowly and carefully as possible. I had no idea how I'd make it in time, and as I pushed open the door to the dining room, it became painfully obvious that I hadn't. Mabel's eyes widened as she just barely escaped being clocked with the panel door. Thankfully, she didn't give me away. Not yet, anyway.

"Do you know where the bathroom is?" I asked, giving her an embarrassed look. The role came to me in a moment—new girl, naïve and confused but very, very innocent. "I'm *so* lost, and I really have to go."

She pointed over her shoulder while giving me an assessing look. "It's by the staircase."

"Well, no wonder I couldn't find it," I whispered with a tiny laugh, then pushed open the door to the kitchen. "I guess I'll have to hold it so I don't interrupt the meeting."

Mabel followed me through the door. "Ava has sent me to get Reverend Brown's coffee."

"I guess it's a good thing I didn't dump the rest of the pot." I reached for it, trying to sound breezy.

"Aren't you renting the apartment over the garage?" she asked, her eyes narrowing with suspicion. "Why didn't you go over there?"

I hadn't heard anyone mention my living situation, but I wasn't surprised she knew. It was obvious they were all fond of gossip. And if they knew who I was, I was like a juicy Georgia peach they simply couldn't resist.

I gave her an intimidated smile. "Miss Ava told me to stay here in case someone needed something. I worried I'd get in trouble if I left."

"She also told you to stay in the kitchen."

"I know, Miss Mabel," I said, adding worry to my voice. "That's why I tried the door that was actually a staircase." I grimaced like I really had to pee. "It won't happen again."

She moved closer, studying my face. "Why are you working for Ava?"

I poured the coffee into the cup. "Cream or sugar?"

"Black."

I extended the cup to her and gave her my best innocent look. "I'm working for Ava because I need a job."

She didn't take the coffee. "But you're—"

"Magnolia Steele. Which is exactly why I need this job. It hasn't been easy for me to find work in this town."

The look of surprise on her face told me that hadn't been her objection. But she also didn't look surprised to hear my name.

"Please don't tell Miss Ava," I begged. "I really need this job *and* the apartment. I promise to stay put from now on."

I forced my eyes to well with tears, and her whole stance relaxed.

"I realize you're new, but Ava doesn't give second chances. You'll do best to remember that." While her face had softened, her voice was firm. She took the cup from me, then headed out the door.

As soon as she left, I dug out my phone to search for Walter Frey's obituary notice. His funeral was at three o'clock the next afternoon at Williamson Memorial Funeral Home.

Did I dare go to Walter Frey's funeral? Mr. Frey hadn't seemed like the kind of guy who frequented dive bars on weekday nights. His wife had seen us together at Mellow Mushroom—had she tied his presence at the Embassy that night to me?

The last thing I wanted to do was upset her, but it might be an opportunity to find more information. What if people involved in my father's disappearance were there? I ignored the fact that I wouldn't know they were the culprits even if they walked up and shook my hand. Sure, it was a long shot, but other than the dentist, it was all I had. But if I was going, I needed a car. I sent Colt a text.

I'm only working at the store for two hours today. Can you pick me up and take me to Momma's house to look at my car before we start at the catering shop at four?

I had almost finished cleaning up the kitchen before he texted back.

Sure. Meet you in the parking lot at 2:15?

I'll be there.

If my car wasn't fixable, I was sure Tilly would let me borrow hers.

I pulled up the information for Geraldo Lopez, then called his office before I could chicken out. When prompted, I pressed the extension for the appointment desk. "I need to schedule an appointment as soon as possible," I said when a woman answered. "I have a tooth that's killing me." I'd have a better chance of getting in to see him if I claimed to have a bad tooth. I'd deal with the fact that my teeth were healthy when the time came.

"Are you a patient here?"

"No," I said. "But I've heard great things about Dr. Lopez, and my tooth hurts so much I can hardly stand it." I made my voice crack to convey my distress.

She was silent for a few moments before she said, "If you can be here first thing tomorrow morning at eight, we can fit you in then."

Eight? Well, crap. Considering the hassle of Nashville's rush-hour traffic, I'd have to be up by six thirty at the latest to be ready in time. But I really wanted to talk with him. "Yeah. That's great."

I couldn't give them my own name. What if Geraldo Lopez recognized it and canceled? I definitely needed the element of surprise. So I gave them the first name that came to mind, then instantly regretted it. "Tilly," I said. "Tilly Bartok."

We went through the customary insurance and personal information questions. I made up most of the information, but gave her my real phone number. When I hung up, I realized Ava was watching me from the doorway.

Oh shit. She definitely looked unhappy. Had Mabel told her that she'd caught me snooping?

"Are you ill?" she asked, sounding disgusted by the thought.

I forced a pleasant smile. "No. I was making a dentist appointment."

She gave me a blank look.

I shrugged, trying to play it off. "I'm due for a cleaning, and now that I'm settled, I figured there was no time like the present."

"I see." She brushed imaginary lint off the front of her skirt. "I would appreciate it if you held your personal calls until after you leave."

I almost pointed out that she'd refused to let me out of my cage to finish cleaning up the rest of the food, but that didn't seem prudent at the moment. "Yes, ma'am. It won't happen again."

"The Bible study is over, so you're free to clean up the remaining refreshments."

I hurried into the dining room, eager to finish so I could get out of here and think about everything I'd learned.

What mess had Walter Frey been involved in? Probably something illegal if his wife had quit their gossip group. If they were all about appearances, they couldn't have a criminal's wife in their ranks—even though I suspected not all their husbands were squeaky clean. But had he and my father been involved in the same mess, or was this something new? And if the "Bible study" group had discovered what Walter was up to a year ago, what predicament had Ava taken care of two years ago? Did it have anything to do with the recent murders? Then it occurred to me: Colt had started to spend time with Ava two years ago, and he said he'd helped her out. But what had he done, and what two issues had popped up after she'd "handled" the situation they'd discussed at the meeting?

One thing was certain—Walter Frey didn't die from a robbery. Despite my promise to my mother, I was going to find out what happened.

chapter thirteen

Colt's truck was in the parking lot when I got off work at the shop. Alvin had quizzed me mercilessly about Miss Ava's Bible study, but I had kept my lips sealed. It didn't take a genius to deduce that getting on Ava Milton's bad side was a very bad idea, and besides, I was hoping to get more information next week.

When I climbed into the cab of Colt's truck, he looked me over from head to toe. "Well, well, you made it out alive." His grin lit up his eyes.

"It's a wonder. I thought Alvin was going to have a coronary when I refused to tell him anything."

Colt pulled out of the parking space and headed for the exit. "I was referring to Miss Ava, but now that you mention it, I've heard Alvin's relentless. It's a wonder he didn't tie you up in the basement and hold you there until you told him what he wanted to know."

The blood rushed from my head. Colt's suggestion hit far too close to what had happened in the basement of that abandoned house ten years ago.

"Jesus, Maggie," Colt said in alarm. "Are you okay?"

Try to act normal, Magnolia. "Yeah."

"You don't look okay."

"It's the heat is all."

He stopped at the exit of the parking lot, ignoring the car honking behind him. "It's not that hot."

I forced a smile, something I'd done a lot of these past few days. "I feel hot. I bet my blood sugar's low. I haven't eaten anything today." Not a lie, and now that I thought about it, my stomach rumbled in protest.

"It's after two o'clock."

I waved him off. "I'll be fine once I eat."

"We'll stop and get something on the way to your mother's."

He went through a McDonald's drive-through and got us both lunch, which we ate on the way to my family home.

He parked in the driveway as we finished. Momma's car was gone, and I felt like I was trespassing, even though she'd given me her permission via text to come check out the car.

"You feeling better?" he asked.

"Yeah," I said with a grimace, irritated with myself for my overreaction. But his offhanded remark had caught me by surprise. I needed to congratulate myself on my quick recovery. "Sorry I got all weird earlier."

He reached over and took my hand in his, looking into my eyes. "I care about you, Maggie. You have to know that by now."

I glanced down, suddenly worried where this conversation was going. "I do. And I hope you know how much I appreciate having you for a friend." I looked up into his uncharacteristically serious blue eyes. "It's nice to know I have a friend I can count on."

A sly grin spread across his face. "You think you said the word friend enough?" I grimaced, but he only laughed. "I was going to say the same thing to you. I usually just sleep with the women in my life and move on. It's kind of nice to have a friend who's a girl to hang out with, no expectations."

"Expectations?" I teased as relief rushed through me. "Is the reputation of your sexual prowess so widespread you feel performance anxiety?"

He leaned back, his eyes full of mock outrage, and pointed his finger at me. "Hey! Watch it now. You don't want to get left here with a busted car."

I laughed. "I'd take it back, but I'm genuinely curious about the answer."

Still laughing, we got out of the truck. Even though Colt had the garage code, I used the front door key Momma had finally given me a couple of weeks before. There wasn't a speck of dust on the floor or an object out of place as we made our way through the dining room to the kitchen, then through the door to the garage. That's where the cleanliness stopped.

Colt let out a low groan as he walked down the two steps. "Jesus. I still can't believe Lila let this happen."

I could see his point. The garage was stuffed with boxes and furniture that my brother had insisted on putting in my mother's garage. But it meant that she couldn't park in it anymore, and my old car was completely blocked in.

"Where did all this shit come from?" he asked as he edged around a leather sofa.

"Roy."

"Why doesn't the bastard rent a storage unit? God knows he can afford it."

"I don't know, and I haven't asked. I'm guessing this is stuff from the bachelor pad he had before he married Belinda."

Colt shot me a quizzical look. "He never had a bachelor pad."

I blinked in surprise. "What?"

"He moved in with your mother after he left college, then moved in with a friend before he and Belinda moved in together. How do you not know any of this?"

I shot him an irritated look. "How do *you*?"

"I've worked for Southern Belles for three years," he said with a shrug. "I hear things."

"You're as gossipy as the women at Miss Ava's *Bible study*," I said, using air quotes.

"So you did hear some gossip?" Colt asked with a grin.

"Nothing I'm going to repeat." Ava knew Colt. What if he was testing me and reporting back to her?

Sure, he was my friend, but it was obvious he'd known her longer.

"So, if this isn't Roy's furniture," I said as I pushed the button to lift the garage door behind my car, "then who does it belong to?"

"That is a damn good question, Maggie Mae." He studied it with more interest than I'd expected.

"You've been here before. Didn't you ever wonder about this?" With a flourish worthy of a *Price is Right* Showcase Showdown, I gestured with both hands to a dresser that was wedged next to a dark wood headboard.

"Nope."

That I didn't believe, but Colt interrupted me before I could call him on it.

"Do you know where the keys are?"

"In the ignition. I tried to start it a couple of weeks ago, after I decided to stay, but I left the keys in the car once I realized it wasn't going anywhere."

"I need to pop the hood, but there's too much crap crammed around it. Let's move some of it into the driveway."

"Okay."

I checked my phone and was relieved to find a text from Belinda. Alvin and I had finally discussed my schedule, and I'd sent her a message letting her know I was free for lunch on Friday. That had been a couple of hours ago, though, and I'd started to get worried.

Sounds good. I'll call you tomorrow morning.

Part of me wanted to call her now, but I was up to my elbows with my own issues.

My pink dress and heels weren't moving-friendly, but I wasn't about to complain. We had a path cleared out in ten minutes, but it had required us to move multiple boxes and miscellaneous pieces of furniture.

"Who do you think it belonged to?" I asked again, handing Colt a bottle of water as we stared at the mess.

He shrugged, focusing his attention on unscrewing the bottle cap. "Beats the hell out of me."

I moved closer and waded into the piles. "It's the contents of an apartment," I said. "One bedroom. Definitely a guy."

"How can you know that?" he asked after gulping half the bottle.

I picked up a lamp shaped like a rifle, but it was in good taste. Like something from a Restoration Hardware catalog. "Exhibit A."

He laughed. "Good point." After he finished the rest of the bottle, he popped open the car's hood and looked the engine over. "Like I said, my guess is that you need a new battery, but we can try backing it out into the driveway and jumping it first."

"Do you think it could be that easy?" I asked hopefully.

He grinned. "With your luck, no. But let's try it anyway."

I got inside and put the car in neutral. Colt pushed on the front end while I steered the car to make sure it didn't back into his truck. Then I put the car into park and hopped out to watch him hook up the jumper cables.

"You seem to be studying this pretty intently," he said, laughing.

"I want to know how to do it, should the need ever arise."

"You've never jumped a car before?"

"I told you that I hadn't driven in ten years. Why would I need to jump-start a car?"

"Good point." So he told me what he was doing and why. But when I tried to start the engine, nothing happened.

"Okay," Colt said, unhooking the cords. "That's what I was afraid of. We'll have to get you a new battery and go from there."

"And if that's not the problem?"

"Let's not borrow trouble."

We decided to leave the car in the driveway until we figured out the problem, so we started to haul all the stuff back into the garage.

"Why would my mother agree to keep someone else's things?" I asked while dragging what looked to be the contents of someone's kitchen back inside. "She hates clutter."

"Probably because your brother asked her to keep it here."

"Obviously she loves him more than she dislikes the mess." I couldn't help my petulant tone.

"She probably rarely goes in there," he said with a shrug. "She parks in the driveway."

"Yeah." But I wasn't buying it. I noticed a ceramic three-foot-tall Dalmatian sitting on its haunches. "This doesn't exactly fit in with the aesthetic, does it?" Then a memory clicked into place, and I gasped in surprise. "Wait. My father had one exactly like this. I bought it for him for his birthday when I was ten."

Colt stopped mid-step with a box in his arms. "What? You're kidding."

I looked up at him in horror. "How many of these things do you think they sold?"

"I don't know." He scrunched up his nose in distaste. "I sure as hell hope there aren't too many. What are you getting at?"

I tore into one of the boxes next to me, finding a bunch of stainless steel pots and pans. Then I moved on to the next: DVDs and CDs of Broadway musicals and jazz.

"Maggie, what're you doing?"

"Seeing if this was my dad's stuff."

"You think your dad had an apartment? What for?" He sucked in a breath. "Oh. God. His affair."

"*He did not have an affair!*" I shouted, then said more dejectedly, "But it's not his stuff." I waved a hand toward the box of DVDs and CDs. "He hated musicals, and he was a classic rock guy. Not jazz."

Tears stung my eyes, but I had no idea why. It was obviously a good thing that they weren't his belongings.

Colt was right. Why would my father have needed an apartment unless he'd been having an affair? But I was so desperate for solid information about his disappearance—hell, even an ambiguous clue would do—that I couldn't help being disappointed.

Colt watched me for a moment, then set the box down and gathered me into his arms. He held me for several seconds before he said, "I know you want answers, but have you ever considered that maybe you already have them? You just don't like what you see?"

I sniffed and pulled away, wiping a stray tear from the corner of my eye. "I don't know what you're talking about."

His mouth pressed into a frown. "Fine. Play it that way, but *I* think you need to accept that he ran off. He loved you—from everything Tilly has said, there's no denying it—but for whatever reason, he took off. Your mother has accepted it, and so has your brother. Now you need to."

Colt was wrong about one thing. They *hadn't* accepted it. Momma was hiding something, and Roy damn sure knew something too, judging from his visit. I just needed to keep digging.

I reached up on tiptoes and kissed his cheek. "You would make a great older brother."

He pressed both hands to his chest and staggered backward with a goofy grin on his face. "That was a mortal blow, Magnolia Steele. *An older brother?* I'm a good two years younger than you."

My eyes flew open, and a deep belly laugh bubbled out of me. "You liar!"

He'd never confessed his age, and neither had I, but he'd known my mother for several years. He was privy to a lot more of my past than I was of his.

We finished putting everything back in the garage, but I gave the dog statue a long look.

Colt walked over and picked it up, grunting as he carried it out and shut the garage door.

"What are you doing?" I asked

He hefted it up with a loud groan, then set it in the bed of his truck. "This thing might be ugly as sin and as heavy as a stack of bricks, but it reminds you of your dad, and it's just sitting in your mother's garage. You should have it."

The gesture shouldn't have meant so much to me—Colt was right; it was pretty darn ugly—yet it did. "Thanks."

We went by the auto parts store for a new battery. I needed to be at the catering business a half hour before Colt, so he dropped me off and said he'd install the new battery before his shift.

I expected Momma to give me the third degree, but she just gave me a long look before returning to the prep of her famous garlic potatoes.

Tonight the Belles were catering an awards dinner for one hundred people, so it was all hands on deck. Tilly put me to work stirring pesto sauce as she and the other employees prepared all the food to be loaded into the vans.

When I was a teenager, I had found Momma's catering work boring and monotonous. The only part I'd enjoyed was serving, especially at fancy events where I could imagine myself as one of the guests. But now I was stuck loading and unloading pans, washing up, and doing the grunt work.

My mother expected me to take over her share of the catering business after she died, but it felt like a death sentence of my own.

Colt arrived five minutes late, but Momma didn't even chew him out—she just glanced at the clock on the wall, muttered under her breath, and continued with her task.

Colt glanced at me and shook his head. "No bueno, Mags."

I groaned, and Tilly looked up from her pot. "What's the problem?"

"I take it you can't get your Audi running?" Momma asked, her tone nicer than I'd expected. "It ran a couple of years ago when I had the oil changed."

Colt shot me a *maybe she's coming around* glance, then turned to my mother. "We replaced the battery, but it still won't start. I'll try to replace the spark plugs tomorrow."

Which meant I wouldn't have a car to drive into Nashville in the morning. I decided to be honest. Mostly. "I have a dentist appointment tomorrow."

All three of them looked shocked.

"Why?" Momma asked. "You hate the dentist."

"I hated the dentist when I was ten years old. I'm an adult now. Besides, it's called dental hygiene."

"Did you make an appointment with Dr. Murphy?" Momma asked.

I had hoped to avoid this. "No," I said, drawing it out and scrounging for a reason. "Dr. Murphy smells like mothballs."

"Magnolia," Momma scolded. "That's ridiculous."

"What does it matter who I'm seeing? All that matters is that I need a car."

"Stay at my house tonight," Momma said. "And I'll take you."

I narrowed my eyes. "I'm a little old for my mother to take me to the dentist. Besides, it's in Nashville at eight. You hate traffic."

Tilly's head bobbed in agreement. "She has a point."

Then Momma asked the inevitable question. "Why on earth are you going to Nashville anyway? There are more than enough dentists who don't smell like mothballs here in Franklin."

"This dentist has a reputation," I said on the fly. "He works with country music artists. He understands the needs of a celebrity."

"Why do you need a special dentist when it's your tits that are famous?" my mother asked, always the voice of reason.

Colt burst out laughing and Tilly's cheeks turned pink.

I gave her a tight smile. "I knew you wouldn't understand." Not that I would have understood either. It was a ridiculous excuse. I should have come up with a better one before bringing it up.

But to my surprise, Momma's face softened. "We'll work something out. I'd let Colt go replace the spark plugs now, but we're running late as it is."

"She can borrow my car," Tilly said. "Lila, you can take me home tonight. We don't have any catering jobs tomorrow, and I was fixing to clean my house. I don't need my car."

"Thank you, Tilly," I said, giving her a warm smile.

"Think nothing of it. Maybe Colt can have your car running by the time you get back from your appointment."

When we had everything loaded, Momma said, "Magnolia, I'd like you to ride with me."

Colt and Tilly shot me looks of surprise and worry, but I steeled my back and said in a breezy tone, "Of course."

I slid into the passenger seat of her car and tried to hide my anxiety, which increased tenfold every second my mother held her tongue. We rode in silence for a good minute. This was going to be bad if it was taking her this long to get to it.

Finally, she said, "I'm sorry."

My eyebrows shot up. "*What?*"

"I was very harsh yesterday morning, but . . ." She paused and seemed to weigh her words. "You need to let the past go, Magnolia. No good will come from digging up graves."

Even though she was adamant I give up my search, I took it as a good sign that she was discussing it at all. I turned in my seat to face her. "Momma, a man died two days ago, and you can't deny it had something to do with Daddy."

"I can and *will* deny it had anything to do with your father if it means protecting you."

"But Momma—"

"Magnolia. Your father is gone. That is the plain and simple truth. No one looks at us and whispers behind our backs anymore. They've moved on. And so should you."

"They're just whispering for different reasons now," I mumbled.

"That may be true, but things are different now. People forget faster. You'll be yesterday's news next week." She cast me a glance. "But I'm scared to death you'll be in tomorrow's obituaries if you don't let this go. I didn't just get you back to lose you."

I leaned forward and studied her intently. "I need to know what you know."

"I don't know a blessed thing."

"Momma," I groaned.

Her face set in a fierce expression. "That's the God's honest truth." She paused. "I knew something was goin' on, but your father refused to tell me what. He said it was better if I didn't know . . . plausible deniability."

"Did it have something to do with his work?"

"What else could it be?" Her voice broke. "But I've wondered over the years if maybe he *did* run off. Maybe he got tired of me and my sharp tongue."

"Momma." My heart was breaking. "Daddy loved you. I know it."

"I used to know it too." She sniffed and wiped at the corner of her eye, her fierceness returning. "Now, no more givin' the police ideas about digging into the past. You hear?"

"Yes, ma'am." I wasn't sure what I was going to do, but I sure wasn't going to disagree with her when she was in this state.

"Now we need to talk about your car."

That surprised me. "I know we moved things around trying to get it out of the garage, but we'll put it all back. I swear."

"That's not what I mean. That garage has been an eyesore since your brother moved all of that crap into it two years ago. I'm talking about getting your car running." She cast me a glance. "I should have suggested we get it running sooner, but I've been tired."

"Momma, I don't expect you to do anything for me."

"I know." She picked up my hand from the seat and squeezed. "And that's why I want to do it. Now, I've been paying the insurance on the thing, and its tags are current, but if Colt can't get it running with the new spark plugs, have it towed to the shop I use, and I'll pay for the repairs."

"You don't have to do that, Momma."

"I know. But I want to." She paused. "But that car's fifteen years old, so when I die, I want you to have mine."

I sucked in a breath. "I don't want to talk about you dyin'."

"And yet, it's still gonna happen." She released my hand and sighed. "But we can talk about practical things another day."

Then she turned up the music on the radio, and we were silent the rest of the way to the banquet hall.

Colt and Tilly waited expectantly at the back of the open van when we pulled up, but my mother began barking orders as soon as she got out of the car.

"What's everyone standing around for? That food's not going to carry itself in." She grabbed a pan and headed inside, leaving the three of us behind.

Tilly turned to me. "Well?"

I threw my arms around her neck and fought to hold back my tears. My mother was dying, and soon there would be no hiding from it anymore.

chapter fourteen

re you sure you've got it?" I asked, climbing the stairs to my apartment with my keys in hand.

"Yeah," Colt grunted. "Who knew a damn plaster dog could be so damn heavy." He shifted the statue in his arms.

I'd driven Tilly's car home, and Colt had followed me in his truck. I'd offered to transfer it to my borrowed car, but he'd insisted on bringing it himself. Now I was grateful I'd let him. "I think it's just awkward," I said as I shoved the key into the lock and hurried to get the door open. "It's tall and narrow, and there's nothing to hold onto."

"Thanks for the analysis," he said sarcastically as he walked through the front door, hefting the dog again. "Where the hell do you want it? Because once I put it down, it's staying there."

The apartment was decorated *Southern Living*-style, while the Dalmatian was more garage-sale treasure, but this wasn't about how it looked. Daddy used to keep plenty of personal objects from me in his office—photos, pictures I'd drawn, and notes—but he'd seemed to love the ceramic dog the most. Colt was undoubtedly humoring me, but I still wanted the statue. The police had held most of the things in Daddy's office hostage while conducting their investigation into his alleged embezzlement. The photos had eventually been returned, but when I'd asked about the rest, Momma told me that Daddy's boss had thrown everything else out.

But it could be no coincidence that I'd found an exact replica of the Dalmatian in the garage. Especially since my brother, who worked for Daddy's old boss, had put it there.

"Maggie!"

"Uh . . ." I shook myself out of my musings. "In the corner." I pointed to the wall and the edge of the bookcase.

He dropped it with a thud, then rose, rubbing his lower back. "So this is what happens when you try to be a nice guy." He shot me a sardonic grin. "Next time I suggest doing something nice, remind me it's only good for getting laid."

I crossed my arms and gave him a mock stern look. "You're not getting laid."

"Dammit." But he was smiling.

I kept staring at the dog, realizing that it wasn't going to work in its current location. I couldn't get the lower cabinet door open if we left it there.

"What?" Colt asked, hesitation in his voice.

He'd said he was only putting it down once. I'd just move it after he left.

"What?" he asked again with a little more force.

"Thanks for bringing it up here, Colt."

"You want to move it somewhere else."

I grimaced. "Maybe . . ."

He released a loud groan. "Where?"

"Um . . ." I spun around in a circle as I scouted out the small space. "Between the chair and the sofa."

He squatted and picked it up, shuffled around the chair, and then started to lower it.

"Wait!" I shouted. "Not there. Next to the refrigerator."

"You're sure?" he asked, giving me the evil eye.

"Yeah."

"Sound more sure, Maggie Mae."

"Yes."

He dropped it with a loud thud next to the fridge, and the dog's front paw fell off in one big chunk. "Oh shit," Colt said as he stood upright. "Sorry."

I leaned over for a closer look. "It's a cheesy ceramic dog. It's no big deal. I'll just glue it back on." But just when I was about to stand back up, I noticed the corner of a piece of paper.

He rubbed a hand over his head. "Sorry."

"You already said that." I got down on my knees to get a closer look.

"Before you start thinking I'm not strong enough to carry that thing, you should know it's freakishly heavy."

I grinned up at him. "I never questioned your masculine strength."

"I could carry you up and down the stairs ten times without getting winded." He thumbed toward the door. "I'll demonstrate now if you want."

I laughed as I pulled out my cell phone to turn on the flashlight and get a better look inside the dog.

"I'll take a raincheck, but I *think* you just insinuated I weigh less than this ceramic dog. So thanks for that."

"What are you doing?" he asked, squatting behind me.

"I see something."

"Inside the dog? Is it literally full of bricks?"

"No," I said. "I see paper."

"It's stuffed with *paper?*"

Upon closer inspection, I realized that the piece of foot that had fallen off had been previously glued. "Someone's hidden something in here."

"What?"

"I don't know," I said. The previously glued crack extended around the entire base of the statue. I glanced up at him. "We need a hammer."

"A hammer?" He sat back on his heels. "I just lugged that thing around trying to keep it in one piece. Now you want me to smash it?"

"Colt, look!" I pointed to the crack. "The entire base was removed and reattached."

"Maybe someone dropped the two-hundred-pound statue and the base broke off; then for whatever unconceivable reason, they liked it enough to reattach it."

"I saw something inside there!"

The look he gave me told me that he was worried for my mental health.

I got to my feet. "Fine. I'll do it." I started to walk around him. "I wonder if there's a hammer somewhere in here."

He released a long, pained groan. "You're a total pain in the ass. You know that, right?"

I batted my eyelashes. "It's a good thing you love me."

"If I crack this open, I doubt there's any chance of putting it back together."

"But the foot broke off—"

"I'm not going to be delicate with this thing, Mags. Either you let me open it my way, or you do it on your own."

I gave the dog a long look. I wanted the dog because it felt like a connection to my father, but that was stupid. The statue wasn't going to bring him back, and I was genuinely curious about what was inside. What if it really *was* the statue I'd given him? What if my father had hidden something inside?

"Smash it."

His eyes lit up with mischief. "Get a towel. We can use it to collect the pieces."

When I returned from the bathroom, Colt was gone, but the front door was cracked open.

He returned a minute later with a tire iron in his hand. "Now we're cooking."

We laid the towel on the floor and set the statue on top. Then Colt wrapped it up and smashed it in multiple places with the tire iron. When he unwrapped it, we both gasped.

"What the hell?" he asked breathlessly. The tire iron was still in his hand, and one end of it was resting on his shoulder.

Several small white bags cinched with draw strings lay among the broken pieces.

"What's in the bags?" I asked in disbelief.

"Could be drugs. Where the hell did Roy get this?"

I squatted down and moved several pieces out of the way to pick up the papers.

"Seriously?" Colt asked in disgust. "You go for the *papers*?" He laid down the tire iron and reached for one of the white canvas bags, which was stuck to a piece of plaster with brittle-looking duct tape. As he lifted it, the bag released a metallic clinking sound.

I cast the bag a curious glance as I unfolded the first paper and saw a list of numbers and letters, like serial numbers. But it was the second paper that caught my attention. The handwriting was familiar, and I almost dropped the note before reading the top line.

Magnolia, if you found this paper, then something has happened to me. Trust no one.

Oh, my God. The note was from *my father*?

"Holy shit!" Colt shouted. "It's gold."

"What?" I managed to drag myself out of my shocked stupor enough to look at him. He'd upended the bag on the kitchen island—revealing multiple small gold rectangles.

Though my heart was beating in double time, and every bit of me longed to finish the letter, I wanted to read these last words from my daddy alone. I folded the letter and stuffed it into my pocket, leaving the other paper out.

His mouth gaping open, Colt picked up something that looked like a slightly oversized bar of Hershey's chocolate. "This is a hundred-gram gold bar, Magnolia," he said in awe.

Why would my father have hidden gold bars?

"How many are in there?" I asked in a strangled voice.

He looked over the pieces. "There are ten in this bag."

I shook my head. "How much is that worth?"

"Thousands of dollars. *Thousands*."

I sucked in a breath and reached for one. The bar was heavier than I'd expected. The word Suisse was embedded on the side, along with 100 g, 999.9, and a series of numbers at the bottom that looked like a serial number.

The serial numbers seemed to match the numbers on the other paper.

"That's a hundred-gram bar, Maggie. There's over two pounds of gold in this bag. No wonder that damn dog was so heavy. Whoever hid the bags taped them to the inside of the statue."

I knew the answer to the whoever question. I couldn't imagine that Roy would leave gold bars inside a statue and stuff it into Momma's garage. Daddy had hidden them. But why?

"What did those papers say?" Colt asked.

I handed him the paper with the numbers. "I think someone listed the serial numbers."

"Shit," he mumbled, looking it over. "I think you're right. What did the other one say?"

Trust no one. The Franklin police were already in question because of Walter Frey's missing cell phone. Now I wondered if I should have given the list to Colt. But he was already handling the coins. What difference did it make if he saw the serial numbers all listed out? But I wasn't going to share my father's note. At least not yet. "Nothing. I think it was there as filler, probably in case one of the bags fell."

Colt gave me an odd look, but if he didn't believe me, he also didn't call me on it. "I counted nine more bags. Let's check them out."

We separated the other bags from the pieces of the statue and spilled their contents onto the counter. Most were more Suisse 100-gram bars, but three bags held two 250-gram bars in addition to the smaller ones, and one held fifteen U.S. twenty-five-dollar gold coins stamped with 1992–1998 and an image of the Statue of Liberty. And sure enough, the serial numbers were listed on the paper.

When we finished, Colt let out a long, low whistle. "There could be a hundred thousand dollars in gold here. What do you want to do with all of this, Maggie Mae?"

"I don't even know." I had to figure out what the treasure had to do with my dad.

"It could be the answer to your money problem."

"That doesn't seem right," I said, thinking about the still partially read note in my pocket. Had my father left the gold for me? Did he want me to turn it in to the police?

"Why don't you think about it?" he asked, stuffing the bars and coins back into their bags. He left one small bar out. "Let me take this one with me to see if I can find out anything about them. Like how much they're worth."

I narrowed my eyes. "Isn't gold's worth determined by weight? Shouldn't it be worth however much it weighs?"

"In theory. But we have no idea how these gold bars found their way into that ugly dog statue. The how is easy enough—they were hidden." He tapped the bottom of the bar. "This is a serial number. This might tell us why they were hidden."

"You think they were stolen."

"It crossed my mind. Why else would they be hidden like this? I can't have you trying to sell stolen gold. We need to know if these serial numbers are hot."

"If I decide to sell it at all."

"You're a little young to be saving for retirement. Especially when you're so broke and working four jobs."

"Four?" I asked. "Momma, the shop, and Miss Ava."

"And singing with me. We have our set tomorrow night."

Crap. In the chaos of my life, I'd forgotten. "I've added more songs, so we need extra rehearsal time." It was the least of my concerns right now, but the note was burning a hole in my pocket. If I tried to cancel on him, it would lead to a longer conversation. Colt was sharp; he might figure out that I was up to something—or a whole lot of somethings . . .

"I can't meet you until late afternoon tomorrow, but I think we'll be fine," Colt said. "Maybe we can rehearse in the catering kitchen. The acoustics are amazing, and the Belles don't have any functions tomorrow night."

"Do you think you'll get my car running tomorrow?" I asked.

He cringed. "I'll go by first thing in the morning and send you a text when I know something."

He reached for the list of serial numbers, but I held on. "Let's just stick to the one bar for now." I'd keep the list in my purse for now.

I expected him to look offended, but he gave me a look that I took as respect.

I followed him to the door. "Thanks, Colt."

He grinned as he tucked the gold bar into his jeans pocket. "That's what friends are for."

As soon as I locked the door behind him, I pulled the note out of my pocket and sat down on the overstuffed chair.

Magnolia,

If you found this paper, then something has happened to me. Trust no one. If you tell the wrong person, you'll be in grave danger. This is much bigger and goes deeper than I ever suspected. Even the people I expected to protect me have let me down.

Take care of your mother and brother. I'm sorry.

Love,

Dad

Tears blurred my vision as I got to the end. This was the only proof I needed: Dad hadn't run off, just like I'd always known; something had happened to him. But I still had no idea what that something was, let alone why he'd filled the dog with gold. Or how he'd expected me to find it. Had he left me clues that I'd missed?

I searched the apartment, looking for somewhere to hide the bags. In the end, I hid them in multiple places. I wasn't sure what to do with them yet, but I couldn't risk anyone else discovering them.

Not until I had more answers.

It looked like I would have even more to discuss with Geraldo Lopez in the morning.

chapter fifteen

Nashville traffic had gotten ten times worse in the years I'd been away. I'd heard Momma and Tilly complain, but this was the first time I'd driven during morning rush hour. The stop-and-go traffic gave me plenty of time to think about the note I'd found in the bottom of the ceramic dog.

I'd stayed up half the night and cried more tears than I had thought possible. While I had more questions than answers, I took satisfaction in the knowledge that Daddy hadn't run off with Shannon Morrissey.

I wanted to tell someone about the note, but who? For the time being, the only thing I knew to do was keep it to myself. Even from Colt. I trusted him not to hurt me, but I wasn't sure if he was as good at keeping other people's secrets as he was at harboring his own. I decided to wait and see what he found out about the gold bar.

Dr. Geraldo Lopez's office was in a multistory office building downtown, two blocks from Daddy's—

and now Roy's—office. After parking in a public parking garage, I headed to the building and took the elevator to the fourteenth floor, hoping something would jar loose from my memory about the day Daddy had taken me to the dentist. While I was nearly certain it was the same dentist, I was hoping for some further confirmation. Nothing was looking familiar. Not that I was surprised. Fourteen years had passed since my visit, and I hadn't paid any attention to the décor.

The waiting room was empty, but an ancient-looking receptionist sat behind an open glass window. Her frown added to her many wrinkles. "You were supposed to be here five minutes ago, Ms. Bartok."

I stared at her in confusion until I remembered that *I* was Ms. Bartok. "Sorry. I haven't had enough coffee this morning."

"So your tooth isn't bothered by heat?"

"No," I said, quickly assuming my role. "Mostly cold."

Her lips pursed as she handed me a clipboard. "I'll make a note of it. Since you're late, you'll only have five minutes to fill out the paperwork instead of the usual fifteen." Then she leaned forward. Up close she looked even *more* ancient. "If you're not ready to go back in five minutes, it'll throw off our entire schedule."

I grabbed the board and pulled it from her firm grasp. "I can write fast." It would be just my luck if the crypt keeper stopped me from seeing Dr. Lopez.

"Make sure it's legible."

I forced a smile, then sat in a chair and wrote an M in the *first name* box before realizing my error. I scribbled it out and wrote Tilly Bartok. Without thinking, I put down my new address instead of the one I'd given the crypt keeper the day before. Time was running out, so I told myself that they'd never compare it, and if they did, it wouldn't be a big deal. I skipped a big section by marking that I didn't have dental insurance—true—then sped through the medical history form, reminding myself not to list the appendectomy I'd gotten at age eight or my sulfa drug allergy. I'd just finished signing the HIPAA forms when a woman who was only slightly less grumpy than the receptionist appeared in the doorway to the back.

"Tilly?" she asked in a stern voice. She probably didn't expect me to be done.

I stood. "Yes."

"Follow me."

I handed off my paperwork and did just that. As we walked down the dark hall, it triggered a memory from fourteen years ago. Daddy had seemed anxious, and his anxiety had passed to me, making me nervous enough that I'd reached for his hand as we walked to the exam room, the last door on the right.

The hygienist led me to the same room.

"Have a seat in the chair."

I did as she requested, looking out the window at the view of the office building across the street. I remembered sitting here before, counting the windows while I waited for Daddy to finish his conversation with Geraldo Lopez.

"Hello, Tilly," a man said as he entered the room several seconds later. "I'm Dr. Lopez."

My breath stuck in my chest. He'd looked familiar in the photos, but in person, there was no denying he was an older version of the man I'd met that day.

"I hear you're having some tooth pain. What exactly is the problem?"

He sounded nice enough. He definitely didn't have the voice of a killer, but then again, I'd only known two alleged killers. The first one was that maniac from the basement, and his creepy voice was etched into my head. The second was Amy, though I still wasn't convinced of her guilt. Then again, I had no idea if Dr. Lopez *was* a murderer. I only suspected him of knowing something about Daddy's disappearance.

On the endless drive downtown, I'd thought about how I should approach this. The smart thing to do would be to question him about his previous clients and mention my father's name to gauge his reaction. But now that I was finally here, I wasn't sure that would work. I decided to be more direct.

He sat in the chair next to me and picked up a dental instrument.

"I sat in this same chair fourteen years ago," I said, looking up into his face.

He frowned. "You must have been a child then. I don't typically take young children."

"I was fourteen," I said, my stomach turning somersaults. "But my appointment was a ruse . . . an excuse for my father to see you."

His face paled and he looked back and forth between my chart and me. I could see the wheels turning. The name was different, but he knew who I was.

"Jackie," he said, looking at the hygienist on the other side of the chair. "Can you excuse us for a moment?"

"What?" she asked in surprise.

"Just for a few minutes." After she stood, he added, "And shut the door behind you."

Her forehead was furrowed, but she complied.

As soon as the door closed, Dr. Lopez pushed his chair back several inches. "You must be Magnolia."

I sat up in the chair, balancing awkwardly because of the incline. "Yes."

He pushed out a long sigh and moved to the window. "I expected you to show up sooner. Walter told me that you'd asked to see him."

That caught me by surprise. "I guess I've been a little slow putting things together."

He slowly turned back around. "Who else have you told about this?"

Trust no one.

My father had turned to these men for help, but neither of them had protected him. Neither of them had stepped up to help find him justice.

I stood. "I'm not sure why that matters."

He took a step toward me, his eyes shining with anxiety. "It's more important than you know." He paused. "Do you know what the police are saying about Walter's death?"

"They're calling it a robbery."

"That's right, but I have firsthand knowledge that he wasn't robbed. The Franklin police are covering it up. Or someone involved with the investigation."

I already knew they were part of a cover-up because of the missing cell phone and paper. I couldn't stand thinking that Brady had something to do with it, but how well did I really know him? What about his friend Owen? I knew nothing at all about him.

But I wasn't going to tell Dr. Lopez any of that.

"Why? What are they covering up?" I asked.

"This goes deep, Magnolia. It all quieted down after your father disappeared, but after Walter . . . He was the fourth person involved in this to be murdered."

"What? Who else?"

"Chris Merritt disappeared three years ago."

"How was he involved?"

"What did Walter tell you?"

"Nothing," I said, even though I couldn't help wondering if honesty was the wrong course. He might be more inclined to talk if he thought I knew something.

"Walter was tired of hiding the truth. He was going to give you information."

Crap. The paper. "I saw a paper in his hand," I said. "I think it listed names. Yours was at the top—that's how I knew to come see you. I remembered visiting your office with my father that day."

He gave me a slight nod. "Who else?"

"The other two were only partial names. His hand blocked the first parts. I saw a word that ended with R-R-I-T-T," I said, spelling out the letters.

He turned back toward the window. "Chris Merritt. And the other?"

I struggled to control my excitement. "And O-G-E-R-S."

He hesitated before responding, "I have no idea who that is."

I wasn't sure I believed him, but decided it would be better to see if he could give me other answers before circling back to this. "Do you think whoever killed Walter Frey knows you and Mr. Merritt were connected?"

"Probably." He pulled the hygienist's chair toward the windows and motioned for me to take his previous seat.

I placed my shaky hands on the low back of the chair, moved it next to his, and sat down.

"People are watching," he said, his gray eyes holding mine. "You were smart to use an assumed name to come see me."

"I confess that I'm a little paranoid at the moment."

"Good," he said. "You should be."

"Do you think I'm in danger?"

"No." His mouth pinched and he glanced out the window. "I think you're fine as long as you don't talk. *To anyone.*"

"I still don't know what's going on. Do you know what my father was involved in or what happened to him?"

"Contrary to what Walter believed, I'm not sure telling you is in your best interest, especially since you can't trust the police." He paused. "I can't stress this enough, Magnolia. You can't trust *any* of them. Look at how they tried to frame you with that music agent's murder a few weeks ago. They would have arrested you if that assistant hadn't confessed and then killed herself."

"You've been watching me?" I asked, trying to hide my fear. Most of the story hadn't been published in the news.

"Since I found out you were back in town? Yes. Your father always expected you to look deeper if he disappeared. He presumed the police would cover it up. Walter and I have always expected that you'd show up asking questions one day."

"And you won't tell me what it involved?"

"I think the less you know, the better."

"And if I disagree?"

A sad smile tilted the corners of his mouth. "I'm afraid I have the upper hand there."

I could threaten him in some way, but I had no idea how, not that I felt compelled to try.

Not yet, anyway.

There might be more than one way to get what I wanted. "Was my father's boss involved?"

"We were never sure of everyone who was involved. They said it was safer that way."

"And *they* were in charge?"

"Yes."

"A person? An organization?"

"I was never sure. I think only one person ran things, but as little as we knew, it could have run deeper."

"The one million dollars that was missing . . . do you know if it was cash or something else?"

His eyes narrowed. "Like what?"

Crap. "Something in small bags. Maybe drugs?"

He laughed, but it sounded bitter. "It was bigger than drugs." He stood and looked out the window again. "When you leave here, you can't come back. You must pretend this never happened. If you tell anyone I talked to you, I'll deny it."

"Daddy was scared. Why?"

Dr. Lopez kept his back to me. "He talked."

"To someone he shouldn't have?"

He nodded, then looked back at me. "You need to go."

"What happened to Shannon Morrissey?"

Worry filled his eyes. "She got too nosy. Just like you're doing now. You need to let this go. And you have to leave. Now."

He'd spoken in vaguenesses, but at least he hadn't denied everything. This was more than I'd hoped to find out. "Thanks for the warning."

He walked to the door, and I got up and followed him. Opening it, he said, "Ms. Bartok, if your molar pain continues from gritting your teeth in your sleep, come in to be fitted for a mouth guard. But what you really need is less stress." He held my gaze. "Take what I've said to heart."

"Thank you, Dr. Lopez," I said as I walked past him.

The hygienist waited in the hall and looked irritated.

"Jackie," Dr. Lopez said, "Ms. Bartok's appointment was a consultation. No charge."

Her irritation grew as she followed me to the front. She opened the door to the waiting room and watched me walk out of the office.

I let out a breath as soon as I got into the elevator. Geraldo Lopez expected me to just let this go, but I needed answers. I owed that much to my dad. I just needed to change the direction of my search.

As the elevator shot down to the garage, I checked my phone. There was a text from Colt.

Your car's up and running.

Thanks. I owe you.

One bar of gold bullion seems more than enough. ;)

Did Colt expect to keep it? Did I have any reason not to let him?

I found Tilly's car in the parking garage, then called her as soon as I was coasting out of the concrete dungeon.

"Hey, Tilly. Colt's already got my car done, so I'm trying to figure out how to get your car back to you."

"Lila and I are going out. She was going to pick me up, but how about you come by here and you can take me."

"Sounds good."

I spent the next thirty minutes mulling over my next steps. I knew what I needed to do to get more information about Shannon Morrissey, but it made me feel like a first-class bitch.

Tilly was waiting on her front porch when I pulled into her driveway, and she climbed into the passenger seat.

"Do you want to drive?" I asked. "It is your car."

She waved her hand. "I like being driven around. Makes me feel like I'm being chauffeured."

I grinned, hiding my anxiety. Tilly lived about five minutes from Momma, which meant I didn't have much time.

"I can't believe you're already back," she said. "That was a fast appointment."

"It was just a consultation." I shot her a glance. "Tilly, I have a question—and you can't tell Momma I asked."

She stiffened. "Oh, okay."

"I'm sorry to do this to you, but it's important."

"Of course, Maggie."

I took a breath. What was the worst that could happen? "I need to know about Shannon Morrissey."

"*Shannon Morrissey?*" She turned in her seat to look at me. "Why on earth do you want to know more about that home-wrecker?" She actually sounded affronted. But maybe she was so used to touting the company line, she fell into it like a duck takes to water.

"So you really think Daddy was having an affair with her?"

"Why else would he have run off?"

She sounded and looked sincere enough that I might have bought it if I hadn't heard her commiserating with my mother over my daddy's safety months after his disappearance. But no point bringing that up now. She could try to convince me of his adultery for all I cared. In fact, I was hoping it would give me the answers I needed.

"I know she was married to Daddy's client, but do you know how they met?"

"Magnolia," she said, sounding torn, "shouldn't you discuss this with your mother?"

"You know she won't talk about it. Is it wrong that I want to know more about what happened?"

She pushed out a huge sigh and sank back in the seat. "No, of course not, sweet girl. I understand."

"I don't want to make you uncomfortable, but I really need some answers."

"I'll tell you what I know."

"Thank you, Tilly."

She took a breath as though trying to steel herself. "You asked how they met. Well, I was there. It was at a fundraiser cocktail party for some charity your father's company helped sponsor. Your mother and I catered the dessert."

"I don't remember that."

"I'm sure you wouldn't. We were known for our cheesecakes back then, and the fundraiser was small, which is probably why I saw them meet. There weren't many other people there."

"She was there with her husband?"

"Yes, but she looked irritated with him."

"So what happened when they met?"

"They exchanged some small talk after they were introduced, but then they disappeared. I went to the kitchen to get something and found them huddled in a corner."

"Did you hear what they were talking about?"

"No."

"Do you know anything about her? Her family? Did she work?"

She laughed. "Work? She was part of Franklin's society life."

I sucked in a breath. "You're sure?"

"Of course I'm sure."

"Thanks, Tilly. That really helps."

She paused. "Her sister never believed it either. She was the biggest thorn in the side of the Franklin police."

"She lives in Franklin?"

"Works here too. Last I heard, she ran the daycare on Murfreesboro Road. Tender Darlings."

"Thanks, Tilly."

"Just be careful, girly," Tilly said. "You might not like what you find."

She wasn't the only person to have told me that, but it was time to shine some light in the darkness.

I'd just have to be ready when the monsters charged.

chapter sixteen

I needed my father's gun.

I'd left it at Momma's when I'd moved to my new apartment, worried that I didn't have a permit for it, but personal safety trumped following the rules, not that I was much of a rule-follower anyway. If I was dropping by Momma's to get my car, I might as well pick up the gun.

Both Momma's car and my old car were in the driveway, so I parked on the street.

Tilly and I walked toward the house together, but I could tell our earlier conversation had bothered her, so I stopped her on the front porch. "Tilly, I didn't mean to upset you."

Worry filled her eyes. "Some things are better left in the past, Maggie."

There was that phrase again. While I agreed with her on some things—my own past, specifically—my father deserved to have his name cleared. "I'll keep that in mind." I opened the front door, surprised to find it unlocked. "Momma, Tilly and I are here."

"In the kitchen."

We followed a savory smell and found Momma pulling a casserole from the oven. "You're both just in time to try my new recipe."

"It smells delicious," I said, grateful I was still in her good graces.

"Colt came by earlier and said your car's ready." She set the dish on a trivet on the counter.

"He sent me a text."

She looked up, holding my gaze. "You two seem pretty chummy."

"I already told you—we're just friends."

"Colt Austin doesn't have friendships with women."

"As you've already warned me," I said with a laugh, sitting on a bar stool. "But I assure you that's all we are. He's never once made a move on me."

She frowned. "Then he's up to something."

"If you question his character so much, then why do you have him working for you?"

Tilly laughed. "She only questions his character as far as women go. Your mother warns every female new hire about his ways."

I grinned. "Does it work?"

"Hardly ever," Tilly conceded. "But your mother feels better if she gives them a leg up."

"Maybe he's scared to screw up a good job, so he knows better than to mess with me." I glanced over at Tilly. "I know he really likes working for you two."

Momma grabbed plates from the cabinet. "How was the dentist?" Something in her voice made me wonder if she knew I was up to something.

"He said that I've been grinding my teeth at night, probably from stress. If I keep having tooth pain, he wants me to come back and get fitted for a night guard."

Momma's eyes narrowed as she put the plates down next to the casserole. "I thought it was just a cleaning."

I shrugged and took the knife from her hand. "I never said what it was for, and I didn't want to worry you. But I'm fine. What do you ladies have planned for today?"

"Lunch. Shopping," Momma said. "You?"

I cut each of us a piece and put them on plates. "I'm going to enjoy a day off in my own apartment. I've never lived alone before."

Both women shot me a curious glance, but they let it go.

"Momma, while Colt and I were getting my car out of the garage, we couldn't help noticing that the stuff in the garage looks like it was from a small apartment."

She looked up at me. "So?"

"Colt said he didn't think Roy ever *had* his own apartment. He says he moved back in with you, then in with a friend, then in with Belinda."

"Colt seems awfully nosy."

"I think he was just looking out for me," I fibbed. "I have a furnished apartment now, but the lease is only good for six months."

She turned up her nose. "Don't remind me. That's six months too long, as far as I'm concerned."

"I think he was thinking I might be able to use some of the furniture in the garage to furnish an apartment when I move."

She stared into my face. "You'll have a place to live once your lease is up."

My eyes widened. Did she mean the house?

The lines around her mouth softened. "Roy's doin' well for himself, plus I paid for all his college tuition. I didn't help you when you were in New York, so the house is yours."

"Momma. I told you that I don't want to talk about you dyin'."

She shrugged. "Nevertheless, it's yours free and clear. No strings. No rules. Sell it and move back to New York if you like. Or stay and make a life here." Tears filled her eyes. "I'd give you more money now . . ."

"*Momma*"—my voice broke—"I don't want your money. I'm used to working hard to get what I want. I only want you."

She reached over the counter and covered my hand with her own. "I don't want to spend the next few months at odds with you. I want you to know that I'm going to make more of an effort to be nice."

I chuckled, blinking to keep the tears in my eyes from falling. "Don't be too nice or I'll think you had a lobotomy."

She and Tilly laughed, and I tried to burn this bittersweet moment into my mind—sitting with two of the adults who had raised me, knowing that Momma would soon be gone.

We all deemed the recipe a success, and Momma and Tilly decided to add it to their brunch menu. Then we cleaned up the kitchen together, and when Momma and Tilly were ready to leave, I pretended to just then remember something I'd left in my old bedroom. Momma agreed that I could lock up. After Tilly pulled away from the curb, I ran upstairs and opened the nightstand drawer. There, wrapped in the towel I'd found it in, was the gun Daddy had hidden in our basement. I grabbed it and the box of ammunition I'd found with it and stuffed them in my purse, where I was keeping Daddy's note and the list of serial numbers.

I was already downstairs again, preparing to leave, when I realized Momma had never told me about the real owner of the things stored in the garage. Had she just gotten distracted? Or had she purposely moved on?

Maybe I needed to do a little investigating.

One side of the three-car garage was empty now, making it easier to dig through the stack of assorted belongings. I dragged a sofa and a pair of end tables to the empty spot, trying to uncover the stacked boxes, which were all unmarked. That seemed odd.

The first few were stuffed with pots and pans, linens, and cleaning supplies. I finally got lucky with box number seven, which looked like it contained the entire unsorted contents of a junk drawer. Pencils, pens, paper clips, plus postage stamps that didn't look like the current forever stamps in use. I stuffed them into the front pocket of my capris, intending to look them up later. I kept sorting—screws and a couple of screwdrivers, a ball of rubber bands. Then a pad of paper labeled: "From the desk of Christopher Merritt."

Was this Chris Merritt who had apparently disappeared three years before? How many men with the same name could possibly be tied to this family? Momma had insinuated that these things had been here for a couple of years.

What the hell was going on?

I went through the rest of the boxes, though I found nothing else to tie the contents to anyone, not even clothing. I closed them all back up the best I could, then restacked them and made a halfhearted attempt to put the furniture back. I was too eager to go inside and use Momma's computer to look up Christopher Merritt to take my time.

I sat down at the desktop computer in her small home office and searched for Christopher Merritt + Franklin TN.

He'd been an accountant, but news reports confirmed that Christopher Merritt had disappeared three years ago, leaving behind a wife and three kids. A few photos of him and his family popped up. They looked so happy.

It had happened to someone else. Just like us. Geraldo Lopez had already told me that, of course, but seeing his family made it more real.

I took a moment to let it sink in. Then I reflected on what little I knew. Daddy had been involved in something with Walter Frey and Geraldo Lopez. Somehow Shannon Morrissey had been mixed up in it too.

According to Dr. Lopez, Walter Frey had felt guilty about not coming forward. He'd planned to bring me information. The paper with those names. Was there anything else on there that I didn't see?

But I couldn't stop thinking about Christopher vanishing without a trace three years ago. Just like my father. What had triggered it? Had he wanted to come forward too?

I grabbed a pad of paper from Momma's desk and made a list of people I needed to talk to—Shannon Morrissey's sister. Christopher Merritt's widow. Momma about when Roy had brought over the stuff in the garage.

Ava Milton.

If Shannon had been active in Franklin society, surely Ava knew something about her. She seemed like she was good at cutting through shit. Maybe she could tell me something about the supposed affair.

It was a good start.

I turned off the computer and locked up the house, excited to have my old car back. Just as I turned the key, my phone rang. Belinda.

"I have most of the afternoon off," she said. "What time would you like to go to lunch?"

I glanced at the car clock, which said it was three a.m. Obviously Colt hadn't set the clock. "I have to run an errand, and I'm not sure how long it will take."

"Call me when you're done. Maybe I can see your new apartment!"

"Yeah. Sounds great."

I hung up, then backed out of the driveway and formulated a plan for talking to Shannon Morrissey's sister. I didn't even know her name. What if she didn't own the daycare anymore? But I'd figure out a contingency plan if I needed one.

The front door of the daycare was locked, so I pushed the call button, suddenly wondering how I would get access. Should I pretend to be a prospective parent? But I didn't need an excuse; the door just opened. I walked into a small foyer, and there was a glass window on the wall to the right that put me in mind of the one at the dentist's office this morning.

A young woman who looked like she was barely out of high school sat at the counter behind the open window. "Can I help you?"

Here goes nothing. "Hi." I gave her a warm smile. "I'm looking for the owner."

"Sydney?" she asked. "She's in her office. Let me get her." She got up and walked through a door in the back of her small room, then returned seconds later. "She says come on back."

A buzzer sounded, and the receptionist gestured for me to go through the door at the end of the foyer. I walked into a large room filled with about thirty toddlers and preschoolers. The women giving them craft supplies gave me a curious glance, and one of the kids started toddling toward me. Being this close to so many small children threatened to make me break out in hives.

A woman's head popped out of an open door to my right. "Can I help you?" She was dressed in a long-sleeved T-shirt with a pair of yoga pants, and her dark blond hair was pulled back into a messy ponytail. She looked down at herself. "I know I look like a hot mess, but I promise we have our sh—stuff together." She gave me a grin. "We're preparing for a state inspection, so we're kind of in frantic cleaning mode."

Talk about bad timing, but I was already here and this would probably only take a few minutes. But right now we were standing out in the open, and I didn't even know Shannon's sister's name. "I'm looking for Shannon Morrissey's sister. Are you her?"

The smile fell from her face. "You need to leave."

While it appeared I'd found the sister, the woman's reaction kind of put a damper on things. "I understand your hesitation, but I promise I'm here to help."

"I'm not giving any interviews. Not anymore. That's what all the police and the reporters promised to do, but then they twisted all my words around." Her angry gaze darted to the tables full of children, then back to me. "It was a long time ago. Let it go."

"Sydney," I said, using the name the receptionist had given. "I can't let it go. I'm Magnolia Steele. Brian Steele's daughter."

Her mouth closed, but she still eyed me with distrust. "Are you here to chew me out for my sister running off with your father?"

"No," I said quietly and took a step toward her. "No. The opposite. I don't believe they had an affair at all. I think they were involved in something else." I paused and looked back into the large room. Several of the daycare workers were openly watching us. "Can we discuss this in your office?"

She studied me for a moment before ducking back into her office. I followed her into the small room decorated with children's artwork and shut the door with the nameplate *Sydney Crowley, Director* behind me. She looked up at me with nervous eyes as she sat in her chair.

"Why are you bringing this up *now*?" she asked, her tone bordering on hateful.

I sat in one of the chairs in front of her desk to buy myself some time. Both Daddy and Dr. Lopez had said, "Trust no one." But I had to give her something, or she wouldn't tell me anything. "I moved away ten years ago. This is the first chance I've had to ask."

She was silent for a moment, looking down at her desk. "Are you here because of Walter Frey?"

I sucked in a breath. "You know about Walter Frey?"

She glanced up. "You mean that he was murdered?"

"That too."

Her eyes narrowed. "What do you want?"

I leaned forward, resting a forearm on the desk. "I want to know what really happened. Like I said, I know there was no affair. My father loved my mother, and he loved my brother and me. Even if he were having an affair, which he most definitely wasn't, he wouldn't have just left his family. Tell me why you think Shannon wasn't having an affair."

She gave me a guarded look. "Because my sister would never do such a thing."

"You know something," I said. "Why else would you have mentioned Mr. Frey?"

Pushing out a long breath, she shook her head and then held my gaze. "I told the police everything back then . . . Magnolia, is it?"

"Yes. Magnolia. I did too, Sydney. I told them that my father never came home after he left to meet Walter Frey."

"That's not the story your mother gave the police."

I blinked. "*What?*" Then I remembered what Brady had said—Momma had recanted her initial statement.

"Your mother told them she knew they were having an affair, and that you were making things up because you couldn't accept the truth. No one took me seriously. Even when I gave them proof."

My heartbeat sped up. "Proof? Proof of what?"

"That my sister was working with Brian Steele to expose her husband's money laundering."

"Money laundering?" Did that have anything to do with the gold I'd found in the statue? Along with the one million dollars my dad and Shannon had been accused of stealing.

Sydney looked irritated. "Look, there's no disputing that Shannon married the shithead for his money. But when the afterglow of having money began to wear off, which happened pretty quickly, she started noticing things."

"What kind of things?"

"I told all of this to the police."

I leveled my gaze. "Obviously they mustn't have taken it seriously."

"Haven't you read the police report?" she asked with a harsh laugh.

"No."

"Are you serious?" she asked in disgust. "You just decided to start asking random strangers questions?"

Basically.

"Look," I said with a defensive sigh. Better to play this totally clueless, which wasn't that much of a stretch. "I'm not a private eye or anything. I'm just a daughter looking for answers."

"Did you stop and think your questions might get you into trouble?" she asked.

"No," I lied. "I just want to find out what really happened to my father."

"My advice is for you to let it go. No one's going to take you seriously, and you'll only end up more bitter and angry in the end. Take it from me."

"Come on, Sydney. Give me something. Don't you want justice for your sister?"

"The best justice I can give my sister at this point is to let it go. Because stirring it up will only hurt my nephew. Kids telling him that his mother abandoned him because he's a loser has been bad enough. Besides, I find it a little . . . coincidental that Walter Frey was murdered right after you came back to town."

She certainly didn't need to know that I'd arranged to meet him that night. But something she'd said jumped out at me. "Shannon had a son? Why isn't he with his father?"

"Because Steve Morrissey isn't his father. Nathan was a baby when she got married. His birth father is a piece of shit who never gave a damn." Sydney leaned forward over her side of the desk. "Magnolia, I know you think you're doing the right thing here, but just let it go."

"I can't."

She stood. "You mean won't," she said, her voice harsh. "You need to leave. I have more cleaning to do."

Feeling defeated, I stood and moved toward the door, but then I turned to face her. "You know how Walter Frey is connected to this, don't you? Because I know for a fact Daddy and Mr. Frey set up a meeting for the night of Daddy and your sister's disappearance. I heard it with my own ears, and my father kissed me goodbye before he left and made sure I knew where to find our handgun. So I know whatever they were doing was dangerous."

Her face paled.

I took a step back into the room. "You were the one who mentioned Walter Frey. Not me. How do you know about him?" When she hesitated, I began to plead. "Please, Sydney. I can get justice for both of them."

"You won't. I already tried."

"Then let *me* try," I said. "I have nothing to lose." That wasn't true, but I'd work it out.

"There were four of them," she said, looking nauseated.

I nearly cried with relief.

She turned quiet. "Your father. Walter Frey. A dentist—and an accountant. They all knew about the embezzlement. Frey was Steve's attorney. Your father was his financial planner. The accountant handled his money."

"And the dentist?" I asked.

"I don't know." She took a shaky breath. "Shannon said all four of them knew he was dirty, and they were planning to take him down. Shannon was helping them."

"So what happened?"

"Steve found out. Your father and Shannon were going to speak to the county prosecutor, but the night before, they disappeared."

"My father went to meet Walter Frey," I said. "Where was your sister going?"

She swallowed. "To meet your father."

I nodded, trying to keep calm. This was big. This was *huge*. "So the police never looked into Steve Morrissey?"

"The other three refused to talk. It was my word against theirs. They knew Steve would have them killed." Fear tightened her features. "Talking to you now could get *me* killed. It got Walter Frey killed."

I reached out and took her hand. "No. Sydney. If he wanted you dead, don't you think he would have had you killed back then, after you talked to the police? Why do anything now?"

She took a deep breath and nodded.

"You don't need to get more involved. I'll get a copy of the police report so I can find your statement and use it."

"No, Magnolia. I only told you so you'll know what's at stake. Steve won't be happy if this gets dragged out into the open again. He knows how vocal I was after they disappeared."

"If anyone asks how I know something, I'll say it's from the police report."

"But you don't even have one."

"No, but I know how to get it."

chapter
seventeen

The police station was quiet when I walked in. I didn't recognize the receptionist at the desk, not that I was surprised. Last time, I'd come in on a weekend.

"Is Detective Bennett in?" I asked as I approached the window. I probably should have called him first, but I was a witness in a murder investigation, which surely gave me a justifiable reason to show up and talk to the detective who took my statement.

But now that I was here, I was paranoid. One, I was sure the police were behind Walter Frey's mysteriously missing cell phone, not to mention the note. And two, by requesting this police report, I was declaring my intentions to Walter Frey's killer. I was also worried Brady wouldn't give it to me. He thought I'd accepted the official storyline about Daddy, and I wasn't sure how he'd interpret my continued interest. I considered asking the receptionist how I could get a copy, but the fewer people who knew about this, the better. Might as well take my chances with Brady.

She gave me a bored look. "What's this in regard to?"

"The Walter Frey murder."

"Detective Frasier is handling that case. Do you want me to ring him?"

"No. Detective Bennett, please."

She narrowed her eyes, looking like she was about to protest, but then picked up her phone and dialed an extension. After speaking with someone in a hushed tone, she hung up. "He's out to lunch," she announced.

"Do you know when he'll be back?"

Her bored look was back. "No. But I'll be happy to take your name and number and have him contact you."

I forced a smile. "No, thanks. I'll just come back later."

I stepped outside and stood in the sunshine, closing my eyes as the gravity of what I'd learned from Sydney sunk in. My father had tried to do the right thing by going to the county prosecutor, and it had cost him his life. Did I really want to pursue this?

"Maggie?"

I opened my eyes, preparing myself to see Brady. He and another man close to his age were walking toward me from the street. "Hi."

The other man gave me a weird look, almost like I was a sideshow freak, but Brady didn't seem to notice.

"What are you doing here?" Brady asked as he stopped in front of me. "Is everything okay?"

"Yeah. Actually, I stopped by to see you."

He gave me the smug smile of a man who just learned he was declared *People's* sexiest man of the year.

I couldn't help grinning. "While your ego is truly astounding, this is an *official* visit."

He laughed and then turned to his friend. "Owen, this is Magnolia Steele. Magnolia, this is Detective Owen Frasier."

Owen could be complicit with whatever was going on in the station—after all, it was his case—so I needed to be very careful. I assumed a role: a young woman trying to win him over because she was interested in his friend. I beamed with a megawatt smile as I held out my hand. "Nice to meet you, Detective Frasier."

He smiled back as he shook it. "Call me Owen if you're a friend of Brady's."

Continuing to play it light and breezy, I shot Brady an ornery smile before looking back at Owen. "I'll keep that in mind, Detective Frasier."

Owen burst out laughing and clapped Brady on the shoulder. "You've met your match with this one, Bennett." Then he turned his amused gaze to me. "I wholeheartedly approve of anyone who doesn't fall at his feet."

I gave him a haughty grin. "No chance of that happening."

Owen laughed again. "I hope to see you again, Magnolia Steele." Then he looked over at Brady. "Good luck, man. I think you need it. See you inside."

I had to admit that Owen Frasier didn't seem threatening, but could I really trust him after only a few seconds of pleasantries?

Brady watched his friend walk inside, shaking his head a little in amusement, before he turned back to me. "We don't know anything new about Walter Frey's case."

"That's not the case I'm interested in at the moment." I paused. "I was wondering if you could get me the report on my father's disappearance."

He took my arm, led me over to a low concrete wall, and then gestured for me to sit with him. "Maggie, I told you the case is closed. Your father was having an affair."

Protesting would likely get me nowhere, but there was another way I could play it, and it might just save my ass for at least a little while longer.

"I know," I said quietly, looking down at my hands in my lap. "I finally realized that everyone is right." I mustered up a few tears, just enough to add to the role but not enough to overdo it. "The thing is, I never got closure. Daddy just left—no note, nothing. I never got to really grieve what happened. But if I had the police report and saw everyone's testimony with my own eyes, I think I could finally let this rest."

He gave me a wary glance.

"I know it might be a lot to ask, especially since I coerced you into investigating it."

He sighed and leaned his forearms on his thighs. "You didn't coerce me. I thought there might be a legitimate angle."

"And now?"

He sat up, looking frustrated. "It still seems pretty damn coincidental that a man you were supposed to meet was murdered. But I've already looked into the only thing linking you two together. Walter Frey was robbed. It was just unfortunate timing." Yet the way he said it made me think he didn't quite buy it himself.

"If it's too much trouble to look it up . . ."

He shook his head. "I have a copy on my desk. It's not a matter of looking it up. I can make a copy for you in a matter of minutes." He studied me. "I think I'm more concerned with what you plan to do with it. Whether there's a connection or not, looking into your father's disappearance is what put you and Walter Frey in the same location that night."

I sat up straighter and swiped at the corner of my eye. "I've learned my lesson about my father, Brady." Only not at all like he presumed I meant. "I hate to put you on the spot like this, but I'm asking anyway. Please?" I gave him a pleading look, and he released a long groan.

"Okay," he finally said, looking none too happy about it. "I'll get you a copy, but I want something in return. Do you have plans tonight?"

Oh crap. He was going to ask me to go out with him. I tried to ignore the fluttering ball of nerves in my stomach and affected a wary look. "Why?"

"I want you to stay home tonight."

I blinked, certain I'd heard him wrong. "*What?*"

"Even though there's no official link between you and Walter Frey's murder, I'd feel better if you stayed home. Or maybe at your mother's. Keep out of the public eye until we have a better handle on who did this."

"You can't be serious. Do you have any solid leads?"

He grimaced. "No. The bar didn't have cameras on the parking lot, and no one's used his credit cards yet."

That was because they hadn't murdered him for the credit cards, but I wasn't going to suggest that. "You're asking me to be a hermit for an indefinite period of time." He didn't answer, and I fought my rising irritation. "Brady, I can't stay home tonight. I already have plans with Colt."

He tried to look nonplussed, but I could see my news bothered him. "Are you working on a catering job with your mother?"

"No." I considered dragging it out to make him suffer, but I didn't see the point, not with a copy of the report on the line. "We're singing tonight. At the Kincaid."

"Are you trying to get signed to a country label?"

"No. I just miss performing. We sang pretty well together at the Embassy, so he asked me to sing with him again tonight. Plus, it's a chance to earn some money from tips."

He watched me with a worried expression. "Do you trust this guy? You can't have known him very long."

I gave him a teasing grin. "I've known him about a half day longer than you."

He didn't smile.

"Brady, tell me what's really going on."

"Officially, you're free to go about your business."

"But unofficially I'm not?"

He rubbed his head in frustration, then turned to face me head-on. "I'm worried about your safety. I have no hard evidence. Just call it a hunch."

Resisting the urge to tighten my hold on my purse, which still contained my gun, I said, "I appreciate your concern, but I'm okay. I promise. I'm being extra vigilant, just like you asked. Plus, you forget I lived in a big city, and cautious was my middle name. Besides, the Kincaid is a large bar. There will be tons of people around."

He didn't look convinced. "That doesn't mean you'll be safe."

"I have to do this, Brady. I can't let Colt down, plus I really *want* to go. I'll stick with Colt the entire time. We're driving there together."

He hesitated and then said, "Please, just be careful, okay?"

"I will."

Standing, he pushed out a heavy sigh. "I have to get inside. Will you be home in about an hour?"

"No, I'm having lunch with my sister-in-law."

"I have to go interview someone, so I'll leave a copy of the report on your front porch."

"You're going to get me a copy?" His reluctance filled me with guilt, although I had no idea why. "Thank you, Brady."

"I may text you later to check on you. I'd appreciate it if you'd respond so I know you're okay." I would have believed he was trying to hit on me, but I saw genuine concern in his eyes, which filled me with renewed fear. What did Brady know that he wasn't telling me? Did he suspect his friend had stolen Walter Frey's phone?

"Thanks," I said, meaning it and wondering if I should rethink this solo investigation.

He started toward the building but then turned back to me and lowered his voice. "One more thing." He paused. "Don't talk about the Walter Frey case or your father's case to anyone."

"You already told me that."

"No. I mean *anyone*. Police included."

Oh, God. He *did* suspect them. Should I tell him what I knew?

He gave me a soft smile. "From the look on your face, I'm scaring you. It's just that a few of the detectives know I'm interested in you. We all tease each other, and I don't want any of them to annoy you." He paused. "Promise me."

It seemed like an odd request, but since I already suspected someone in the department might not have my best interests in mind, I had no problem agreeing to this one. "I promise."

I left the police station a lot more frightened than when I'd arrived, but the gun in my purse gave me reassurance. Once I was in the car, I pulled out my phone and called Belinda. "I'm headed to my apartment, if you want to meet me there."

"I'm finishing up a proposal, but I'll be there in about twenty minutes."

"See you then."

After I drove to my apartment, I parked in the spot next to the garage and headed for the stairs, but the swaying of the curtain in the house's kitchen window caught my eye. I already had Ava's attention. I might as well talk to her now.

I walked over to the back of the house and rapped on the wooden screen door. She waited a few seconds before opening it.

"What are you doing here?" she asked, looking me up and down. "It's not Wednesday."

I latched on to her opening. "Actually, I don't think we set a time for me to come on Wednesday."

"You said you wouldn't know until you got your schedule. Do you have it?"

"Uh, no. But if I'm off, what time would you prefer for me to come over?"

The look she gave me told me she wasn't falling for my ruse. "Eight."

Ugh. *Eight?* But I had brought this on myself. "Thanks. I'll let you know as soon as I find out."

She continued to watch me through the screen, waiting for my next move.

"Miss Ava," I said, wishing I'd thought this through better. "I know you have your hand on the pulse of the city—"

She looked down her nose at me, which was impressive since she was several inches shorter than me. "Is that your way of calling me a gossip?"

I had to salvage this situation, and fast. "What? No!"

"What do you want to know?"

"I want to know what you know about Shannon Morrissey and my father."

Her eyes widened, and then she grinned. "You don't beat around the bush, do you? You're just like your mother."

My back stiffened. "I'm going to take that as a compliment."

"As long as you're not going against me, it is." She shifted her weight. "So what do you know about them?"

"I—"

She pushed the door open. "Maybe you should come inside to discuss this."

I walked past her into the kitchen. "So you believe all the rumors."

"Sit." She gestured to the small table.

I did as she said and placed my hands in my lap. "What do you know?"

"You need to learn patience, Magnolia Steele."

"I've been patient for fourteen years, Miss Ava. I'm done with patience."

She grabbed the tea kettle from the stove, then moved to the sink. "After waiting fourteen years, five minutes isn't going to cost you a hill of beans."

Of course she was right, but it still ticked me off. She was playing with me. We both knew it, but there wasn't a damn thing I could do. She was going to tell me gossip about some torrid affair, and I was going to have to sit here and listen, because that's why I was here. To find out what everyone had said.

After she filled the kettle, she set it on the stove and turned on the burner. I was surprised when she sat down across from me and folded her hands on top of the table. "There were rumors, of course."

I watched her and waited, and this obviously pleased her, because she graced me with a satisfied smile. "The key is that those rumors popped up *after* their disappearance, not before."

It took me a second for her words to register. "Wait. Are you saying they weren't having an affair?"

She straightened and slightly turned her head, giving herself a regal air. "I have no idea if they were or weren't. All I know is that rumors don't usually start floating around after two people have disappeared together. An affair starts quietly, discreetly, and then the couple gets cocky. Sloppy. There was no sloppiness."

Disappointment washed through me. I'd hoped she would reject the idea of an affair altogether. "So you're saying they were clever."

"I'm not saying any such thing. I'm only saying if they had an affair, it was either brand new or they were more careful than most."

I pushed out a breath as I looked down at my hands.

"Shannon wasn't happy in her marriage. Steve Morrissey is not an easy man to live with." She paused. "He had peculiar proclivities."

I glanced up. "What does that mean?"

Her mouth pursed. "Ladies do not speak of such coarse things."

"So it's about sex."

Her lips pinched tighter.

"Steve Morrissey had a fetish," I said, more than asked. "Did Shannon know before she married him?"

"I highly doubt it. Their courtship was a whirlwind. She told him she was pregnant, and they married a month or so later."

"I know she had a son before she married him, but I didn't realize they also had a child together."

"They didn't. She miscarried shortly after the wedding." She gave me a smug look that suggested she didn't believe it. "Rumor had it that he didn't introduce his peculiarities until after her miscarriage, but once he began to make his demands, she started looking for a way out that wouldn't leave her destitute."

My brow furrowed as I tried to read between the lines. Then it hit me. "Mr. Morrissey had a prenup."

She tapped the side of her nose and nodded.

"But she'd get his money if he went to jail, because they'd still be married, right?" Still, that didn't sound quite right. If he was laundering money, wouldn't all his assets be seized?

Miss Ava gave me a sideways glance. "What on earth makes you bring up jail? She stole his money and left. And so did your father."

"She left her son behind? Just like my father supposedly left his family behind."

She lifted her shoulder into a slight shrug. "People in love do strange things."

"Only, they weren't in love," I said quietly. "She was using my father to get what she wanted—out of her marriage but with the money." When she didn't contradict me, I asked, "Why do people believe the other story?"

"Who's to say your version is the truth?" Miss Ava asked with a sharp stare. "Who's to say your father wasn't using *her*?"

I let that settle in for a moment. "Maybe it was a mutual decision. Mutual payoff."

"Or maybe they were simply having an affair and they ran off with Morrissey's money. That's the least preposterous of all the suggestions."

The kettle began to whistle, and Miss Ava got up and walked over to the stove. "Do you prefer Earl Grey or an herbal tea?"

I shook my head. "Neither, thank you. I need to go." I stood, suddenly exhausted.

"Suit yourself," she said, moving the kettle to another burner. "Maybe another time."

I nodded. "That would be nice," I said absently as I made my way to the door. It occurred to me that while Ava had made this a neat and tidy package, she wasn't privy to all the information. Would she know anything about the gold? With my hand on the doorknob, I turned back to look at her. "Do you know anything about Mr. Morrissey's assets back then?"

She looked surprised. "Well . . . I heard things."

"Which is why I'm asking you."

"He used your father as his financial planner, and rumor had it that he'd withdrawn a large chunk of his money from your father and was looking for a more stable investment. Something more traditional. Like utility stocks."

"Or gold?"

She hesitated. "Yes. I'm sure there was gold."

I opened the door. "Thank you."

"Magnolia," she called after me as I walked out the back door.

I glanced back at her.

"Be careful. Sometimes just because you know something doesn't mean you have to act on it. Some things are better left in the past."

I'd heard that again and again lately, but only now did it strike me as odd. We were talking about two people whose disappearance had devastated two families. Not only did my family deserve answers, but so did Shannon Morrissey's family, and Christopher Merritt's and Walter Frey's, and slowly but surely, I was getting them. Besides, Miss Ava was wrong. If my father's investigation into Steve Morrissey had been act one of the man's takedown, this was act two.

I just had to be careful.

I headed up the stairs to my apartment and waited for Belinda to show up. Now that the sun was out, it reflected off shiny pieces of the ceramic dog. While Colt had contained most of the mess with the towel, then dropped them in the waste bin, some pieces had still escaped. I grabbed a broom and dust pan and was in the process of sweeping them up when I heard Belinda's knock.

As soon as I opened the door, she pulled me into a hug and then gushed, "Oh, my word! This place is darling!"

"Come on in." I stood out of the way and looked at the door to see if Brady had made good on his promise, even though it hadn't been an hour yet.

"How in the world did you find it?" she asked as she walked into the kitchen.

"Colt. He knows Miss Ava."

Her smile faded slightly. "Oh."

I narrowed my gaze. "What do you know?"

"Nothing really," she said with a slight shake of her head, making the ends of her strawberry-blond hair brush her shoulders.

I pushed her down on a barstool. "Spill it."

She gave me a patronizing smile. "Ava Milton has a lot of power."

"So I've heard."

"And she and your mother are at odds."

"Which I also know." When she started to protest, I held up my hands. "I had no idea until after I signed the lease."

"It just seems so odd, don't you think?" she asked, searching my face. "It all happened so quickly."

Something in her voice caught my attention. "What are you suggesting?"

"Nothing."

I sucked in a breath. "Don't bullshit me, Belinda."

"Magnolia," she said in a disapproving tone.

"Belinda, I need you to be honest."

She hesitated for a moment. "Then I need you to be honest with me too."

I eyed her cautiously. What was she talking about? "I thought I had been."

"Did you have anything to do with Walter Frey's murder?"

I felt the color bleed from my face. "Did Momma tell you that?"

I hadn't told Belinda I was meeting Mr. Frey. In fact, I hadn't told *anyone.*

Something sparked in her eyes. *Oh.* She'd been fishing, and I'd just given her confirmation.

"I didn't kill him."

She rolled her eyes. "I *know* that. But you were meeting him, weren't you? Did he tell you anything?"

"No. He showed up before I did and took off for the back. The bartender told me where he'd gone, so I went to check on him. I found him out back, all right. Dead."

She reached over and rubbed my arm. "How awful. Are you okay?"

"Yeah. I'm over the shock now." It was mostly true, which bothered me. Was I getting used to seeing murder victims?

"What are the police saying?"

"They think it's a robbery. That it had nothing to do with Daddy."

She stiffened slightly. "Why would it have something to do with your father?"

"Belinda, don't you think it's odd that I set up a meeting with the man and he was killed right before he could meet with me?"

"Well, of course, but you do have terrible luck. Look at Max."

"True, but—"

Her eyes widened with fear. "Have you felt threatened since?"

I couldn't very well tell her *yes, your husband tried to beat me up*, even if I *had* warned her that I'd pissed him off. But despite our combined efforts to track down Max Goodwin's killer, I wasn't going to tell her about my extracurricular sleuthing either, not when Roy was already so riled up. Besides, it was too dangerous for me to involve anyone else. "No, of course not. Say, do you know anything about the stuff Roy has stored in Momma's garage?"

She looked taken aback by the quick change in topic. "Why do you ask?"

"Colt helped me get my car running, and we had to move some things to get it out. It looks like the contents of a one-bedroom apartment. A nice one. I realize Roy has his shit together more than most people, but it seems even out of his league, especially if it's from a place he got after college."

"It belongs to his friend. He was transferred to Hong Kong for a few years, so Roy said he'd keep his things."

"Was it the guy Roy lived with before he moved in with you?"

She was still smiling, but there was a hint of fear in her eyes. "Why so many questions?"

"It just seems odd. First of all, I can't believe Momma agreed to it. And second, why didn't he get a temperature-controlled storage unit? I can't imagine the Tennessee summers are good for the furniture."

"His friend left in a hurry, and they couldn't find a place. It was supposed to be temporary, but then Roy forgot about it, I guess."

"Did Roy have any of his own things mixed in with his friend's stuff?"

"What are you getting at, Magnolia?"

Why did she look so nervous? Did Belinda know something about the stuff in the garage, or did she just know it was important to Roy for some reason?

"Roy's going to have a fit if he finds out you moved any of Todd's things around," she went on.

"I won't tell him, Belinda. Besides, you had nothing to do with it." I took a breath, then plunged on. "Did you tell him about our discussion at Mellow Mushroom?"

"Roy's been very busy this week. He's been getting home late, and he's been . . . stressed."

I understood. She couldn't outright say that she kept secrets from him. And I was sure he kept plenty of secrets from her too. Like his housewarming visit the other night. "So that's a no?"

"No." She took a breath. "Did you disturb the things in the garage?"

Why was she so worried? "It's Momma's garage, and she was also storing my car. She gave me permission, Belinda."

"How much did you move?"

I sure wasn't going to tell her I'd been snooping through the boxes. "Hardly anything. Just enough to get my car onto the driveway."

She was silent for a moment. "Okay."

"Where do you want to go to lunch?" I asked. "I don't care as long as it's not Taco Bell."

She gave me a strange look, then asked, "Do you have anything you need to be back for?"

"No, but . . ." I paused, wondering if I should tell her my plan for the afternoon, then decided if anyone would understand, it would be Belinda. "I want to go to Walter Frey's funeral."

"Oh." She seemed to think about it before she asked, "Do you think that's a good idea?"

"I don't see why not. He was a business associate of my father's." I took a breath. "I feel like it's the right thing to do."

"But it just seems so . . ."

"I'm going," I said in a firm voice.

She took my hand. "I'm sorry. I just worry about you is all." The earnest look in her eyes told me she meant it.

"Nothing's going to happen," I said, squeezing her hand.

She studied my face, then nodded. "Of course. You're right. I was planning to go to the funeral too. I planned their daughter's wedding, and I grew very attached to Shelby. I'm sure she's devastated. We can go together if you'd like."

The thought of facing Walter Frey's distraught family almost made me change my mind. But Belinda's sympathetic face gave me the strength to believe I could handle it. I had no idea how I'd become so attached to her in such a short period of time, but now I didn't know how I'd get along without her. I squeezed her hand tight. "I'd like."

A soft smile spread across her face. "We'll go to lunch first and then head to the funeral together. I can drive."

"Thanks." I paused, hesitating to say, "I've missed you." My kinship with Belinda had caught me by surprise. We'd taken to meeting for lunch several days a week, and I'd even helped her with a wedding the previous week—although I suspected Roy didn't know. But I hadn't seen her since lunch on Tuesday, which was the longest we'd gone without seeing each other since I'd returned to Franklin.

She gave me a tight squeeze. "I've missed you too." Dropping my hand, she took a step back. "Now show me around."

I chuckled. "There's not much to see. It's a one-bedroom, but it's all I need. Besides, Ava has some very strict rules about entertaining gentleman callers."

She laughed. "Gentleman callers?"

"Don't ask. I'm already in trouble for three in one night." Oh shit.

Her eyebrows rose. "Three men?"

I shrugged.

Her face lit up. "Oh, no! You're not getting off that easy. Who?"

"It's not nearly as exciting as it sounds," I lied. "Especially when she included the pizza delivery man in the count."

"She got upset over the pizza delivery man? Are you sure you want to live here?"

"Things will settle down. I really like this place, and I've never lived on my own. It's like a dream come true."

"Did it come furnished?" she asked, wandering into my bedroom.

"Yeah, and the rent is very affordable."

"It almost seems too good to be true."

The hairs on the back of my neck stood on end, but I couldn't deny the same thought had occurred to me. Everything had fallen into place so easily with the apartment. It would have been easier to accept if I believed in fate. "I'm starving. Let's get going." But rather than leave right away, I walked to the sink and opened the cabinet door, pulling out the trash can. It was full of pieces of the ceramic dog, and I'd forgotten to take it out before I'd gone to the dentist. "I'm going to take this down to the garbage bin on the way."

I pulled the bag out of the container, the pieces clinking together.

"Did you break some dishes?" Belinda asked as she walked out of my bedroom.

"No, just a statue."

"Isn't Ava going to have a fit?"

"It wasn't hers." After her freak-out about the garage, I couldn't tell her I'd taken the dog statue. "Colt gave it to me right after I moved in." Technically true.

"Oh, dear," she said. "Will he be upset?"

"He'll get over it." I grabbed my purse and headed toward the door. When we reached the landing, Belinda took the trash bag from me so I could lock the door.

"What was it a statue of?" She peered inside the bag. "Is that a *dog head*? A Dalmatian?"

I put the keys inside my purse. "Yeah."

"There are a lot of pieces."

How closely was she acquainted with the things in the garage? "It was a big dog."

"It looks like it was smashed." When I didn't respond, she gave me a sympathetic smile, then turned and headed down the stairs. "I hope Colt doesn't find out you broke his gift."

"He already knows," I said. "He was here when I broke it."

We were both silent until we got into her car, but I could sense Belinda was struggling to put something into words. "You're spending a lot of time with Colt," she finally said, turning to look at me.

"I've already told you half a dozen times that we're friends."

"Just be careful, Magnolia. Okay?"

I considered arguing with her, but she clearly seemed worried. "I'm fine, Belinda. I promise. Nothing's going on between us but friendship."

She started to say something, stopped, started the car, and then turned back to me. "I probably shouldn't tell you what I'm about to say, but I care about you, Magnolia."

My shoulders tensed. "Okay."

Her mouth twisted into a grimace. "I'm not sure you should entirely trust Colt."

"I already told you that I—"

"No. Because of his criminal past."

"He has a criminal past?" It didn't totally surprise me. He'd admitted that he had once been associated with some dangerous people, and there were plenty of indications he wasn't proud of his past, but this was the first I'd heard about any criminal activities on his part. "Does Momma know?"

"Yes." She pressed her lips together. "She says she's giving him the benefit of the doubt."

"What was he arrested for?"

"Grand larceny, but his charges were dropped."

"Well, then he mustn't have done it."

"He made a plea bargain with the D.A."

"What did he supposedly steal?"

"I don't know. Roy was worried about your mother, so he tried to get the report. But the records were sealed."

"Why would the records be sealed?"

"I don't know."

"How long ago did it happen?"

"I don't know that either."

Was this Colt's big secret? I was dying to know, but did I have a right to ask? Because if I demanded answers from him, he might ask the same of me.

chapter eighteen

There's a lot of people here," I said as Belinda and I looked for a place to sit in the funeral home. There had to be at least one hundred fifty people packed into the room, and there were more people waiting behind us.

Belinda leaned over and whispered in my ear, "I'm not surprised. Walter Frey was a respected member of the community."

Thankfully, my sister-in-law seemed like her normal self again. She'd exchanged multiple texts with someone at lunch before rushing off to the restroom with her phone. When she'd returned, she could barely look me in the eye.

"Is everything okay?" I'd asked.

"Of course." She'd picked up the menu and looked it over.

"You don't look okay."

She'd looked up and smiled. "A disgruntled bride. Not to worry. It will blow over. Part of the job territory."

But she'd been quiet through the rest of our meal, and I couldn't help wondering if it had something to do with my brother.

Funeral home employees were adding folding chairs to the ends of full rows of mourners. One of them motioned for Belinda and me to take two seats a few rows from the front.

Several people acknowledged Belinda by offering a smile or a nod as we passed. I had suspected she knew a lot of people in town, but this was proof. It was yet another sign that she had a life outside of my brother, so why did she stay with him? I had to make her see that she didn't need him. That she could live without him.

After we settled onto our seats, I took a discreet look around the room. I gasped when I recognized Chris Merritt's wife from the internet photos, sitting in a row in front of us.

"Magnolia?" Belinda asked in concern. "What's wrong?"

"I just saw someone unexpected."

"Who?"

"Christopher Merritt's wife."

She looked surprised. "You know Karen?"

"Do *you?*"

Belinda uncrossed her legs and leaned closer. "I met her at the Arts Council of Williamson County. She's only attended a few meetings. How do you know her?"

"Her husband worked with my father."

"He worked at JS Investments?"

"No," I said. "They shared some clients."

I looked back at her, and her eyes widened as the pieces clicked into place.

"Magnolia." She grabbed my arm. "Please tell me you're not here to question Karen."

"No," I said. "Of course not. I had no idea Karen would be here." But it was certainly odd that Karen Merritt was at Walter Frey's funeral. Then again, maybe Walter and Chris had done other business together.

"You're not here to question Walter's wife either, are you?"

"No," I said without sounding defensive. I could see why she might think that, but even I had my limits. "I'm here to pay my respects."

And to look for anything suspicious that I could follow up on later. But Belinda didn't need to know that part. Nevertheless, it felt like a long shot.

Several minutes later, the pianist began to play "How Great Thou Art" as the family walked down the aisle to their seats in the front row. A middle-aged woman with a teenage boy and a twenty-something couple—Mr. Frey's daughter and son-in-law?—entered first, followed by an elderly couple and two more middle-aged couples with their children. Once they took their seats and the service started, it occurred to me that the woman sitting in the front row wasn't the woman Walter Frey had met at Mellow Mushroom. Had she been a client? I couldn't ignore the way she'd studied me as she walked up that afternoon—as if I was some kind of threat.

Was she Walter Frey's lover?

I dwelled on it for a few more moments, but an unexpected swell of emotion overcame me. Walter Frey was most likely dead because of me—I'd known that before now, of course, but it suddenly felt more real. He hadn't wanted to meet me that night. I'd insisted.

I'd killed Walter Frey.

The proof of my destruction sat three rows in front of me as his widow leaned her head on the shoulder of her son. As her daughter's back shook with her sobs.

I had done this.

A pressure built in my chest and the walls felt like they were closing in. My breath came in quick pants, and Belinda turned to me in concern.

"Are you okay?" she whispered.

I shook my head. "I'm sorry," I forced out, trying not to panic even more as I felt a massive anxiety attack brewing. "I need to go to the restroom."

Worry in her eyes, she swung her legs to the side so I could make my escape. I forced myself to walk as slowly as possible to keep from causing a scene, but as soon as I was free of the room, I bolted across the large entryway toward the bathroom.

Once inside, I placed my hands on the counter and leaned my head against the mirror as I concentrated on my breathing, slow deep breaths in and out. I centered my whirling emotions on my happy place—the same memory I'd used to center myself in New York whenever panic and fear had threatened to consume me.

I focused on my father. Or, more specifically, a warm summer night when I was nine. We had reclined on a blanket in the backyard, looking up at the stars. Roy had been there too, but even then he hadn't wanted to be with us—Daddy had insisted. So we all lay on our backs, listening to the locusts in the trees, the warm summer night's breeze rustling our hair. Daddy pointed out several constellations, and then, as we lay there in silence, I reached out my hand to his. He laced our fingers and squeezed tight. In that moment, I had felt like nothing could hurt me. That Daddy would protect me from everything.

Deep down I knew it wasn't true. Would he have protected me the night I'd been held hostage, beaten, branded with the killer's knife, and forced to listen to that poor woman's screams as she was murdered?

Because the sad truth was that Daddy hadn't even been able to protect himself.

After several minutes, I began to calm down and my face stopped tingling. I was grateful I hadn't burst into tears, because I definitely didn't have the makeup in my purse to fix a hot mess. When I felt more in control, I studied my face in the mirror and created a character to play. I was a woman accompanying her friend to a family friend's funeral. I was the pillar for my friend to lean against. I was not a helpless victim.

I took a deep breath, assumed my role, and walked out the door, already feeling stronger.

When I returned to the service, everyone was standing, singing, "It Is Well with My Soul," so my entrance went unnoticed by most people, except for a woman toward the back. She was standing in front of one of the hastily added folding chairs, and her eyes met mine as I passed her. It was the woman who Walter Frey had met for lunch.

I recovered from my shock and slipped past Belinda to take my seat.

"Are you okay?" she mouthed.

I nodded and looked down at her hymnal and began to sing, resisting the urge to look back to see if the woman was watching. I hadn't seen her when I'd made my escape, but I'd been too focused on reaching the bathroom door to notice.

The service ended soon after that, and we watched as the casket was wheeled out the side door, with the pallbearers walking beside it. I glanced back to catch a glimpse of the woman, but she was gone. I wasn't sure I could go to the graveside, but Belinda looped her arm through mine and tugged me along with the other mourners.

Clouds from an imminent storm were brewing to the west, kicking up a breeze and a chill. Although the coffin was brought to the gravesite in a hearse, most of us traveled on foot behind.

I only had on a light sweater, so I shivered from the cold and nerves as I kept my eyes on Walter Frey's son. His face was stoic as he helped pull the coffin from the hearse. His mother and sister held hands as they watched, tears glittering in their red eyes.

Belinda gave my arm a squeeze. As if reading my mind, she said, "It's not your fault, Magnolia."

I gave her a tight smile and lied. "I know."

We stood toward the back of the crowd of fifty or so people—some had left after the ceremony—and I realized I'd never gotten this closure with my father. Sure, I'd used it as an excuse to get the report from Brady, but standing here now, the truth of my supposed lie really sunk in. Daddy had simply disappeared, and I'd lived with the uncertainty ever since.

Karen Merritt stood behind Mrs. Frey, her hand on the new widow's shoulder. Mrs. Merritt hadn't gotten her closure either.

I zoned out for the rest of the short graveside service, only realizing it was over when I heard Belinda telling an older woman that we wouldn't be going to the church for the potluck early dinner afterward.

As the woman wandered off, Belinda turned to me. "I need to talk to Mrs. Ramey about something related to the Arts Council fundraiser tomorrow night. Will you be okay if I leave you for a minute?"

"Of course. I'm fine."

She gave me a wary look before she moved closer to a woman on the other side of the group.

"She's wrong, you know," I heard a woman with a raspy voice say from behind me.

I spun around to face Walter Frey's lunch date, my heart lodging in my throat.

"It was your fault."

Find a role. Find a role, a voice chanted in my head. I quickly settled on a woman accused of a crime she didn't commit, an easy role to assume since I'd played it so recently. I gave her a haughty look. "I'm sorry . . . have we met?"

She assessed me, and the look in her eyes seemed to say, *Okay, if that's how you want to play it.* "We inadvertently met last Tuesday at the restaurant, although we were never introduced. You're Magnolia Steele."

I titled my head slightly, giving her a bitchy look. "And you are . . . ?"

"Unimportant. I know why you were meeting Walter that night."

I cocked an eyebrow and asked with a smirk, "Why would you think we were meeting? I was just saying hello to him at the restaurant."

Anger flashed in her eyes, and she grabbed my arm and dragged me several feet away from the group. "Don't play dumb with me, little girl. You have no idea what you've stirred up."

I tried to jerk loose from her hold, but I didn't want to cause a scene.

"Walter Frey was murdered in a robbery," I said, proud of myself for maintaining my role. "I have no idea why you'd try to pin that on me. I doubt my presence in Franklin has inspired robbers to start murdering people."

Her face leaned closer to mine, and her fingers pinched deep. "Stay out of this, Magnolia. Let sleeping dogs lie. Before you get someone else killed." Then she released me as if it offended her to touch me and turned and walked away.

"Oh, my word," Belinda gasped beside me, sounding out of breath. "What just happened?"

Had she run over to intervene? Thankfully, no one else seemed to have noticed the woman's verbal assault.

I brushed my arm, plastering a distasteful look on my face. "Apparently she wasn't a fan of my YouTube videos."

Belinda's eyes narrowed. It was clear she didn't believe me, but she didn't question me either.

"Did you recognize her?" I asked, glancing over at the woman. She had reached the asphalt path and was walking toward the parking lot.

"No."

"I thought you knew everyone," I teased, forcing myself to laugh.

She turned her concerned gaze on me. "Are you sure you're okay?"

"Of course," I said, still reeling from the woman's accusation. This man's death was on my shoulders, and I had no idea how to atone for it. Should I tell his widow that I wasn't sure I believed the robbery story?

If I did that, I'd be stealing closure from her and her children, not to mention possibly putting them in danger. She wasn't the person I needed to talk to.

No. That person was standing on the opposite side of the crowd, his eyes firmly glued to me.

Brady Bennett.

What the heck was he doing here?

Belinda realized I was watching him and gave me a questioning look.

"Come on, let's go." I didn't want to talk to him within earshot of Belinda.

"Do you know him?"

I started walking, and thankfully she followed. "That's Brady."

Belinda gave me a sly smile. "*Brady?*"

Crap. I needed to set her straight. "*Detective* Brady Bennett."

That caught her off guard, but she didn't look all that alarmed. "You're on a first-name basis with a police detective?"

"I *do* seem to be hanging out with a lot of them lately."

"Not funny." She cringed. "I saw the way he was looking at you. I need more of an explanation than that."

How was he looking at me? With the concern he'd shown earlier or the naked interest with which he'd watched me sing? I didn't dare ask. "I met him a few weeks ago. During the last investigation."

She narrowed her eyes, but a grin tugged her lips. "You never told me about Detective Brady Bennett."

He must have given me the hungry man in front of a buffet look. "That's because it was . . ." How did I describe what happened between us? "Neither of us knew who the other was the first time we met. Then the second time . . . let's just say while there was chemistry, the fact that he works for the Franklin police put a damper on anything happening."

"And this time?"

"I called him when I found Walter Frey." When she gasped, I added, "Brady had saved his number to my phone, so when I found Walter Frey, I called him. He was the first person on the scene, and he called it in."

"*You* found Mr. Frey's body?"

I cringed. "I didn't tell you that part?"

She took a second to process, then asked, "So he's investigating the murder?"

"Not exactly." I resisted the urge to look over my shoulder to see if he was following us. "He wasn't on duty, so he handed it off to his friend. But Brady took my statement and has kept me informed."

She eyed me for a moment. "Why do I think there's a whole lot you're not telling me?"

"What makes you say that?"

Her eyes twinkled. "Because Alvin called to ask me what I knew about you and Franklin's most attractive police detective."

"Belinda!" Then I lowered my voice in case Brady was close enough to hear. "You knew?"

"I was waiting for you to tell me yourself. I hear he asked you to dinner. Why won't you go out with him?"

Crap. How did I get out of this one?

"Because he hurt me, Belinda."

I quickly explained his betrayal over the Goodwin case.

Belinda stopped in her tracks. "Magnolia! Why didn't you tell me?" Then she looked back toward the grave, obviously searching for Brady. My gaze followed hers; he was talking to someone in the crowd, although I had no idea who the man was.

I shrugged and started walking again. "There was a lot going on. I never told anyone. Except for Colt."

She scowled. Obviously her opinion of him hadn't changed in the last couple of hours. "I heard you two are playing at the Kincaid tonight."

"How'd you hear that?"

"Tilly. She got pretty excited when I told her what a big deal it was."

It was my turn to stop. "Whoa. Why would you tell her that?"

"Because it *is* a big deal."

I gave her a blank stare.

"Are you *serious*? You really don't know? Magnolia! It's where a lot of artists get discovered. I would have given anything to play there."

I'd almost forgotten that Belinda had come to Nashville to become a country music star. I still had to wonder how she had handed in that lifestyle to be my brother's Stepford wife. I knew she couldn't be happy. The question was why she stayed.

"How did this come about?" she asked.

"Colt and I sang at the Embassy. Then he told me he was playing at the Kincaid and asked me to sing with him."

Her eyebrows lifted. "You two sang together?"

"How else would he know if I was any good or not?"

"How about the fact you were a Broadway star?"

"I was a Broadway star for about two seconds. And while we *did* sound great, I have no desire to be a country music artist."

"Then why did you agree to sing with him?"

I shrugged again. "I don't know. I guess because I love being onstage. I know it's only been a few weeks, but I miss it. And sure, singing is performing, but all the touring and sleeping in a different bed every night? No, thanks."

She gave me a look of stern reprimand. "Then you better tell Colt, because most musicians play there for a reason. I'm sure he thinks he has a better shot of getting a record deal if you're with him."

"You mean because of my name," I suggested dryly.

"Oh, honey. I didn't mean it that way. I just worry about you. I would hate for someone to use you. And while Colt is a charmer, he's most definitely a user."

Her concern was almost humorous. Belinda was one of the most genuinely sweet people I knew. I was usually the more jaded one.

"Trust me, Belinda. I know exactly what I'm getting when it comes to Colt, his criminal past aside."

"Are you sure of that?" she asked with worry in her eyes. "He pulled one over on you with the Kincaid."

Dammit. She had a point.

The wind picked up, and the air felt heavy with impending rain. I saw a flash of lightning and started hurrying. "Let's get to the car before it starts raining."

"I need to get back anyway," she said. "We got a new shipment of wedding dresses that I left for my assistant to steam." She gave me a sly look. "You should come try some on."

"I'm off on Monday morning. Besides, it's about time I went to see your shop."

"*Really?* I expected you to say no."

"Why? Just about every girl likes to dress up like a princess, and isn't a wedding dress like the ultimate princess gown?"

"Are you a secret romantic, Magnolia?"

I laughed. "Hardly. But what's not to love about a dress that makes you look and feel like royalty? I might as well wear one when I can."

"But someday you'll get married. You'll wear one then."

I snorted. "I'm never getting married."

She turned back to me, her eyes wide. "Why?"

I couldn't tell her the real reason—that I could never let anyone get close enough to get married. I had too many secrets that I could never, ever share. But thankfully I already had a pat answer. "Too selfish," I said with a snooty air. "The theatre is too demanding for me to have enough energy left over to devote to making a marriage work."

"But you're not acting now. Don't you wish you had someone to share your life with? Don't you get lonely?"

"No."

"Not even just a little? When was the last time you had a serious boyfriend?" she asked, watching me like I was a goldfish in a bowl. "And don't tell me Griff, because from what you've told me, he doesn't count."

"I don't know," I said, starting to get irritated. "Can we stop psychoanalyzing my life? Tell me about the dresses you got in."

She seemed to give it serious thought before she said, "I'm really good at helping my brides pick their dresses. I bet I can pick the perfect dress for you."

We reached the car, and I opened the passenger door. "I can tell you right now that I've watched so many episodes of *Say Yes to the Dress* that I know I wouldn't want a mermaid style."

She got in on the driver's side, then said, "See, most people think that it's all about body type, but there's so much more to it than that. It's also the person's personality. The essence of them, if you will."

It seemed like a new age philosophy, which surprised me. I would have pegged Belinda as a staunch conservative.

"Let me give this some thought," she said, her brows furrowed with concentration as she started the car.

It seemed so wrong to be discussing a wedding dress for a wedding I'd never have as I walked away from the grave of the man I'd gotten killed. But the funeral had left me shaken, and it felt good to have a harmless distraction.

Belinda was quiet long enough that I was sure she'd dropped the subject, but as she pulled onto the road, she added, "You're classical, but you like attention."

I forced a laugh. "You just figured that out?"

She ignored me. "At first I thought of a ball gown because you made the princess comment, but while a ball gown is an attention grabber, it seems too innocent, too girlish for you."

She was right. I'd never go for that style.

"I have a new dress that came in. A fitted A-line dress with a full skirt, a beaded lace bodice, and beads and rhinestones fading down the skirt."

She said she picked the dress for the bride, not necessarily the body type. I was curious. "Okay. I'll bite. Why that dress?"

"The full skirt because you like to feel feminine. You wear a lot of dresses and skirts. The rhinestones and beads because you like attention and handle it well. But the back is lace-covered. It gives a hint of skin while still keeping it covered. Despite the fact that you're often in the public eye, you're still very closed off, avoiding close connections with people."

The hair on the back of my neck stood on end. Belinda stopped at a red light, and she was quiet for a moment, as if mulling over what she was going to say next.

When the light turned green, she continued driving and said, "Lace edges the scoop neck of the dress, which is perfect because you carry your secrets close, guarding them as if your life depended on it."

My heartbeat picked up. "Why in the world would you say that?"

She turned to me with innocent eyes. "Because it's true, isn't it?"

How did she know? *What* did she know? She couldn't know about the murder I'd witnessed on graduation night. Did she know that I'd shared my suspicions about my father with Brady? I hadn't told her about my discussion with him after the murder, but then she knew that Brady had asked me out to dinner—and that I'd declined. What if Roy had told her a detective came to see him? She could very well have put it all together.

Maybe I should tell her everything I knew. Lord knew I needed to tell someone. The secrets and lies and dangers and half-truths were all welling up inside me, making me liable to burst.

Trust no one.

Of course, Daddy hadn't even known Belinda. My biggest concern was asking her to keep a secret from her husband. Would she agree? Would she tell him anyway to protect herself?

I couldn't take that risk.

chapter nineteen

I was hastily coming up with a response, but I jolted when I heard my phone start to ring. I pulled it out and looked at the screen. Brady.

I pushed the mute button. I couldn't talk to him yet.

"What are you talking about, Belinda?"

Her nose wrinkled. "All those years in New York on your own. You're not very open about what you were doing."

Relief washed through me, but I tried not to let it show. I was being paranoid and ridiculous. What had I expected her to mean? I gave her a teasing grin that I hoped didn't look too insincere. "What exactly do you think I was *doing?*"

"Nothing bad," she said in a reassuring voice. "It's just that I know it had to be lonely for you." She pulled up to the curb outside of Ava's house and put the car in park. "I'm sure it was harder than you let on."

I reached for the door handle. "No sense dwelling on the past."

"Why was that woman talking to you?" she asked quietly. "What did she want?"

Anger rose up out of nowhere. Maybe it was because I was so tired of hiding. Maybe it was because I so desperately wanted to share my secrets with her, yet I couldn't trust her. Because I knew she'd choose my abusive asshole brother over me. But that alone was irrational and unreasonable. She'd known Roy a whole lot longer than she'd known me.

Still, my anger won out, flooding every cell of my being. Fight or flight kicked in, and instead of answering, I said, "How about I tell you after you tell me why you let my brother beat you?"

The color drained from her face.

"That's right. I know. But then, you already knew that. We just don't discuss it. You may let him hurt *you*, but *I* won't tolerate it, so tell your husband if he shows up at my apartment again, I'll do a whole lot worse than kick him in the balls this time. Brother or not."

If possible, her face paled even more. "Roy came to see you?"

"Yeah, the night I warned you that he was pissed. Why don't you ask him about it?" I sneered, then got out of the car and stomped to my apartment. As I heard her car pull away, I was overwhelmed with regret and shame. Magnolia Mae Steele, master of pushing people away. I'd just hurt the one friend who'd given me a chance.

God. Sometimes I really could be a cold-hearted bitch.

When I got to the top of the steps, there was a large manila envelope waiting for me. It was propped against my front door, attached with several pieces of tape. I pulled it off and went into the apartment, close to tears. I had to apologize, but what could I possibly say to make things better? *Sorry, Belinda. I didn't mean to admit that I know my brother beats you* didn't seem appropriate.

What a mess.

My phone rang. It was Brady again, so I answered with a sigh, already weary of the conversation I knew we were about to have and the excuses I would have to fabricate. "Hey, Brady. Thanks for checking in. I'm fine."

He didn't waste any time getting to the point. "Why were you at Walter Frey's funeral?" he asked, sounding irritated.

I considered protesting his question, but it didn't feel fair. After all, just a few hours ago, I'd promised him I'd leave well enough alone. "I was there to pay my respects." The fact that it was a partial truth made me feel better.

"Why am I having a hard time believing that?"

"Brady, you have to see this my way. Even if he was killed in a robbery, he was there because I asked him to go. If he hadn't been there, he wouldn't be dead."

"You feel guilty."

It took a second to speak past the lump in my throat. "Wouldn't you?"

His voice softened. "Maggie, it's not your fault."

"So why were *you* there? Did you think the burglar was going to rob the body?"

"Criminals who get off on what they've done sometimes feed off the grief of the victim's family."

"That's disgusting." I started to pull the documents from the envelope, but out of the corner of my eye, I noticed the covers on my bed were messed up. It had definitely been made before I showed Belinda around the apartment—I'd made a point of it.

"It's rare, but—"

"Someone's been in my apartment," I said, my heart leaping into my throat. Was it Walter Frey's killer?

Brady turned professional. "Are you there now?"

Why would the killer have broken into my apartment? The way the bedding and my clothing had been tossed around, it looked like the intruder had been looking for something. "Yeah." Maybe it was Roy seeking retaliation. But he seemed more like a smash and destroy kind of guy. Besides, he was probably in his office in downtown Nashville, over a half hour away depending on traffic.

"Get outside and wait for me by the street. I'm on my way."

"I don't think they're still here." Surely, if the killer were here, he would have jumped out at me already. But then it struck me why someone would be searching my apartment.

The gold.

"*Magnolia.* Get out *now.* I'll be there in a few minutes."

But how could anyone know I had it? The only other person who knew about it was Colt.

"Magnolia!"

I shook my head. Brady was waiting for an answer, so I said in a huff, "*Okay.*"

I hung up before he could respond, then immediately called Colt as I began to search my hiding places.

As soon as he answered, I cut off his greeting and didn't try to hide my panic. "Who have you talked to about the gold?"

"What?" His voice hardened. "What happened?"

"Someone's been in my apartment, and they were looking for something." I lifted the edge of the mattress. Sure enough, the two bags I'd hidden there were missing. "They've got at least one of the bags."

"Are you there now?" he asked, sounding breathless. "I'm on my way."

And so was Brady. "No! You can't come. Brady's coming over right now."

"*You called the police?* Are you insane?"

"No! I was talking to him on the phone when I realized someone had been in the apartment. He figured out what was going on, so he's coming over. You can't show up too."

"Why not?"

"Colt!"

"Just checking to make sure you still had some sense in your head," he grumbled. "You can't tell him about the gold, Maggie. He's going to ask you where it came from, and the minute you say your brother put it in your mother's garage, you lose all possession of it. It's not legally yours."

Only it was. Kind of. If my father hadn't stolen it, of course. But that reminded me of Colt's task for the day. "I'm not stupid. I'm not going to tell him. But someone knows it's here. You talked to someone about that bar you took, didn't you?"

"It was very discreet, Maggie. And I swear I didn't tell them where I'd gotten it."

"Did you find out anything about it?"

"No. I went to a guy in Nashville. He's going to get back with me. I trust him. He wouldn't tell."

"Well, someone did."

"Did they get it all?"

"I don't know," I said, stumbling over a pile of clothes and digging through my closet. "They got the bags between the mattresses . . ."

"Oh, my God. Under your mattress? That's the first place people look."

"I hid them in other places too, Colt!"

"You better check them before Detective Eager to Get You out of Your Pants shows up."

"I'm not wearing pants," I said, grabbing one of my black leather three-inch-heel boots.

"All the better for him," Colt said in a disgusted tone.

I turned the boot over to dump the contents into my hand, but I already knew the bag was gone. The boot felt too light. "They got two," I groaned.

"You need to check every hiding place, and quick," he said. "He's gonna have his guys rip the place apart, and if they find one—"

"I'll look. But I have to go."

"Call me when you're done."

I hung up and stuffed the phone in my pocket, already racing to the next hiding place. If Brady had still been at the cemetery, he'd be here in ten minutes or less. I'd checked nine places and turned up empty. I was reaching for the tenth, underneath the kitchen sink, when I heard a pounding on the door.

"Magnolia!" Brady shouted. "Open the door."

"Just a minute!" I pulled out a tall container of antibacterial wipes, pushing out a breath of relief when I felt the reassuring weight of it.

"Magnolia!"

I pried off the lid and dumped out both the wipes and the bag of gold. There wasn't time to put it back together, so I threw the container in the trash can and tucked the bag into my purse, where I'd been keeping the gun along with Daddy's note and the list of serial numbers, before opening the door. An irate Brady was waiting on my front porch.

"I told you to wait by the street."

"No one's here, Brady."

He pushed past me and stood in the center of the room, glancing at the TV and my laptop on the island. "They didn't take the electronics. Can you tell if they took anything else?"

"No. I don't have much, which is why I rented a furnished apartment. I left everything but my clothes in New York. I don't have anything worth stealing."

He moved into the bedroom. "Well, they were looking for *something*." He turned back to look at me. "Do you have any idea what it could be?"

"No."

He held my gaze as though waiting for me to change my answer. A scowl crossed his face as he turned back to my closet. "Was the door unlocked? I didn't see a sign of forced entry."

"No, it was locked. I have no idea how they got in." And that scared the crap out of me.

"Does anyone else have a key?" He moved in front of me. "Colt?"

I knew he needed to ask, but his tone pissed me off. "No, Colt doesn't have a key, not that it's any of your business."

"As the detective who is currently investigating your break-in, it definitely is."

I glared up at him. "Then I want a new detective." But I didn't. Not really. I just needed to get Brady to back off. He wasn't going to find anything that would help. I doubted he would even look for prints since nothing had been stolen. Well, nothing I could tell him about.

But my threat was enough to soften him. "I'm only trying to help you, Maggie."

He was right. I sighed. "No one has a key except for my landlord."

"And he owns the house?" he asked.

Dammit. I'd had a very pointed conversation with Miss Ava, and I suspected she knew a lot about a lot of people's business. Had she come in here looking for something? But as soon as the idea popped into my head, I dismissed it. I had a hard time picturing Ava Milton, the pillar of Franklin society, ransacking my apartment.

"She," I said absently. "Ava Milton."

His slight reaction suggested he knew of her. In my opinion, any smart law enforcement officer should.

"I think I'll walk over and check if Ms. Milton saw anything," he said.

That was actually a good idea. Nothing slipped past her.

"But I want to look around first." He left the bedroom and headed into the kitchen. Of course his glance immediately landed on the container of antibacterial wipes in the trash can. He glanced at me. "Did you throw this away?"

"Yeah . . ." I tried to sound confused.

"It's brand new." He leaned closer. "And the wipes are still wet."

What could he be thinking? "So?"

"Why would you throw it away?"

"What are you, the waste police? What does it matter?" When he continued to stare at me, I used the first excuse that came to me, no matter how much of a diva it made me sound like. "I didn't like the smell."

His eyebrows lifted slightly. "So you took the lid off and dumped the entire thing into the trash can? Wouldn't the smell bother you even more that way?"

"Are you serious?" I asked, getting angry. "You're asking me about throwing away wipes when someone broke into my apartment? I never asked you to come over, Brady. I sure didn't think you'd accuse me of anything."

The tension eased from his shoulders. "I'm not accusing you of anything, Maggie. I'm just trying to figure out what happened."

"I don't *know* what happened."

He moved closer and put his hand on my shoulder. "You don't have to know what happened. That's for me to figure out."

"But they didn't take anything."

"Are you certain?"

"Yes."

He pulled out his phone and swiped the screen.

"What are you doing?"

"I'm getting someone over here to dust for prints."

Maybe I was being stupid, but I didn't want the police all over my apartment. "No. I don't want to file a report."

Lowering his hand, he gave me a worried glance. "Someone broke into your apartment. I already told you that I have a bad feeling about your safety. Please let me make the call."

What if he got the prints of whoever did this? That would be useful information. But the thief surely hadn't been stupid enough to leave prints behind. "No."

"Maggie! What the hell are you doing?"

What could I tell him that wouldn't make me look more suspicious? "Because I might know who did it."

His eyes narrowed. "You said you didn't know."

"It only just occurred to me. I think it was Roy."

"Your brother? Why would he break in?"

"Momma gave me a necklace that belonged to her mother," I said, making it up on the fly. "Roy demanded that I give it to him."

"Your brother broke into your apartment to take your mother's necklace?" Just when I was sure he was going to accuse me of being the liar I was, his eyes filled with anger. "I think I need to go have a talk with your brother."

"What? No! You'll only make things worse."

"Maggie, the man physically hurt you during the Max Goodwin investigation. Was he the one who was at your apartment before I showed up the other night?"

"Let it go, Brady."

"Not if he's breaking into your apartment. He's dangerous."

"You don't know that."

"I talked to him two days ago. I know what he's capable of."

I froze. "What does that mean?"

He shook his head and glanced around the room. "How did I not see this when I was here before? It wasn't Colt. It was Roy, after all."

"I'm not filing charges, Brady." I grabbed his arm and started to drag him to the door.

He pulled me to a halt. "Why the hell not?"

"He's my brother. This will kill my mother."

"Do you really think your mother wants him hurting you?"

"She's dying."

His eyes widened.

Dammit. I hadn't meant to let that slip. "She told me when I came back. That's part of the reason I'm still here. She only has a few months left, and she loves my brother. Asshole or not, he was here for her when I wasn't. It would destroy her if he was charged with anything, especially if it was against me. I can't do that to her. I'm not sure she'd forgive me, and our relationship is shaky as it is."

"Maggie."

Genuine tears filled my eyes. "I can't. You have to understand that."

He sucked in a deep breath, then pushed it out. "I'm worried about you. Surely you can understand that you're in danger."

"He wouldn't hurt me."

"Yet he already has. I saw it with my own eyes."

"He was angry when I saw him a few weeks ago. I still know how to push his buttons, and I pushed a few too many. I'm sure he didn't mean to pinch me so hard."

And then I realized I sounded like every clichéd victim. Was that what Belinda told herself?

He looked into my eyes. "And the slap mark on your cheek?"

My face burned with embarrassment.

"Yeah. I saw the faded shape of his hand print on your cheek when I stopped by the other night."

I dropped my gaze, feeling a kinship with Belinda that made me squirm after what I'd just said to her.

"He's dangerous, Magnolia. I can't believe your mother would want you to leave yourself vulnerable."

"I'll be more careful."

"Did he get the necklace?"

I kept my gaze down, unable to look him in the face while I was lying to him. I already felt like a bitch because of how I'd treated Belinda. Now I'd elevated myself to first class d-bag. "I'll go check."

I stepped around him and walked into the bedroom, stepping over my pile of clothes. I opened the drawer in the bedside table and pretended to look inside. "It's gone."

I stood upright and stared at him, feeling even guiltier, if that were possible.

"Did your brother know Walter Frey?"

"What?" Oh, God. Had he jumped from point A to point C? Was Roy now on his short list of suspects for Mr. Frey's murder? "I don't know," I stammered.

His mouth pinched into a line. "I think it's better if you stay with your mother for now. And I really think you should cancel your concert tonight."

"It's not a concert. It's just a set. And I already told you. I can't."

"And staying with your mother?"

I was missing the old security of the front door of my childhood home, so his suggestion was tempting. "I can't," I said truthfully. "She'd want to know why I was there, and I can't tell her." And I didn't want to bring any more danger to her door.

"Do you have any friends?"

"No." The admission hurt. "Not anymore."

"What about Colt?"

My mouth dropped like a trap door.

He released a pained laugh. "Now you see how truly worried I am."

I really didn't want to stay with Colt, but I could see he wasn't going to let this drop. "I'll ask him."

He gave a sharp nod and looked around. "Is there any way I can convince you to file a report?"

"No."

Disappointment filled his eyes. "If your brother breaks in again or threatens you in any other way, I want you to swear you'll tell me."

"He won't."

"Not good enough, Maggie," he said with an edge in his voice. "Swear it."

Why did he care so much? He hardly knew me, but I had to admit that he was wearing me down. "Okay."

I glanced over at my purse, thinking about the bag of gold that was hidden beneath my wallet, along with the gun. I needed to find a new hiding spot, but obviously nowhere in my apartment was safe. Then again, maybe it was. Whoever had broken in probably thought they had gotten them all. Unless they knew how many bags there had been. But Brady saw the direction of my gaze and thought I was looking at the manila envelope.

"You found the report," he said.

"Thanks for getting it for me."

He held my gaze when I looked up at him. "Why am I having a hard time believing that you let this go?"

I really didn't want to lie to him anymore. "I'm fine," I said softly.

"I want to help you, Maggie. But you have to let me." Then he turned around and walked out the door, leaving a slimy feeling in my chest.

Was it wrong that I wanted to trust him? That I wanted to tell him what I knew? I had a hard time believing that he'd manufactured feelings for me so he could use me. He seemed genuinely concerned. But it was hard to ignore that he'd thought I was in danger even before my break-in, which meant he might be involved in the phone cover-up.

What the hell was I doing?

My phone rang, startling me out of my stupor. I wasn't surprised to see it was Colt.

"Is he gone?" he asked.

"He just left."

"Did they get it all?"

"All but one bag."

"Shit."

"I know."

"You didn't tell him about the gold, did you?"

"I'm not stupid, Colt."

"You are when it comes to him."

I started to protest, but maybe he had a point. At least I hadn't told him everything. "How did someone know about it?"

"Like I said, I didn't tell anyone other than Big Mike, and I swear to God he doesn't know where I got it. There's no way he could tie it to you." He paused. "What if your brother noticed the dog was gone?"

"How would he know there was gold inside?"

"Maggie, someone put the gold inside that statute. We can't ignore the fact that your brother stored that dime store ceramic dog along with a bunch of nice stuff. Doesn't that seem weird to you?"

Someone *had* put the gold there, but it had been my father. "How would Roy know I had the statue?"

But as soon as I said the words, it hit me.

Belinda.

She'd seen the pieces in the trash bag. It would explain her weird behavior at lunch, not to mention all those texts she'd sent.

But Colt was oblivious to my revelation. "Roy knows we've been messing around in the garage. Maybe he went to see if we'd disturbed anything."

"Maybe." I wondered if I should share my concern with Colt, but there was no way Belinda would betray me.

Would she?

chapter twenty

I can be at the Belles in a half hour," Colt said. "Do you want to meet there? I can drive us to the Kincaid."

I was still trying to shake the idea that Belinda had told Roy what she'd seen. But the dog had been in pieces—how would she have even recognized it? Then I remembered the dog's head had still been fairly intact. She'd even commented on it. "Sure. Sounds good."

I hung up, and since I had a few minutes, I put all my clothes back into the clothes hamper and straightened my bed. I decided to leave early and stop at the deli to pick up a sandwich for dinner, so I grabbed the envelope with the police report, folded it over, and stuffed it into my purse. Good thing I was used to carrying a large bag from when I lived in New York.

The storm had blown over without dumping any rain, but the air was cooler. I considered going back upstairs to get a heavier jacket but decided I'd warm up as I walked.

But just as I started to head toward the street, the house's back door cracked open and Miss Ava called out, "Magnolia Steele."

I fought the urge to run. "Good afternoon, Miss Ava." She didn't sound happy, but maybe I could use this opportunity to ask her about Christopher Merritt.

"Your merry-go-round of male suitors is still continuing."

"I don't have any male suitors, but you probably noticed Detective Bennett. I believe he was here twice today. Did you see someone else?"

"A shifty-looking man. He wore one of those hooded sweatshirts that covered his head and most of his face. I couldn't see anything about him other than his jacket, jeans, and his white tennis shoes." Her superior tone suggested that Brady hadn't stopped by to question her after all.

"You don't say?" I asked, trying to sound breezy. "Do you remember how tall he was?"

"About as tall as that police detective who's been at your apartment twice today." Her eyes narrowed. "Are you in some kind of trouble?"

If only she knew. "No."

But hearing her talk about the guy made my hair stand on end. While I'd seen the evidence of someone ransacking my place, hearing her description made me uneasy. I considered telling her the truth, but I worried she'd think it was too risky to rent to me. Either that or she'd want to see the police report about the break-in. Since I wouldn't let Brady file one, that made things tricky. "He's a handyman I hired to look at . . . a leaky faucet."

"If you have a leaky faucet, you're supposed to tell me. I want my own handyman to look at it. I'm not paying for your guy."

"I planned to pay for it myself. I don't want to be a troublesome tenant."

Her mouth pursed as though I'd already gone past troublesome and well into irritating.

"Did you happen to notice how long he stayed?" I asked. "I didn't have a chance to see if he fixed it."

"Maybe fifteen minutes. And I'd prefer for you not to give your key to strange men in the future."

Brady had commented that there wasn't any sign of a forced entry, but how would the intruder have gotten a key? Ava had surely rented the apartment before. Maybe he'd gotten it from a previous tenant, but I had to admit the idea seemed preposterous. Had someone had access to my own key over the last few days?

I needed to get the lock changed.

"Miss Ava, at the risk of upsetting you, I've been thinking . . ."

She narrowed her eyes. "Go on."

I was counting on the fact that she really wanted to keep me in her apartment to irritate my mother. "I was wondering if you'd changed the locks after your last tenant. After some videos were posted of me on the internet, I've attracted interest from certain . . . unsavory individuals. I'd feel safer if I had a more secure lock. And maybe one of those cameras. I'll be happy to pay for it, of course." I hoped I could afford it.

From the twist of her mouth to her narrowed eyes, she was the picture of a woman about to give an eviction notice, but to my surprise, she said in a short tone, "I've already arranged to have new locks and a deadbolt installed tomorrow morning."

"Uh . . ." I stammered. "Thank you."

"But if you give your key to any other strange-looking men, you'll be out in a day."

"Yes, ma'am." I started to walk away, then turned back, not surprised to find her still standing in the same place. "Since I'm here, I was wondering if I could ask you about Christopher Merritt."

Her face was a blank slate, but I could tell I'd taken her by surprise. "Why are you asking about Christopher Merritt?"

"I've been away for several years, so I had no idea he'd gone missing. I felt terrible when I found out."

"What makes you think I know anything about Christopher Merritt?" Her careful manner told me it wasn't a run-of-the-mill disappearance, if there even was such a thing.

I decided to use her pride to my advantage. "Miss Ava, I don't think people can take a dump in Franklin without you knowing it."

I wasn't sure how she'd react, and while shock made her mouth sag slightly, a hint of pride filled her eyes. "I may know a thing or two." She paused. "But it's quite interesting that you're asking me about Chris Merritt after asking me about your father earlier."

"Is it?" I asked. "What did people say about Mr. Merritt's disappearance?"

"They didn't say he had an affair."

"So there weren't any rumors?"

"I didn't say that."

"So what did they say?"

"That he and his wife were arguing and he took off."

Similar to my father, but not exactly the same. "Were they actually arguing?"

She stood a little bit taller. "No."

"Do you know what happened to him?"

"No." Then she slammed the door shut.

"It's been great chatting with you too," I muttered.

As I walked the few blocks into town, I mulled over everything she'd said, both now and earlier. Had Steve Morrissey had my father and his own wife killed because they were about to expose something? Chris Merritt disappeared eleven years later. Maybe he had been on the verge of confessing his knowledge about Daddy and Mrs. Morrissey? How did Steve Morrissey have so much power?

When I reached the deli, I put in an order for both Colt and myself. I guessed on what to get for him, but he seemed like the kind of guy who wouldn't complain about free food.

Momma had given me a key to the catering business, so I let myself in the front door and dragged a stool to the stainless steel table in the middle of the kitchen. I pulled out the envelope and started to look it over, but my guilt over Belinda made it difficult to concentrate. Not only had I hurt her, I'd also thought her capable of betraying me.

My paranoia was getting the better of me. My sister-in-law had always gone above and beyond to help me and be my friend.

Before I changed my mind, I sent her a text.

I'm sorry. I know I hurt you, but I hope you can forgive me. I feel terrible.

She answered back within seconds.

There's nothing to forgive, Magnolia. I know you don't understand, but you have to trust me.

There was that word again. Trust. How could people throw it around so casually? Just about every person I'd trusted had ended up hurting me. Griff. Momma. Even Daddy. Trusting someone gave them power. But it was appealing in the way many dangerous things are.

Time to read Daddy's police report and search for any threads of truth among the lies. I scanned the first document, a handwritten Missing Persons Report. The officer had taken my mother's statement (her husband had left for the evening and never returned), including a note that I had insisted my father had gone to meet a local attorney named Walter Frey. The officer had questioned Walter Frey, however, and both Frey and his wife had insisted it hadn't happened. The police had ultimately found my father's car at the Nashville airport—a piece of information I had never heard before.

Also included was the Missing Persons Report for Shannon Morrissey, which had been filed by her sister, Sydney, the day after my father's disappearance. Shannon had never shown up to their lunch date. Sydney was particularly worried because Shannon had left her two-year-old in her sister's care the previous afternoon. When Steve Morrissey was questioned, he said he'd found out that his wife was having an affair with his financial planner and that he had kicked her out the night before. Shannon's car was also found at the airport. When questioned the next day, Mr. Morrissey said a suitcase was missing, along with Shannon's passport and clothes. And one million dollars from one of his accounts, to which she wasn't supposed to have access.

The next page was a follow-up with Momma. She said there was no money missing from her joint bank account and there were no missing suitcases or clothes.

Next were copies of all of our statements—Momma's, Roy's (which stated he didn't know anything), and even mine. Days later, Momma had changed her statement to say she thought my father had run away with his mistress, Shannon Morrissey.

But Bill James, Daddy's boss, had made the most damning statement of all. He said that Daddy hadn't been acting like himself for the last few months and that Shannon Morrissey had been stopping by to see him more frequently. Bill had called Daddy into his office and told him he didn't approve of his behavior with his client's wife, and he either needed to end the relationship or find another job.

Daddy had disappeared the next week, along with one million dollars of Steve Morrissey's money.

An interview with Mandy Pinkel, Daddy's assistant, corroborated Bill James's statement about Shannon Morrissey's visits.

But if Shannon Morrissey had been working with Daddy to turn Steve Morrissey in for money laundering, it made sense that they would have had meetings about it. Sudden doubt stabbed into me: what if my brother really had seen Daddy meet Shannon one night? At the time, he'd been a twelve-year-old boy who wasn't particularly interested in his sister's life. He would neither have known nor cared what I was doing.

I quickly flipped through the pages to find Sydney's statement, but there was no sign of it. A second flip-through didn't fare any better.

Had Brady removed it, or had it not been included in the report he'd seen?

I was about to read a report about the evidence—or lack thereof—found in my father's car when the back door opened. I jolted in surprise, then lowered my hand to my purse as I swung around. It was only Colt.

"What has you so jumpy?" Colt asked.

"Nothing," I said, gathering the papers. "You just caught me off guard."

But Colt snatched the stack from my hand. "What is this?"

"It's none of your business," I said, reaching for the file.

He quickly scanned the top before turning to me with his mouth dropped open. "Your father's Missing Persons Report? Why are you looking at that?"

"Curiosity. Now give it back."

He held it over his head. "Fine. I'll give it back after you tell me about Miss Ava's Bible study."

"You've already asked. I still don't have anything to tell you."

"I guess I'll just settle in to read," he said as he plopped onto a stool.

I'd given it a lot of thought since the day before, and now I couldn't help but wonder if my suspicions of the group were partially due to my paranoia. What difference did it make if their entire meeting wasn't a Bible study? Secret, genteel women's societies weren't entirely unheard of in the South. The problems they'd referred to were probably no more sordid than someone's weedy flower bed.

"There were about fifteen women there besides Miss Ava," I said. "And they loved to gossip."

He put his elbow on the table and rested his chin on his hand, his eyes alight with mischief. "Go on."

"You're terrible."

"I've never claimed otherwise. Anything else?"

I shrugged. "I *may* have overheard some of their meeting."

"How did that come about?"

I didn't want to confess to finding the secret staircase, so I said, "I eavesdropped."

"And what did you hear?"

"Nothing that made any sense. Things about problems cropping up. Nothing specific besides Mr. Frey's murder. Then the reverend showed up. I didn't realize that reverends went to Thursday morning Bible studies."

"Me either."

I was expecting him to give me more of a fight, but he let me snatch the file back from him. As I stuffed the papers into the envelope, he said, "I had a visit from your favorite Franklin law enforcement officer earlier, about midafternoon."

"What?" The papers were only halfway inside the envelope, but that stopped me short. "Brady?" He'd told me that he was headed to an interview. I hadn't realized it had been to question Colt.

His face turned serious. "Detective Bennett to me. He was there partially on your behalf."

"*What?*" I asked in horror.

"He wanted to know about our relationship. How long I'd known you. If I had any prior arrests. He seemed particularly interested in knowing if I had any assault or domestic violence charges."

I stopped again, my eyes sinking shut as I groaned. "Oh, no. I'm sorry."

"The not-so-subtle message I received was to keep my hands off you, and I'm not talking in a biblical sense. Why would he think I'd hurt you?"

My eyes flew open. "Colt, I am so, so sorry. I never, ever insinuated that you would do anything of the sort."

"Then why would he think I did?"

"Brady came by on Wednesday night to give me an update on . . ." I paused, trying to decide how much to reveal. "The case."

"He couldn't give it to you over the phone?" he asked sarcastically. "So what happened to make him think I'd hurt you?"

Shit. What did I confess to? "Roy stopped by after you dropped me off. He was pissed, and he made a bit of a mess before he left."

Colt's face reddened. "I'm pretty damn sure there's more to it. *Detective Bennett* told me if he finds out that I hurt you, he'd deal with me without his badge and gun. *Why?*"

I cringed. "Let's just say he saw evidence that Roy had been unhappy and leave it at that." I leaned forward, holding his gaze. "But now he knows it's not you. I made sure he believed it."

He got off the stool and took several steps away, anger radiating from him. "Why the fuck didn't you tell me that your brother hurt you again?"

"What good would it do?"

"But you told *him*."

Brady. Was Colt jealous? It was far more likely that he was worried I'd put too much trust in a police officer. "Only so he'd stop harassing me to file a police report about the break-in. I lied and told him I thought Roy had broken in to steal a necklace that belonged to my mother."

"Good thinking," he grudgingly admitted.

"But I have some information about the person who ransacked my apartment."

That caught him by surprise. "*What?* How?"

"Miss Ava, of course. She saw a man with a hooded sweatshirt open my apartment door as though he had a key. He was in there for about fifteen minutes."

"Did she say anything else about him?"

"He wore jeans and white athletic shoes. She said he was as tall as Brady." When Colt narrowed his eyes, I added, "He was there twice this afternoon." Great, that wasn't any better. "He dropped off the police report while I was at lunch and then came back to investigate the break-in."

"So that narrows it down, since it only applies to about a third of the male population in the Nashville area."

"Yeah." I cocked my head. "You said I was partially the reason for his visit. What was the other?"

"He wanted to know if I had a connection to Walter Frey."

I gasped. "*What?* What did you tell him?"

"That I'd never seen him before in my life until the day you pointed him out at the Mellow Mushroom." He turned to look at me. "What's he up to, Mags?"

"They don't have any leads on Walter Frey's killer, and he's worried about me. Around lunchtime today, he pretty much admitted he didn't trust you, and then the break-in freaked him out—hell, it freaked me out—but he took it as evidence that I'm in danger."

"Are you?"

"Honestly? I don't know."

He sat back down and rubbed his hand over his mouth. Then he lowered his hand and looked me in the eyes. "What do you want to do?"

"Brady doesn't want me to be alone tonight. He wants me to stay with you."

His eyes widened. "You're shitting me."

"After I set him straight about Roy, he must have decided to trust you."

"So what do you want to do, Mags?" he repeated.

That was a very good question, but my mind reached for a distraction instead. After all, I'd had years of practice. "I want to rehearse so we don't look like fools tonight."

But I couldn't help thinking I was already a fool. I just hadn't figured out the how of it yet.

chapter
twenty-one

Colt and I stood backstage at the Kincaid, waiting for the manager to give us our cue. When he'd asked how to announce us, I'd had a moment of panic—we'd never discussed what to call ourselves—but Colt had quickly blurted out "Maggie and Colt." He'd turned to me and winked as the manager walked onto the stage. "Better to keep it simple," he said in his lazy Georgia drawl.

Our rehearsal had gone well. The biggest issue for me was learning all the lyrics, but I was used to memorizing vast amounts of lines in a short time. Even though we'd originally discussed singing no more than a few songs together, we'd unanimously decided we should sing most of the songs in the forty-five-minute set together. Somehow we'd briefly forgotten I was part of another murder investigation and possibly in danger. The thing I loved about being with Colt was how easy it was. We laughed and joked, and my heart felt light and free—even if it was only for a few hours in the safety of my mother's catering kitchen.

If our performance turned out anything like our rehearsal, we'd be golden. But I was surprised to feel the prickle of nerves as I stood to the side of the stage, eyeing the large Friday night crowd. While in some ways singing was similar to acting, it made me feel more exposed because there wasn't an obvious role to hide behind. It was like I was giving the world a glimpse into my soul.

Colt reached over and squeezed my hand. I looked into his eyes.

He winked. "You've got this."

"Is it that obvious I'm nervous?"

His gaze held mine. "It wouldn't be to most people."

I started to ask him how he could sense it, but the stage manager was already in front of the mic, saying, ". . . give a warm welcome to Maggie and Colt!"

The crowd's response was warmer than it had been at the Embassy but wasn't overly enthusiastic, not that I could blame them. No one knew who we were or what to expect from us.

I suddenly found that thrilling.

As we walked onto the stage, Colt with his guitar slung over his shoulder, I realized I could be anyone I wanted on this stage. I wasn't Magnolia Steele, failed theatre actress. I could be Maggie, country music ingénue.

Colt sat on his stool and shot me a quick glance as he adjusted his guitar. When I grinned, a smile spread across his face as he turned to the audience. "We're gonna start tonight with the song that brought us together, 'Need You Now' by Lady Antebellum."

After the intro, I sang the first female verse, and then Colt joined in for the chorus. The energy of the crowd made us even better.

For the next forty-five minutes, we sang a variety of songs, including the ballad from *Fireflies at Dawn*, which I'd sung for Brady on Main Street what seemed like an eternity ago, as well as a couple of songs Colt had written that were actually really good. Between songs, we exchanged some humorous banter, so that by the time we finished, the crowd was totally invested.

That was what I missed about the theatre. Holding the audience spellbound and pushing their emotions one way or another, sometimes with just an expression. But I also realized how much I'd used acting as an escape from my real life. Being someone else onstage kept my anxiety at bay.

When we finished, we took our bow and went backstage for Colt to put his guitar in his case. The manager had gone back onstage to introduce the next act, but he grabbed us before we left.

"You two were great. The crowd loved you and have been generous with tips. I'd be happy to have you back."

Colt finished fastening his case and stood. "Thanks. We'll get back to you."

"While you're waitin' to settle up, I know there are a few fans who'd like to buy you both a drink. And there's an agent who'd like to chat with you."

Colt gave me a questioning glance.

I knew that part of the gig was networking, and even if *I* wasn't in this for a record deal, Colt was. "Yeah, sounds good." Not to mention I wasn't in any hurry to get back to my apartment. While I reasoned that the person who had ransacked it wouldn't be back, I was still freaked out. They probably had a key, and there really wasn't anything in the apartment I could use to barricade the door. I was giving serious consideration to sneaking into Momma's house and crashing in my old bed.

Colt left his guitar backstage and we entered the main room, creating some interest as we headed to the bar. Several of the patrons knew Colt, and they gave him claps on the back while giving me appreciative grins.

Colt put his hand on the small of my back and led me to the bar. The newest group onstage was loud and a lot more rock than country, not that the crowd seemed to mind.

A man with neatly trimmed dark hair, slightly shorter than Colt, approached us and held out his hand. "I'm Justin Kasper. Do you two have an agent?"

Colt shot me a quick glance as we both shook hands with the man.

"No. But we're not usually a group."

"I know." The man lifted his beer bottle. "I was listening, and I liked what I heard." Then he waved his bottle toward the room. "And so did everyone else."

"Maggie Mae's not looking to sign with anyone," Colt said, "but I'm in the market."

Justin made a face. "You have to know that I'm interested in the two of you as a partnership." He handed Colt a card, then glanced at me. "If you change your mind, let me know."

As he walked away, I leaned into Colt's ear. "I'm sorry."

"No harm, no foul," he said, sounding more easygoing than I'd expected.

The bartender walked over and smiled. "The manager says drinks on the house for you two."

I ordered a beer. When I was in a crowd, I was über vigilant. I knew a few women who had been dosed with something through their drinks. It was a lot harder to drug a small-mouthed beer bottle that never left my hand. Here in Nashville it seemed a little paranoid, but in light of all the other threats in my life, paranoia seemed appropriate.

Several women approached us and wanted to know if we were a couple. As soon as Colt confirmed that we were only friends, they swarmed him. I sat on my stool several feet away, shaking my head indulgently while I watched him in action.

"I take it you two have an open relationship." I recognized the voice all too well.

Steeling myself, I turned to face him. "What are you doing here, Brady?"

"Enjoying the music, just like everyone else. Imagine my surprise when I discovered you were singing."

I narrowed my eyes. "I told you I was singing here."

"Okay. So I was curious." But he scanned the crowd as he talked. His gaze landed on Colt, and a slight frown tugged at his mouth.

"You're checking up on me."

He shrugged. "So it kills two birds with one stone. It made me nervous that you'd be out in such a busy place." His gaze landed on Colt again, and his disapproval was clear. Brady had expected Colt to play babysitter.

He flagged down the bartender and ordered his own beer, then turned back to face me, leaning close so he couldn't be overheard. "Have you felt unsafe? Has anyone around here made you feel uneasy?"

"You mean other than you?" I asked with a straight face.

He cringed, clearly uncomfortable.

I leaned closer and held his gaze. "Brady! I was teasing."

He still looked uncertain.

"At the risk of regretting this later, I feel better knowing you're here." It was true. While I still questioned if I could trust him, I had to wonder why he'd go to so much effort to watch over me if he didn't have my best interests in mind.

But maybe I was being naïve.

I thought he'd gloat at my admission, but while his discomfort vanished, he simply smiled and leaned his arm against the bar.

"You sang that song. The one you sang on the street a few weeks ago. It was from your musical, wasn't it?"

"Yeah. That was my big break." I turned my back to the bar and glanced up at the all-male, good ol' boy-looking band on the stage. "You said you never watched the videos—"

"I didn't."

"I'm sure you heard the rumors."

"I met you before I heard the rumors. I never gave a shit about them."

I turned to look at him, trying to determine if he was telling the truth, but the bartender interrupted the moment by returning with Brady's beer.

Brady dug his wallet out of his jeans and handed him some cash. "I can stay here and keep you company until Colt's finished *socializing*"—I was surprised he didn't choke on the word—"or . . ."

I tensed. "Or?"

"My friends would like to meet you."

"*What?*"

"I'm here with my friends. You met Owen this afternoon, but there are a few others."

"Why do they want to meet me? What do they know—or think they know?"

His eyes filled with understanding. "They know you were amazing onstage, and that I've met you before . . .

and that I like you. But with the exception of Owen, they have no idea that you're *the* Magnolia Steele."

I really didn't feel like pretending tonight. Being onstage had helped relieve a lot of my stress, and I was feeling pretty good. To go with Brady meant I'd have to put my mask back on, and it suddenly seemed like an exhausting prospect. But Colt was totally engrossed in conversation with his women about his workout routine, which meant I'd be sitting here bored and alone and probably fending off countless guys trying to hit on me. What if one of them was after something other than a night of fun? Colt was distracted, and it would be easy for someone to discreetly point a gun at me and coerce me to leave without causing a disturbance.

But even more convincing was the fact that Owen was the lead detective on Walter Frey's investigation. Getting information out of him was unlikely, but I needed to know if he'd found that note in Mr. Frey's hand. Or if someone else had taken it.

"Okay."

I was doing this for strategic reasons, but there was no ignoring the slight flip of my stomach when he instantly smiled and stood upright. Again, I expected him to gloat, but he just looked happy and relieved. "Great."

"I need to tell Colt."

A sarcastic look washed over his face. "Do you think he'll even notice you're gone?"

I glanced back and saw that Colt was—literally—surrounded by beautiful women.

I gave him a stern glare. "Very funny."

His eyes darkened. "No, actually it's not. Why do you put up with that?"

My anger flared. "My relationship with Colt is none of your business."

He scowled but gave me a curt nod.

Maybe this was a bad idea after all.

No. I just needed to be careful.

"Colt," I yelled over the racket of a not-up-to-par Dierks Bentley song as I hopped off my stool and moved closer to him. "I'll be right back."

"Where are you goin'?" he asked. Then he glanced over his shoulder and sat upright, his smirk falling off when he saw who was standing behind me. "Are you in trouble?"

"No."

He pulled back and gave me an irritated look.

I leaned close to his ear. "I know what I'm doing. I'm going to meet his friends."

"Already?" he asked in a sarcastic tone. "Doesn't that usually wait for the second or third date?"

"It's not like that." Lowering my voice, I said, "He's here with the detective who took over the murder case."

"So?"

"So. I need more details."

He gave me a long look, his eyes full of worry. "Be careful, Mags."

"I will."

"Not just with your secret."

I was about to ask him what he meant, but I already knew, and it wasn't just about digging for info—the more time I spent with Brady, the more likely I was to get hurt or entangled in something that wouldn't end well. Besides, he'd already turned back to his groupies, then ordered drinks for everyone. No wonder he was always broke.

But I had bigger things to worry about. Like how to pry information out of Owen Frasier.

chapter
twenty-two

Brady was watching me intently as I turned back toward him, and I had to wonder how much he'd picked up from my conversation with Colt. Hopefully not much.

I gave him a tight smile. "Lead the way."

I followed him through the crowd to the other side of the room. He stopped at a small table surrounded by three men and two women. "Maggie, these are a few of my friends." He pointed to the man at my right, then moved counterclockwise around the semicircle. "You already met Owen. This is Drew, Drew's wife Stacy, and Mary and her boyfriend Steve." He glanced down at me and smiled. "Everyone, this is Maggie."

I lifted my hand and gave them a small wave. "Hi."

Stacy leaned forward. "You were amazing, Maggie!"

I gave her a broad smile, deciding to fill the role of a confident young woman who *might* be interested in the man standing next to her. "Thanks."

Drew laughed. "I figured Brady was shitting us when he said he knew you." His eyes lit up with mischief. "How much did he pay you to come over and pretend to know him? It's okay, you can tell us. We'll double it."

Grinning, I shook my head. "He didn't pay me to come over. We *do* know each other."

"So tell me this," Owen said with a teasing glint. "Brady seems to think he has a chance with you, but I'd like to throw my hat into the ring if you're single. Do I stand a chance?"

"That depends," I said, reminding myself that this charming guy might not be as nice as he seemed. I, of all people, knew how easy it was to play a role. But I was playing one too, and if he wasn't what he seemed, I couldn't give him any reason to be suspicious of me. "You work for the Franklin police, don't you?"

His grin turned hopeful. "Why? You got a thing for cops?"

"The opposite," I said, taking the seat next to him and leaving Brady with nowhere to sit. Then I said in a teasing tone, "I don't date cops."

I didn't turn around to see Brady's reaction, but everyone at the table was laughing.

"Are you a professional singer?" Stacy asked.

"Nah," I said. "I just came to help Colt out tonight." I took a sip of my beer, then glanced around the table and forced a friendly smile. "Y'all been here long?"

"We caught the act before yours," Mary said. "But they weren't as good as you and Colt." She glanced up at

Brady, who had dragged over a chair and sat next to me. "Have you and Colt been singing together long?"

I could smell a thinly veiled question from a mile away, but this one seemed safe. I hadn't answered Owen's question, and she wanted to know if Colt and I were together. Brady's friends might be giving him a hard time, but they had his back and wanted to make sure I didn't hurt him. I could respect that. "No, we haven't," I said. "Believe it or not, this is only the third time we've sang together, if you count our rehearsal earlier."

"You said that one song was from the musical *Fireflies at Dawn*," Mary continued. "Isn't that the play where the actress—"

Brady took a sip of his beer and leaned back in his seat. "Would you believe that I was one of the few people lucky enough to see their first performance? She and Colt sang in a hole-in-the-wall bar, and she sounded amazing."

"Is that how you met her?" Stacy asked Brady.

I glanced back at him. "Yeah, Brady. Tell them how we met."

He laughed and glanced at his friends, then turned to me with a grin. "It was at the deli downtown. She has the most beautiful eyes in the world, and when I grabbed her bag by mistake, I knew I had to get to know her better."

His eyes held mine, and his smile was huge. He was overselling it, as though purposely embellishing his story for entertainment. But I had to wonder how much of what he said was true. He'd made no secret of his interest in me.

I broke his gaze and turned to his group, grinning like it was the funniest thing I'd heard in ages.

Steve groaned. "Dude, that is the cheesiest line ever."

"You stole her *sandwich?*" Mary asked.

Brady laughed. "What can I say? She had me flustered."

"*You*, flustered?" Drew asked.

"So you were taken with her eyes and stole her sandwich," Stacy teased. "But have you been out?"

Brady sipped his beer, then grinned and said, "The timing hasn't been right." His grin spread and he snuck a glance at me. "But I'm hopeful."

"No pressure." Mary laughed, then winked at me. "Hold your ground, Maggie. Brady gets just about everything he wants. Make him work for it."

I smiled playfully as I lifted my bottle. "I'm not looking for a relationship right now, but if I change my mind, I'll keep my options open."

The group broke out into uproarious laughter, and even though it was at Brady's expense, he was still grinning and having a good time. I'd dated plenty of guys who couldn't handle it when people took pot shots at their egos. Brady obviously had the confidence to take a few hits, which only made him more intriguing.

But Brady Bennett was off limits, and I needed to remember that.

I stayed with them longer than I'd intended, especially since I didn't get the chance to ask Owen anything pertaining to the case, but his friends were fun. They teased Brady mercilessly, and he gave as good as he got. The unspoken rule seemed to be that I was off limits. I suspected they knew how much he liked me and didn't want to scare me off.

I'd sat with them for about a half hour when Brady said he had to go to the restroom. After he left, Owen said he was going to make a drinks run.

Sensing an opportunity, I said, "I'll go with you. I need to check in with Colt."

"Is he your brother?" Stacy asked, taking advantage of the fact that Brady wasn't there to head off anyone's questions.

I grinned. "No. He's definitely not my brother."

Owen gathered everyone's orders, and the two of us headed to the bar. The band after Colt and me had ended their set and the new one hadn't started yet, so I decided to take advantage of the lower decibel level as we walked.

"So you and Brady are friends?" I asked. "But not partners."

He gave me a meaningful look. "I know his partner Martinez came across as a total hardass when you met her, but she's usually not that intense."

I had to wonder what he'd heard about my "performance" during her interrogation. Brady's partner had asked a lot of questions based on the information I'd given him the night before, and I'd played a cold, calculating bitch. "And why would I care about Brady's partner?"

"Because if you're part of Brady's world, you'll have to get used to having her around."

My mouth lifted into a smug grin. "And who says I want to be part of Brady's world?"

He shrugged, but his eyes sparkled with mischief. "Fair enough."

We stopped at the counter and Owen placed his orders, then turned to me.

"Water."

He seemed surprised, but he didn't question me. While we waited for the bartender, I cast a glance at Colt, who had narrowed down his group to two women.

"You're not really dating that guy," Owen said, lifting his finger and pointing to Colt.

I could lie, but I didn't see the point. "Colt and I are . . . complicated."

"But you're letting Brady think you are?"

"That's complicated too."

He nodded. "Fair enough."

"How long have you and Brady been friends?"

"About eight years," he said with a grin. "We went through police academy together."

"So that's why he called you the other night," I said. "Because he can trust you."

His smile faded. "He wanted to make sure you were treated fairly this time. What you went through with the Goodwin murder . . . it bothered him. A lot."

I'd already suspected as much, but the confirmation was nice. "So if you had shown up first and I didn't know Brady, would I be under suspicion?"

Confusion washed over his face. "Why would you be? I know it's odd that you stumbled upon two bodies in such a short period of time, but there was nothing to tie you to this one."

I stared at him for a few seconds before it clicked. Brady hadn't told him that I had arranged to meet Mr. Frey that night. But why not? Was he trying to make up for what happened with Martinez? What if word got out that he'd covered it up? But I kept my face perfectly emotionless while all of that flitted through my head.

"And you think it was a robbery?" I asked.

"Yeah. Wrong time, wrong place. His wife said he said he was going out, but she had no idea where or why. After talking with her, I could see why the guy would go someplace like that to drink. Why would you think you'd be a suspect?"

I shrugged, trying to play it off. "I didn't have a very solid alibi, and then there's the fact I found the body."

"What are you talking about?" He pointed his thumb over his shoulder. "Colt over there is your alibi. Both he and Brady confirmed that you were there to sing. When you went to the restroom before you sang, you heard a noise out back, and you found Walter Frey when you went to investigate."

Why hadn't Brady told me about the lie? What about Chuck the bartender? He knew I'd gone to the bar to meet Mr. Frey. And what about that note?

I suddenly felt sick.

"Maggie," Owen said. "Is there something I don't know?"

"What?" I blinked up at him, looking confused. "Of course not." I shook my head. "Sorry. Talking about this makes me relive the whole thing all over again."

Colt glanced over, and after taking one look at my face, he whispered something to his companions and hopped off his stool.

"I still need to talk to Colt," I said to Owen. "If you'll wait, I'll help you carry the drinks back."

"Sounds good," he said, but he kept his attention on digging out his wallet.

Colt met me halfway. Putting his hand on my shoulder, he leaned into my ear. "What happened?"

"Did you and Brady discuss your statement about the night at the Embassy?" I blurted out, looking up at him to gauge his reaction.

His eyes hardened. "The only discussion I've had with your detective was this afternoon when he threatened to kick my ass. Why?"

"What did you tell them?"

"That I found you at the bar and invited you to sing with me."

"You didn't say that I specifically came to the bar to sing with you? Or that I found Walter Frey right before our set because I heard something near the restrooms?"

"No. I told them what I just told you."

I was certain he was telling the truth. Which meant Brady had lied on an official report. Did Owen suspect?

He'd looked genuinely confused when I'd asked if I could be a suspect.

But then I realized this was why Brady had told me not to talk to anyone—police included. I was in the middle of a cover-up.

Why?

Colt's jaw set. "What's going on, Mags?"

Casting a glance at Colt's pouting admirers, I said, "I'm going to ask Brady to take me home."

His eyes flew wide. "Do you really think that's a good idea? I can see you're shaken up about something."

"Brady's friend Owen has no idea that I was there to see Walter Frey. Brady lied in his report."

Colt rubbed his jaw, looking back at the women who were still waiting for him. "Why would he do that?"

"I don't know, but what worries me is that other people know it's not true, like the bartender and Belinda. What if it gets out?"

"Belinda won't tell anyone."

"What about the bartender?"

Worry filled his eyes.

"I have to find out why Brady lied."

"Isn't it obvious? He wants in your pants."

"By lying on a police report? That could get him fired. I'm definitely not *that* good in bed."

I expected a crass retort—I needed a joke right now. Instead, he studied me for a moment and then nodded. "It's a good idea to talk to him. Just be careful. Call or text if you need me."

I stood on my tiptoes and kissed him on the cheek. "Thanks, Colt. I don't know what I'd do without you."

A smile spread across his face. "Of course you don't. Let me know what you find out." Then he was off, and the girls squealed—actually squealed—as he walked toward them.

Good Lord.

Owen was waiting for me, several glasses in his hands, but he'd left a couple of beer bottles and a glass of water on the counter.

I picked up the beers and turned my back to the bar.

"You didn't get your drink." He smiled at me, and although it was innocent enough, the hair on my neck stood on end. Something about his mood seemed to have shifted, though I couldn't put my finger on it.

I'd completely forgotten about my water. Not that I wanted it anyway—it had been sitting there for a few minutes, within reach of anyone.

"That's okay," I said. "I've got my hands full."

"You walked all the way over here; you should at least get your own drink." He put his drinks on the counter, grabbed the two beer bottles and cradled them to his side with his arm, and then picked up the remaining drinks. There were only two left for me to carry—one mixed drink and the water. "What kind of guy would I be if I let you help, but we left your drink behind?"

"Thanks." I picked up both glasses, forcing a smile.

We headed back to the table, and I stayed close to Owen, deciding to press my luck. "I know you've determined Mr. Frey was killed in a robbery, but have you figured out who did it?"

"No. We don't have any suspects yet. Unfortunately, the building didn't have any security cameras and absolutely no witnesses have turned up."

Brady had already told me that. "What about the note?" I asked, deciding to throw caution to the wind. I wanted to see his reaction since the note hadn't been listed on the report.

Owen hesitated for a moment, then gave me a curious look. "What note?"

I shook my head, feigning confusion. "I'm sure it's nothing, but I thought I saw a note."

He stopped and studied me. "What kind of note?"

He either hadn't seen it or was pretending that he hadn't, so I needed to back away from this as smoothly as possible. "I thought I saw a piece of paper next to him, but I probably imagined it. I *was* pretty traumatized." But not enough to have dreamed up the note. The question wasn't if there had been a note—it was who had taken it.

But Owen continued to watch me. "Did you see anything on the note?"

"No, like I said, it looked like a piece of paper." I cringed. "But I was pretty shaken up, so I probably read more into it than was there. Forget I said anything."

He gave me a patronizing smile. "It was probably a piece of trash that blew away in the wind."

"Yeah," I agreed. "You're probably right." Only, Brady had said the exact same thing before blowing off the idea.

I was starting to rethink my decision to see if he would take me home.

Brady was standing next to his chair when we got back. He took the drinks from my hands and then leaned close to my ear. "I wasn't sure you were coming back."

I looked up at him, suddenly wary. "I wouldn't just leave like that." But I quickly glanced away and sat back in my chair. I needed some time to think.

"Hey," Stacy called out. "I know you're busy making goo-goo eyes at Maggie, but maybe can you hand me my drink?" she said, harassing Brady.

He handed her the glass, then looked around the table with my water in his hand.

"That's Maggie's," Owen said, pointing from the glass to me.

Brady set it down in front of me and took his seat, and I told myself to calm down and consider this situation rationally. Was it as simple as Colt had suggested? Had Brady lied to protect me? It didn't make sense—after all, we barely knew each other—but he *had* promised he wouldn't let me be railroaded into being a suspect again. I couldn't believe that was the reason, though. So what was going on?

He and his friends carried on with their conversation, but I tuned them out, trying to put all the pieces together. Was Brady protecting me from someone in the police department?

"Maggie?" Mary asked, and the way she said it made me realize I'd missed part of the conversation.

I had no good reason not to drink it, but I wasn't about to accept his challenge. I stood. "Brady can stay. I can find a ride on my own."

But Brady stood when I did. "No, I'm ready to go too."

Drew sat up straighter, wearing a huge grin. "You never go home before midnight."

Stacy shoved her husband's arm. "Shut up, Drew!" Then she smiled up at me. "It was great getting to meet you, Maggie. We hope to see you again."

"And Brady's hoping to see even more of her now."

Stacy gasped and shoved Drew harder.

Brady grimaced. "And *that's* our cue to leave. Drew's had so much to drink he's lost his internal censor."

"That's right," Drew said. "Shit's about to get real."

Shaking his head, Brady gave a wave to the table. "I'll see you all later, and Owen, I'll see you tomorrow."

Owen didn't look happy, but he lifted his beer in salute as we left.

"Do you need to get anything?" Brady asked as we headed to the bar.

"My purse is in Colt's truck."

Colt was still close to the bar with his new friends, but he looked up and watched us walk toward him. "I need to get my bag."

Colt shot Brady a glare, but handed me his keys.

It was awkward having Brady trail me out to the parking lot, and I waffled between feeling safer in his presence and overwhelmed by all the unknowns.

"I'm sorry," I said. "I'm really tired. It's been a long day. I'm thinking about calling it a night." I started to reach for my water glass before remembering that I hadn't had my eyes on it the whole night. As I pulled my hand away, I noticed Owen watching me from the corner of his eye.

"Do you think Colt's ready to leave?" Brady asked, watching me closely. "You rode with him, right?"

My original plan to ask Brady to take me home no longer seemed wise. And to make matters even more complicated, I wasn't sure I even wanted to stay at my place. My mother's house was looking pretty good.

I scanned the bar area and, sure enough, Colt was still flirting with his two very attentive companions. "Colt seems a little preoccupied. I can just get an Uber."

Brady turned to me. "I can take you home, Maggie."

I was torn between wanting answers and protecting myself. But bottom line, I had a hard time believing that this man watching me with so much concern in his eyes was capable of hurting me.

I really hope I don't regret this.

"Are you sure you don't mind?"

"You guys can't leave yet," Owen shouted loud enough for the entire table and several surrounding ones to hear over the noise. "It's not even eleven. Maggie just needs to get her second wind." He shoved my glass toward me. "Down this water, and then you'll be good as new."

He held my gaze and fear slithered down my spine. Could I trust Owen?

I quickly grabbed my purse from under the passenger seat, then hurried back to the bar to return Colt's keys. Before I knew it, Brady was leading me back out to the parking lot.

I spotted his car, a dark, generic sedan that I recognized from Tuesday night. I suddenly knew one way to help me feel in control. "I'm driving," I said, turning around and walking backward as I reached out my hand.

"I'm not drunk, Maggie."

"I've seen you drink two beers in about forty-five minutes. I told you I can protect myself, and this is me proving it." I stretched out my hand farther. "Keys." I'd feel a whole lot better about this situation if I were in control.

He turned serious. "I would never drive drunk or even buzzed. I barely touched my last beer."

"Keys."

He dug into his pocket and placed them in my palm. "It's important you know that I would never hurt you."

He had no idea how much I was counting on that. How would he react when I started asking questions? "I guess we'll find out if that's true or not."

Brady looked like he wanted to argue the point. Instead, he walked to the driver's door and opened it, then gestured for me to get in. Once I was behind the wheel, he walked around and got into the passenger seat. I turned over the engine, and classical music filtered through the speakers. That surprised me. Brady didn't seem like a classical music guy, but it only reminded me that I didn't know him very well.

"Where are we headed?" he asked as he reached for the volume knob and turned it down.

"My apartment." Once I got there, I'd pack a bag and head to Momma's.

He watched me, his cop face returning.

Dammit.

I adjusted the seat and mirror, then backed out of the spot and headed out of the parking lot. Thank God I'd paid attention when Colt had driven to the club hours earlier.

We were silent until I pulled onto 65 South, and a male radio announcer's voice spoke, reminding listeners that the NPR station was collecting donations.

When a Beethoven sonata began to play, Brady turned to me. "Why did you really want to leave?" he asked, his tone neutral.

I shot him a glance. "I told you. I'm tired."

"Something happened when you and Owen went to get drinks. You were different when you came back. So was he."

So much for the element of surprise with my questions.

We drove in silence again before he said, "You're not driving because you think I drank too much. You feel like things are out of control, and this is your way of taking charge of the situation."

Fear raced through my blood. How had he deduced that?

"You're scared of something, Magnolia. I'm trying to figure out who or what it is, but you're making it damn difficult."

"Maybe there's nothing to figure out. Maybe I'm scared because you told me I was in danger."

"No. You were scared before that. Hell, you were *terrified* the first two times I ran into you weeks ago."

"Of course I was. I was a person of interest in a murder investigation."

"No. You looked like you were running from the murderer yourself."

My heart began to race, and I struggled to catch my breath. He wasn't that far from the truth. "That's ridiculous. Amy was the murderer, and I was never scared of her."

"That's just it. I don't think she was the one you were running from."

How was he coming up with this theory? I had to get control of this situation. Fast.

"Maggie, I want to help you," he pleaded, turning in his seat to face me. "Let me *help* you."

"And here I thought you already were," I said in a snotty tone. "You said you showed up tonight to make sure I was safe. Was that a lie to try to get me to sleep with you? Because I'm not going to your place."

"No. I'm honestly worried about you, and I think you know it." He paused and lowered his voice. "But I know what you're doing. You're trying to get me off track so I'll stop asking what you're hiding."

"How can you know that? You hardly know me."

"I suspect *no one* knows you. Not really."

"And how have you surmised that?" I asked, ramping up my bitchiness. It was the strongest weapon in my arsenal, but it wasn't even making a dent in his calm exterior.

"From watching you. From our conversation the night you came to the police station. The way you answered my questions, both about your life and who had hurt you. You're very good. Very careful. And I suspect you've fooled just about everyone."

I felt everything spiraling out of control, and my panic threatened to take over. "And what exactly do you think I've fooled everyone about? You think I'm some kind of con artist? Like everyone accused my father of being?"

"*No.* I think you've hidden how terrified you are."

"I'm not terrified of anything," I said, my voice rising. "Except of what *you're* hiding from *me!*"

"What the hell are you talking about?"

"You hid the fact that I was meeting Walter Frey at the Embassy. Why would you do that?"

I turned to gauge his reaction—shock filled his eyes, quickly replaced by determination. "I already told you why."

"Your answer was bullshit, Brady. Does Owen know?"

He hesitated. "He knows what I told him."

"Does he suspect you lied?"

His pause was longer this time. "He knows I haven't handled this in the usual way, but I'm sure he attributes it to the fact that I'm interested in you."

"He's not asking questions?"

"No."

But Owen did know *something*, and based on his reaction, I was sure he'd seen the note. Maybe he was even the one who'd confiscated it and the phone. Had Owen taken Brady at his word until I'd brought it up? Did he suspect me of something now? "What happens if he finds out you lied? What happens if it gets out that I *did* know Walter Frey?"

"*It won't.*"

"What aren't you telling me, Brady?"

"What aren't you telling *me*?" He leaned closer. "I know you think you're in control, Magnolia, but you're missing things. I *let* you take my car keys—because I know how to play the game too. I let you think you were in charge so you would be more at ease so I could ask questions. And if you missed that, what other dangers are you putting yourself in?"

I shot him a look, gripping the steering wheel with both hands so he wouldn't see me shaking. "You think you let me *think* I'm in charge?" I was proud of the edge in my voice—the way it hid my fear.

Then, before he could say another word, I checked the rearview mirror and whipped the car across three lanes of traffic on the interstate, barely making the exit.

"Who's in charge now, Brady?"

He braced himself against the dashboard. "Holy shit, Magnolia!"

Ignoring him, I barely slowed at the stop sign, thankful it was late enough for there to be hardly any traffic. I turned left through a red light, the tires squealing in protest.

"What the hell are you doing?" Brady shouted.

"Do you still think you're controlling me, Brady?" I shot back, pushing the gas pedal and gunning the car across the bridge. I whipped into the back of a hotel parking lot, then slammed the car into park. After turning off the engine, I scrambled out of the car and dug my cell phone out of my pocket.

Brady bolted out of the car, his hands raised in the air in a sign of surrender. "Okay, obviously wrong way to try to get my point across."

My fingers were shaking as I tried to unlock my phone. Who should I call to come get me? Pure panic had flooded my head. I knew I was acting irrationally. *I knew it*, yet I was powerless to stop. I felt trapped and ready to lash out. "I want an answer and not some bullshit generic *I'm protecting you*." I took a breath. "Do you think I killed Walter Frey?"

"No!"

"Then why did you lie?" When he didn't answer, I put my hands on my hips and stomped my foot. "You're messing with *my* life. I have a right to know, dammit!"

He put both of his hands on top of his head and began to pace along the length of the car. He lowered his hands as he turned to face me. "I'll tell you," he said, though he still looked torn, "but you have to give me something."

"Give you *what?*"

"You're hiding something, probably *several* somethings. You agree to give me one credible piece of information, and I'll tell you why."

I turned away to think. I could lie, but I didn't want to do that. What would I tell him, though? Twisting around to study his face, I said, "If you give me a bullshit answer, not only will I not give you anything, I'll walk away and never speak to you again."

"Fine." He moved in front of me. "But we're not discussing this out in the open. Let's do it in the car."

I narrowed my eyes. "I'm still driving."

The corners of his mouth twitched. "Yes, Maggie. You're in control."

"Don't you fucking patronize me."

He sighed. "That came out wrong. You have the potential to screw me over in this deal since I'm giving you my information first. You really are in control."

I wasn't so sure I believed him, but I let it go and walked back to the car, getting behind the steering wheel.

Brady walked around to the passenger side, and once he closed the door, he took a deep breath and then pushed it out. "When I said I'm trying to protect you, I meant it, but not from who you think." He turned to me. "Maggie, you have to swear to keep this to yourself. You can't tell your mother. Or Colt. Not anyone. Swear it."

"I swear."

He rubbed his forehead as though trying to decide whether he should follow through. "I'm not sure who I can trust," he said, looking through the windshield.

"What does that mean?"

"Someone in the department is dirty. But I'm not sure who."

I had a pretty good idea, but I didn't think he wanted to hear it. "You didn't tell Owen, did you?"

"I think it's safer if he doesn't know."

"How does it involve me?"

"I don't know for certain it does. It's just a hunch, but after Detective Holden tried to railroad you, I think it's a legit concern."

"So Holden is the one who's dirty."

He shook his head. "No. He may be, but . . ."

"Why do you think someone's dirty?"

He shook his head. "That's for me to worry about, but I'm sure it's credible. In the meantime, maybe you should go somewhere on vacation. Or visit a friend in New York."

"For how long?"

"I don't know."

"Indefinitely?"

He didn't answer.

"I could leave for a few days, maybe a week, but that's it. I can't leave my mother."

"You're no good to her dead, Maggie."

"If someone was going to kill me, don't you think they already would have?" Which made me wonder if it was safe to go home to the apartment after all. "I'm not going anywhere."

"Do you believe me?"

"Yeah." Because I already suspected it was Owen.

"So you owe me information."

I still hadn't decided what to tell him. Part of me wanted to tell him everything, but I didn't trust him enough to go that far. And what happened to me ten years ago was out.

How about if I gave him a real case to investigate? Because if he solved it, he might find answers to my father's disappearance.

"Christopher Merritt."

His brow furrowed. "Who is that?"

I turned on the engine, and the radio announcer's voice filled the space, reporting the local news.

"Magnolia. Give me more than that."

"*Wait.*" The radio announcer was talking about a missing Nashville man, and the hair on the back of my neck stood on end. I reached for the volume knob to turn it louder.

"*Magnolia.*"

He reached for the knob, and I pushed his hand away. "*Listen.*"

The male announcer continued, "—called to the scene of an abandoned car, left running in the middle of this downtown Nashville parking garage. Nashville police aren't releasing much, but they have confirmed that the car belongs to a Nashville dentist, Geraldo Lopez."

Another man was missing, and once again, it was my fault.

chapter twenty-three

I sucked in a breath, and Brady's eyes widened as he studied me.

"His staff says he left for lunch and never returned," the radio announcer said. "The police suspect foul play and are asking for leads from the public. We'll report more information as soon as we have it."

I started to hyperventilate.

"Magnolia?" Brady asked in alarm. He put his hand on my shoulder. "Do you know him?"

Tears stung my eyes as I nodded.

Understanding washed over his face, followed by horror. "Oh shit. It's the dentist. The one you saw with your father."

I nodded, trying to catch my breath.

"You remembered his name."

"Yes." My face tingled, and I cupped my hands in front of it as I tried to regain control.

He was silent for a moment. "*Oh, fuck.* You went to see him."

I started to freak out even more as Brady put together the connection.

"Okay. Okay," he said, leaning his head back against the armrest. He took several breaths, then said, "I'm going to find out what's going on with the investigation, but I need to place a call to my friend in the Nashville Police Department." Brady pulled out his phone and called his friend while I tried to figure out what I was going to tell him. He'd insist on telling Owen, but I wasn't sure that was a good idea. Brady trusted Owen and he sure wasn't going to listen to a warning from a woman he hardly knew. I was going to have to get him to agree to keep this a secret until we figured out who to trust.

Brady hung up and turned to me with a grave look in his eyes. "My friend says a 911 call was placed around noon today. A woman found Lopez's car running in the parking garage. The driver-side door was open, and there was a small amount of blood on it."

"Do they have any ideas about what happened?"

"No. The camera that covered that area had been knocked out about fifteen minutes before the call was made. It was premeditated."

"Like Walter Frey," I whispered.

"Maggie, I need to know what you know."

"Who says I know anything?"

His eyes narrowed. "Don't bullshit me. A man's life might depend on what you can tell me."

Dr. Lopez's insistence that the police couldn't be trusted looped in my head.

"Magnolia!"

"You can't tell anyone."

"No." He shook his head. "I can't agree to that."

"Then I'm not telling you anything. You said yourself that someone in the police department is dirty. What if there are multiple someones? You have no idea who to trust, and I don't trust any of them. I barely trust you."

"What have I done to make you distrust me?"

"You lied about my involvement in Walter Frey's case. You turned me in to your partner."

"Dammit, Magnolia."

"You either promise, or I tell you nothing."

He flung the door open, climbed out, and began to pace again.

Was I doing the right thing? All I knew was to trust my instinct, and it told me to tell Brady, but no one else. Sighing, I turned off the motor and got out too, standing at the back of the car as I watched him.

"Fine," he said, sounding resentful. "Tell me."

"That's not good enough. I want your promise." I was counting on Brady Bennett being a man of his word.

"I promise," he grunted.

I understood his resentment, but I wasn't going to let that sway me. "Christopher Merritt was an accountant. He worked with Walter Frey. He also knew my father. Christopher Merritt disappeared three years ago."

"*What?* How do you know this?" He gasped. "Oh shit. The dentist."

"I went to see him at his office this morning."

"What did Lopez tell you?"

"Not much. He gave me Christopher Merritt's name." I considered telling him more about Dr. Lopez's suspicions of the police, but since Owen was heading up the investigation into Walter Frey's murder, I wasn't sure Brady would believe it. "Dr. Lopez, my father, Walter Frey, and Christopher Merritt had been working together on something. They answered to someone, but Dr. Lopez didn't know who."

"So this thing spans fourteen years?"

"Yes. But that's not all," I said, deciding to tell him as much as I could. "I also talked to Shannon Morrissey's sister."

He watched me for a second. "Did she have anything helpful?"

"Yes. She said Shannon was suspicious of her husband's behavior. She suspected money laundering, and she and my father were supposed to go to the county prosecutor the day after their disappearance."

Brady shook his head. "I didn't see any of that in the report."

"I didn't either."

"Do you think she's making it up?"

"No. She looked terrified and insisted I leave it alone. She thinks Steve Morrissey killed my father and her sister. She's certain he killed Walter Frey for coming to talk to me. Then Dr. Lopez . . ."

"He might be coming for you next."

Where was Dr. Lopez now? Probably dead. But Brady *had* said a man's life might depend on my information.

"Do you think Dr. Lopez is still alive?" I asked with a shaky voice.

"Do you know that he's *not?*"

Tears stung my eyes. "I think he's dead."

"At least let me tell Owen."

"No one."

"He's my friend. I can trust him."

"No."

Brady grunted his frustration and began to pace again, rubbing the back of his neck. After nearly half a minute, he stopped and looked at me. "What if you call in an anonymous tip?"

"What am I supposed to say?"

"Say Walter Frey's murder is related to Geraldo Lopez's disappearance. Maybe even say it's tied to the accountant's disappearance."

"They'll trace my call."

Without a word, he got into the car on the passenger side, and when he came back, he had an ancient-looking cell phone in his hand.

"It's a burner. No record tying it to anyone. You can call from this."

I narrowed my eyes. "Why do you have a burner phone?"

He held it out to me. "Use it."

I took the phone but hesitated, wondering if it was some kind of trap, but I had to do something to help Dr. Lopez.

"Call the crime tip line." He spouted off the number, and I entered it into the phone. "Don't leave your name; just tell them you think it's related."

I nodded. "Okay." I placed the call, gave the person the information, and then hung up before she could ask questions. I glanced up at Brady, feeling guilty over the conflict in his eyes. "I need to call Sydney."

"Who's Sydney?"

"Shannon's sister."

"Do you have her number?"

"No."

"What's her last name?"

"Crowley. She owns Tender Darlings Daycare."

He started typing on his phone and then rattled off a phone number. Sydney answered after a few rings, sounding sleepy. "Hello?"

"Sydney, this is Magnolia Steele. I think you're in danger."

"What? What happened?" She sounded much more awake.

"Dr. Lopez is missing."

"Who?"

"The fourth man. I met with him this morning, and I just heard on the news that he's missing."

She was silent for a moment. "I'm leaving town."

"That's probably a good idea."

"You should too."

I glanced up at Brady. "No. I'm not running."

"I warned you that you were stirring up shit. You should have left this alone."

I had to wonder if she was right, but it was too late to fix things now. I could only do damage control. "Let me know when you get somewhere safe."

"And tie my phone to yours?" she demanded. "Haven't you done enough damage already?"

"It's a burner. It can't be tied to me. Please, Sydney. I just want to know that you're safe."

But she hung up.

I handed the phone back to Brady, suffocating in guilt. How many people's lives had I destroyed in my quest for answers? For justice?

"You shouldn't stay at your apartment tonight," Brady said.

"I planned to stay at my mother's."

"I'm not sure you should stay there either. If someone is looking for you, they're probably going to look there next."

Fear raced through my blood, but anger blazed up in its wake. "I can't just leave my mother there unprotected if someone might go looking for me there!"

"Then let me tell Owen. He can help protect you *and* your mother."

"No." I didn't trust the man near me, let alone my mother. What if someone took her next?

"Dammit, Magnolia!"

I steeled my back and gave him a fierce gaze. "No. I don't trust anyone. *I'll* protect her."

"And how the hell do you propose you're going to do that?" When I didn't answer, he shook his head. "No. I'll watch over you both. I'll sleep on the sofa tonight, and we'll revisit this tomorrow."

I wanted to argue with him, but I was too exhausted. Not about him sleeping on the sofa—that gave me more reassurance than felt comfortable. But if he thought I might change my mind about talking to Owen, he would be sadly mistaken.

I only hoped I could trust him to keep his word.

chapter
twenty-four

When I pried my eyes open the next morning, I was lying on my old bed, still wearing the dress I'd worn last night and twisted in the linens. I blinked, momentarily confused, before the previous night came rushing back.

Geraldo Lopez was missing. I'd told Brady more than I probably should have. Brady had slept on my mother's sofa.

Oh crap. Brady was downstairs on my mother's sofa.

The clock on the nightstand read 8:06, and my mother was routinely up by seven.

I had a lot of explaining to do.

But when I got downstairs, I was hit with a delicious smell of something savory, reminding me that I hadn't eaten since early the evening before. Momma was sitting at the breakfast table drinking a cup of coffee while staring out the windows at the woods, and there was no sign of Brady.

"Did you sleep well?" she asked, her back still to me.

I grabbed a mug and poured a cup of coffee. "You're not gonna ask why I'm here?"

"I figured you had your reasons. There's a breakfast casserole in the oven."

I pulled the dish out of the oven and served myself a piece before I sat next to her. Had Brady snuck out before my mother got up? I'd left my cell phone upstairs.

"Your new place not everything you thought it would be?"

"It's being fumigated."

"Your car's not here."

"Someone gave me a ride."

"The police detective who questioned me about your father?" She turned to look at me with raised brows. "I saw him sneaking out this morning." A grin tugged at her lips. "He offered to come back and give you a ride to your car, but I told him that wasn't necessary."

Oh crap. "I can explain."

She waved her hand, looking slightly amused. "I don't want to know. Are you working at your other job this morning?"

"Yeah. From ten to two—until I need to come work for the Belles."

Her grin fell as she picked up her coffee and stared out the window into the trees.

I used to love them too, but now I couldn't so much as look at them without remembering *that* night. My whole life was a nightmare, but I was the one who'd brought this current one to our doorstep. It wasn't fair to my mother. Especially since she'd warned me to let it go.

She turned to me. "I know you, girl. Drama follows you like a swarm of flies follows a pig in a sty. That detective was here last night watching over you because you've stirred up shit."

"*Momma.*"

"And the personal touch is because you also draw men like flies. Always did."

"Momma," I said, feeling exhausted. It was clear she was only getting warmed up, so I prepared myself for another character berating.

"You've always been *so damn independent*, even when you were a girl, never wanting a lick of help. The only person you'd ever let help you was your father, and after he left . . ." She took a sip of her coffee, and her tone changed. "You wouldn't let me help you, Magnolia, and I suppose that's my fault."

I stared at her in shock. "What are you talking about?"

She looked into my eyes. "I know something happened that night of your graduation. I was so terrified when no one knew where you were. It was like your father all over again. He'd brought his own problem on himself, and you're so much like him, I was sure you'd brought something down on yourself too." She shook her head. "You were no angel, Magnolia."

I should have been pissed that she was rehashing my slightly rebellious teenage years, but shock left little room for other emotions. This was uncharted territory for us. "I know."

"I'd lost your father. I couldn't lose you too, and I was so *angry*. How could God take you from me too? How could you be so careless? But then you stumbled into the house covered in mud and looking like a drowned rat, and all of my anger was still there, burning like a furnace inside me, and it rushed out. So I lashed out at you, even though something deep in my head registered something wasn't right. Something had happened." She took a breath. "I could see it in your eyes. You were terrified."

I held my breath. I couldn't let her try to pry this mystery apart, yet I could see that she needed to get this off her chest. Momma was dying and she was trying to make things right.

"I sent you to bed, thinking I'd be calm enough to discuss what happened in the morning, but then all kinds of things rushed through my mind about the horrible things that could have happened to you. Except you were already at home and asleep in your bed, so my mind twisted your disappearance the night before into a personal affront to me."

"Momma—"

She shook her head, her eyes narrowed. "No. It didn't make sense, but I rationalized it anyway. When I saw you that morning, I knew I needed to calm down before I found out the truth, so I left for work. Tilly took me to task for the cruel things I'd said to you. I knew I was in the wrong, but I'm a proud woman, and it's hard for me to apologize. So I planned to take you to dinner to tell you how sorry I was and find out what really happened, but you were gone."

Tears welled in my eyes. "It's okay, Momma."

"No, Magnolia. It's not okay. Nothing was okay after you left." Her voice cracked. "I had no idea where you were. You refused to answer your phone. I filed a Missing Persons Report, and the police found your car at the airport. Just like your father." She paused and took a breath. "Days later, you finally sent a text saying you'd left, and I knew I'd deserved it. I'd brought it on myself. But I still hoped . . ." She released a hiccup. "I always hoped you'd come home."

Was that why she hadn't done anything to my room? Why she'd kept my car?

"I'm a fool, Magnolia. I always believed family comes first, but I'm an even bigger fool because I let my anger get the better of me, and it cost me my daughter."

"I'm back now, Momma. We're getting there, don't you think?"

"Your father was a fool too. He was idealistic to think that some wrongs were so heinous they needed to be righted. I thought he was on a fool's errand, and I made no effort to hold back my disapproval. We quarreled the day he disappeared, but even though I knew I was wrong, I couldn't bring myself to apologize. I'll carry that shame to my grave soon enough."

"Daddy loved you, and he knew you loved him. He understood you."

She nodded and a tear spilled down her cheek. "You're more like him than I can take some days. You're on a fool's errand too." I started to protest, but she held up her hand. "I'm supposed to die before you, Magnolia. A mother's not supposed to bury her child, but if you keep pursuing this nonsense, you'll be in the ground before me."

A lump formed in my throat. "I'm sorry."

She shook her head and stood. "You need to do what you think is right, Magnolia. This is bigger than me. Just be careful."

My stomach twisted. Could I do this to her? Did I have a choice? I'd started this snowball rolling, and I was pretty sure it had picked up enough steam that there was no stopping it now.

She got up and took the cup to the sink. "I'll be ready to drop you off at your apartment in about twenty minutes." Then she turned to face me, tears still on her cheeks. "I love you, Magnolia. I'm proud of the woman you've become." With that, she went upstairs.

I washed up the dishes, then went upstairs and found my phone. Brady had sent me several texts.

I'm heading out before your mother wakes up. Text me when you get up.

Then:

Your mother saw me, but she didn't ask questions. Sorry.

An hour later:

Maggie, CALL ME.

I took a deep breath as I hit the call button, worried about what he had to tell me.

"I was about to come back over and check on you," he said when he answered.

"I left my phone in my room, and my mother and I . . . had a chat."

"Was she upset that I was there?"

"Not how you think." I pushed the bedroom door shut. "Do you know anything about Dr. Lopez?"

"It's a little difficult to ask questions about a case I have no part of without looking suspicious. Let me at least tell Owen, and he can say he's working on a hunch that his case is related."

"So I take it that's your roundabout way of saying no."

"Maggie."

"I don't want to have this conversation on the phone. My mother is taking me to my apartment so I can shower and change. Meet me there in an hour." I needed time to think.

"I'll be there in half an hour. I have to work later." Then he hung up.

Was he right? Brady and Owen had known each other for years. Was it possible Brady could be so wrong about him? But Dr. Lopez had seemed so certain the police were dirty, and there was the not-so-small matter of Walter Frey's missing cell phone and note. Suddenly it struck me: Owen Frasier was in charge of *that* case, but who'd been in charge of my father's case?

I reached for my purse to pull out the envelope, then slid out the papers, searching for the detective's name on the report.

Detective Gordon Frasier.

Oh shit.

I opened the search app on my phone and looked for Gordon Frasier. It didn't take much to find out he was a retired police detective from the Franklin Police Department. A little further digging told me that he was Owen's uncle. Double shit.

"Magnolia!" my mother called out from the hall.

"In here." I stuffed the papers back into the envelope as the door opened.

She gave the envelope a curious glance. "Are you ready to go yet?"

"I haven't made the bed. I'll be down in a minute."

Momma nodded, then shut the door behind her.

She was quiet during the drive to my apartment, and I was busy wrestling with how to tell Brady I was sure his best friend was crooked. Momma pulled up to the curb and curled her lips. "I suppose you've already been inside her house."

"Yours is nicer, Momma. Hers is pretentious."

To my surprise, she said, "That's my girl." And then, as if I wasn't shocked enough, she grabbed my hand and squeezed. "Be careful, Magnolia."

"I will."

I walked down the driveway, not surprised to see Miss Ava standing at her back door as I passed. The woman seriously needed to get a hobby.

"Good morning, Miss Ava."

"Is that your mother pulling away?" There was no mistaking the snide tone in her voice. "She didn't want to see your apartment?"

I forced a smile. "She had to get back to work." I cast a glance at my front door at the top of the stairs. "Any word on when the locks will be changed?"

She pushed open her screen door and stood in the opening, holding out her hand. Silver keys dangled from her fingertips. "Already done."

The locksmith must have shown up at the butt crack of dawn, which made me even more thankful I'd spent the night with Momma. "Seriously?"

"I never joke, Magnolia."

No, I suspected she didn't. "Thank you." I took them from her grasp, then asked, "No one else has had access to them, right? Just the locksmith and you?"

"And now you." Her eyes bore into mine. "Don't share them with anyone else."

"I won't."

I started to head toward the stairs, then turned back to face her. "Do you know anything about the missing Nashville dentist, Geraldo Lopez?"

She made a face. "Why would I be concerned with some *Nashville* dentist?" Then she shut the door.

So did that mean she did or she didn't?

I now had fifteen minutes before Brady showed up, and I needed to lay on the charm to get my answers. Which meant I had to hurry so he didn't show up while I was in the shower.

I was showered and dressed, and was putting on my mascara by the time I heard the knock on my door. When I stared out the peephole, I saw Brady holding a drink tray with what looked like two coffees and a pastry bag.

Looked like I wasn't the only one planning on doing some buttering up.

I opened the door—mascara tube in hand—and slipped into the role I'd planned to play: a strong young woman who was willing to do whatever it took to stay safe and get answers. Admittedly, it looked like I might have to use Brady to achieve that goal. The role didn't do much to help the slimy feeling in my chest. "Brady. You brought breakfast."

I stepped out of the way, and he gave me a tight grin before walking past me. "And coffee."

He set the bag and tray on my small kitchen island, then handed me a cup. "I ordered what you got the night we took our walk."

I lifted an eyebrow. "You remembered?"

His gaze held mine. "I remember details. That's part of what makes me a good detective."

"Arrogant much?" I asked before I thought better of it.

His answer wasn't smug, but it was confident. "If it's true, why hide it?"

I cocked my head, not entirely sure I liked this change in attitude. He thought he had the upper hand. Why?

Turning back to the counter, he opened the bag. "I wasn't sure what you'd like, so I got a blueberry muffin and a croissant. You pick."

"I already ate at my mother's."

He simply shrugged and pulled the blueberry muffin out of the bag. Then he perched on a stool, but when I didn't follow suit, he cast a glance at me. "Are you going to just stand there?"

I lifted my brows in challenge.

"You said you wanted to talk in person." He took a bite of his muffin before adding, "I'm ready to talk."

What was going on with him? "I'm not quite ready yet." I waved the mascara tube. "I'll be out in a second." Then I set the cup on the counter—still untasted—and went into the bathroom and finished putting on my mascara. I hadn't washed my hair, but I'd pulled the sides back from my face. My makeup was understated, and I had chosen a pink and yellow floral dress with a pair of low-heeled wedges—a fashion decision I was sure I was going to regret by the end of the day.

Brady had polished off the muffin and half the croissant by the time I walked out.

"I have to be at work in a half hour."

"Then I guess you better start talking," he said, spinning in his seat to face me.

I pulled the second stool several inches from the counter—and from him—and sat down. Brady Bennett was pretty damn sure about himself, and I needed to proceed with caution. "You said you thought someone was dirty in your department, but you don't know who."

"That's right."

I already knew he didn't want to tell me why, but what if I asked in a roundabout way? "When did you first suspect?"

He hesitated. "A few weeks."

I'd arrived in town a few weeks ago. "Does Owen know?"

The corners of his mouth lifted into a half-smile. "Yes and no. Not about the current situation, but when I mentioned my suspicions a few weeks ago, we'd both had a few beers too many. He called me a crazy conspiracy theorist and then blew it off as me being shit-faced. I let him."

"Why would he call you that?"

He ran a hand through his hair. "People in our department have been accused of a cover-up before."

My eyes widened.

He pushed out a sigh. "I'm going to be honest with you, Magnolia."

"Finally."

He scowled but otherwise ignored my statement. "My boss didn't know I was looking into your father's case this week."

That caught me off guard. "Why not?"

"Because the disappearance of your father and Shannon Morrissey is the case that sparked the original conspiracy theories." He paused. "Shannon Morrissey's sister was very vocal in her insistence that there was more to it."

"You knew this?"

He grimaced. "I didn't put it together until I took your report. Your father's disappearance triggered a vague memory, so I did some digging and realized the connection."

"But Sydney's statement wasn't in the report."

His brow furrowed. "I know."

"And that doesn't bother you?"

"It bothers the shit out of me. It was in the original report, and now it's gone."

"Brady. I know who the lead detective was in my father's case. I searched for it in the report. Gordon Frasier is Owen's uncle."

It was his turn to look surprised that I'd figured it out.

"How well do you know Owen?"

"You're barking up the wrong tree, Maggie."

"I'll be the judge of that. How long have you known him?"

He gave me an obstinate glare, then sat back in his seat. For now, he was humoring me. "We met in the police academy eight years ago, and we just synced. We've been best friends ever since. We lived together for a while, until he moved in with his girlfriend a few years ago."

"His girlfriend wasn't there last night," I said, thinking about Owen's joke about making a play for me.

"They broke up several months ago."

"Is he living with you again?"

"No. We both value our friendship too much." He flashed me a grin, but it faded quickly. "I can trust him."

"I understand, but I'm not sure *I* can trust him. I've talked to two men about my father in the past four days. One is dead and the other is missing. Not to mention that your best friend's uncle was in charge of a case that has a missing report. I'm not going to trust anyone."

"Someone pulled Sydney's statement after it was filed."

"How can you be certain?"

He glanced around until his eyes landed on the envelope sticking out of my purse on the coffee table. When I nodded, giving him permission, he grabbed it and brought it back to the counter. "There are pages missing. You can see that from the sequence." He pulled out the pages and flipped through until he stopped in a particular spot. "Sydney Crowley's statement should have been next, but there are four pages missing, which means it was originally filed with the report." He slid the papers toward me and pointed to the numbering on top.

He was right. There were pages missing.

He leaned closer. "Sydney's testimony rattled some cages. Nothing came of it, but it didn't stop some people of accusing Owen's uncle of a cover-up. He was cleared of wrongdoing, but he was bitter and he left the force. These pages were included in the original report, and at some point after Gordon was cleared, someone removed them."

Did Brady think I was stupid? I turned to him in disbelief. "So you think this is all a coincidence?"

"No. Not at all. I'm convinced Walter Frey's murder and Geraldo Lopez's disappearance have something to do with your father and Christopher Merritt."

I shook my head in confusion. "But you just said there wasn't a cover-up."

"Owen has always believed his uncle was railroaded. If we take this to him, he'll help us. He'll want to prove his uncle's innocence."

"What?" I asked in disbelief. "That makes no scnse whatsoever. Something happened to all four men, which pretty much proves something's rotten, starting with the investigation that began fourteen years ago. If Owen wants to fix his uncle's reputation, he's going to shove this under the rug so fast we won't have time to find a broom." I stood and moved to the other side of the island. "No. We definitely can't tell him now."

Brady groaned. "Maggie, I need help in this. I can't do it alone. Not outside the department."

"I know." That filled me with more guilt. But my mind flashed back to Brady's behavior when he'd first arrived. He'd seemed so confident, so full of energy. "What else aren't you telling me?"

"What makes you think there's something else?"

I rolled my eyes. "Please. What is it?"

"I pulled Christopher Merritt's Missing Persons Report."

"And?"

"His car was found at the Nashville airport, just like your father's and Shannon Morrissey's."

"Anything else?"

"A hundred thousand dollars was pulled from a client's account, then sent to an off-shore bank account."

I sucked in a breath. "Steve Morrissey's?"

"No. Walter Frey's."

chapter twenty-five

I placed both hands on the counter. "What?"

"Merritt was Walter Frey's accountant and had access to several of his accounts. The conclusion was that Merritt ran off with Frey's money."

I stared at him in shock. "You're kidding." No wonder Brady had been so damned smug, carrying around a bombshell like that.

"Maggie, we can use this to open this case from a different angle."

"So you don't need my information."

"I'm not saying that at all. I'm saying you can feel safe to provide it."

I walked over to the cabinet and grabbed a glass. "You really believe that?"

He hesitated and his voice sounded flat. "You obviously don't."

"Have they found Dr. Lopez yet?" I filled the glass with ice from the refrigerator door.

"You know they haven't."

I turned around to face him, my glass still in my hand. "No." I didn't trust Owen as far as I could throw him. But did I dare tell Brady about Walter Frey's note? Sure, I'd mentioned it in passing, but I'd played it down…

No, there was another way to put doubt in his head. I spun back around and filled my glass with water. "There's something that hasn't been answered to my satisfaction."

"What?"

"What happened to Walter Frey's cell phone?" While I was willing to bring up the missing phone, I planned to keep the note to myself.

He blinked. "I told you. It was stolen."

I slowly shook my head. "No. I saw it in his hand."

"You were confused and—"

"No. I saw a cell phone in his hand, and if you're honest with yourself, you'll admit that you believe me."

His cop face was back. "What do you think happened to it, Magnolia?"

I held his gaze. "I don't know, Brady. Why don't *you* tell *me*?" He didn't answer, but he didn't look away either. "I saw his cell phone in his hand right before you pulled up, so if we're following a chain of custody, I passed it off to you. Did you take it?"

"I can't believe you asked me that!" he shouted, getting to his feet. "Do you really believe that?"

I set my glass of water on the counter with a thud, sloshing water over the side. "If I thought you took his phone, you sure as hell wouldn't be in my apartment right now."

"Then who do you think took it?"

"You're the big shot detective who notices all the freaking details!" I shouted back. "Why don't *you* tell *me?*"

To my surprise, his face darkened and he turned around and stomped out of my apartment, slamming the door behind him.

Well, crap.

But a quick glance at the clock made me realize I was on the verge of being late, so I gulped down my water along with a couple of ibuprofen, then locked up my apartment—which I still hadn't completely straightened up after the break-in. But I'd noticed that there was a new inside chain lock, along with an impressive-looking deadbolt and new doorknob lock. I'd have plenty of time to clean up after the Belles' big catering job tonight and my day off tomorrow.

I barely made it to work on time, but Alvin didn't seem to notice. The morning went by in a blur, and the only thing that shook me out of my funk was when Colt walked in through the back door at around noon.

I gaped at him in shock, but Alvin broke my stupor as he called out, "Magnolia, are you going to introduce us?"

How did he even know Colt was here for me? Probably the way Colt was staring at me. Also, I doubted this was the kind of place someone like him would be caught dead under normal circumstances. "Alvin, this is

Colt. Colt, Alvin. Colt works with me at Southern Belles Catering, and Alvin is my boss."

A customer walked in through the front door, and as soon as Alvin left to talk to her, Colt's smile fell. "What happened last night?"

There was no way he could know about Geraldo Lopez, and I wasn't about to clue him in. "Nothing."

"Nothing? I thought you were going to question Brady"—he said his name like a curse— "about what he knows about the case."

The less Colt knew, the better, although I hated lying to him. Other than Belinda, he was the only real friend I had here. "He took me to Momma's house, and that was it."

He lifted an eyebrow, his skepticism apparent. "Oh, really?"

"He didn't give me any answers, and I decided not to push. I'll just steer clear of him from now on." After the way he'd stormed out of my apartment, I had a feeling that it wouldn't be that difficult.

"Then why did Lila find him slinking out of her house this morning?"

Oh shit. I couldn't believe she'd told him. "It wasn't like that."

His eyes narrowed. "Like what, Magnolia?"

I knew I was in trouble when he used my full name. "He was protecting me, Colt. Momma too."

He slowly nodded his head, but the look in his eyes told me I had his vote for the biggest idiot in Franklin. He pushed out a breath of frustration, then looked around the store before saying, "I actually have another purpose for dropping in. You weren't answering your phone, and I thought I should let you know that my friend got back to me." When my eyes widened, he said, "The piece I showed him hadn't been stolen, and it's worth several thousand dollars."

I gasped. "But there were enough pieces that—"

"Yeah, someone stole nearly a million dollars' worth of gold from your apartment."

I felt lightheaded and placed my hand on a display table to stay upright, the significance hitting me square in the face. What if Steve Morrissey wasn't missing a million dollars? What if he was missing a million in gold?

Had my father really stolen it?

"I've been thinking. What if we take that list of serial numbers and report that the gold was stolen? They'll be reported the moment someone tries to sell them. We can find out who took it."

"Yeah," I grumbled. "While that sounds like a great idea, we'd have to report it to the police."

"Then tell your new boyfriend. I'm sure he'll *protect* you *and* your remaining gold."

I clenched my fists, seething. "He's not my boyfriend."

His scowl deepened and he leaned closer. "Then there's another way. I can have my friend take care of it."

"Are you serious? How?"

"Since it was a local job, they might try to take it to him. If we give him the serial numbers, he'll keep watch and let me know if someone shows up. But he'll put a flag on the numbers, so if the gold is taken somewhere else, it'll say it was taken from him."

"What's his cut?" I asked sarcastically. There was no way Colt's friend was going to go to this much trouble out of the kindness of his heart.

"Five percent."

I groaned, but five percent seemed worth it if we could find out who'd stolen the gold. My life might depend on it. "Fine. Do it."

"And just because that one piece wasn't stolen doesn't mean the rest wasn't. It's a good idea to check."

"I already said yes," I grumbled. "No need to sell me on the idea." I went behind the counter and grabbed the list out of my purse, then hurried back over. "It's my only copy, Colt, so make a copy or two and hide them before you take it to him."

He nodded as he took it from me. "We'll get this figured out."

"Thanks." But the cynical me wondered why he was so invested. Maybe the reason Colt was so certain Brady had ulterior motives was because he did too.

Brady walked in through the back door of the shop right at two, wearing a scowl. Alvin looked like he was about to say hello until he noticed the detective's dark expression. He turned to help a customer instead.

Smart man.

I wasn't so sure I wanted to talk to Brady either, but despite the fact that Rhoda was asking him about some serving dish he'd bought for his cousin's wedding, I knew I was the reason he was here.

I grabbed my purse, relieved to have it on my person again, where it wouldn't be as easy for someone to steal the gold or gun inside it. Maybe I should look into getting a safety deposit box.

I didn't say a word to Brady as I walked past him onto the sidewalk, but he trailed me out of the store. Right before the door closed behind him, I heard Rhoda stage-whisper to Alvin, besmirching my character for sleeping with two men at once. Probably wishful thinking on her part.

"I take it you're here for a reason?" I asked dryly. "Is it official since you're on duty?"

"Have you eaten?"

I put a hand on my hip. "Funny, I would think a crack detective like you might know the answer to that question."

"It's been a long fucking day already, Magnolia. Do you want to hear what I have to tell you or not?"

Some of my bluster faded. "I do." I only had a half hour before I needed to be at the catering kitchen, but surely that was enough time for him to fill me in.

"Good. I'm starving and I'm getting something to eat, so either come with me or don't—I don't care. But I'm not talking about it out here."

As we walked toward the deli, I couldn't help wondering if he was mad at me or himself. Probably both.

We both ordered and Brady insisted on paying the bill. Neither of us said a word to each other until we sat down with our food. I kept resisting the urge to apologize, although I wasn't entirely sure what words I could use to express myself. *I'm sorry I accused your best friend of stealing evidence* didn't seem the best course, especially since I still believed Owen was guilty.

Which was why I was so pissed when he broke the silence with, "I went and talked to Owen."

"And when you say you talked to Owen, I take it you weren't chatting about your plans for tonight."

"Maggie, hear me out."

"You betrayed me."

"No. *I didn't.* I asked him if there had been any new developments in the Frey case. I wanted to know if he'd done anything about the tip that had been called in."

"Had he?"

"No. He said it seemed too out there, that he was working on another lead, but I convinced him to at least check it out. I suggested he look for connections between the three separate cases."

"Did he bite?"

"No. He said he had something better."

That didn't surprise me. If Owen had seen the paper—and I suspected he had—then Geraldo Lopez's name was at the top of the list. He sure wasn't going to agree there was a connection.

"Didn't he think it was weird that you'd interfere?" I asked.

"No. I told him you were worried because we hadn't caught the perpetrator—that you feared for your safety and I had promised you I'd check on things."

I'd mentioned the note to Owen just last night, and now Brady was telling him I wanted answers.

I was in big trouble.

"So that was that?"

"No. I went to see Steve Morrissey myself."

I blinked, sure I'd heard him wrong. "You *what?*"

"I figured I had nothing to lose."

"What happened?"

"When I asked him about Lopez, he said he was his dentist when he was married to Shannon, but he found a new one after she disappeared. As for Merritt, he said they had some work connections in common, but as a banker, he's worked with many local professionals."

"So that's it?" I asked in disbelief.

"Until the department digs deeper, there's nothing I can do. I couldn't take him downtown." He paused. "But he was nervous."

"Yeah," I said sarcastically. "Because the police were finally taking him as a serious threat. I'm in just as much danger as I was last night. Maybe more, after you showed up at Morrissey's door."

"And today was the second time I talked to him," Brady said. "Remember? I visited him on Wednesday when I was digging into your father's disappearance."

Crap. I'd forgotten about that. "I'm in deep shit."

"Then go with me to talk to Owen."

"No." He had to see for himself that he couldn't trust Owen. He was never going to take my word over his best friend's.

"Magnolia. Please."

"I have to get to work." I got up and threw my trash away. Glancing back, I saw Brady fumbling with his bag, so I took advantage of his distraction and headed out the door, jaywalking across the street and down the parking lot behind the buildings toward the catering shop.

I wasn't surprised when Brady fell into step beside me. "I can't help you if you don't let me."

"I never asked you to."

"Don't be so stubborn. Someone has possibly killed five people. You need protection."

I was scared shitless, but I wasn't convinced the police weren't as much of a threat as whoever had done this. I stopped outside the back door to the catering shop. "Then follow Steve Morrissey around and make sure he doesn't hurt me or anyone else."

"You know I can't do that."

"Then what good are you, Brady?" I closed my eyes as soon as I uttered the words. "I didn't mean that."

"I'll arrest you," he said, his jaw clenched.

"What? On what grounds?" I shouted in disbelief.

"Obstruction of justice. You have information that could help a missing man, and you won't go to the authorities."

"I did go to the authorities!" I shouted. "I went to you!"

"And you made me swear not to tell!"

"Then tell them, Brady!" I flung out my hand, pointing in the direction of the police station. "Go tell them right now!"

"You know I can't do that." He sounded defeated.

Because I had made him give his word. And now I was destroying him.

The door jerked open and Colt filled the doorway, his jaw set. "Is there a problem here, Maggie?" he asked, but he kept his eyes on Brady.

"No," I said, then swallowed the lump in my throat. "Detective Bennett was just leaving."

"Maggie," Brady pleaded, his tone softening. "Let me help you."

Colt stepped closer. "You heard the lady. You need to go."

I slipped past Colt. Brady squared his shoulders and looked like he was about to follow, but Colt blocked his path. "Do you have a warrant to enter this property, Officer?"

"Goddammit, Maggie!" Brady shouted as I took the coward's way out and walked into the kitchen.

In the bustling workspace, everyone's eyes lingered on me, and I had to wonder how much they'd heard. My mother gave me a dark look—obviously they'd heard enough to get me into trouble. Enough to make Colt come investigate.

Even though I was early, there was plenty to keep me busy. The event was an Arts Council fundraiser. Belinda had helped secure the contract, so Momma and Tilly were under plenty of pressure to make sure everything went okay. Momma had to be desperate because she set me to work on salad prep, stating that surely I couldn't mess up some simple chopping.

A few hours later, we had the vans loaded and I found myself sitting in one of them with Colt. He'd ignored me since his interception of Brady, and it hadn't seemed like a good idea to bring up the subject before now.

As soon as he pulled the van out of the parking lot, he asked, "Did you tell him about the gold?"

"No. Of course not."

"Then what does he want you to go to the police about?"

I sighed. "The less you know, the better."

"He knows your secret?"

"No." I released a bitter laugh. "I'm a complicated woman with plenty of secrets to go 'round."

Colt reached over and grabbed my hand. "That's what makes you such an *interesting* woman, Maggie Mae. You're cloaked in a shroud of mystery."

I couldn't help smiling at the grin in his voice. "I'm going to take that as a compliment."

He pulled up to the back of the Factory, an old factory that had manufactured ovens back in the early twentieth century. It had been repurposed as a shopping and dining venue, and there were several event spaces. The Arts Council event was being held in the room aptly named Art Gallery, an open loft space on the second floor, overlooking the open commons area below. A few of the staff set up the food staging in a room next door while Colt and I set up high-top tables with tablecloths. I was putting a tablecloth on a rectangular table, where we planned to put warming dishes, when Belinda walked into the room and stopped dead in her tracks. Her eyes locked with mine; then she jerked her gaze away and went to talk to a woman who was examining an art display.

I tried to ignore the sick feeling in my gut, but I couldn't pretend that being estranged from Belinda didn't rip me apart.

The party started off slow, but was in full swing within an hour. Colt was playing bartender, Momma and I were in the back, and Tilly kept running in and out of the other room, checking on the wait staff and the food. But at some point in the second hour, she burst into the staging room, her face red and her shirt soaked with sweat.

"Tilly!" Momma exclaimed. "What on earth?"

She practically tossed the pan she was carrying on the table. "Hot flash!" she shouted as she tugged at the buttons on her white dress shirt.

"Tilly!" Momma shouted. "What on earth are you doin'?"

"I can't stay in this thing for another minute!"

"You can't take off your shirt!"

"Watch me!" Tilly's fingers shook as she fumbled with the buttons, until she released a loud cry of frustration. She ripped the shirt open to reveal a sparkly gold bra. I watched with my mouth gaping open as Tilly shrugged off the offending piece of clothing and tossed it to the floor. "I'm on fire!"

One of the servers walked through the door. "Tilly, we're out of pita chips for the—*oh, my God!*"

Tilly had picked up a dishtowel and was flapping it around as if trying to fan herself. "I'm not going anywhere near those warming trays!"

Momma glanced from the server to me, and I groaned. "I'll take Tilly's place."

"You can't go out there," Momma said. "Look what happened last time."

"Last time was a fluke," I said. "How many men get killed at parties around here?" I glared at her over my shoulder as I picked up a pan. "Don't answer that."

She looked like she was about to protest, but Tilly was now digging in the ice container, about to pour it over her head.

"Tilly!" Momma shouted, rushing toward her. "Why can't you just go on hormone replacement like everyone else?"

I carried the pan of pita chips out to the warming pan and refilled it, and I was about to go get more spinach and artichoke dip when I heard someone call out my name.

"Magnolia Steele."

I didn't recognize the male voice, but it didn't sound friendly, so I prepared myself as I spun around.

And looked into the face of Steve Morrissey.

"Mr. Morrissey," I said in surprise, although I wasn't sure why. He was a banker and part of the local community. It seemed like the sort of event he'd attend.

"You and I need to have a chat." He stopped in front of me, and the look on his face told me it wouldn't be a friendly one.

I took a step backward, holding the empty metal pan between us. "Now's not a good time. As you can see, I'm busy."

He glanced around the room, then back at me. "It's a good time for me."

I tried to step around him, but he blocked my path. "I'm not sure what you could possibly want to discuss with me. But I'll be sure to tell Roy I saw you."

"There's plenty to discuss. Let's start with the policeman who showed up at my front door today."

The blood drained from my face, but I faked a condescending smile. "I guess you should have paid those parking tickets, huh?" Then I bolted around him and slipped into the prep room, hoping Momma or Tilly's stripper show would scare him off.

The prep kitchen was empty, but the door to the hall was open, and I heard Momma calling after Tilly as they ran down the hall. "Where do you think you're going?"

Mr. Morrissey followed me into the makeshift kitchen and grabbed my arm. "Why do the police think I had something to do with Walter Frey's murder?"

"I'm not sure what Roy's told you, but I haven't joined the police force. I'm working as a shopkeeper and for my momma as a caterer." I tried to jerk free, but his fingers dug deeper.

"Don't get smart with me, young lady," he said, his face turning red. "That policeman said—"

The door burst open and Belinda came barreling through it. "Magnolia! There you are! We have a catering emergency, and I need you *immediately*." Looping her arm through mine, she pulled me free from Mr. Morrissey's hold. Without so much as glancing back at him, she dragged me through the door and back into the event area. Belinda didn't stop until we were on the other side of the room. Then she searched me up and down and asked, "Are you okay?"

"Yeah."

"You look pretty shaken."

I *felt* shaken. I was next on Steve Morrissey's list.

But Belinda was still worried about me, and I refused to drag her into this. "I'm fine," I forced out. "I just didn't expect to be verbally attacked so soon. That has to be a new record—I was verbally accosted within five seconds of entering the main room."

"What did he want?"

"He thinks I accused him of murder."

"Did you?"

"That's beside the point . . ."

She sighed. "Where were your mother and Tilly?"

"Tilly got a hot flash that seemed to be melting her from the inside out, so maybe Momma was looking for a fire extinguisher."

"I want you to stick with me until they get back. We're not going to let you out of our sight."

"But yesterday afternoon . . ." I said, feeling terrible. "I said the most awful things—"

"Magnolia," she said with a smile. "We're family. Families fight, but they have to make up."

I was pretty sure Roy didn't feel the same way. Neither did I, when it came to him. "I'm so sorry."

"Already forgotten. Now you can make the rounds with me."

Belinda seemed to know everyone in town, so I took mental notes as she talked to just about everyone in the room. Thankfully, Steve Morrissey seemed to have disappeared. I imagined he was lying in wait for me. As soon as I could get away from my new guardian angel, I planned to call Brady and fill him in.

Another half hour had passed and I was ready to head back to the kitchen to do my job—Momma was going to be furious I'd been gone so long—when a woman burst into the room, sobbing hysterically.

"Help!" she shouted. "He's dead! My husband is dead."

My words to my mother raced through my head: *How many men get killed at parties around here?* Then it hit me that I'd seen this woman three weeks earlier—with her husband, whom I knew all too well.

Steve Morrissey.

chapter
twenty-six

I wasn't too shocked when Brady showed up fifteen minutes later, but the nervous look in his eyes did catch me by surprise. He looked like he wanted to talk to me straightaway, but instead he started with Steve Morrissey's now-grieving widow.

I wasn't entirely sure what had happened, but Morrissey's wife said he'd been upset and on edge all afternoon. She'd insisted they go to the event despite his wish to stay home. He'd been distracted all evening, and then he'd disappeared. She'd made several calls, all unanswered, before heading out to the parking lot to see if he'd actually left, and that's when she found him—dead in his car.

I shot a glance over to Colt, who was still at his bar, offering drinks to nervous partygoers. This was bound to put a damper on Franklin social life.

Brady's partner, Detective Martinez, took over with the crying widow, and Brady got up and headed straight toward me.

"He looks like he means business," Belinda whispered nervously. She reached down and squeezed my hand.

After our conversation earlier today, I wasn't sure what to expect.

"Magnolia, we need to talk." This was Detective Bennett, all cop.

"All right, but I would prefer for Belinda to stay with me."

"I'm afraid that's not possible."

Belinda had already pieced things together. "Detective Bennett, if you're thinking Magnolia had anything to do with this, then you're climbing up the wrong tree. Magnolia's been by my side for nearly the last hour."

"Literally every minute?" he asked. "No bathroom breaks? No going to the kitchen?"

"No," Belinda said, holding her chin high. "Mr. Morrissey confronted her about an hour ago, wanting to know what she'd told the police. He was aggressive and upset, and Magnolia was completely blindsided, so I came to her rescue and have kept her by my side the entire time since. I wanted to make sure she was protected." Her gaze held his.

He glanced from me to Belinda. "And other witnesses will confirm this?"

A smile ghosted on her face. "Detective Bennett, I had a prearranged list of guests to attend to tonight. I'll be happy to provide it to you, and then you can question each guest individually if you'd like. Their visits also overlapped."

Brady's brow furrowed. "That seems very structured."

Belinda gave him a look that wouldn't have been out of place on a momma bear. "I thrive on structure, Detective Bennett."

He cast a glance to the back corner, where Colt was offering his liquid consolation. "And him?"

"Colt?" she asked in surprise. "He's been there the entire time too. It's an open bar, and we can't afford for him to take a break. The more the attendees drink, the looser their pocketbooks become."

Brady didn't say anything before he turned and walked away.

As soon as he was out of earshot, I said low enough so no one could hear me, "Brady's right. It does seem very premeditated."

She was scanning the crowd, but she swiveled her head to look at me. "The fact that I have a schedule for visiting with donors, or the fact that I had you at my side every moment after he accosted you?"

I was tired of playing games, so against my better judgment, I said, "Both."

"You think I had something to do with killing Steve Morrissey?"

My brain hadn't made that leap, but now I realized it all seemed suspicious. Still, this was Belinda we were talking about. "God, no. I'm just saying you know how the police love to twist things around when it comes to me."

I was surprised Momma and Tilly hadn't come looking for me since the police had shown up, but while Belinda had been parading me around the room, I'd seen Tilly through the swinging door to the kitchen, strutting around in her pants and a bra.

Then it occurred to me that Momma and Tilly had left right around the time Steve Morrissey had found me. Would they be suspects?

"I need to find Momma and Tilly," I said.

Belinda nodded. "Good idea."

We found them in the kitchen. Tilly was wearing a pink T-shirt that looked two sizes too small, but she'd topped it with an apron.

"Are they trying to tie this to you?" Momma asked.

"Why would they—" I started to say, then stopped. "They might have, but Belinda had me by her side the entire time. I have close to two hundred witnesses to attest to my alibi, thanks to her."

My mother gave my sister-in-law an appreciative look, which Belinda responded to with a tight smile. What in tarnation was that about?

"Where did you two run off to?"

They shared a meaningful glance, then both looked at me. "We went to the catering van to get Tilly a shirt," Momma said.

Tilly nodded. "After I stood around a bit in the cool night air."

"Mr. Morrissey's wife said she found him in his car. Did you see anything?"

They both shook their heads. "Not a thing."

About ten minutes later, Brady came and found me, his face softer. "Maggie, can we have that talk now?" When I hesitated, he said, "You'll want to hear this, but I can't tell you in here."

I had to admit I was curious. "Okay."

I followed him out of the kitchen, down the stairs, and into the now-quiet common area. When he stopped, I stood in front of him, my arms crossed over my chest.

"What I'm about to tell you is official police information that we're not releasing until we conduct a more thorough investigation, but I want you to feel safe."

I shook my head in confusion. "Safe? What does that mean?"

He leaned closer. "Steve Morrissey committed suicide."

"What?" I said with a gasp. "Are you sure?" Despite all of his wife's wailing, she'd never told us his cause of death.

"Yes. Gunshot wound to the head."

I closed my eyes and cringed.

"It was dark when Mrs. Morrissey found him, so she didn't see all the blood in the back of the car." He hesitated. "He shot himself through the roof of his mouth."

I felt like I was going to be sick.

"Maggie," he said, his voice even lower. "There's something else."

I opened my eyes and looked up at him.

"There was a note."

"What?"

"He admitted to killing your father and Shannon fourteen years ago. He also admitted to killing Christopher Merritt, Walter Frey, and even Geraldo Lopez."

My knees buckled, but Brady put an arm around me and led me to a bench. "I don't believe it."

"I know," he said. "After all these years, you finally get closure."

I glanced up at him. He was right. That's what I'd wanted, so why did I still feel empty inside? It felt too neat and tidy, like something wasn't right.

"I don't want you to be scared anymore."

"Thank you."

"I ask that you keep this information to yourself. Don't even tell your mother or your sister-in-law." His eyes darkened. "And definitely not Colt Austin."

I nodded, still feeling numb. "Okay."

"You're free to go." He paused. "But if . . ." He shook his head. "Good night, Maggie."

Brady headed toward the doors to the parking lot, and I turned the other direction. It was then I saw a face in the shadows—a face that looked a lot like my brother's. I considered chasing him down, but it just then occurred to me that I hadn't seen my brother all evening, which was a surprise since so many professionals with money were in attendance. But if Roy was here, why was he hiding?

I found Belinda upstairs. She looked surprisingly calm given all the drama that had unfolded tonight.

"I just talked to Brady," I told her. "And he's confirmed I'm not a suspect, so I'm free to go home as soon as Momma lets me."

Relief washed over her face. "Thank God."

"Say, Belinda. Where's Roy tonight?"

"Roy?"

"I haven't seen him all night. This seems like his kind of party."

Her eyes lost their sparkle. "He had a prior engagement."

"I thought I just saw him downstairs."

She shook her head. "Your nerves must be getting the better of you. He's in downtown Nashville, attending some boring dinner."

I was nearly ninety-nine percent certain she was wrong, but I didn't want to be the one to convince her of it. Besides, Roy had become a point of contention between us, and I didn't want to argue with her over my stupid brother.

"I'm pretty much done here—we don't expect people to donate money after what happened. So how about I take you home?" she asked.

"I should probably stay and help Momma and her staff."

"I've already talked to her, and we all agreed it would be best if you went ahead and left. You've had enough of a shock today."

They probably wanted to ensure I didn't create an even larger disturbance, but I wasn't complaining. "I'm going to tell Momma goodbye."

I headed into the kitchen and found her and Tilly packing up pans and various serving implements. Momma looked up, her eyes filled with questions. I went to her and pulled her into a hug. "I'm fine, Momma. I'm not a suspect. In fact, everything is okay now."

She leaned back and searched my face for further explanation, but I couldn't give one to her. Not yet. As hard as it was not to let her know that Daddy hadn't run off with Shannon Morrissey. That I wasn't in danger anymore. That this portion of my nightmare was over.

"I'll talk to you tomorrow." I paused. "I love you, Momma."

She placed her hand on my cheek and looked into my eyes. "I love you too, girl." Then she dropped her hand and went back to work.

I found Colt before I left, assuring him I was okay and not a suspect. He looked relieved, then offered to come hang out with me for the night so I'd feel safe.

I shook my head. "I don't have to be worried or scared anymore." At least not in regard to my father's death. The murderer from the night of my graduation was another matter, but I doubted he'd be coming for me tonight. I hadn't heard from him since the night of Mr. Frey's death.

"Any word from your friend?" I asked. Brady hadn't said a word about the gold, but that didn't mean Mr. Morrissey hadn't mentioned it in his note. Still, it was another unanswered question, another loose thread.

Colt shook his head. "No. Sorry, Mags."

I was out in the parking lot before I realized my purse was locked in one of the catering vans, but I didn't want to go back and get the key. I didn't need the gun anymore, at least not for tonight, and it might be a good idea to hide the last bag of gold somewhere other than my apartment. I had my phone and my keys in my pocket. I could get my purse in the morning.

Belinda was quiet on the drive home, but as we got closer to my apartment, I felt the need to make things right between us. "Belinda, I know I apologized earlier, but it doesn't seem nearly enough. I hurt you, and you have no idea how angry I am at myself over it."

"Magnolia," she said softly. "Please don't be so hard on yourself. I know you don't understand. Some days *I* don't understand. How did I get in this position? I was a strong independent woman." She pulled up outside my apartment and turned to face me, grabbing both of my hands in hers. "Can you keep a secret?"

"Of course."

"I have an exit strategy."

"What does that mean?"

"It means I have a plan, and everything is falling into place. But I might need your help shortly. Will you help me?" She grimaced. "I hate to ask—he is your brother—but it sounds like he's hurt you too."

I turned my hands over and squeezed hers. "Belinda. I'm here for you. No matter what. No judgment. It was unfair of me to judge you earlier, and I'm sorry."

She shook her head. The corners of her mouth tilted up, and tears shimmered in her eyes. "You're the best thing to happen to me in a very long time."

Her words carried a responsibility that would have ordinarily made me feel stifled. But now it felt good to be needed.

"I feel the same way about you."

I got out of the car and walked toward my apartment, my mind buzzing with questions. Why would Steve Morrissey have killed himself in the parking lot? Had he hoped to talk to me before he did it? Could I have prevented it? That question caught me by surprise, enough so that when I unlocked and opened the front door to my apartment, it took me a good three seconds to realize a man was sitting in the dark on my overstuffed chair.

"Good evening, Magnolia," the voice said. When I recognized it, I was sure I was hallucinating or dreaming.

"*Dr. Lopez?*"

He flipped on the lamp, momentarily blinding me. But I quickly recovered and started troubleshooting an exit plan. The door behind me seemed the best solution, but two things hindered my escape: the door was closed, and he had a gun in his hand.

Well, shit.

"I thought you were dead," I said, but it sounded stupid as I said the words out loud.

"It was best if everyone thought so. I have the Goodwin case to thank for my solution."

I slowly shook my head in confusion.

"I thought you were brighter than that," he said in disappointment. "The suicide note."

Amy's suicide note. "Mr. Morrissey didn't kill all those people. You did."

He grinned, but it looked more like tried patience. "If you think you're getting a confession out of me, you're barking up the wrong tree. I'm Catholic. The only person I'll confess to is a priest."

"Then why are you here?" I asked, irritation washing through me. "What do you want?"

"The gold, of course. The missing bag."

"You know about the gold?"

He rolled his eyes. "Keep up, Magnolia. I *own* the gold. It's mine. Your father stole it, and I want it back. You tipped me off that you had it when you asked if the million could be something other than money and in small bags." He stood, still pointing the gun at me. "Now where is it?"

What was I going to do? Once I gave it to him, I'd be dead. But then again, it was in the catering van, which was parked on the north side of the Factory, not too far from where Mr. Morrissey's car was swarmed with police.

"It's not here."

He gave me a disappointed look. "Of course you'd say that."

"In this case, it's true. I was worried whoever ransacked my apartment would come back to get it, so I hid it somewhere else." That someone was him, of course. He'd staged his disappearance around noon yesterday, then had come to Franklin and burgled my apartment. How fortunate for him that I'd listed my real address on my paperwork.

"Where?"

I considered making something up, but its actual location seemed the best route. If he took me with him, I'd have a chance to attract the cops' attention, maybe escape. "It's in a catering van. Parked on the north side of the parking lot of the Factory."

He nodded, then grabbed my arm and dragged me toward the kitchen. Fear made me clumsy. "What are you doing?"

"I'm putting you somewhere until I find out if you're telling the truth." He released me to open the small utility closet, grabbing the trash can and throwing it behind him to make room.

This would not end well.

I took advantage of my moment of freedom to bolt for the front door, but he caught up with me. Grabbing the back of my shirt, he jerked me backward.

"Not so fast." Then he shoved me toward the open closet and pushed me inside. He was about to shut the door when he pulled it back open and held out his free hand. "Your phone."

"I don't—"

He slapped me with his left hand. "Don't insult me, Magnolia. I don't want to hurt you any more than necessary, but if you play games with me, I'll play games with you. Your phone."

My ears rang and I was about to cry, but I swallowed my tears as I pulled my phone out of my pocket and handed it to him.

He took it and sighed. "I only hope you're telling the truth. Otherwise I'll be forced to punish you. Last chance to change your mind."

"There are two vans," I said, proud that my voice didn't break. "My purse is under the front passenger seat of one of them."

He unceremoniously shut the door, plunging me into darkness in the tight space as I heard the sound of scraping metal on the wood floor.

As soon as I heard the front door shut, I tried to get the utility closet open, but the knob barely turned and the door didn't even budge. I wasn't getting out of this closet of my own free will. Which meant I needed to create an escape plan. Geraldo Lopez was coming back one way or another, and when he came back, he was going to kill me.

My only hope was that the police or one of Momma's staff saw him breaking into the van.

Time seemed to stand still as I stood there paralyzed with fear. Memories of that night in the basement, the night I'd witnessed a murder, gripped hold of me. I struggled to catch my breath and soon felt lightheaded from hyperventilating. I knew I needed to calm down and regain control, but knowing something and acting on it turned out to be two very separate things.

Maybe someone would come looking for me.

But I doubted that was true. While I'd kind of repaired things with Brady, he wouldn't be coming over tonight. And Colt had no reason to.

I was alone.

But I was a survivor. I could figure this out on my own. I had no other choice. I just had to calm down, formulate a plan, and execute it when Geraldo Lopez returned. Otherwise I was as good as dead.

I was in the utility closet, so various cleaning supplies were stored over my head. I reached for the shelf over my head, but there wasn't enough of a gap between the door and the shelf for me to grab anything. I placed my hand on the flat wooden shelf and pushed, but it barely budged.

Dammit.

But I wasn't giving up. For what seemed an eternity, but was probably more like ten minutes, I continued to ram the shelf with my hands, finally working it loose and tilting it sideways. The cans and bottles of cleaners rained down on my head, but I ignored the pain and the welt already swelling on my forehead as I felt for the bottle of all-purpose cleaner. That should be close to pepper spray.

Now all I had to do was wait.

Fortunately—or not—I didn't have to wait long. I barely heard the front door open and the approaching footsteps over my own breathing, but there was a clatter on the floor as the closet door opened, and I found myself face to face with an angry Geraldo Lopez.

I didn't give him time to say anything. I already had the bottle raised and gave several squirts aimed at his face, then used the broom in the closet to jab him hard in the stomach as he cried out and stumbled backward. I ran for the door, frustrated to find it locked. I had gotten the deadbolt unlocked and was turning the doorknob when I was jerked backward by my hair.

He threw me to the floor, and as I looked up into his angry face, I knew not only would I die tonight, but I would suffer before it ended.

"Where is it?" he asked through gritted teeth, spittle flying out. He was hefting the broom I'd used to hit him.

"Where's what?"

"The gold!" He struck my shoulders with the broom handle, and I covered my head with my arms. "Where's the damn gold?" I curled up on my side as he continued to hit me with the broom handle.

"It was there," I choked out through my tears. "In the van."

The broom handle hit my back, and I regretted the snap decision to use it as a weapon. I'd no doubt given him the idea.

He hit me several more times in various places before he stopped and grabbed my hair, pulling me to a sitting position. He squatted and leaned his face into mine. "Let's try this again, shall we?" His hand ran down the side of my face, sliding over my tear-slicked cheek. "I don't want to hurt you, Magnolia. I only want what's mine."

I wanted to be brave, but I knew I wouldn't survive this. Besides, I had nothing else to tell him. The impassive look in his eyes told me he would beat me for the rest of the night if that was what it took to get what he wanted. "It was there," I choked out. "In my purse. I swear."

He slowly shook his head, disappointment filling his eyes. "I found your purse, but no gold."

What about the gun? If it had been there, surely he would have mentioned it too, but I didn't have time to dwell on it before he stood and hit me several more times with the broom handle.

Then he squatted next to me again, cupping both cheeks this time. "Magnolia, you're such a pretty girl. I'll move to your face next unless you tell me where it is."

I needed a location. Anything to get him to leave. Even if he locked me back into the closet, it would give me time to formulate a plan. "The catering business," I said through my tears, instantly realizing my mistake. I had hardly given myself any time at all.

He grabbed my arm and tugged me toward the door. "You're coming with me this time." His car was parked in front of the garage. Holding my arm, he dragged me down the steps, but my body protested from the pain he'd already inflicted. He was smart. Enough to make me suffer, but nothing even close to life-threatening. He was good with torture.

My mouth gaped as he opened his trunk and gestured toward it.

Good with torture. Could Geraldo Lopez be the man who'd tied me to a pole and carved the scar into my leg ten years ago?

He pointed his gun at me. "Get in."

A decision lay before me. I'd rather die here than out in the woods where they might never discover my body. But I'd rather not die at all, so I decided to take a stupid risk.

I moved closer to the trunk, pretending I was going to comply, then shoved his hand toward the car at the last instant. The gun went off, the sound a loud bang in the quiet night. And a new hope filled me. Ava Milton. She never let anything slip past her. Surely she must have called 911 by now. But I didn't let myself dwell on that hope. Instead, I stomped on the inside of his heel before lifting my knee up high and hard into his crotch.

He let out a whoosh of air as he hunched over, and I made a split-second decision to run back up the stairs to my apartment. I could take off running, but it was late enough that people would be in bed sleeping. I'd waste valuable time waking them up. Also, the police station was close, but still a half mile away. Geraldo Lopez had a car and would easily catch up. My apartment seemed to be the best option, mostly because Geraldo had left my phone on the kitchen island.

I could call Brady.

Several gunshots rang out as I stumbled up the steps. By the time I got inside and locked the door and turned the deadbolt, I expected to realize I'd been shot, but thankfully I didn't see any blood.

I grabbed my phone and pressed Brady's speed dial number, starting to cry in relief when he answered on the first ring.

"Brady, he's here. He's going to kill me."

"Maggie? Where are you?" he asked. His voice was calm, but I heard worry there too.

"My apartment. He has a gun, Brady. He's going to kill me."

I heard him shouting the order to send units to my address. "Who's trying to kill you, Maggie?" he asked, his voice deceptively calm again.

"Geraldo Lopez."

"But Lopez—"

"He's here," I said, terror washing through me again as I heard heavy footsteps on the stairs. "He killed Steve Morrissey. He wrote the note to make it look like Morrissey killed everyone and then himself."

"What does he want from you? Why's he there?"

I could trust Brady or not. The fact that I'd called him proved that I did. But he would have to put it in his report, and I wasn't ready for that—not when I still wasn't sure if I could trust everyone on the force. Yes, Geraldo had obviously lied to me, but there was still that missing paper . . .

So I answered truthfully. "He thinks I have something that my father had. He thinks my father stole it from him."

Gunshots rang out, and then the front door bounced open.

"Oh, God," I gasped.

Geraldo Lopez filled the doorway, pointing his gun at me. "I want to kill you, but I need your answer first. I will make you suffer until you tell me where it is."

"Maggie!" Brady shouted in my ear.

I dropped the phone and took a step backward. "I don't know," I said, my voice breaking. "I swear to God."

He moved around the island and grabbed a butcher knife from the wooden block on the counter and held it up. "Remember what I said about your pretty face."

"Please," I begged, considering making a break for the door, but I was sure that he'd shoot me. "I swear. I don't know."

He advanced toward me, but then I heard a man say in a low, threatening voice, "Put the weapons down, Lopez. It's over."

It was Owen.

Dr. Lopez lifted a look of surprise to the door. "You think you're going to get away with—"

Two gunshots rang out and I ducked, huddling next to the bookcases.

Geraldo Lopez fell to the floor, and Owen burst in through the door. He squatted next to the body, then pulled out his phone, saying something about how the suspect was deceased.

Owen squatted next to me. "Magnolia?" he said gently. "Are you okay?"

I nodded, unable to find the words to speak.

"Let me help you up, okay?"

I nodded again and let him lead me outside and down the steps. Flashing lights were bouncing off the houses and the driveway, and I wondered when they had shown up. I hadn't heard the sirens.

"Someone get her a blanket," Owen said, and only then did I realize I was shaking uncontrollably.

"Maggie!" The sound of Brady's voice jarred something in me, and I started to cry.

He rushed through the crowd, looking me up and down as he approached me. "Are you okay?"

I nodded, crying too hard to speak.

"She's in shock," Owen said quietly. "We need to have her looked over for injuries. There were multiple gunshots before I showed up."

I shook my head. "I'm okay. He didn't shoot me. He missed."

"Where is he?" Brady asked, his eyes murderous.

"Dead," Owen said. "When I showed up, he had a gun and a knife and was threatening to cut her face. I told him to drop his weapons, but he lunged for Maggie, and then I shot him." He paused. "I had to protect her."

"Thank you," Brady said, pulling me into a hug.

But I flinched as he put pressure on the bruises and welts on my back. Before I realized what he was doing, he scooped me up and carried me to an ambulance parked on the street.

I started to protest, but I was too overwhelmed.

He set me down on a stretcher, and the EMTs took my blood pressure.

They made me lie down, but I wasn't having it. "I'm fine," I finally said, trying to sit up.

Brady pushed me back down. "Your blood pressure is low from shock, so just lie still for a few minutes. Okay? Please don't scare me more."

"You were scared?" I asked in surprise.

"I was terrified." His eyes looked wild as he ran a hand over his head. "I thought he was going to kill you. Thank God for Owen."

"Yes," I said, closing my eyes. "Thank God for Owen."

But I couldn't help wondering why I remembered things a little differently than how Owen had described them.

Did it matter? Owen had saved my life.

Or had he saved his own?

chapter twenty-seven

Brady wanted me to go to the hospital to get checked out, but I refused, especially after the EMTs said it didn't look like I had any broken bones or other injuries. Hospitals had always freaked me out, and I already felt traumatized. My fragile psyche couldn't take it.

So I gave my statement to Owen in the back of the ambulance. Leaving out any mention of the gold, I told him that Lopez had come to the apartment looking for something. I'd pretended to know what that something was—assuming he would kill me otherwise—and told him it was in my purse in the catering van in the hopes that Brady or someone would catch him trying to break in. But he had come back angrier than ever and decided to beat it out of me. I'd escaped from him while he was trying to stuff me into the trunk of his car.

Owen studied me after I finished giving my statement. "So you have no idea what Lopez was after?"

I gave him a long look, feeling nervous over the way he was watching me. I hadn't contradicted the statement he'd made to Brady about Geraldo Lopez. Did he know I'd picked up on his lie, or did he think I'd repressed the memory out of terror?

I shook my head. "No. Not really, but I have to wonder if it had something to do with the missing million dollars."

Brady was sitting on the gurney next to mine and leaned his elbows on his knees. "Maybe it was a safety deposit key."

"Maybe," Owen replied, but his tone suggested he didn't believe it. Did he know what Dr. Lopez was really looking for? Was that why he'd shot him?

Owen hopped out of the back of the ambulance and went to talk to a uniformed officer, leaving Brady and me alone.

Brady was quiet for a moment before he placed his hand over mine. "We might never know what he was after, Maggie. All the key players are dead. We're not sure what really happened with the five of them, but we *do* know that your father was murdered. And that's what you were really after, isn't it? Proof that your father hadn't abandoned you?"

I blinked back tears. "Yeah." But now that I knew part of the story, I was greedy to know it all.

"Maybe Sydney Crowley can help us piece it all together," Brady said, but I doubted she could. She'd already told them everything she knew.

Brady lowered his face to look at me, and the compassion and worry in his warm brown eyes stole my breath. "You can't stay here tonight, so where do you want to go? Do you want to go to your mother's?"

I didn't trust Owen. I suspected he knew about the gold, and that he knew I knew. Just like the note.

I'd figured out the first partial name, but what about the second? Who was "—ogers"? I was still fair game. While I hoped he would be smart enough to let things go, I couldn't count on it. There was only one person I felt could protect me. He'd proven himself to me several times.

"Actually . . ." I looked down at his hand still covering mine and then back up into his face. "I was hoping I could stay with you."

A warm smile lit up his eyes. "Of course, Maggie. You can have the guest room if you'd like."

"Thank you," I said. "But you can say no . . . after this afternoon."

He leaned over the gurney I was sitting on and carefully wrapped an arm around my back. "We had a disagreement. It happens. It's how you handle it afterward that makes the difference. As far as I'm concerned, it's a moot point. I still want you to stay."

His words brought tears to my eyes. "Why are you so nice to me?"

He leaned back, put a finger under my chin, and lifted my face until I was staring into his eyes. "Because you're worth being nice to."

I lowered my head to his shoulder, overcome with exhaustion. "Do you know where my phone is? I need to call my mother. If she hears this from someone else . . ."

"How about we get you settled in my car and I'll go find it?"

"The last place I saw it was in my kitchen. When I called you."

He helped me out of the ambulance, and I was surprised at how stiff and sore my body had gotten in less than an hour. Tomorrow was going to be torture.

I sat in the passenger seat of his car and watched him head down the drive next to Miss Ava's house. I couldn't help wondering what she thought of all the chaos. I couldn't imagine living in that apartment again. With any luck at all, she'd let me out of my lease. Of course, considering the chaos I'd brought to her door, she'd probably be happy to see me go.

Then it occurred to me—how had Geraldo Lopez gotten into my apartment after I'd had the locks changed? I was even more thankful to be going home with Brady.

He returned ten minutes later and handed me the phone. "I have to stop by the Morrissey murder scene. I left my partner there to work it alone, and I need to at least check in with her now that we know it's not a suicide. I'll leave you in the car, but I'll be close enough for you to yell at me if need be. Will you feel safe enough?"

"Yeah," I said, leaning against the headrest and closing my eyes. "Thank you."

I stared at the phone in my hand, wondering how I was going to make this call. How Momma would react to the news. But when Brady pulled into the parking lot, both catering vans were still there, which meant Momma was still there too. Calling her was the chickenshit way out. Truth be told, staying with Brady was the chickenshit way out too. I was barely stomaching one cowardly act. I couldn't handle two.

"My mother's still here," I said as Brady started to get out of the car. "I need to tell her this in person. I need to tell her that her husband didn't leave her for another woman." I was pretty sure that she already knew it, but surely she needed closure too.

He looked back at me and nodded. "Do you want me to go with you?"

"No, I need to do this myself." But as strong as I'd felt in the car, I felt vulnerable and terrified walking across the now mostly empty parking lot. I was perfectly safe. In fact, I could feel Brady's watchful gaze on me as I walked, but my imagination ran wild at the thought of what boogeymen might be hiding in the night.

As though reading my mind, the phone in my hand vibrated with a text and my heart leapt when I read,

Good girls keep their mouths shut. Can you continue to be a good girl, Magnolia?

Disappointment bore down on me. While I'd realized how unlikely it was that Geraldo Lopez was the murderer from my memories, I'd hoped it was true.

I typed back:

I can keep a secret.

He didn't answer, and I tried to get myself together before I found my mother. But then I remembered seeing Roy earlier. Had he actually been here? If so, why? Was Belinda covering for him? Or was she really clueless? What was her escape plan?

Once again, despite how far I'd come, I had far more questions than I did answers.

I found my mother sitting with Belinda, which meant Belinda hadn't gone home after all. The rest of the staff was gone, including Tilly and Colt, and all the equipment was packed up.

"Magnolia!" My mother gasped when she saw me, and Belinda's eyes widened in fear. She probably saw my bruises and thought Roy had paid me a visit.

"I'm fine," I said, trying to make myself sound stronger than I felt. "What are you still doing here, Momma?"

"Someone broke into both vans, so we're waiting for them to finish their investigation."

"I came back to keep your mother company," Belinda said, patting my mother on the leg.

"What are *you* doing here?" Momma asked warily. "What happened?"

"I'm the reason you're still here. Why the vans were broken into."

"You broke into the vans?" Momma asked in disbelief. "Why didn't you just ask for the keys?"

"I didn't do it, but I know who did and why."

I grabbed a chair and pulled it in front of her. "Momma, Daddy didn't run away with Shannon Morrissey."

She rolled her eyes and groaned. "Magnolia, we've been over this—"

"Momma. No." I shook my head. "Steve Morrissey left a suicide note that said he'd had several people killed. Walter Frey. Christopher Merritt. And Daddy." Sure, Brady had told me not to share the information, but now we knew it wasn't true anyway.

Belinda gasped and grabbed Momma's hand.

My mother's face paled. "What?"

I put my hand over Momma's and Belinda's clasped ones. I was thankful that they didn't shrug me off. "But the note was only partially right. Steve Morrissey didn't kill them. A dentist named Geraldo Lopez did. He killed Mr. Morrissey and made it look like a suicide."

"Why?"

"I guess so he could get away with his crime without falling under suspicion."

"Get away with what crime?"

"Taking a million dollars." I took a breath. "I don't know what was going on, and maybe we'll never know, but somehow Daddy, Geraldo Lopez, Walter Frey, Christopher Merritt, and Steve Morrissey were all tied up with the money. Shannon Morrissey's sister said Shannon thought her husband was laundering money, and she and Daddy were about to turn them in. She thought Steve killed them to keep them quiet."

"And the others?"

"I don't know about Mr. Merritt, but Dr. Lopez told me that Walter Frey was coming to see me to give me proof of what happened. I suspect Dr. Lopez killed him for obvious reasons."

"So your father was a criminal," she said in a flat voice. "That's worse than an adulterer."

"No, Lila," Belinda said in a soothing tone.

"Not necessarily, Momma. He was helping to turn Mr. Morrissey in. But at least we know the partial truth."

"Do we?" she asked, sounding weary.

"No. I guess we don't."

Momma's eyes narrowed. "Dentist. The one you went to see yesterday?"

I hesitated. "Yes. He paid me a visit tonight, but the police arrived just in time. I'm fine."

Momma stood. She was thinner than I'd ever seen her, and the lighting gave her a sickly pallor. "Belinda, can you take me home?"

"Of course, Lila."

Part of me wanted to go home with her and take care of her. I'd risked my life to prove my father wasn't an adulterer, but Momma was right. Was finding out he might have been a criminal any better? Had I risked my life and put my mother's safety in jeopardy over nothing? And wasn't staying with Brady putting him in danger too? The murderer who was stalking me wasn't liable to be happy I'd allied myself with a policeman.

I had no doubt that everyone in my life would be safer—and probably happier—without me. The selfless thing to do would be to leave—catch an early morning flight back to New York—but I couldn't do it. And if that didn't make me a selfish bitch, I didn't know what did.

"Momma," I said, my voice breaking. "I'm sorry."

To my surprise, she pulled me into a tight hug and clung to me for several seconds. "I made my peace with your father's absence years ago. You're the one still struggling, Magnolia. I hope you find your peace too." She kissed my cheek, and I watched Belinda lead her away.

"You okay?" Brady asked from behind me.

I turned to face him. "I can go stay with my mother tonight if it's more convenient for you."

"No, you scared the shit out of me tonight. I'd feel better if you stayed with me."

"Thanks."

"I'm done here. So let's go."

We drove to his place in silence, and I didn't comment on the nice condo building he lived in. We rode the elevator to the third floor, and he led me down a hallway to a door marked 307. After he'd unlocked the door and pushed it open, I took in the well-decorated apartment. It looked like a guy's place—big-screen TV and leather furniture, a small kitchen with dark cabinets and black granite counters.

"Make yourself at home, Maggie," he said. "Unlike your place, there's food in the fridge."

I smiled and that seemed to make him happy.

"I know you don't have any clothes, but I can give you a T-shirt to sleep in. We'll pick up some of your things tomorrow if you want to stay for a while."

"Thanks." I wasn't sure how long I'd want to stay. Surely Owen wouldn't hurt me if I was staying with his best friend.

"Do you want to take a shower?"

I thought about teasing him, but I didn't have the energy. "No. I just want to go to bed. But do you have any ibuprofen?"

Worry covered his face. "Have you changed your mind about going to the hospital?"

"No. Just preventative."

He got me a glass of water and two pills, along with a T-shirt. He even dug up an unopened toothbrush so I could brush my teeth. When I was finished in the bathroom, he was standing in the hallway, pacing.

"Why do you look so nervous?" I asked with a chuckle.

"I still think you should go to the hospital."

I shook my head. "I got mugged once, and it was worse than this. I didn't go then. I'm fine."

He started to say something, but then stopped himself. "Let's get you into bed." He started to lead me to a room, but I grabbed his arm.

"Brady."

He stopped and looked down at me with such compassion and concern it brought tears to my eyes. No man had ever looked at me like that before. Which made what I was about to ask him equally difficult and easy.

"I'm not ready to start a relationship with you yet, so I have no right to ask this."

"Ask, Maggie. I want you to ask."

"I don't want to be alone. Can I sleep with you? Not *with* you but—"

"Yes. Of course." He led me to his room and pulled back the covers to his made bed. I climbed in and tucked my phone under my pillow. I didn't want Brady to get a look at any incoming texts before I did.

He got ready for bed and crawled in next to me, wearing a pair of sweatpants and a T-shirt.

"Sexy," I teased, already half-asleep.

I was lying on my side and he spooned behind me, carefully draping his arm against my side. "I usually sleep in the buff," he whispered in my ear. "But maybe you can find that out later for yourself."

Soon his breathing leveled off, and even though I'd been sleepy before, his comment about our possible future made me anxious. Did I dare take a chance with him?

My phone buzzed with a text, and I pulled it out from under the pillow, wondering if Belinda had checked in with a report about taking my mother home. But it was from Colt, and if I had hoped that learning the truth about my father's disappearance would bring me peace, his text proved otherwise.

I heard back from my friend. The serial numbers are all clear with the exception of three bars. All three were made and reported stolen ten years ago.

Four years after my father had disappeared.

Call Back
(Magnolia Steele Mystery #3)

To find out more about Denise Grover Swank's releases and to have access to bonus content, join her newsletter!
www.denisegroverswank.com/mailing-list/

About the Author

Denise Grover Swank was born in Kansas City, Missouri and lived in the area until she was nineteen. Then she became a nomadic gypsy, living in five cities, four states and ten houses over the course of ten years before she moved back to her roots. She speaks English and smattering of Spanish and Chinese which she learned through an intensive Nick Jr. immersion period. Her hobbies include witty Facebook comments (in own her mind) and dancing in her kitchen with her children. (Quite badly if you believe her offspring.) Hidden talents include the gift of justification and the ability to drink massive amounts of caffeine and still fall asleep within two minutes. Her lack of the sense of smell allows her to perform many unspeakable tasks. She has six children and hasn't lost her sanity. Or so she leads you to believe.

For more info go to: DeniseGroverSwank.com

82755393R00237

Made in the USA
Columbia, SC
05 December 2017